Re
Copper … series
by HEIDI CULLINAN

The Doctor's Secret

"Cullinan weaves themes of racism and Asian culture, family pressures, and the value of friends, home, and love into a deeply satisfying romance."

—*Publishers Weekly,* Starred Review

"If you like slow, trope-filled romances with high stakes and happy endings (and a side of codes and gurneys), this is a must-read. Cullinan knows how to keep her readers hooked!"

—Love Bytes

"I stayed up past my bed time to finish this book and it was totally worth it."

—Two Chicks Obsessed

The Doctor's Date

"…the story's magic is in how their affection for each other helps them individually achieve self-confidence and self-love. This tear-jerker is a captivating winner."

—*Publishers Weekly*, Starred Review

By HEIDI CULLINAN

With Marie Sexton: Family Man

COPPER POINT MEDICAL
The Doctor's Secret
The Doctor's Date
The Doctor's Orders

TUCKER SPRINGS
With Marie Sexton: Second Hand
Dirty Laundry

Published by DREAMSPINNER PRESS
www.dreamspinnerpress.com

THE DOCTOR'S ORDERS

HEIDI CULLINAN

Published by
DREAMSPINNER PRESS

5032 Capital Circle SW, Suite 2, PMB# 279,
Tallahassee, FL 32305-7886 USA
www.dreamspinnerpress.com

Mass Market Paperback ISBN: 978-1-64108-140-5
Trade Paperback ISBN: 978-1-64080-851-5
Digital ISBN: 978-1-64080-850-8
Library of Congress Control Number: 2018907111
Mass Market Paperback published August 2019
v. 1.0

Printed in the United States of America

This paper meets the requirements of
ANSI/NISO Z39.48-1992 (Permanence of Paper).

This novel is dedicated to my patrons, who waited so patiently for a whole year while I did almost nothing but write this trilogy. Thanks for being my rock, guys.

Rosie Moewe
Anu Harvey
DeAnna Ferguson
Carole Lake
Lauren Adams
Michele Crissinger
Raybo Sparkles
Kaija K
Heather Nelson
Susan Freedman
Katherine DuGarm
Carlamia Sciberras
Kim Heath
Dana Fine
Mandy Anne
Susan Romito
Leslie Juhlke
Hils
Aerielle Kaiser
Laura Ryder
Olivia Ventura
Sandy C
Jennifer Harvey
Aurora Willow
Kenyon
Maureen Murray
Sueann Snow
Ninna
Debel-Hansen
Karen Mathre
Erin Sharpe
Lisa Strimple
Terri Hawkins
Joellen Shendy
MtSnow

Liliane Menard
Amanda Briggs
Juli-Anna Dobson
Kirsten Madden
Emilie
Olivia Orndorff
Amanda Hobson
Lois Bradbeer
John Brandt
Kyl James
Chris Klaene
Christine Weingart
Elaine Corvidae
Karen Ray
Maggie White
Trista Dunaway
Jess Severe
Theodore Loucks
Brian B.
H Lie
Carin Bockleman
Kathryn Martino
Melissa
Melanie Köhler
Jessica Lynn
Kimberly M. Lowe
Brook Savage
Tracy A Faul
Marti
Liz Cowan
Ruth Staunton
Krista Holtz
Mary Dolphin
Melissa Walton
Harrison Hicks

Wanda Gibney
Cindy Kennedy
ABL
Shannon Curry
Erika Fawcett
Melissa Valentine
Jennifer Rice
Nikki Cheah
Attenbrough
Sharis Ingram
Hattie
Lauren Weidner
Gitte
Nichole Lacy
Savannah J.
Frierson
Laura
Deandra Ellerbe
Daith Garlington
Annika Bührmann
Kate Ferguson
Libby Mills
Marsha
Michelle Thorla
Margaret Mills
Geraldine Austin
leahjberg
Emilia Agrafojo
Liberty Vasquez
Kimberly
Curington
Tina Marie
Nanette Kerrison
Janet Linton
Brittney Musick

Katy
Caryn
Jessica O'Rourke
Linda Hansson
MHH
Kim D
Kari Blackmoore
Sarah Evans
Delfina
Kardas-Kotlicka
AllAskewe
Jennifer Richards
Janet Ann Black
Shawn Griffin
Becky Gotthardt
Molly Lathrop
Amelia
Nina L
Bethãnia
lae raal
Geri Olson
Suzanne Bibeault
Kaitlin Bryant
Maria Lima
Rachael Waring
Sarah
Tish Lopez
AnnMarie Fasano
Leanne Carroll
Kathleen Harry
Kira Delaney
Emily Johnson
Mink Rose
Heather C
Eileen Haggerty
Stephanie
Steinberg
Mary Eagan
Kathy Wallace

Giselle
Alicia Ramos
Jo Morris
Antonia Aquilante
Victoria Golar
Victoria Poulter
Michelle Coleman
Elizabeth Andrews
Tanzi Melton
Lara Adair
Peter Cornes
Kim Williams
Jennifer
Drummond
Evelyn Maire
Emily Seelye
Dawn Duhon
Amanda Kelsey
Colette
Renee Spalding
Rachel Maybury
Kelly M. Gonzalez
Linda
Galexis
Liza Q Wirtz
Christina Maria
Rose
Heather Cat
Eugenia M
Jess Lane
Joanne Vukman
Stephani M Rozier
Kathleen Koskie
Lea
Tamara Gal-On
Laura DeMay
Nicola Jennings
China Bower
Lesha Porche

Jordan
blkshp
CurlyQ
Leta Blake
Kezia Shugrue
Cheri Nauman
Jane Coulter
Mari Kane
Amanda McLeod
Amy Irwin
Hamykia
Josephine Myles
Raven
Barbara Armstrong
Mary Balkon
Liz Madrox
Silvia Park
Jules Lovesbooks
Sherry Lynn Burke
Carl Lindström
Jewel Cardwell
Saskia
Bert Jones
Layla Lawlor
Rebecca Cartee
Ann Bryant
Anne Jost
Carolyn Hill
Anu
Jenny Scott
Sarah Moore
Felix Kimmel
Sara Lake
Monica N.
Lin Z Bee
Brandon Witt
Samantha Pilon
Lori MacNabb
Emptycicada

ACKNOWLEDGMENTS

THANK YOU to Sonali Dev for help with the Amin family's names, and to Eliza David and LaQuette for beta reading. I couldn't have put this book together without you guys and hope this story lives up to your generous guidance. Thanks to Lillie for the indispensable story bible and deep proofing, to Sasha for holding my hand through my year of mess, and to Dreamspinner Press for letting me bring my team to this trilogy.

CHAPTER ONE

ONCE UPON a time, Nicolas Beckert went to weddings without a heavy pang in his heart.

He'd attended plenty in his day, between his Copper Point cousins, relatives in Milwaukee, and friends of the family. For several years it felt like every weekend there was yet another gift his grandmother or mother picked out, waiting for Nick to amplify it with a little extra cash and a handwritten note wishing the couple a bright future. Nick had always happily gone to these weddings. As the one who had understood without being told it was his job to live up to the legacy of service and grace his father had left behind, Nick knew his duty, and he took pride in fulfilling it, never once begrudging even a penny of those cash packets tucked into the card or a second of those busy Saturday afternoons.

Lately, though, the weddings themselves underscored the fact that while he was present at these events, he was separate from them in a way he couldn't ever let anyone know.

The wedding of his third cousin at the New Birth Baptist Church in Copper Point was particularly uncomfortable, and it wasn't just because the first Saturday in June had dawned uncharacteristically muggy and hot. People were gossiping as they always did, but the topic du jour made him distinctly uncomfortable.

"Did you hear, the surgeon and nurse finally picked a date for their wedding? Coming up fast too. First weekend in October." The speaker, one of Nick's distant relations, raised her eyebrows knowingly, fanning herself with a paper plate as she stood in line for the buffet. "Going to be a big to-do, since Dr. Wu has his family coming from Taiwan."

Nick's great-aunt clucked her tongue. "The things we see sometimes."

The group around them made ever-so-slightly disapproving noises.

This was spoken a bit loudly, for the benefit of Dr. Kathryn Lambert-Diaz, whose first cousin was the bride. Kathryn was attending with her wife, Rebecca, whom she'd married years ago in a ceremony among friends and accepting family members while Kathryn was doing her residency at the University of Iowa. Nick watched them both, worried Rebecca in particular would say something, but they only continued to chat politely with Kathryn's parents. They didn't have plates of food in their hands and looked as if they were about to leave.

"The other couple hasn't set their date yet, but they're next." By *other couple*, his great-aunt meant Dr. Owen Gagnon and Erin Andreas. "Should have never thought to see the day."

"All of them working at the hospital too." Uncle Billy leaned around his wife to address Nick, who stood close enough to easily be drawn into conversation. "You best keep your people in line there, son."

His wife swatted Billy with her fan. "You leave the boy alone. He's had enough work, with the embezzlement scandal. He don't need your sass too."

Pastor Robert came up behind Nick and rested a hand on his shoulder. "I have faith in our Nick. He's done a wonderful job with the hospital. I daresay we've never had better leadership in place there, thanks to him. We certainly haven't had a better CEO." He winked at Nick. "If all it comes with is a bit of unusual community color, I suppose we can count that as a blessing."

Everyone at the table chuckled, and Nick inclined his head. He wanted out of this conversation. "I should go check on my grandmother and mother, to make sure they don't need anything. If you folks'll excuse me?"

They shooed him away gleefully, but Nick could hear them talking about him as he disappeared, and a perverse instinct kept him nearby but hidden so he could eavesdrop.

"He's the next one we need to see married off."

"Get him a wife and a couple of kids, and we'll have ourselves the Copper Point Obamas!"

"What's taking him so long, though? He never dates anybody."

"Well, he's been busy with all those scandals."

"Scandal's been done and dusted. Besides, a man's got needs. It's not right, him never dating."

"You don't think our Nick…."

Nick's stomach turned over. Wiping his mouth to cover the grimness of his countenance, he moved out of earshot before he heard the rest of that sentence.

He didn't get three feet, though, before he ran into the choir director, James Grant.

James greeted him with his usual wide smile. "Nick, looking good, brother." His grin faded as Nick failed to mask his unsettled emotions fast enough. "You all right? Something happen?"

Nick fished up a smile. "Nah. No worries. Too much to do, is all, too much on my mind."

James raised an eyebrow. "Things haven't calmed down at the hospital?"

"Oh, you know how it goes." Nick couldn't quite catch his groove. That last remark kept echoing in his head. *You don't think our Nick….*

James put a hand on Nick's shoulder. "Hey. You want to go sit somewhere for a minute and talk? You don't look so good."

Talking was the last thing Nick wanted to do. And much as he loved James, sitting with *him* and having an intimate heart-to-heart would only fuel the flames of what people were apparently thinking about *their Nick*. He held up his hands. "Thanks, but honestly, I'm just doing a little too much these days." He took a step sideways and kept walking as he spoke. "I gotta go check in for a second. But we'll talk soon. The choir is killing it, by the way."

"All right." James waved him away, looking sad. "We'll talk later."

Nick gave himself a moment behind a bush to gather his composure before hunting down his family. His mother, grandmother, and sister were together at the table where the groom's closest relatives had gathered, Grandma Emerson holding court. She was in the middle of telling some story as Nick approached, but his sister broke away to greet him.

"Hey, you." She nudged him with her hip. "You going to get down with me later?"

"Can't. Got the reception for Dr. Amin."

She sighed. "Oh right, I forgot you had to leave early."

"Erin's covering for me, letting me show up late." He tugged at his tie and reached into his pocket for his handkerchief to dab at his neck, which dripped in the heat. "Need to go home and freshen up before I head out to the country club."

"Country club crowd." Emmanuella wrinkled her nose. "How bad will *that* be?"

"Standard hospital donor schmoozefest. Pretty dry and crusty, but they made the cardiac unit possible. I wish you would've agreed to be my date so you could meet Dr. Amin. She's amazing. You'll love her."

"I'll meet her sometime when she's *not* at one of those dog and pony shows, thanks. The dedication ceremony was more than enough for me." She punched him lightly in the arm. "Besides. It's time you get a proper date for yourself instead of hauling me around to these things."

"She wants to meet the family, though, since she wasn't in town for the ceremony."

"You should invite her family over for dinner. Mom and Grandma would love it." She leaned in closer and spoke quietly. "Did I hear right, the Ryans will be there?"

The Ryans were Jeremiah Ryan, their father's longtime friend and sometimes business partner back in the day, and his daughter Cynthia. Since then, Ryan had made quite a name for himself in the hospital industry, to the point that now he was the CEO of a corporation managing several medical centers in the Midwest. Nick nodded, stealing a careful glance at their mother. "Was she the one who mentioned it?"

Emmanuella snorted. "I can't believe she hasn't bothered you about it yet. You know she's always dreamed about Cynthia Ryan as a daughter-in-law."

Yes, Nick was painfully aware. He didn't comment, choosing to wipe his mouth with his hand and send his gaze out across the crowd. It landed on the bride and groom, who stood hand in hand as they greeted their guests two tables over. They looked so happy.

Nick fought another pang in the center of his chest.

His mother spied him then, smiling wide and waving him to her side. "Baby, come sit and eat. I made you a plate, and it's getting cold."

Though Nick wasn't remotely hungry, he held up his hands in apology, dredged up his most charismatic grin, and settled into the space beside her. "Sorry, was making my rounds." He reached across the table to shake hands with the groom's family. "Wonderful ceremony. Thanks so much for having us."

Mrs. Hill beamed and pressed her hand to her chest. "We're so glad y'all could come. Especially since your mother tells me you have another event yet today?"

"Reception for the new cardiologist, yes."

Mr. Hill's chest puffed up at being prioritized over the fancy country club shindig. "I'm telling you, Nick, your daddy would be so proud to see the work you've done with that hospital. Not just becoming the CEO, but cleaning up all the mess those fools made for so many years. You're a credit to his name."

Nick inclined his head. "Thank you, sir."

Mrs. Hill elbowed her husband with a sly wink. "Now we have to help find *him* a lovely wife too."

Nick pushed the potato salad and baked beans around his plate, doing his best to ignore the leaden feeling in his stomach.

As the table conversation resumed, allowing him to drift into his own thoughts again, Nick focused on the sea of guests. People were happy and laughing, caught up in the festivities. It was a humble gathering, with homemade decorations and family and church members helping cook and serve the dishes in lieu of a catered lunch. It was practically more picnic than wedding, except everyone was dressed in their finest outfits, and in the case of many of the ladies, hats. Nick loved the children the best, in their frilly dresses and suits and ties, chasing each other and giggling as they ran about the lawn, mothers and aunties occasionally hollering at them to mind their clothes or sit and finish their food.

Everything was warm and wonderful and perfect.

The bride and groom glowed as they reveled in their special day. They were good people, and Nick looked forward to watching them make their family together. Except though he celebrated their union and their happiness, it pained him too. With every tinkle of laughter the couple inspired, each beaming smile they shared, the yearning inside Nick grew, until eventually he excused himself from the table and flitted around the reception once more.

When the time came for him to bid people goodbye and get ready for the country club party, he was almost relieved. As he stopped by his family to let them know he was leaving, his grandmother put her hand on his arm. "There's a bag on the table in the kitchen, a small gift for the Ryans. Give it to them, will you, when you see them this afternoon? And be sure to say hello to Cynthia. Tell her to stop by the house the next time she's through."

"Of course." With a squeeze of her shoulder, Nick went on his way.

He found the gift—locally roasted coffee and a loaf of Grandma Emerson's famous banana bread tastefully tucked inside tissue paper in an elegant bright blue gift bag—where she'd said it would be. It smelled wonderful, and he lingered to savor the mingling scents. Then, setting his keys beside the package so he wouldn't forget it, he hurried upstairs to shower.

Shutting his eyes under the spray, Nick saw the smiling faces of the bride and groom once again in his mind's eye. So happy. So celebrated. So protected. Everything laid out before them, the community ensuring their path stayed clear.

What would that be like, he wondered?

Adjusting the plain silk bow tie over the tips of his shirt collar, he stared at his reflection. He felt much stiffer in his tuxedo than he had in the tan suit and gray-striped tie he'd worn to the wedding. He tried out a few expressions in the mirror, searching for one that allowed him to remain guarded but still seem dignified.

He grabbed the gift bag along with his keys, and to boost himself on the way to the country club, he blasted The Weeknd on his stereo. He sang along, winding down the long, scenic road leading to the country club on the top of the hill overlooking the most beautiful and expansive part of the bay.

Pulling up to the gates, he clicked off the radio, put his work face on, and presented his member card to the guard.

The party was in full swing as he handed his keys to the valet and entered the crush. The women were in elegant dresses, the men all in tuxedos or suits—excepting Rebecca Lambert-Diaz. She and Kathryn had already arrived, no longer dressed in airy outdoor wedding clothes, but while Kathryn wore a simple black evening gown, Rebecca had donned a smart black pantsuit with glittering rhinestones on the collar and cuffs. They seemed a bit more at ease at this party than the one they had left, laughing and mingling with the guests.

Nick took his place in the crowd as well, moving from group to group, smiling and shaking hands, ensuring people felt welcomed. His reception here was markedly different than it had been at church. Here they were wary of him, the young upstart who had changed so much about the tidy lives of Copper Point.

As far as they were concerned, he'd broken all their rules. Nick had been hired to be a pawn. Oh, no one had ever come out and said as much, but he'd understood things with one glance. A hospital CEO, at his age? He didn't have the experience. His suspicions had been confirmed as soon as he'd come through the door. No real power, no backing. Even so, experience was experiencc, and it was nice to stay close to home. He'd told himself he could put up with it for a while, until it was time to upgrade.

Except part of him hadn't been able to shake the idea that he could dig under the rotten surface of the institution and dismantle the system that had broken his father's spirit and nearly ruined their family. A few years on the hospital board had been enough to catch the attention of the power players at the hospital in a way that dogged him even after he'd been voted out. They worked behind the scenes to ruin his business and nearly cost him his home—and ultimately, through his failing health, had cost him his life.

Nick hadn't really thought he'd be able to avenge his father, had only dreamed of it. But with the help of Erin and the others, he'd done just that. Now there was a new board, a new balance of power, and a new day at St. Ann's. For many of the people in this room, though? Oh, Nick was still *that man*. It didn't matter that the board members who'd embezzled a scandalous amount of money were all in jail and that Nick had helped put them there. These people still didn't like him. They didn't like how he'd gone out of his way to make the new hospital board reflect the diverse population of Copper Point. There was a lot of rumbling from this set about "the way things used to be," their gazes turned toward the past with longing.

Well, Nick thought as he sipped a glass of champagne he'd collected from a passing tray, if they'd rather have the crooks than progress, then screw 'em.

Jeremiah Ryan beamed when he saw Nick, waving him over. Cynthia waved too, her expression welcoming and warm, reminiscent of the faces he'd left at the wedding reception. It also carried the whiff of something more, something hopeful.

Nick smiled back, ready to make his way to this important donor, this friend of the family, this man who understood his difficult position better than anyone, this woman he admired and considered an important friend. But before he reached them, he bumped into another guest, and as soon as he saw who it was, his carefully constructed image fell apart.

"Sorry." The man, fair-haired and tall, but not as tall as Nick, held up his hands and stepped aside. As their gazes met, the man's smile fell away. "Oh. It's you."

Yes. It's me.

It's you.

They both had their masks down as they regarded one another. Nick was conscious of the heavy beating of his heart, of the ache and longing he always felt when he stood this close to Dr. Jared Kumpel. He looked devastating in his tuxedo, crisp and neat, dark-blond hair gleaming in contrast to the dark fabric, his light skin glowing in the dim light.

He was beautiful in a way that stole Nick's breath and short-circuited his brain. This man had stirred him ever since he could remember, since the moment Nick had been, at last, able to understand why he felt so different than everyone else around him.

Jared spoke first, his voice thin and forced. "How was the wedding?"

It took Nick a second to register what Jared had said, to remember he shouldn't simply stare at the seductive curve of the man's upper lip. "G-good. It was good." He cleared his throat. "Hot."

"Yes, it's a muggy day out, isn't it?" The conversation, such as it was, broke off and dangled.

Nick tugged at the cuffs of his shirt and glanced away. "I should…."

"Of course." Jared's voice was flat, dead, as if he couldn't wait to get away. "I'm sorry to keep you."

And just like that, they parted, Jared wafting over to the bar, Nick resuming his trajectory toward the Ryans, plastering on the expression he'd practiced in the mirror as the leaden weight settled all the more deeply onto his heart.

DR. JARED Kumpel wanted to find a dark broom closet, put a bucket over his head, and scream.

It was supposed to be an evening of celebration. The physicians, board members, and local donor class were gathered at the Copper Point Country Club to toast the arrival of Dr. Uma Amin, who would start work next week. After years of embezzlement scandals and a complete overhaul of the hospital board of directors, at last things were peaceful. Perfect, even.

Except for the part where Nick Beckert had a smile for everyone in the room but Jared. The memory of Nick's bright expression melting away at the sight of Jared, the way he'd hurried off as if escaping the plague, drove Jared directly to the bar, where he sipped his drink and tortured himself by watching Nick pull out the charm for everyone else.

Goddamn it.

Jared had absolutely no right to feel so proprietary, which only made him crankier. Nick wasn't his boyfriend, was barely his friend, despite the fact that once upon a time they'd been so intimate he could have identified the man by the sound of his breath. For the past four years, Nick had been Jared's employer, in a sense, though the contractual relationship between clinic physicians and St. Ann's Medical Center was complicated. For years the two of them had silently agreed to pretend the past never existed, and this strategy, while frustrating, had mostly worked out for the best.

It was just lately they'd gotten along, talking casually, playing racquetball, hanging out in the safety of large groups. Jared realized he'd allowed these interactions to engender false hope and perhaps a bit of expectation. He wasn't ready for Nick to start freezing him out.

Before the embezzlement crisis, Nick had focused entirely on work, and Copper Point had seemed willing to leave him to his monkhood. But then Nick had taken out the embezzlement ring in the old board and overseen funding for the long-overdue cardiac center, dedicated in his father's name. He was the shiniest man in town, and everyone wanted him on their arm.

So many damn *women* wanted him in their bed.

Watching yet another woman brush a manicured hand along the sleeve of Nick's tuxedo jacket, Jared told himself it didn't matter. *He's never going to admit who he is, even to himself, so who cares who flirts with him?*

I care, damn it. Turning away with a glower, Jared finished off his drink and wandered into the crowd. Except he didn't feel like mingling, so he found a table as far from Nick as possible and sat, ready to bury himself in his phone.

He hadn't had so much as a chance to reach for his pocket before someone joined him. Dr. Owen Gagnon, the anesthesiologist at St. Ann's Medical Center and one of Jared's best friends, pushed a glass in front of Jared and plunked down at the table beside him. "Doing all right? You seem off your game."

After taking a sip of his drink, Jared waved a breezy hand. "Fine. Not feeling the hospital function vibe, is all."

With a grunt of agreement, Owen peeled back the panels of his tuxedo jacket and settled in. "Jack has to be jealous we didn't throw him a party when he arrived."

Jack was Dr. Hong-Wei Wu, St. Ann's resident general surgeon. "Knowing Jack, he's indifferent. I'd think he wouldn't want the fuss but would have endured it if we'd arranged it for him. Though maybe you're right. Maybe he was quietly offended we didn't treat him better. He holds a lot of cards close to his vest."

Owen snorted. "He's all about doing things up properly. I bet he was mad we didn't give him more of a welcome. He sure as hell deserved it."

Jared felt better not thinking about Nick. He tried to keep the conversation going. "By the way, the quintet sounded great, but of course it always does. Your solo was particularly good."

As usual, Owen ignored the compliment and wrinkled his nose. "I don't love how every time we have one of these gigs I have to play Pied Piper. Sometimes I want to sit and grouse about having to show up in my monkey suit with the rest of the doctors."

"If your fiancé hears you, you'll be sleeping in the garage tonight."

"Yes, well, the good news is the garage in the mansion is climate controlled." Owen glanced around. "Still, there's no reason for Erin to have to hear."

This time Jared didn't have to fake his grin. "Have you seen Jack or Simon?"

"Jack's talking with Dr. Amin. Simon, I'm not sure."

"Probably with Jack, since he's not with us. He feels out of place at these things. Until he was Jack's plus-one, he never had to come."

"As the nursing rep on the hospital board, he'd be here anyway. He needs to get comfortable." Owen leaned in closer, eyes sparkling with mischief. "So, Mr. I-Know-All-the-Gossip. How's Copper Point's elite handling yet another physician who isn't a white male evangelical Christian?"

"Oh my God. Where do I start?" Jared rolled his eyes and picked up his drink, sipping it as he moved closer to Owen so they wouldn't be overheard. "The retired college president's wife was in a private chat group pitching a fit because the new cardiologist isn't only from India, she's Muslim. Someone pointed out there was nothing wrong with that, and the end result was the country club scrambling to find someone they could send into the women's locker room to break up a fight when the online spat went abruptly offline. Then on Copper Point People someone else—no one of note, some random MAGA—complained about how it was obvious St. Ann's had an antiwhite hiring policy."

Owen buried his face in his hands. "That Facebook group is trash."

"Wait until you hear how it got resolved. People argued back and forth for two days, but when everyone was starting to cool off, someone came in as the 'mediating' voice and pointed out at least she was straight this time."

Owen sat up slowly, drawing his fingers down his face and staring sightlessly at the table decorations in front of them. "Tell me again why we live here?"

"Because Simon couldn't bear to leave his family when we were looking for somewhere for us to get jobs together after med school. Plus now you're marrying one of the founding sons. Just because we're stuck in this crazy town doesn't mean we can't get our quiet revenge by living well, though. I think you and Erin should adopt a horde of children and raise them Wiccan. It's the only way to heal this place."

Owen rubbed his jaw. "I dunno if I'm organized enough to be Wiccan. Aren't there a lot of meetings and rituals? I could do casual pagan."

"I think it depends on the type of Wiccan." Jared lifted an eyebrow. "Are you ignoring the hordes-of-children part, or is this your way of telling me you've changed your opinion on fatherhood?"

"Well. I mean, I don't know about *hordes*. But yeah, we've talked about it some, and it doesn't seem such a terrible idea, when I think about it with Erin. Oh." He straightened, his face transforming into a youthful, slightly ridiculous grin as he waved to someone across the room. "Speak of the devil. I need to go. You sure you're okay here?"

You fine being alone? That was the translation.

Jared got out the fake smile, wrestling it into something genuine. "Nowhere else I'd rather be. Go see your man."

After Owen left, Jared sipped his drink and people watched for a few minutes, telling himself everything was fine, but his gaze kept drifting to Nick. The DJ switched to a slow song, and one of the women surrounding Nick took his hands to lure him onto the dance floor. He didn't fight her.

It was the daughter of the investor from Milwaukee. Cynthia Ryan. The two of them looked stunning together, her dark hair swept up in a breathtaking style no white woman in the room could emulate, her brown skin glowing against her goldenrod evening dress.

If Nick took Cynthia home to Grandma Emerson, she'd give her blessing in the span of a sigh.

Setting his teeth, Jared finished his drink, then rose and went to get a refill.

Matthew Engleton was at the bar, collecting change for a vodka sour, and he grinned at Jared as he approached. "Dr. Kumpel. Good to see you."

It wasn't a dismissive greeting, which Jared found interesting. He knew Matt, vaguely, because you couldn't live in Copper Point and not know the Engletons, especially if you ever had to buy a suit from their family store. Matt was on the hospital board now too, so they'd gotten a bit closer.

Jared smiled back politely. "Good to see you as well. Enjoying yourself?"

"Oh, as much as I can at these sorts of things." Matt leaned an elbow on the bar and gestured at the crowd of Copper Point elite and St. Ann's higher echelon. "What about you? You aren't with your usual crew."

"We're all busy networking bees. They want the doctors talking to the potential donors, so if we stay in the corner and drink, it defeats the purpose."

Matt laughed. "Difficult to hide, I suspect, when one of you is engaged to the vice president." He motioned to the bartender. "Let me buy you a drink, and you can network with me."

"But you're a board member."

"I'm also one of the potential donors. Dad always gives liberally to the hospital, but he never comes to these functions anymore. He says he needs me to be the representative now. So I have double duty." He raised his eyebrows. "You'll have to charm the money out of me, Doctor."

Oh my. Was Matt… hitting on him? A closer inspection of the man's focused gaze told Jared yes, he was.

Well. He hadn't seen this coming. Jared had assumed Matt hid his orientation in deference to the family business. Apparently he was wrong, or there was an exception clause for local pediatricians.

Did he *want* Matt to hit on him? He hadn't thought of Matt as anyone but the polite man who sold clothing well before, and now was also the man who sat in boring meetings beside him. He supposed he was cute enough….

"What'll you have?" the bartender asked.

"Old Fashioned," Jared replied.

A familiar feminine laugh behind him made his shoulders relax. "Someone's ordering an Old Fashioned? Dr. Kumpel must be at the bar."

He turned around in time for Rebecca Lambert-Diaz to catch his cheek in her hand and give it a gentle tweak. He playfully swatted it away. "Hello, Rebecca. Where's your wife?"

"Hiding in a corner. She hates these things, and we already had to endure a family wedding this afternoon." Rebecca smiled at Matt. "Hello again, Matthew. How's the store?"

Was it Jared's imagination, or did Matt's expression dim a little? "Everything's going well, but we'd do better if our favorite lawyer came by and checked out our new summer line."

"Always a salesman. But now that you mention it, you're right, I haven't been by in a while." She withdrew a twenty and waved it at the bartender. "Let me get my glass of wine, we'll find a seat, and you can tell me what you have in stock. I do need a new suit."

The three of them ended up back at the table Jared had vacated, Rebecca in the middle as she and Matt spoke intensely about women's clothing. Jared sipped his drink and scanned the room, more concerned about where people were. Jack was with Dr. Amin, poor Simon appearing as lost as Owen had said. Owen was with Erin, talking with the leader of the Copper Point string quintet.

Where was Nick, though?

Jared's lip nearly curled when he found him. He was with Cynthia Ryan, and didn't they look *cozy*.

Grumbling under his breath, Jared took a fortifying drink of alcohol, the burn fueling his ire.

"Don't you think, Jared?"

He snapped out of his funk at Rebecca's question. "Sorry, what?"

She gestured to herself, miming dress parts as she spoke. "I enjoy a double-breasted suit, but I think what's best on me are those single-breasted smooth pieces that don't have a crease. You know what I'm talking about?"

Jared frowned at her, his attention officially drawn away from Nick. "Well, yes, it's the most flattering option for you, but it isn't as if you can wear the same thing all the time."

Matt held out his hands. "*Thank you.* I've been trying to convince her of this for months."

Rebecca waved airily. "Whatever, I'll let the two of you dress me."

Jared snorted into his Old Fashioned. "You won't ever give up control so easily, but nice try."

"Who I'd really like to get into the store is Jared." Matt bumped Jared's arm, lingering a little longer than necessary. "It's been a while since you've treated yourself to some new clothes. Unless you've been cheating on me with other clothing stores?"

Rebecca laughed. "Jared, leave town to shop? Good luck with that."

No question about it, Matt was trying to flirt with Jared and was getting lesbian cock-blocked at every turn. Well, Jared supposed he could do worse.

He cut a glance to the other side of the room. Matt was as nice as any number of men, but Jared's attention was firmly fixed elsewhere.

Jared's gaze landed on the woman's hand sliding down Nick's arm, and his teeth set.

"Did you want another drink?" Matt shook Jared's glass, which he was shocked to discover was empty. "Or maybe you want to get up and walk around?"

Jared couldn't look away from Nick, though he knew he needed to. He felt a hand on his arm as he stood—Rebecca gave him a questioning look.

"You've seemed off all evening. And honestly, you haven't been yourself lately, period. Is there something going on?"

How could he tell her or any of them the truth? He bent and kissed her on the cheek. "I'm fine, but thank you."

She caught his shoulder and kept him down long enough to whisper. "You're not. You might have fooled the others, but you haven't fooled me. Who's giving you a ride home?"

Oh, Lord, now he had Rebecca mothering him. Sighing, he patted her shoulder. "Seriously. It's not a problem. Okay?"

Matt frowned at him.

Jared squared his shoulders. He *was* fine. He was absolutely perfect, and he didn't need a babysitter. Maybe he'd start an affair with Matt Engleton, what the hell. Maybe sweet little Matt would surprise him and he'd be the next one of their group to find a happy ever after.

Sweet, boring Matt.

"You okay?" Matt asked.

God, they needed to *stop asking him*. Jared's face was going to break, he was stretching it so far for these damn smiles. "Absolutely."

Except as they rounded the corner of a group of chuckling old men, he got another glimpse of Nick as the music shifted. It was Prince of all the damn things, and not only Prince but "Kiss."

Like magnets, Nick and Jared's gazes met and locked.

You're not boring, baby. Not boring at all.

And I haven't forgotten a thing.

When two new women appeared beside Nick, giggling and tugging him forward, Nick turned away, and Jared couldn't stand it anymore.

Jared threaded his fingers through his hair in an attempt to hide his shaking hands. "Actually," he said to Matt, "I think I wouldn't mind stepping outside."

Matt beamed. "Great."

Yes, let's get out of here.

Except Jared knew from experience it didn't matter how far he ran. He couldn't get away from Nick.

CHAPTER TWO

NICK DROPPED his focus from Jared for two minutes, and Matt Engleton was draped all over him.

Whenever Nick was in the same room as Jared, he was keenly aware of the man's presence, but usually they were at work and Jared was only looking fine in a white doctor's coat and whatever shirt and tie he had underneath, or scrubs if he was doing his turn in the ER. Tonight, however, Jared was in a tux, and it took everything for Nick to keep from feasting his eyes. And what was his reward for good behavior?

Matt Engleton. That puppy.

Good God, the man couldn't stop touching Jared, hands drifting dangerously close to his ass. During a Prince song, no less.

The hell this was going to stand. Seeing them stalled by Rebecca, Nick longed to stalk across the dance floor and wrench Jared away.

Except of course he couldn't do that.

Obviously he couldn't do that. It was just….

"Something wrong?"

Cynthia Ryan's voice, ringed with concern, brought Nick to reality. He wrenched his attention away from Jared and back to her. "Nothing at all. I'm sorry. What were you saying?"

Jeremiah laughed and clapped Nick on the back. "I was trying to get you to sit down with me and talk about this deal again."

Nick did his best to tuck away his frustration. "Mr. Ryan. You know how much I love spending time with you, but you *also* know I can't make any decisions without the hospital board."

Ryan waved this objection away. "I know, I know. But your board listens to you. Besides, I like an excuse to sit and drink with a fine young man." He winked and elbowed Nick. "Be careful, or I'll have Cynthia convince you instead."

"Daddy." Cynthia's voice was a warning, though she smiled too. Some of that warmth lingered as she turned once more to Nick. "Of course we understand you can't do anything without the board. But we'd love to go over the plan again to see if we can't win you over to our way of thinking. You do know this has nothing to do with taking over your hospital and everything to do with supporting someone we see as family."

She really was the crack negotiator of their team, and it was difficult to say no to her. He opened his mouth to gently skirt the issue, but before he spoke, his gaze darted to the bar against his will, where he saw Engleton's hand firmly planted on Jared's shoulder, their hips so close they might actually be touching.

Goddamn it.

Unaware of Nick's inner conflict, Ryan playfully wagged a finger at Nick. "Let us invest in St. Ann's and protect the legacy you've made."

Cynthia stepped closer, pitching her voice low. "And let us keep you safe from the vultures swarming around."

They didn't move their gazes to the cluster of chuckling men fifteen feet away, but they didn't need to.

Ryan raised one eyebrow slightly. "You did well, the way you handled that embezzlement scheme last year. And with Dr. Wu's leadership in surgery and his connections in the field, you've put in the work to turn this failing ship around. But you know as well as I do this place can't rebound so quickly after decades of mismanagement."

Cynthia nodded. "Your budget won't rearrange itself. It had to have been a trick to get this cardiac unit into place, and you already admitted to us you're more in debt than you'd like."

Nothing they said was untrue. While the new board had a solid plan to get out of debt, it hinged on no surprises upending their efforts. These fund-raisers and glad-handings were insurance. Nick pursed his lips.

"Let us help you," Ryan urged. "Because if it's not us, it's going to be a vulture like Jordan Peterson who comes for you."

Nick held up his hands. "Never fear. St. Ann's has no interest in being picked over, by Peterson or anyone." Before the Ryans could launch into another pitch, he checked on Jared. Matt's hand had traveled down to settle onto Jared's waist. Nick couldn't afford to be polite any longer. "I'm terribly sorry. If you can excuse me."

Yes, Matt had his hand on the *small of Jared's back* now, brazenly leaving it there as if it were his right, and Jared was letting him. Nick had to work his jaw to keep from setting his teeth. Why wasn't Jared moving away? Was this what he wanted? Nick had thought they'd made some headway lately. He'd thought they'd healed their relationship a bit. He'd thought....

What, you thought it could go somewhere? That because you were somewhat friendly on occasion, he'd never look at another man?

You thought, what, that you were going to start something up with him again? You know that can't happen. Ever.

He stopped walking, undone by his own thoughts.

"Nick."

He slow-blinked, hating himself and his hesitation. He didn't bother with too much of a smile as he turned toward Peterson and his clutch of friends, but he of course couldn't afford to be rude either. "Mr. Peterson. What can I do for you?"

Peterson waved Nick over like he was calling for a waiter. "C'mere. I was telling a story to these guys, and I know you'd love to hear it."

Oh, Nick was quite certain he'd not enjoy it at all. Nevertheless, it was his job to stand next to boors such as this and pretend he didn't mind.

"I was telling the story," Peterson began as soon as it was clear Nick was obeying him, "about the Iowa hospital we bought last week. Such a wreck. Damn place is in the middle of nowhere, and over half the town is on welfare." He held up his hand as a shield that hid absolutely nothing and whispered, not at all sotto voce, "*Indian reservation*."

The rich white men tittered knowingly. Nick moved his face into a more neutral position and called on his patience.

Enjoying his audience, Peterson continued. "Anyway. They wouldn't budge for years. Mismanaged everything, then refused help until they were so far underwater they almost had to close. They're just lucky we came in and bought them out."

Nick considered saying nothing. It would have been his preference, since clearly Peterson's whole goal was to bait him. Even a year ago, Nick would have hesitated to wade in no matter what. However, it wasn't a year ago, and it was obvious the other donors listening to Peterson's nonsense took him seriously.

Packing away his patience, Nick quietly drew the sword he was starting to get comfortable waving around.

"I'm not sure what part of that I was meant to enjoy." Nick tucked his hands behind his jacket and regarded Peterson carefully. "However, I do know the hospital to which you're referring. Iowa privatized its Medicaid system, causing unending issues for rural hospitals and anywhere with an aging population. I can see how it's of concern in their state, where population growth is declining, especially among the younger generations. As for the mismanagement, I'm afraid it's all on the state level. I completely disagree about the rescue, however. I happen to know Smithstown did everything they could locally. They retained as many services as they could, because they're so remote they knew going without a hospital was the one thing their community couldn't handle. Ah, but that's the first thing your corporation does when it swoops in, doesn't it, cut services?" He smiled. "I'm afraid such an arrangement isn't an opportunity for Copper Point."

Peterson's audience became alarmed, clearly not understanding the story in quite that light, and Peterson himself sputtered in quiet fury. "You're deliberately misrepresenting things, Beckert. Mark my words, you're *going* to need us, and sooner than you think."

"Not while I'm the CEO of the hospital, we won't." Seeing Matt and Jared heading toward the country club balcony, Nick decided he'd played with these fools enough. "If you'll excuse me."

Crossing the room with swift, purposeful strides, Nick cut Jared off before he reached the door.

"Dr. Kumpel." He purposefully ignored Engleton, because if he made eye contact with the man, he'd give too much away. "I hope you weren't planning to leave without greeting your new colleague properly."

Jared gave him a withering glare. "I'm stepping out for some air. It's a little stifling in here with all the sucking up going on."

What was with this snippy attitude? "You're starting to sound like Owen."

"Well, someone has to be the resident smart-ass. He's softened too much since falling for Erin."

"Someone doesn't, in fact, need to fill that role." Nick nodded at Matt. "Sorry, I need to steal Jared for a bit."

"Of course." Engleton looked frustrated.

Good.

Unfortunately, Jared was also annoyed and let Nick have it as he was dragged away. "I already met Dr. Amin, and you know it. What was all that about?"

"You didn't meet her here tonight."

"Hell."

"Stop swearing."

Dr. Amin stood in a cluster of people at the side of the room, the belle of the ball, such as it was. She was talking with Jack and Simon, but her smile widened as Nick approached with Jared.

"Mr. Beckert. Dr. Kumpel. Hello. Thank you again for such a lovely party. I certainly don't deserve it."

Nick inclined his head to her. "We're fortunate to have you. Have you settled in?"

"Yes, yes." She slipped a lock of hair behind her ear. "The kids are obsessed with the idea of swimming in the lake, though. They won't listen to us when we tell them the water is cold."

"Well, it's not as awful right now as it can be, especially if they're only wading, but it can be pretty dangerous if you don't know what you're doing. We should have a picnic, though." Jared nodded at Owen, who chatted with a group of people nearby. "We could have a private welcome for the Amin family at the beach." He leaned around Nick and shouted at Owen. "Hey, Gagnon. You learn how to drive your boat yet?"

Dr. Amin's eyes went wide. "Oh, a boat? They'd love that."

At first the conversation went well. Owen joined them, and so did Erin, and it seemed as if they were making plans, the six of them and the Amins. Except when Nick's shoulder brushed Jared—somewhat accidental, somewhat on purpose—Jared didn't let *him* linger the way he did Matt. Instead he pulled away as if he'd been burned. To make matters worse, he excused himself.

"I'm so sorry to be rude, but I need to see someone before they go. I'll be right back."

Jared left, and everyone stared after him in bemusement. Nick wasn't sure what to do, until he saw Jared heading toward Engleton.

Oh, hell no.

Excusing himself as well, Nick followed Jared, not wasting time as he herded him toward the door.

Jared turned to him, glaring. "What exactly are you doing?"

"Have you been drinking?" Nick leaned in and sniffed him. "You have."

"Nothing else to do. Everyone else is off being lovey-dovey."

Yes, like you with Engleton. Obviously Nick couldn't say that. He had noticed the others hadn't been with Jared most of the evening. They were supposed to split up and focus on donors at an event such as this, but if it led to Jared ending up with Matt....

Nick's mouth tightened. "He doesn't suit you."

"What do you care who suits me or not?"

"Hush." Nick glanced around. They were off to the side, away from people, but still, he didn't need any rumors.

Jared shoved at him. He was definitely tipsy. Probably too many of those damn Old Fashioneds. "Matt suits me fine. He's sweet and cute. Maybe I'll go flirt with him."

Nick caught Jared's elbow. "You need to mingle with more donors."

Jared rolled his eyes. "Fine."

Jesus. "First you need to sober up. Let's get you some water and go outside."

"I was *going* outside when you stopped me."

Yes, he'd been going outside with Matt.

Well, maybe Nick should have left him alone. Maybe he was butting in where he wasn't wanted.

Nick leaned onto the bar, hoping to get the bartender's attention and a bottle of water, but the server was on the other end and busy flirting with a woman who was trying to get a drink discount. Nick hesitated, wondering what to do, but he was rescued by Kathryn, who slipped onto the stool beside him.

"The service on this end is bad." She raised her eyebrows at Jared, who was clearly trying to escape out the side door. "Were you guys going outside? I could get you something and bring it to you."

"That would be great," Nick said at the same time Jared called out he was fine. Nick fished out his wallet with one hand and withdrew a ten-dollar bill. "Would you get a couple bottles of water? You can text me, and I'll get them."

"Oh, no, I'll bring them out. Gives me an excuse to escape the crowd." She winked at him. "Just don't tell my boss."

Jared glared at Nick as he headed for the door. "Are you coming, or what?"

As Kathryn grinned at him, Nick touched her elbow gratefully and let Jared pull him out the door.

There weren't many people on the balcony. The temperature had settled into something far more tolerable, but the fish flies were starting to come out. Not enough that the outside lights had to be turned off, but enough to make most people think the bay would be better viewed through a window.

Jared had never cared about the fish flies. When they'd been boys, they'd run off together to watch them swarm, laughing at how gross the insects were. They lived for the weeks when the eggs hatched and the bugs were so thick the city had to shut off streetlights or risk traffic accidents because so many bugs were drawn to the glow.

When they'd been a little older, they'd learned fish fly nights were good cover for other activities they didn't want discovered.

Nick studied Jared's profile in the early sunset, bay breeze whipping his blond hair until its baby-fine strands glinted like gossamer spider threads. He had a whisper of a goatee, common for him during the winter. It was nearly summer now, though. Nick wondered why Jared hadn't shaved it off yet. It looked soft, though Nick suspected it wasn't.

He wanted to find out.

He *didn't* want Matt Engleton to.

Jared leaned on the railing and stared out at the water. "So are you going to date one of those women?"

Nick blinked. What brought this on? He glanced around, ensuring they were alone.

This apparently annoyed Jared. "The only other people out here are Mr. and Mrs. Larson, and they're both so hard of hearing you'd have to shout into their ears for them to eavesdrop. Are you dating one of them or not?"

"Am I dating Mr. and Mrs. Larson?"

"Oh, don't get cute."

"Well, I don't know who else you're talking about. Who am I supposed to be dating?"

You. I've been thinking about dating you.

There was no way he could say that out loud, though. If he hinted he was thinking about such a thing, Jared would….

Well, he didn't know what Jared would do anymore. That was the problem.

"I'm talking about your damn harem." Jared gestured vaguely at the building behind them.

"My harem?"

Jared turned around, patience lost. "The women who've been hanging on you all night long."

The women…? What women? Nick frowned at Jared. "You've been drinking too much."

Jared laughed. "You're kidding me. You're so gay you can't tell when a horde of women are hitting on you? All they've done all night is try to climb you like you're a tree, or unwrap you like a Big Mac."

Oh. He meant the group of people who had gathered around him inside, complimenting him on his accomplishments, who had clearly been attempting to make contact with him to further the interests of their families' businesses. He supposed several of them had been women.

And of course Cynthia Ryan was a woman. She certainly wasn't unwrapping him, though. Had anyone done that? What did that *mean*?

While it pleased him to hear Jared had kept such tabs on him, he didn't appreciate being outed, even if there didn't seem to be anyone around. "Keep your voice down."

With a *hmpf*, Jared faced the bay.

Nick leaned against the rail beside him, daring to stand close enough to let their elbows and upper arms touch as he spoke softly. "None of them wanted me. They only wanted connections. St. Ann's has the most growth in Copper Point right now. For decades the hospital has been hanging on by threads, held together by shady backroom deals. Now it might truly move forward. I'm trying to make sure that's what actually happens."

"So what you're saying is you weren't looking at these women at all, you were fixated on work, and it was me who was acting a fool, sitting alone in a corner getting jealous."

Nick's heart quickened at that confession, and he closed his eyes, taking in a deep, slow breath. A fish fly hit the top of his head, tangling briefly in his curls, and another smashed into his chin, but he didn't care. It only further served to take him back to his youth, to the times they'd stood together like this, daring to touch each other more and more, until one day… one day….

Maybe this time I can get it right….

Maybe, somehow, this time it'll all work out….

But the moment broke as Jared moved away, and when Nick opened his eyes, he saw Jared frowning at the bay, heard the iron in his voice when he spoke. "I should just date Matt and get over you. Date anyone and get over you."

Nick's breath caught.

Get… over me?

He gripped the rail as his thoughts tangled into each other. Jared wasn't over him? After all this time?

But they'd just been a fling. Youthful indiscretion. Nick's mistake. His greatest lapse of judgment.

I'm the one who can't get over you. But if you've been thinking of me all this time too....

Nick shut his eyes on a long blink, head spinning.

Jared kept talking. "It'd be a lot easier if I didn't have to see you every damn day. And if you didn't look like Idris Elba."

"I look like Idris Elba?"

Jared waved impatiently at him. "You know you're hot as hell. Don't fish for more compliments."

Nick wanted to whip out a net and collect them all. He wanted to scoop up Jared too.

All this time... have you really thought about me, all this time?

He lifted his hand, tried to speak.

No words came.

The door opened, and Kathryn appeared with a smile and two bottles of water. Jared pushed off the railing, weary and sad. "I'm going inside with Kathryn. Please leave me alone for the rest of the night."

Nick didn't want to let Jared go. He wanted to take him into his arms and confess everything, to tell him how he felt, how he'd always felt. Except he didn't know what came after that confession.

I can't change everything. Not now.

He watched Jared walking away and felt his heart tug.

I can't change, but I want to.

IT TOOK everything in Jared to make a somewhat dignified exit, so he couldn't offer any explanations to Kathryn as they left. Besides, given the way

Rebecca had shadowed him all night, he was pretty sure the Lambert-Diazes were already in the know when it came to how he felt about Nick.

This thought was cinched when Rebecca herself ambushed him. Flanked by the wives, Jared was marched into a secluded corner of the room and plunked into a chair.

Kathryn gave him the water, looking concerned. "Jared, what's going on? Are you and Nick fighting?"

"More like they're having foreplay," Rebecca remarked wryly.

Jared made no comment, downing half the bottle of water in one gulp. God, he hadn't realized how thirsty he was. He wiped his mouth with the back of his hand. "Are we allowed to leave yet? Because I want to get out of here."

Rebecca raised an eyebrow. "Tell me what's going on between you and Nick, and we can leave right now."

Jared smiled acerbically. "That'll be easy. Nothing whatsoever is going on. Can we go?"

Kathryn frowned at her wife. "Nick seemed so concerned about Jared earlier. He had me buy him water."

"Oh, you should have seen his face when Matt was flirting with Jared."

Kathryn put a hand to her lips. "Matt was flirting with Jared?"

Oh yes, Jared was going to follow up on that. Except he couldn't do it tonight. He was too tired. Exhausted all the way to his bones. "I'm going to find Owen and get him to take me home."

"We can do that," Kathryn insisted.

He held up his hands and wobbled to his feet. "No, I'm fine. I'll go with Owen." Owen wouldn't interrogate him. He was too busy being newly in love.

Kathryn and Rebecca tried to keep him there, but he declined firmly, and once they gave up, he slipped away, sipping his water and mingling with the crowd. He smiled at people he passed, putting on his mask. It was a little trickier than it should have been.

Nick was right, he'd had too much to drink. But all he needed was a good night's sleep, and he'd be fine.

Just have to go back to the house by myself, where I'll wake up alone too.

Jared aggressively finished the last of the water.

Owen was still talking to Dr. Amin, or rather he was listening as she told a story. Erin was too, and as Jared came closer, he saw Jack and Simon were with them. They waved as Jared approached.

"I hear you're planning excursions on our boat." Erin, ever the VP, was cool and slightly scolding at once.

"Well, someone has to goad you into pulling it out of storage." Jared inclined his head to Dr. Amin. "My apologies for stepping away."

"Oh, no trouble at all," she assured him.

"We can't wait until you join us officially," Jack told her.

"Her house isn't far from yours or our condo." Simon looked pleased. "We're going to help her move the last of their things in when they arrive next weekend. You'll help, won't you, Jared?"

"As long as I'm not scheduled for the ER."

"Oh, I'll make sure you're not," Erin promised.

It was clear Jared wasn't getting a ride anytime soon, so he sucked it up and mingled with the others, chitchatting and plastic-smiling until he had almost sobered up. He was so wrung out he wanted to collapse in a heap.

As Jared had asked, Nick left Jared alone. For the rest of thc evening, Jared saw him across the room, but Nick never came close again and didn't glance at him anymore.

It annoyed the hell out of Jared.

He tried to hide his frustration, but Owen noticed something was wrong with him right away, and when they went together to get the car, he commented on it.

"What's going on? You looked grim in there."

Jared rubbed the back of his neck. "Too much to drink, long day. I need to go home and sleep it off."

Owen winced. "Shit. I told Erin we could swing by the hospital on the way home. I'll tell him we have to drop you off first."

Jared shook his head. "No, actually, I want to stop there anyway."

"You're not going to do rounds smelling like bourbon, are you?"

"For God's sake, of course not. I'm a pediatrician, do you think I'm insane? No, I think I forgot my lunch bag there yesterday, and everything will be gross by Monday if I don't bring it home."

"I could grab it for you."

"It's fine, really."

Owen laughed. "You want to see if there's new gossip."

Jared lifted his chin. "I prefer to call it information gathering."

Grinning, Owen slung his arm around Jared's shoulders. "Why don't you come stay at our place tonight? I miss hanging out with you all the time."

Should he take Owen up on his offer? If Jared went home, he'd only end up feeling sorry for himself. He hated being the single extra feature, but the truth was, they didn't make him feel that way when they were together. He made himself feel that way, and it had everything to do with Nick.

Jared sighed. "Yeah. Sure, I'll stay over. Thanks."

"There's more going on with you than you're telling me, and it's starting to piss me off."

Nodding, Jared bumped his friend with his hip. "Well, you never know. Maybe tonight's the night I'll fill you in."

Owen didn't bother him about it any more, only held the door for him as they got to the car.

He didn't bring it up, either, as Owen soothed his frazzled fiancé, who was full of worries over whether the event had gone well. He'd collected Owen's violin, and as they drove, Erin held it in the front seat with him. Erin brightened, though, when he heard Jared was staying overnight with them.

"Oh, good. It'll be like old times." Erin smiled at Jared. "I miss having you in the kitchen when I wake up."

I miss having everyone around, period. Jared swallowed this and smiled back. "Well, I'll be there tomorrow morning."

The hospital was quiet as they arrived, not much going on in the ER, which was good. Jared lingered with the nurses on shift there, getting information on the cases from the evening and general dirt that had nothing to do with the hospital. He also found out about some surprise new hires.

"I don't care for the new security guys," the nurse's aide working the ER told him. "They're weird."

Jared hadn't met any of them, and Erin hadn't mentioned picking people up. "What's weird about them?"

The nurse's aide made a face, and Don, the ambulance guy who was loitering in the hallway, chuckled. "Oh, Trish, you don't like them because one of them gave you grief about double-parking."

Trish wrinkled her nose. "He didn't have to be so *rude* about it."

Jared wanted to learn more about these new security guys, to find out if they were locals or people from out of town, but Owen and Erin had already gone ahead, so he meandered after them, taking the elevator to the second floor to collect his lunch.

The elevator doors hesitated when Jared entered, and he thought it felt a little jerky on the ride up. He met Kevin, the custodian on duty, on his way to the doctors' lounge, and mentioned this to him.

"Oh, yeah." Kevin rubbed his head and grimaced. "There's some sort of electrical glitch, I guess. Elevator B is completely out of service, and Elevator A is acting funny. The company is coming to look at it tomorrow."

Jared lifted his eyebrows. "Thank God it's not a state inspection week, I guess. But seriously? Electrical glitch, and they're waiting that long? Is it safe to let people use it?"

"They ran some kind of test from their end and said everything's fine. I think they don't want to drive all the way up from Madison on a Saturday night. They were grumbly enough about tomorrow."

"But they swear it's safe?"

"Yeah, just going to be uncomfortable is all. Guy gave his personal guarantee."

"He better be right, because if anything goes wrong with it, we'll use it in court."

Kevin grinned. "Yeah, we have the barracuda on our board now. Nobody better mess with us."

Jared picked up his lunch in the lounge, still turning over Kevin's comment in his mind. That hadn't been the first time a staff member had felt pride about their new board, even though every single member was young and green when it came to hospital matters. Jared was one of the physician advisory representatives, a new addition to the crew Nick had invented. Doctors and nurses alike were thrilled to have this kind of representation.

Nick was doing good things. Nick had come into his own, found his stride, and everyone was noticing. Finally.

I should get over him and simply admire him as my boss. It's the responsible thing to do.

Despite Kevin's assurance about the elevator, Jared took the stairs to the third floor. Swinging his lunch bag from his finger, he headed to Erin's office. "Sorry I took so long, guys. I was chatting—"

He cut himself off as Nick emerged from the adjoining office, glancing at Jared as he locked the door.

"Looking for Erin and Owen?" Nick continued to fuss with the lock. "They went downstairs. Told me to tell you to meet them in the parking garage."

Jared folded his arms over his chest. "Why didn't they text me?"

"They did, apparently, but you didn't answer. Owen worried you'd left your phone in the car."

Jared patted his pockets, then blushed. "I suppose I did." He ran his hand through his hair. "Well, thanks for letting me know. I'll be going, then."

"Hold on. I'll walk with you."

Too bad he didn't have the excuse of being drunk anymore, because that would have been a handy explanation for the reason his cheeks turned so red. Jared tucked his hands into his pockets and studied the wall, the carpet, and the ceiling until Nick walked beside him, long strides sending his intoxicating scent toward Jared in a wave as Nick caught his elbow gently to propel him forward.

"You're looking better than you were at the party."

Jared clutched the strap of his lunch bag. "Sorry I looked like shit earlier."

"Not what I was implying. I'm saying you seemed upset." He wiped his chin, grimacing. "Sorry if I was part of that."

Glaring at the button for the elevator, Jared punched it angrily. He hoped to hell this thing didn't act up. All he needed was a lurching elevator on top of everything else. God help him if he freaked out and Nick comforted him.

Because the truth was, if the man tried to take him into his arms again, he'd go. And he knew that wasn't a good idea.

Though he wouldn't mind Nick being thrown off his damn game for once. Maybe Jared could be the one to comfort *him*.

The way I used to do.

The doors opened smoothly this time, and Nick stepped to the side as Jared followed after him. He pressed the number for the first floor, then stood beside Nick—close, but not too close—as they descended.

At least it wouldn't be a long ride. It was a slow elevator, but it was only three floors to the parking level.

"Jared," Nick began, and Jared tensed, all too familiar with that tone. It was his lecture tone, his scolding tone, his *we need to end this* tone.

We haven't even started anything, Jared thought, and braced himself to hear something that would piss him off.

But before Nick could say a word, the elevator lurched.

Nick grabbed the back wall and Jared, steadying him instinctively. "What in the hell?"

Damn the man, he didn't even startle without being sexy. "Apparently the elevator has some electrical glitch. It's no big deal, they said, it won't—"

The elevator lurched again, but this time there was a horrible grinding sound and a terrifying metal *snap* that made Jared lose his breath.

As the car slid free from its cables with the scream of a metal-eating banshee, Jared teetered off-balance, and Nick swept him tight into his arms as they tumbled together to the floor.

CHAPTER THREE

FOR A terrible moment, Nick thought the elevator car wasn't going to stop until it hit the bottom of the shaft. He felt the sides shuddering, heard the cables snapping and metal groaning, and he truly feared this was how he was going to die.

With Jared in my arms. Heart clenching, he drew him tighter to his chest, trying to wrap himself around the man like a human shield.

As abruptly as the nightmare began, it ended. With a jolt, the car stopped and tilted slightly to one side, sending Nick and Jared on a slow slide into the farthest corner. The lights above flickered, then went out. Even the emergency lights were off, leaving them in complete darkness.

In the cradle of Nick's arms, Jared tensed, then began to shake.

We're alive. Nick let out a shuddering breath of relief.

He felt Jared's hands on his face. "Are you all right? Are you hurt?" Soft, cool hands examined him carefully, expertly. "You took the brunt of our fall. Did you break anything? Do you have a sprain? Cut?"

"I'm fine. Maybe a few bruises, but I've had worse tripping over my sister's things on the way to the bathroom in the middle of the night." He touched Jared's neck, but he wasn't checking for vitals. "How about you? Are you okay?"

"I'm fine. You—you…."

Nick cupped Jared's cheek, and Jared leaned into his hand.

Inside the breast pocket of Nick's jacket, his phone buzzed. Shifting so he didn't have to let go of Jared, he fished it out, checking the caller ID. It was Erin.

"*Nick*, we can't find Jared—please tell me he's somewhere with you—"

"He's with me."

Nick slid his fingers from Jared's face into his hair. He floated in a strange dream, the shock of the accident, the displacement of being trapped in the dark, all of it unlacing the thin remains of his control.

Erin's voice in his ear pulled him out of his trance. "Where are you? Did you hear the elevator? I think it may have crashed or something—"

"We're in the elevator together."

"*Oh my God*."

"We're both okay." He should focus on talking this through with Erin, but it was as if his common sense had been tossed around inside the car and hadn't yet settled into place. Maybe it was shock? Maybe this was his reaction to the accident? Too much stress built up?

All he knew was Jared felt so good in his arms he ached. His free hand shifted, tracing the outline of the man beside him. How could Jared feel the same as he had when they were teenagers? Physically, they'd both grown. They were years older. But the feelings were so familiar Nick wanted to shake. In the dark, everything was instinct and emotion and memory. The shape of his face was the same, but Jared's skin wasn't as taut as it was when they were sixteen, and he had facial hair. The beard hadn't been there before, and it wasn't soft. Well, it was both soft and coarse somehow.

He made the same noises, though. The whisper-soft intakes of breath that lit Nick on fire, made him feel like ten million goddamn dollars.

Nick let out a slow, ragged sigh. "We're okay," he said again, maybe to reassure Erin, maybe himself. "There's no light in here, though. The car is tilted sideways, as if it's off the cable. The emergency lights didn't go on."

"I thought I heard a snap." Jared spoke quietly, his voice inches from Nick's face. He must have been able to hear Erin too.

"I'm going to call the fire department and get you out." Erin was calmer now, but still intense.

Jared sat up. "Put it on speakerphone."

Nick did, and held the phone between the two of them. He could see Jared for the first time, his stern face lit by the phone's glow.

"Erin." Nick saw Jared purse his lips in the phone's dim glow. "You need to stay calm."

"You're in a crashed elevator, what do you—?"

"We're fine. I don't think it's going to do much more moving, not in the immediate future. You need to call emergency services, yes, but *you* in particular need to maintain your composure, because right now you're the face of the hospital. Before you're off the phone with me, the town will be full of wild stories about what's happened and whether or not St. Ann's let a faulty elevator go unchecked. You should speak to Kevin the custodian about the elevator company."

Nick frowned in Jared's direction. "What about the elevator company?"

Jared ignored him and kept talking to Erin. "Tell him to tell you what he told me earlier. Above all, make sure the stories about what's going on here don't go wild and don't damage the work you and Nick have done. At the very least, don't contribute to the hysteria."

Who's the CEO here? Normally Nick would snap at Jared for stepping on his authority. This wasn't normal, though. He felt as if he'd been knocked off his center along with the elevator.

I just need a minute to get myself together. How he was going to do that with Jared in his arms, he had no idea.

"Jared, who's the gossip I need to sit on over this?" This was Owen. Erin must have put his phone on speaker as well.

Jared sighed. Nick kept his hand at his neck, loosely now, and Jared reached for it absently. "Probably the nurses. It's going to be too late, but they have to understand the importance of not spreading stories. The problem is they're all going to know about the elevator acting up, and they'll exaggerate it. Also there are apparently some new security guards. I don't know anything about them or what they know, but somebody talk to them and make sure they toe the party line."

"Oh, you're talking about Tim Shephard and Allen Adamson?" This was Erin. "Yes, we hired them a few days ago. They're doing extra shifts after that string of retirements. They seem fine. I interviewed them myself. Why? What's wrong with them?"

"Nothing, I don't think, but I'm saying I don't know how they'll react to this. I planned to hunt them down and get a read on them, but I was trying to catch up to you guys."

Nick snapped out of his haze. "Hold on. The elevator was acting up before we got on? Why didn't I know about this?"

"I guess it started a few hours ago. None of us were around." Erin sounded despondent. "There's a work order, and all the proper procedures were carried out when you look at it on paper, except if I'd been in the building when I heard the *elevator wasn't working*…."

Jared shook his head. "It won't matter if you followed the procedures. The story will be how it was all day and you dropped the ball. Get on top of it."

"I will. Right after I call someone to get you out," Erin promised. "I'll keep you informed."

The call ended. After a few seconds, the phone stopped glowing, and they were in darkness once again.

Jared started to let go of Nick's arm, then seemed to think better of it, clinging loosely.

Neither one of them wanted to let go of the other. Nick only wished he knew if this were because of the shock, panic, or…

Or what, exactly, he didn't know.

Well, he had nothing else to do right now but find out.

Definitely he should stop touching the man quite so intimately. He withdrew his hand from Jared's hair.

Jared clamped it down, trapping it on his own neck. "Please don't let go." His breath tickled Nick's face.

"Are *you* all right? You were so focused on me. Are you hurt?"

"No." His voice had a tremor in it, though, and he slid a hand to Nick's shoulder, holding on. "I… I'm fine."

Translation: he was a quiet wreck but didn't want to talk about it. No problem. Nick could work with that, but he wanted some boundaries. "Do you want to lean on me, or…?"

"I felt better when you were petting my hair."

Was it wrong to feel a rush of lust during an administration crisis? Yes. Except there wasn't much administration Nick could manage from here. Erin had to handle that part.

The only person he could take care of was the man in his arms.

It's okay. No one is here but the two of us. It's okay to let go right now.

"So." Nick ran his thumb along the thick, tense muscle on the side of Jared's neck, testing out the touch. He liked how Jared's breath hitched, how his own blood tingled. They were in a strange cocoon away from the world. "Why am I not surprised you knew about the custodian and the elevator? But it does make me wonder why you let us get on."

"I was flustered. Besides, Kevin said the company swore it would be fine, that it was just a glitch."

"I'm going to have Rebecca sue the company within an inch of its life."

"Funny, Kevin mentioned Rebecca too." His grip on Nick's arm tightened. "I know I asked you to do it, but… why are you touching me so much?"

Because my life flashed before my eyes, and when I got a second chance, you were in my arms. He wasn't ready to say that. Which meant he shouldn't be doing it.

Except he wanted to keep touching Jared. It was like every time he'd been at a convention and seen the right guy at a bar after too many drinks. Like when in college he couldn't take it anymore and had gone to *those bars* even while telling himself he couldn't, he shouldn't. This moment was the same except louder, sharper, deeper. Because it was the man who had cracked open the door to this part of himself. The man who had become his friend again after all these years. The man who had just confessed he'd been thinking of Nick all this time.

This moment was more because it was with Jared.

Nick knew what this meant to him. What did it mean to Jared? What did *he* want? What was fair to him?

Nick's hand stilled. "Did you want me to stop?"

"It depends on why this is happening. We were fighting at the country club, and now… here we are."

With a sigh, Nick let his hand fall away. No. He had no right to push this, not when he knew damn well they'd end up with the same tragic end they'd had when they were teenagers. "What do you think are the odds they can get us out of here with any kind of ease?"

"Given the way the car pitched and how we're sitting slightly on our side, it's going to require specialized equipment to get the car righted."

"Don't you think they can pry the top off with the Jaws of Life or whatever?"

"The Jaws of Life aren't can openers, and this isn't a motor vehicle. They'll have to stabilize the elevator car first, and the shaft as well, if the integrity of it was compromised. All of this should be within their purview, since they're the largest and only non-volunteer fire department in the area. If it gets too specialized, however, they'll have to call for a consultation."

Damn but Nick wished he could see Jared's face. "How the hell do you know all this?"

"Dated a firefighter when I was in college."

Well, this wasn't an image Nick needed. Because his mind wasn't conjuring visions of Jared out to dinner with said nameless firefighter, of course—despite this being taunt enough. No, Nick went right to Jared making out with a hot, strapping stranger. A muscular man who pinned him to the bed and—

Nope, Beckert, shut this line of thought down right now. You don't need to torture yourself.

But goddamn, he hated that image.

The silence went on a little too long. Nick couldn't help glancing around, despite the fact that this was a fruitless endeavor. *Talk about something else. Anything else.* "Now I really wish I'd taken a piss before I got in here."

He winced. *Smooth move, Beckert.*

Of course, no subject was TMI for a medical doctor. "They'll drop a portable urinal in here if we ask for one."

"I'm damn well not going to let it be the first thing I request."

Jared's soft laughter crawled under Nick's skin.

Did the firefighter make you laugh like that?

Nick cleared his throat. "So. You dated a firefighter. Anyone else? Paramedics? Other doctors?"

He wanted Jared to flip him a smart answer about how he wasn't going to wait for him forever, but once again Jared made everything serious too fast. "Where are these questions coming from? Why do you want to know?"

Funny, normally he'd backpedal. Of course, normally he wouldn't have come to this moment. The safety of the darkness was powerful. "From when the damn elevator was falling and I thought it might be too late to ever tell you the things I wanted to tell you."

"You have things you want to tell me that involve running your hands over my hair and down my arms?"

"You're damn right I do."

He desperately wanted to know how Jared was going to reply, but before he got a chance, his phone rang again. Possibly he answered the unknown number a touch more gruffly than necessary. "Beckert."

It was the fire chief, calling en route. "A crew is arriving and assessing the scene as we speak. You'll hear them scraping and banging above you, but don't be alarmed. The first thing we're doing is setting up lights and reinforcing the cables. You're unfortunately in the worst possible spot, just below the third floor but tilted with the access door away from us and trapped by the cables. I don't know what fool designed this, but I want to give him a piece of my mind. You're high enough I don't want you falling farther, but you're far enough out of reach we can't get to you in the way we want. I guess the bright side is at least it didn't damage the other elevator shaft. That said, it's going to be some time before we can access the car and get you supplies. I understand Dr. Kumpel is with you as well?"

Nick had put the phone on speaker immediately, so Jared spoke for himself. "Yes. Both of us are fine, though I've taken Mr. Beckert's word for it and haven't formally examined him. It's difficult in the dark."

"I'm fine," Nick said, a little annoyed.

"So long as no one's hurt or in shock, I'm happy for now. I won't lie, it's a relief to have a doctor on the scene. Sorry to make you work your own emergency, Kumpel."

"I'm sure you have worse stories, Tim."

The fire chief laughed. "We'll get you out of there, and I'll take you for a drink and fill your head full of tales, how's that?"

"Sounds like a plan."

Tim said he'd keep them updated when he had more information. Nick was in the process of tucking his phone away when the banging started above them, accompanied by male voices shouting to one another.

"Not promising, that bit about the access door," Nick said.

"No." Jared stiffened as the cables creaked and the banging became louder. "I hope Owen is keeping the nurses away from the scene so they don't hear any of this, but I bet it'll be all over Copper Point People before the chief gets here."

Nick seriously hated that Facebook group. "Well, we'll deal with the fallout, whatever it is. Or rather, I will. You don't have to bother, you know."

"What, you think I'm going to leave you to—"

There was no warning, just a snap and scream of metal as the elevator pitched and fell. For one terrible second they lifted off the floor, then crashed into each other, Jared's terrified gasp cutting the air like a knife.

Jared grabbed Nick half a second before the car stopped, slamming them much harder into the wall than the last time. Jared's cry told Nick he'd been hurt, and Nick hadn't escaped this time either. He hissed through clenched teeth against the pain in his right shoulder.

It was a primal response, something inside Nick moving his body, shifting to pull Jared closer, to cradle his face in his hands. Jared didn't fight him, didn't ask him why he was doing this or what it was for. He only melted into Nick's touch, trembling, and when their foreheads bumped together, a soft sob escaped him.

"Nick," he whispered.

Jared.

Shutting his eyes, Nick did what he'd kept himself from doing for twenty years: he drew Jared Kumpel's mouth to his own.

JARED WAS stuck in an elevator that had attempted to kill him, and all he could think about was how Nick Beckert's mouth was softer and more full of temptation than he remembered. And he remembered quite a lot about how it felt to be kissed by this man.

Jared had seriously thought they were going to die when the elevator fell that second time. All he could think about was that they were just below the third floor, and he knew there was a basement to this elevator—not accessible without a key, but the space was there in the shaft, which meant plenty of space to fall.

In that second they'd gone airborne, all he could think was, *Will we fall far enough for this elevator to kill us?*

That and, *Will I die without ever kissing Nick again?*

Apparently Nick had the same thought. If they died today, at least they wouldn't have this regret.

Shifting Jared on his lap, Nick deepened the kiss, one hand on Jared's neck, the other in the center of his back, closing a tight fist against his tuxedo jacket. Jared yielded to him, tilting his head to the side, opening his mouth wider. The scent, the taste of him, filled Jared's senses, making him dizzy with desire, drunk on emotion.

God, I've missed him so much.

There were shouts above, and more scraping, but the two of them ignored it all and simply held fast to one another, not breaking the kiss until the buzzing in Nick's pocket forced them to. He answered on speaker, but he pushed Jared's head to his shoulder as he hit the button.

After confirming they were both safe, the chief explained what had happened: one of the few remaining support cables had broken loose, and they were now hanging by a frayed cord, the elevator car wedged more severely sideways.

"Whatever you do, don't move from where you are right now unless you have to."

Nick pressed a silent kiss against Jared's forehead. "We won't."

The chief also told them the plan had changed; while they waited for a more specialized team to arrive from Duluth, they were reinforcing the car from below with temporary support beams, so when they heard scraping and banging underneath, that's what it was.

"How much battery life do you have?" the chief asked.

"About 50 percent."

"Then I don't want to waste it. We won't call you unless we need to from now on, but if you need to contact me, don't hesitate."

As soon as they hung up, Jared nudged Nick. "Call your family."

"He just said to preserve the battery." But there was longing in his tone.

"It doesn't have to be for long. Have them put you on speaker, and tell them you're safe, that I'm with you so they know you have a doctor beside you. Tell them everything will be fine."

"We damn well don't know it'll be fine."

Jared ignored this. "Make sure they're talking to Erin. If the chief isn't keeping them updated, Erin will. Plan what you're going to say, and it won't have to be a long conversation."

Nick's sigh was ragged, and his hand on Jared's back tightened. "All right, but they're going to tell me I should save my battery."

"They'll be glad all the same."

"What about you? Don't you want to call your parents?"

"No. If I thought we were actually going to die, maybe, but not now."

"So you don't get on with them after all this time?"

Jared didn't know how to start this conversation. "I'm not interested in pretending beliefs and attitudes don't matter, that we can agree to disagree."

Nick didn't reply, and soon the phone lit up with his mother's name and number. He didn't keep it on speaker, but Jared could hear enough of the conversation to feel a pang of jealousy the way he did when he listened to one of his friends have a positive interaction with their family. His estrangement wasn't on the level of Owen's—he greeted his parents when he met them in town, dropped by major events to say hello—but he'd given up pretending they'd ever have a warm relationship. His sister was a little better, as were his cousins, but the overall connection had felt severed for some time.

Not Nick. He'd always been close to his entire family, from his grandmother to his cousins who lived in Milwaukee to the handful of distant blood relatives in town. He had cousins here, and some friends of the family who were unofficial aunts and uncles. It had confused Jared when they were young. He asked Nick one day, "How many sisters and brothers do your parents have?" Nick had laughed and explained it was a Black-culture thing, and it had been one of the many times he'd been an awkward white boy who wasn't in the know.

God, he'd loved being in Nick's house, though. There was warmth there like he'd never felt before, notable since if he were to describe the environment, he'd have to say it was stricter than anything he'd ever been in. The Beckert family taught Jared that discipline done right was caring. They gave him space at first, leaving him out of their loving bullying, but over time they started to nag him too, and Jared had treasured that acceptance.

Then abruptly, along with Nick, it had gone away. They were civil and polite to him when they saw him in town after he and Nick were estranged, but that was all. Jared often wondered how much they had figured out. He knew Nick wouldn't have told them anything.

When Nick hung up, Jared put a hand to Nick's chest, hoping he took it as a comforting gesture. "You okay?"

"Yeah." He wrapped his arms around Jared.

For a while neither of them spoke, only held each other in the darkness.

When the banging started below, Jared startled, and Nick pulled him closer.

Past the point of shame, Jared buried his face in Nick's neck. "I don't want to fall again."

"I'm not letting you go. If we fall, I've got you."

"Yes, but I don't want you hurt either." Jared touched Nick's shoulder gingerly, pressing his lips together when Nick hissed. "Dammit, you're really injured this time. Let me look at it."

"No. What are you gonna do in here? You don't have any supplies, and you can't see a thing."

"Hush." Jared sat up, feeling Nick's joints carefully, directing him into diagnostic movements. "I'll want to do a better exam in the light, but I think you strained some tendons. Possibly you separated your shoulder, but that's the worst-case scenario, and it's not bad. Still, be careful with it."

"Yes, Doctor."

Jared settled into him, resting his fingers against the silk of Nick's bow tie. "The elevator is going to be out of commission for weeks, isn't it?"

"I'm sure the state inspectors aren't going to love the idea, no. We still have the dedicated surgical elevator, but it's just that: dedicated for ER and surgery. It's going to be a major issue, having one elevator for guests, staff, and patients. And I suspect it's going to be out of commission longer than weeks. Try months." Nick sighed. "Why this hospital isn't a single story, I don't know. It's the strangest setup for such a small institution. I've *never* seen a county hospital with multiple stories."

"It's an incredibly old building at its core. The original building, where we have the clinic offices now, was built in 1930. The current hospital was added in 1950. It should have all been razed then and built anew, but it wasn't, and now here we are."

"That was the most Copper Point thing I've ever heard."

"Well, if you're looking to build a new building, this incident is good incentive to help the conversation along. You won't believe how expensive it's going to be to repair this."

"I believe it'll be so expensive I'll be eating antacids for all my meals for the next week."

"We'll help you. All of us on the board. You're not facing this alone."

Arms hugged him closer. "I'm glad you're there. I appreciate having your help."

The darkness, the closeness, the rich, woods-and-cinnamon scent of him, unlaced Jared, sent words tumbling out of the deep recesses of his heart. "I'd do anything for you."

"Don't go out with Matt."

As if he could after this. Even if Nick went back to ignoring him, Jared wouldn't be able to look at another man, not anytime soon. Not after these embraces, not after that kiss. Except even as he thought that, he felt heavy. He'd held a torch for Nick all this time, and what had it given him? An empty house and lonely heart.

Jared forced a smile in the darkness, trying to push lightness into his tone. "What right do you have to tell me that, hmm?"

"This right," Nick said, and kissed Jared again.

It was something about the darkness, Jared decided, making them both come undone. Part of him wanted to pull away and demand answers—what was Nick thinking, kissing him like this not once but twice, where did he intend to take this?—but he couldn't bring himself to do anything but respond to Nick's slow, steady burn of desire.

Couldn't do anything but answer with the flare of his own.

They were both burning, all right. Jared didn't know where the man had practiced his kisses—honestly, he didn't want that question answered—but whoever had taught him, Nick had been a good student. This kiss was slow and tantalizing, Nick drawing on Jared's lips before delving inside, his tongue playing lazily along Jared's own, as if they were tucked away in a bedroom, not trapped in a perilously balanced elevator shaft.

Nick ran his fingers along Jared's jaw, breaking the kiss long enough to smile. "Your beard tickles when I kiss you. Not used to that."

Why did it feel so hard to breathe? "I'll shave it."

"Don't." Nick nipped at his chin, then kissed the underside of his jaw. "This is good too."

Everything felt so surreal. Jared tried to float on the moment, but when the banging below them became too loud, he tensed up more and more, and when the elevator jolted once again, he cried out, clenching at Nick's shirtfront.

Nick tucked him in close, threading fingers into his hair. "It's all right. It's going to be all right."

"I was going to go to bed," Jared whispered into Nick's neck. "But I needed a ride home, and I was lonely, and so I said I'd go home with Owen and Erin."

The hand in his hair kneaded gently. "I'm sorry you were lonely. I don't want you to be."

Do you understand you're part of the reason why I am? Except that wasn't fair. It wasn't Nick's fault Jared couldn't let go. Though this elevator interlude was setting all his progress back twenty years and then some. "What's going to happen when we get out? Are you going to pretend this didn't happen?"

"No."

Jared's heart beat faster. He opened his eyes, but he couldn't see anything. He could smell, though. Nick's scent, his cologne, the spicy Nick-ness of him everywhere, in Jared's nostrils, on his tongue. He wanted to dive into that, but he wanted answers more. "What does that mean, no? What's going to happen between us now?"

"I don't know yet. But I'll figure it out." He shifted his legs and rolled his sore shoulder, grunting softly in pain. "I'm also going to find a way to start lobbying for a new hospital building."

"I agree this is what we should do, though I assume it's going to be a trick with our budget. Didn't you say there were two different investors coming to Dr. Amin's welcome party? What about them, would they be any help?"

"Not really. Jeremiah Ryan's investment company is a good one, but they privatize small hospitals and make them part of their group. I don't think it's the right path for Copper Point. But the other one—Peterson—he's the worst. He wants to scoop us up and make us part of a corporation too, but he wouldn't work with us or the community. Everything that group touches turns to ash for the hospital and money for the investors. Except we've got to do something. I don't want anything like this to happen again."

"There's plenty you can do. Hire an independent firm to find code violations and give recommendations. This gives you a perfect reason to get such a report, and I can promise it's going to come back in your favor. The building was last upgraded seriously in the 1980s and hasn't been well-maintained."

"How is that going to help? It just plays into Peterson's hands."

"Because once you have the information, we can use it to budget and talk to the community and *our* investors. We aren't without our own resources. Erin's father might donate a little more money, as he needs to do everything he can to get back in the community's good graces. Look what Jack did, getting all our specialists here, and now Dr. Amin. He's been here two years, but he's shaped so much of this hospital. You have too. And now you and Erin have built this amazing new, young board. Leverage that. Get your information and fight for what you need. We're all behind you."

Nick pressed his lips to Jared's forehead. "You're so damn smart, baby."

Okay, Jared could get used to this. "Mmm."

This time their kissing was more languid and unhurried, and mostly they sat together, bodies tangled. Several times Jared almost nodded off, but the banging and shouting underneath them kept him awake.

"I'll sing to you," Nick offered, when Jared complained about it.

He smiled. "What are you going to sing to me? A lullaby?"

Nick didn't answer with words. He simply began singing Prince songs softly into Jared's ear.

Prince had always been theirs. They'd both been fans in middle school, but Nick had scoffed at Jared, saying he didn't *truly* know the artist, and when put to the test, Jared conceded Nick had him beat, then asked to be educated. So during book club, they'd sat for hours in Nick's room, listening and discussing, dreaming of running away to a concert or at least making a pilgrimage to Paisley Park.

They'd never managed either before they'd become estranged, and Jared hadn't had the heart to do anything solo. When he'd heard of the pop idol's death, he'd been heartsick on so many levels. He'd missed his window to see the artist live, and he couldn't mourn with his best friend. It seemed to seal their separation forever.

Now here he sat in an elevator, half laughing, half crying as Nick crooned a slowed-down version of "Kiss" in his ear. After "Kiss" he sang "Alphabet St." and "Sometimes It Snows in April." Jared could hear the banging below, and the car shifted again, but this time the elevator leveled out. Shortly after, Nick received another call. Jared didn't listen, hovering on the soft haze Nick had created with his voice.

Nick filled him in when he hung up. "The elevator is secure, but they don't want to do anything until the Duluth team arrives. They'll be on the scene within the hour." He stroked Jared's back. "Also, Erin sent me a text. Your parents are in the lobby." Nick kept stroking him. "So are the news crews from three cities."

Now Jared sat up. "Oh no."

"Yeah. Rebecca's there too, though, helping Erin frame what he says from a liability standpoint, and she's already working with the hospital's lawyers to draft a suit against the elevator company. Jack's going to examine us for injuries when we get out. Don't fight it. It's part of the investigation."

Jared rested his head on Nick's shoulder.

Nick smoothed his hair. "Also, apparently everyone admitted to St. Ann's has been sent to a different hospital."

Hold on. "The hospital was evacuated? Why?"

"They didn't tell me. I assume it was some sort of precaution because of all the work they have to do to access us. I wanted to press, but I didn't want to take more of his time."

Jared had been tired before, but now he was exhausted. He was off this weekend, so he didn't have any official patients except for one long-term one, but practically every child in town was his patient in one way or another. If anyone under eighteen was admitted, he knew about them and at least consulted. He hated the idea of them being sent hours away to unfamiliar surroundings because he was stuck.

Nick rubbed Jared's shoulder. "It'll be all right. It's almost over."

"Did you tell Erin about pushing for a new building?"

"He figured that out on his own."

"Or Owen nudged him. He and I have wished for a single-floor hospital since we got here."

"The bottom line is we're safe, and we're getting out. They're probably going to stabilize it further, open the access hatch, or make their own. They'll lift us one at a time onto the second floor. Erin says Jack, Owen, and Simon will take us away to be examined, but I'll make a quick statement before that."

Jared felt as if their protective bubble was already popping. *I don't want this to end.* Ridiculous. He couldn't confess such a thing, but… "Will you… stay? Tonight?"

Oh, this was much worse. He sounded too needy. He wished he hadn't said a thing.

The hand down his back, trailing his spine, made Jared's skin break out in gooseflesh. Nick sighed against his hair. "My family will expect me at home."

Jared's heart sank. So this would end here. Nick could say what he liked about figuring it out, but Jared knew him well enough to understand how this was going to go. Nick Beckert didn't move unless he felt the path was safe and clear. Jared had tried to force the issue before, and the strategy had blown up in his face. He'd been sixteen, granted, but he didn't think the results would end up differently now.

What he did know, there in the dark, was that he loved Nick as much as he ever had, possibly more. There was no reason to consider dating Matt or anyone else.

Nick cradled Jared to him once again, encouraging him onto his good shoulder. "Get some rest while you can. I'll sing to you some more, if you want."

"Please," Jared whispered, then smiled, heart full and aching as Nick smoothed the hair away from his ear and crooned "Sexy M.F." to him until he drifted gently into a fitful sleep.

THINGS MOVED quickly once the Duluth rescue team arrived, half of them working underneath to make sure the car didn't fall farther, the others focused on how to retrieve Nick and Jared. Nick spoke on the phone with them until they cracked the edge of the access door enough to toss him a walkie-talkie. They also gave them bottles of water, hand wipes, a few meal bars, and as Jared had said they would, portable urinals. Nick wanted nothing to do with the latter, but when Jared pointed out how long it was going to be until they were out and how much attention he was going to get, he caved.

"This is embarrassing," he murmured as he fiddled with the plastic container.

"I'm a doctor. You have to work hard for me to find bodily functions embarrassing, especially in a situation like this."

Nick didn't know what to make of that dismissal. Objectively, he knew Jared was right, but Nick wasn't able to downshift from making out to practicality so easily. His bladder didn't care much about his sensitivities, however, so he faced the wall and did his business.

Jared utilized his portable urinal as well, and after that they cleaned up a bit, ate and drank, and in between updates from the team, prepped for how they'd behave once they exited. Mostly Jared prepped Nick.

"Don't let them push you around." He straightened Nick's collar and smoothed his jacket. "You've come too far and gained too much."

"You talk to me as if I don't know how to do my job."

"You know very well how to do your job. You're amazing at it. You were never more amazing than when you took down Erin's father and the embezzlers on the board last year. You gave me chills."

"Yeah, well, their friends are always lurking, waiting for me to mess up. And I'm not kidding about Peterson. He's a shark. He wants to eat this hospital and everyone in it, and me for standing in his way."

"I have faith you can handle him."

Nick's head was starting to hurt. "Yes, but I'm damn tired."

He hadn't meant to say that out loud, but he was glad it had slipped out. The only place he ever let his guard down this far was at home. Being with Jared like this reminded him how they used to be, how once upon a time Jared had been a different kind of safe space.

God, but I want that back.

Jared stroked Nick's neck. "I imagine you are. And I'm sorry, I didn't mean to imply you have to take all this on. Well… you do, somewhat. But I didn't intend to dismiss your frustrations. I'm guilty of being starstruck by everything you've accomplished here and in your life in general. But… but if you ever want to vent your frustrations to me, I'm happy to listen."

Nick touched Jared's cheek. "Thanks."

"Also, you didn't mess anything up about the elevator. This wasn't your fault."

"The janitor should have told someone immediately about the elevator at the first sign of trouble. That's going to be on me."

"I'm telling you, keep everybody honed in on commissioning a study of the safety of the building, prioritizing improvements or new construction, whatever they advise. And they'll advise new construction."

Nick tipped his head against the wall. "People will be pissed about property taxes going up."

"The construction companies will be over the moon, though. And if you can keep talking about the new jobs it's going to create, good for you. Work with Erin."

"It's not going to be as simple as raising some taxes. The finances for this place are precarious at best. We barely had it balanced to add cardiac care. That will pay off in the long run, but we can't add this at the same damn time. The timing couldn't possibly be worse."

"We'll figure this out. All of us."

Nick slid his hands down Jared's shoulders. It was nice to be able to see him properly, at least. "I'll work with you. You've got some good ideas, Dr. Kumpel."

Jared stroked the stubble of Nick's jaw. "I can only work with a patient who's getting adequate rest and stress relief. Can you promise me you'll give yourself regular release, Mr. Beckert?"

"Mmm. Not sure. You might have to give me a prescription. Maybe some personal visits."

Jared smiled and nipped Nick's jaw. "If I must, I must."

Nick couldn't help but notice Jared looked a little sad, though.

The rescue team had tossed a portable light into the shaft as well, and even as it was a relief to be able to see without worrying about using up the phone's battery, something about the return of his vision made Nick all too aware of the impending end of their cocoon.

This setup was directly out of a romcom: two people trapped in an elevator, emerging at the cusp of love. Except he and Jared had gone in primed. He'd told himself their high school infatuation had been a fling, a lapse in judgment, the folly of youth, but as he'd grown older, unable to deny who he was, he'd had to admit what he'd felt with Jared was real. When he came back to Copper Point and worked side by side with Jared, even before they'd become closer working on the embezzlement investigation together, Nick had known their old flame had never gone out. They'd only ever needed a match to set things alight again.

Passion had never been their problem. It was the logistics of being together they needed to sort out, not their feelings. In the darkness, Nick had told himself they could face it. Something about the light, even the dim glow of the lantern, drew his self-doubt back to the surface.

Their intimacy began to erode when the Duluth team used the Jaws of Life to cut the top off the elevator since the access door was jammed and wouldn't open more than forty degrees. As the metal scraped and whined and debris began to fall, Nick and Jared rose, moving far away from the area, and though they touched one another, they were more subdued than they'd been when they were together in the dark. Nick wasn't sure what he thought should happen, but he'd at least hoped for one last flare between the two of them, a final kiss, a glance over Jared's shoulder. Ridiculous, since all that mattered was the two of them getting out. But as he helped lift Jared into the rescue team's arms, then held his throbbing shoulder and watched Jared disappear into the shaft, all he knew was that Jared was leaving. Their time alone together was over. By the time Nick emerged into the main hallway, he got a quick glimpse of Jared being ushered away by Owen before he was beset by reporters.

It's done. The moment with Jared is gone.

With a hand on his elbow, Erin appeared beside him, smiling at the press as he spoke sotto voce to

Nick. "Thank them, promise to give them a statement after you've been cleared by the medical team, and let Jack escort you to a room."

Dr. Wu was indeed standing by, stern-faced and agitated. Nick nodded, indicating he understood what Erin wanted him to do.

Erin didn't pull aside and leave him to it, not yet. "You're all right? You said you were, but you look haggard."

"From the way he's lowering his shoulder, I want to run a CT scan on it." Jack glared at them both. "Finish this so I can do my job."

Nick wasn't entirely sure what he said to the crowd, but he managed a smile while he did it. He was glad Jack insisted the nurse take him away in a wheelchair instead of letting him walk. He kept his chin up until he was wheeled into a private room, which smelled of his mother's perfume, his grandmother's baking, and his sister's weeping.

As Jack shut the door and the three women folded him into their arms, Nick let himself crumble a bit.

"We were worried sick," his sister said, squeezing his hand and kissing the side of his head. His mother didn't say anything, only stroked his face, her eyes brimming with tears. Grandma Emerson sat beside him, rubbing his back as if he were a little boy who had stumbled and fallen down.

He wasn't allowed their comfort long. Jack was apologetic and gracious as he removed him from their care, explaining he was taking him to run some tests. On the way down the hallway—carefully clear of all reporters—he asked Nick questions about his shoulder injury, and paused to have him demonstrate some range of motion.

"I think you're probably fine, but Rebecca wants us to run full tests on the both of you because it'll look better in the paperwork." Jack took up the handles of the wheelchair again. "And I hate to point it out, but because of the location of the CT scanner—"

Nick tensed. "Oh, *hell.*"

"Yes. We'll have to take the elevator to the first floor. Trust me when I tell you it's been thoroughly inspected by three different fire crews, and the likelihood of you having a repeat of the incident which landed you here is next to nothing, but I do understand your hesitation."

Nick wanted to lobby for walking down the stairs, but he was exhausted on a level he didn't know how to describe, so he shut his eyes and told himself over and over *it's going to be fine, everything will be fine* as he went into the elevator car. When it jolted to a start, he couldn't help startling, and Jack put a hand on his shoulder.

"This one is rougher than the other. Which is unfortunate as it's what we'll have to use for months to come. The damage to the shaft on the main one is extensive."

"Jared thinks I should lobby for a new building." Maybe if he kept talking, he wouldn't panic as much.

"It isn't the best design, this one. And depending on how expensive the repair bill comes out to be, especially if there are other improvements that should be done, we might be better off building new. The timing isn't the best, is it?"

How was it possible this elevator was slower than the other one, which had practically been a snail? "Where's Jared? Is he all right?"

"Owen is with him. I haven't heard anything, but your rooms are next to each other upstairs. I'll tell the others to make sure he checks in with you before he goes home. Except I'm going to try to get you both to stay overnight for observation. The hospital will cover the cost anyway."

Home. No, Jared would leave with Owen and Erin. He'd invited Nick to come too. Maybe he should have said he'd go. He *wanted* to go. There was no way he could, though.

It was already over, wasn't it? They'd had a moment in the elevator, and it was all they'd have.

No. I want more.

God, but hc was so tired. And sore. He rolled his shoulder again, but it felt stiff and sent a dull ache through him.

"Nick?"

Someone was calling him. Jack? Or was it Jared? Blinking, he rubbed his shoulder and glanced around. It was raining.

In the elevator?

No. He wasn't in the elevator. He was under the bleachers, and Jared stood in front of him. It was confusing, because one minute he was young Jared, lanky and thin, and the next he was Dr. Kumpel, wearing a white coat and a tasteful beard. The two spoke in unison, together, voice changing between young and old.

"I just want to be your boyfriend. Officially. I want to hear you say that's what this is, not send me guilty glances like we're some horrible mistake. Is it such a terrible thing to ask for?"

It wasn't, but it was too much for Nick. It had been then, and it was somehow even more impossible now. Except it hurt more at thirty-six than it had at sixteen to turn him away.

"I don't want you to go away again."

"Nick." Someone shook him gently, and when he opened his eyes, blinking, he saw Jack Wu regarding him with concern. "Nick, stay with me. The elevator's about to open, and we'll get you to an exam room immediately."

It was too late. Jared had already left. No reason for Nick to stay, then. "Tell him I always loved him," he murmured, and as people shouted, doors opening to let in bright light, Nick gave in to his exhaustion and slumped forward in the chair.

CHAPTER FOUR

WHEN JARED heard that Nick had collapsed on the way to the CT scanner, he tried to go see him. Owen immediately pushed him back into the bed.

"You're a patient right now, not a doctor." Owen adjusted the tape on Jared's IV. "Jack will take care of him. I sent Simon to help, if it makes you feel better."

It did, but what would make Jared feel best would be helping Nick himself. "Why did he pass out, though? Is his shoulder that bad?"

Owen gave Jared a long look. "You were trapped in a small dark space for five hours. It's a traumatic event. The poor man had to ride in a damn elevator to get to the scanner."

Oh no. "Nick can't have panic attacks about elevators now, that's no good." The rest of what Owen said soaked through Jared's overwhelmed brain. "Wait, we were in there for five hours? And he passed out? I need to see him right now. I need to verify that he's okay."

"*Chill.* Nick will be fine. You'll be fine. Everyone is going to be amazing. The whole hospital will be sprouting flowers and rainbows before you know it."

Jared ran a hand over his face. "When are you letting me out of here? I just want to sleep in a bed."

"You're funny, you know? If you glance down, you'll notice you're in one. Sleep anytime you want. Would you like me to prescribe something to help you relax?"

Jared pulled his hand away, regarding Owen in horror. "You bitch. You admitted me?"

"Doctors do make the worst patients. You're completely dehydrated and exhausted. You're so over-stimulated you're shaking. Most importantly, though, you're a physician at this hospital and your health is essential for the health of this community. Yes, I admitted you. They'll bring the papers by in a minute. If you try to refuse them, I'll send in Erin."

Sighing, Jared lay back against the pillows. "Fine. But I expect to go home in the morning." He frowned as he did a mental calculation on the time and realized it was morning, albeit very early.

"We'll discuss that after you rest." Owen was seated on a stool beside Jared, focused on the laptop serving as the physician access port to the electronic charts. "Also, while you're already cranky, as soon as we're done here, your parents want to see you."

Jared swore under his breath and stared at the ceiling.

Owen raised an eyebrow. "Want me to ship them off? I will."

"No, it's fine." He grimaced. "I mean, it's not, but send them in. It's less trouble than ignoring them."

Owen didn't look up from the computer. "I'll stay and force them out when you've had enough." He rubbed his jaw. "They seem subdued, if it helps. We were all scared to death out here. I think things have calmed enough I can tell you this now, but there was a fire danger until the Duluth crew got here and stabilized things."

Fire? With them trapped in the elevator. Jared gripped thc bedrail. "That's why you evacuated everyone."

Owen nodded, grim. "Yes, and it's what got the news networks in such a frenzy. Erin was trying to keep a lid on it, but there wasn't a chance. If anything had happened with the two of you in there, they weren't sure they could have gotten you out in time."

Jared's limbs felt weak. "You're kidding me. It was that bad?"

"Yes." When Owen turned to face Jared and took hold of his hand over the top of the blanket, his eyes were glossy with unshed tears. "So you'll forgive us for being fussy with the two of you, all right? We're just thrilled we're visiting your obstinate ass in a hospital room and not your corpse in the morgue."

Taking deep breaths had suddenly become difficult. Jared pushed his thumb against the side of Owen's wrist. "Say, Doc. How about you put a little lorazepam through that IV port?"

"I'll get it right now, before I let your parents in."

"Perfect."

Owen rose from the stool and bent over the bed, pressing a kiss against Jared's forehead.

Jared caught his shoulder weakly and held him there, drinking the contact in.

The bliss of Ativan injection hit him as soon as Owen slid it into his IV line, and the short-term anti-anxiety med smoothed out the jagged edges creeping uncomfortably close to his psyche when he thought about the elevator. He felt reasonably ready for his parents too, and when the door opened, he managed a small smile and even a wave. Chemicals were such a wonderful thing.

His mother shuffled forward, hugging her purse, and his father came in behind her with his hand on her shoulder. They looked absolutely ragged, and it occurred to Jared a round of Ativan for the whole Kumpel clan wouldn't have gone amiss.

Jared tipped one side of his mouth a little higher. "Hey."

They hurried over and hugged him together, his mother touching his face and his father ruffling his hair. They fussed and said all the things he expected, telling him how worried they'd been, how they'd been so afraid they'd lose him. It was a nice moment, and the lightness of the drug let Jared think the ridiculous thought that maybe he should almost die more often so they could all forget the awfulness between them.

Except it wasn't five minutes before they started in.

"I just can't believe who you had to be caught in an elevator *with*," his mother murmured.

Owen, pretending to enter things into the computer, paused.

Jared pulled his hand away from his mother, his heart sinking. Right. Fool he, to think a mere brush with death would get them past this.

Jared's father patted his wife's shoulder. "Now, now. We're going to focus on how glad we are Jared's alive."

No, Jared decided. *I'm going to push back, because I don't want to pretend when I know where this is going to end.* "Nick was amazing in the elevator. I owe him so much. I'd likely have a concussion if it weren't for him. Every time it fell, it pitched us sideways and knocked us around, and he'd grab hold of me, wrapping his body around me so he took the brunt of the assault."

He stared at his mother, daring her to make a comment.

She stared back, her lips puckered as if she'd eaten a lemon.

His father looked uncomfortable and said nothing.

Owen turned to Jared. "You didn't tell me this. No wonder he passed out. I'll get a message to Jack. I think they're finished downstairs now. I saw activity in the room next door, and the two of you are the only patients. Though, give us an hour to change that. It's a full moon."

Jared stared at the ceiling again, unwillingly remembering. "Yeah. We were in a corner, but when it shifted, there'd be pretty much no warning, and it was completely dark. The time I about lost it was when we lifted in the air. I think that's when he really hurt his shoulder." He shut his eyes. "It's starting to hit me now what it could have been like, what it would have been to endure that alone. I'd just ridden the thing to go up to the second floor. It *could* have been me alone." His stomach became queasy, and his hands began to shake.

Owen squeezed his hand. "I'll put a standing order in on the Ativan. Also, FYI, Simon and Jack took up the shift tonight, and I'm working for free. You're going to have to Skype the peds patient we shipped out of town once this is over. He heard the news and was terrified you were dead."

"Nick mentioned that in the elevator. I'll do it as soon as someone gives me my phone."

"He's in bed by this point. No nurse will let him take a call, and your doctors won't let you make it. You can talk to him in the morning. As for your mobile, though, I'll let you have a few minutes with it." Owen tossed Jared's phone onto the bed. "I shut it off because it was blowing up, and that was stressing me out when we weren't sure what was going to happen."

"Jared."

He turned toward his mother, honestly having forgotten she was there. "Mom, Dad. Thank you for coming. But if you start anything, I'm kicking you out."

His mother appeared genuinely hurt. "How can you say that to me when I've come to see my son who nearly died?"

"Because I'm the son who nearly died. And I know how much you can hurt me with the casual things you say about Nick, that you mean to do it. Today of all days, I'm not in the mood. So if you can't sit here without making a jab at him, you'd better get going."

For several seconds they regarded one another, a quiet standoff. Jared's dad was usually ready to smooth everything over with a platitude, but for once he stayed quiet. Eventually Jared's mother rose, holding her purse to her side, lifting her chin high. "You're tired and need to rest. We'll come see you tomorrow."

"You'll have to behave then too," Jared called after them.

The second the door closed, Owen turned on him. "What in the hell was that?"

Jared considered his options. It would be easy to pawn him off. Owen wasn't going to push him on anything tonight.

But maybe Jared wanted to be pushed. Or maybe he simply wanted to spill on his own.

In the silence, Owen kept going. "I know you're mad at your parents because they've tilted conservative the last few years, but… are you telling me they're so racist they're mad you were trapped in an elevator with a Black man? What the hell? Do they just not like Nick? What's going on? I feel as if I came in on the wrong episode of a soap opera."

Yep. Jared was going to tell Owen everything.

Everything.

"My mother was always two-faced when it came to the Beckerts, but she laminated her racist card when I was sixteen." Jared stared at the ceiling. So weird, after all these years, to finally tell his best friend. "When she caught Nick and me having sex in my bedroom."

Owen shut the laptop with a sharp *snap* and turned to face Jared fully. "*Shut. Up.*"

Jared cocked an eyebrow at him. "Which part has you gobsmacked? The bit where my mother is more horrible than you knew, or that I had a relationship with Nick?"

"You had a *relationship* with Nick?"

Jared listened to the clicks and whirs of his IV machine as he pondered how to start the story. "Well. *He* wouldn't say that. He had a lot of words for it at the time, and I hated all of them. Fooling around. Having fun. Letting off steam. But yeah, it got heavy toward the end, and it went on for several months after building for years."

"I had no idea. I knew you were friendly with him at school, but that was it."

"We kept our friendship—and everything else—to ourselves. It was the way he wanted it. You know how he was, always quiet and a little standoffish."

"Yeah, he never hung out with anyone at school. Sometimes the other Black kids, but not even that group very much. I remember him being a loner more than anything else."

"We were close, in private. He knew a lot about us, though. The three of us, I mean. He'd talk about you and Simon a lot."

Owen blinked. "He did?"

"Yes. He worried about you and your dad. I never said anything because you wouldn't have wanted me to, but he's highly observant. And loyal." Jared smoothed his hair from his face with his hand that didn't have an IV line. "Anyway. We became close when my mom got into book clubs. Nick's mom was one of the hosts. Their place was perfect, so they hosted a lot. I usually went along since Mom didn't like me home alone, and that's how I started playing with Nick. Even when I was old enough to stay alone, I kept coming if the Beckerts were hosting because it was fun to hang out with him. We'd already become close enough, though, that Aniyah often asked if I wanted to stay for a sleepover."

"So is this the stereotype where one night at a sleepover one of you rolled over and kissed the other one?"

Jared smiled, remembering. "Not quite. We were fifteen, and I can't speak for Nick, but I'd had feelings for him for some time. Though we'd sometimes played together in elementary school at recess, he didn't seem to want to hang out much together in middle school, and I thought maybe it was because I'd come out. It hurt, but I didn't want to break the friendship, so I stayed quiet. But when we were alone together in his room or walking around in the park, it was great. One afternoon when no one was at the house, we were in his room listening to Prince, and I forgot myself and sang to him with my feelings hanging out. It was 'Kiss,' and there may have been a bit of dirty dancing going on."

Owen chuckled darkly. "Smooth operator. What'd he do, grab you and throw you on the bed to have his way with you?"

"Well, the awkward teenager version of that. Grabbed me, we stared at each other in shock a few seconds, then after he stared at my lips too long, I decided I couldn't stand it anymore, and I kissed him. Rather chastely, because for all my coquettishness I was a complete and utter virgin and scared to death of looking like an idiot."

"What'd he do then?"

"What you said. Pushed me onto the bed and showed me what a real kiss was. The high school edition, anyway."

Owen wolf-whistled and fanned himself.

"It pretty much progressed from there, in fits and starts. He would make out, but he wouldn't talk about it. He insisted he wasn't gay, despite a hell of a lot of evidence to the contrary. It bothered me, but I had so many feelings for him, and, well… he was hot and good with his hands. I kept hoping eventually he'd be okay with it, and then we could be an official couple."

"So what happened? Was it because your mom caught you?"

"Partly. That's actually a side story, but it sparked me wanting him to come out and make us legitimate. I wanted to show her we were a serious couple. She knew I was gay and had, I thought, accepted me, so in my logic, showing her Nick was my boyfriend, not some guy I was sleeping around with, was an important distinction. Also, I'd worried his family suspected us. It was a matter of time before the same thing happened with them. So I said we should at least tell them, even if we didn't tell anyone else."

"Logical. I take it he didn't agree?"

"Oh my God. He didn't just reject the idea, he was furious. He doubled down on all his insisting he wasn't gay, which made me angry. So I pushed him harder, determined that if he could just see himself for who he was, if he could admit that to himself and to me, maybe we could move forward. In hindsight I know it was the wrong move. I know coming out is different for everyone, that his reasons are his reasons and I can't tell him how to feel about it. But at the time it hurt like hell. I tried to wait him out, but we went from making out all the time to always fighting. Then

I did a stupid thing. I threw it out as an ultimatum, that he had to come out or we had to break up."

Owen flinched and sagged in his chair. "Oh, Jared. You didn't."

"I did. I was a proud idiot, only considering myself. I honestly assumed he'd put our relationship first."

"It was a sleaze move. Had I known you did that, I'd have decked you."

"It wasn't the sort of thing I was sharing with the class. And by the time I had a better working knowledge of psychology and figured out I'd been an ass, he was gone to college, and so was I. I considered trying to contact him over break, but I didn't know what to say. Sorry, obviously, but…." He sighed. "All right. I was a bit eaten up by pride. But I couldn't forget him. I always knew he was the reason I couldn't find a lasting relationship, and no amount of telling myself it wasn't ever going to happen got me anywhere. When he showed up as the CEO of St. Ann's, I wanted to start over as friends. At first he was more closed off than before with no space for me at all. It was maddening, because I could see those old bastards screwing him over, and he was just standing there taking it. I had no right to say anything to him, but God knows I ached to. When you guys started doing the racquetball tournaments last year, I jumped at the chance to make him my partner, and I was shocked when he said yes. I was so excited that we were able to start over. I was determined friendship could be enough. It wasn't, though. I've been pining for him like crazy, worse every day, and at the welcome party for Dr. Amin, I swear every woman in town was flirting with him. I thought, 'Oh my God, he's going to marry a woman so he doesn't have to come out—'"

"Jared, you're really a jerk."

"Yes, I'm awful. What does Simon's mother always say? Stinking thinking. And it doesn't help that everyone else is not only partnered up but engaged, and here I am hung up on my high school crush who won't look at me. I felt so pathetic." When Owen's glower turned to sympathy, Jared waved him away. "Don't. Listen to the whole story, because it gets interesting."

"Yes. You crashed in an elevator with your crush. That had to have been intense."

"It was, especially the part where he kissed me until I couldn't breathe." Jared drew his knees closer to his chest, knowing he was blushing like a schoolboy. "I had no idea it was coming. I don't know what to make of it. Probably it was the intensity of everything, our sense that we might have died. Now I'm worried it'll go back to the way it was, which depresses me. I wish I could tell you I could be content to be his close friend. I can't." He put his hands to his face, rattling the IV line. "At the very least, I want to find out how much better an adult Nick is in bed. Those kisses got my imagination going. Plus he was so sweet and protective. I want to scold him into next week for hurting his shoulder, but it was all to protect me, like we were in some kind of action film and he was the big buff hero keeping me safe."

Owen's smile was soft and knowing. "It doesn't sound as if he feels indifferent about you."

"Yes, but he has even more reason for us to be secret now. I'm not making the same mistake twice, but how on earth am I supposed to have a secret relationship with the CEO of the hospital in a town as gossipy as Copper Point?"

"That's a question for Jack and Simon, since they were the secret lovers of our group."

"What are you talking about my love life for?" Simon pushed the door open and came into the room with his nurse's cart. "Also, Dr. Gagnon, who isn't supposed to be working, why are you bothering my patient?"

"I'm working pro bono, so hush. Jack asked me to admit him, and it's not like I'm going home anytime soon. Also, you're going to want to bother him once you hear the juicy story he's got."

Jared shut his eyes. "I'm not telling it again."

"It's all right, I'll do it. I assume you don't mind him knowing, since you told me?"

Did he mind? Jared didn't know about anything anymore. "Sure. Just don't embellish."

Owen only did a little, but the tale was rather salacious on its own, and Simon got too distracted taking Jared's blood pressure twice and eventually gave up until Owen finished. "Wow," he said when he was caught up. "Just… wow. I had no idea. I mean, I sensed things between you and Nick, but I never dreamed…."

Owen frowned. "Say, what was all that with your mom? What happened after she caught you, and what does this have to do with why you guys don't get along?"

Jared legitimately was getting tired, but it was too precious to have his best friends here, the story out in the open between them after all these years. "When I was young, I didn't pick up on it, not on a conscious level, but over time I think part of me realized my mother didn't care for Nick's family. My mom doesn't like a lot of people. She wasn't nice to Nick either, when he was in our house, and it made me mad—I said something once, and she got prickly, but she was better after that, until she caught us. In hindsight, I can see it so clearly. At the time, however, no one had taught me to see it, and I certainly didn't want to. There wasn't much getting away from it when she yelled at me after Nick left and said, 'I can barely stomach you being a homosexual as it is, but you're certainly not going to go carrying on with some Black boy, not while I'm alive.'"

Neither Owen nor Simon said a word.

Jared continued, the sick awareness of the memory returning. "I stood gaping at her like an idiot for a long time. 'No, my mom can't be one of *those people*. She goes to church and smiles and gives good hugs.' I waited for her to take the words back, to tell me she didn't mean it, that I'd misunderstood. But to this day, she hasn't so much as hinted she might have been in the wrong."

Owen's expression had become wooden, but Simon as usual had his emotions all over his face. "I'm so sorry."

"To be honest? Largely I felt foolish. I left the house, shaking and sick, and when I came back she acted as if nothing had happened—this was my cue, you see, to fall in line. But I didn't. I started watching her with my eyes wide open. I listened too. Plenty of people in Copper Point say horrible things like 'the neighborhood has gone bad' as code for 'Hispanic immigrants of lower economic status have moved in,' but she always went further and said 'those people' in a tone that meant 'those things.' They're the people that if you pointed their errors out to them, they'd bluster and get angry, saying it's not what they mean, that they don't think such horrible things, but it's absolutely what they think. They're the people who would never admit they have bigoted or white supremacist thoughts and yet have them every single day, those subtle, subversive ones so embedded into our culture they're broadcast on the evening news. I didn't have the lingo for all of that then, but her comments cracked something open in me, and I started to see it, in them and in myself. I saw more than I ever dreamed I'd see. I lingered in places they didn't think I was and heard them talking politics and realized they were supporting people who said some seriously awful things about gay people. In short, people like me. Like all of us.

"I kept a journal of everything they were doing and saying, and when I was eighteen, I confronted them. They got angry, said I was twisting their words—which was rich, since I was literally repeating them word for word. So then they switched to saying I was taking them out of context. Eventually I gave up and said we were done. I didn't need anything from them. I said I'd do college on my own, and I promised I'd be ten times more successful than they were, how I'd be an out doctor loved by my patients. That I ended up being able to keep my promise here in town was just a perk. So now here I am, their out gay son and the town pediatrician, vocal flaming liberal. The only consolation they had was I never openly dated here."

"But they didn't like that you were in an elevator with Nick?" Owen frowned as he folded his arms. "What, because of the optics?"

"Precisely. They haven't changed."

Simon looked crestfallen, but Owen was only grim. Not surprising. Simon had good, understanding parents who rarely let him down. Owen was so estranged from his he'd leave the room if they entered it.

"So what happens now?" Simon asked.

Jared picked at his blanket. "I don't know. I wanted to talk to Nick, but he needs to recover and be with his family."

"Well." Simon nodded at the door. "He's in his room, resting. Emmanuella is staying overnight with him, but his mother is taking their grandmother home now that they know he's all right. I can get you a wheelchair and take you over."

No. This time I'm going to do it right. "Ask him, first, if he wants to see me."

Smiling, Simon squeezed Jared's hand and rose. "I'll go do that."

NICK WASN'T sure when he'd last felt so physically and mentally drained.

He'd passed out on the way to the CT scan, woken up in the ER, and, after a lot of fluids and some drugs, gotten the scan after all. Jack had been convinced Nick had a minor PTSD reaction to the elevator, which Nick had tried to brush off until they had to ride it upstairs. He'd exited it sweating and breathing so shallowly the world lost color for a moment. The idea that he might now have a fear of elevators upset him.

He hadn't had time to dwell on that, because his mother, grandmother, and sister had descended on him as soon as he entered the room. They'd fussed over him, touching him everywhere, hugging him carefully and asking him if he was all right.

He'd wanted to go home and rest in his bed, but he didn't attempt to fight Jack on his admission, especially since he could barely lift his arm to sign with the electronic pen.

His mother sat beside him, stroking his hair over and over. "Baby, we're not going to stay too long, because we want you to rest. Emmanuella's going to sit with you overnight, and Mom and I will be back in the morning, first thing."

"I'm going to bake you the pineapple upside-down cake," Grandma Emerson declared, leaning on her cane beside the foot of his bed.

It was his favorite cake, a lush Bundt treat she made for his birthday and during the summer when they were having fancy company. When he was little, he'd eat it at the high counter with his feet swinging, and he'd close his eyes, the sugar and fruit making his whole body tingle. He'd sigh and shut his eyes and say, "It tastes like Hawaii, Grandma!"

She'd tease him then, asking him how would he know, since he'd never been. He always insisted he was sure it did, and someday he'd take her there so they could find out together. He hadn't come through on his promise, but she always made him that cake when she wanted to show him love.

He smiled at her, his heart in his throat. "I'll eat it all up."

She swatted his leg lightly. "You'll share with those caring for you. And save some for the doctor with you in there. Isn't he the one who used to be your friend when you were younger?"

Now his heart was pinched for other reasons. "Yeah. He is."

His mother kept stroking his hair, his face. "I thought I wouldn't get to see you again. I'm so glad you're safe, baby."

Nick hated how much he'd made her worry. He took her hand and squeezed it. "I'm going to hire a company to go over the safety of the whole hospital, Mama. Nobody's going to get hurt like that here again. If we can't fix this building, we'll build a new one."

She had tears in her eyes as she patted his cheeks. "Look at my boy. You're barely out of your own situation and you're trying to protect other people. Just like your father."

His chest swelled with pride, but it also pinched on a bittersweet ache.

Emmanuella, stationed on the other side of his bed, made shooing motions at their mother. "All right, now. Simon and Dr. Wu both said he needed to rest, and if you two stay, he's gonna keep trying to make you feel better. Leave him to me, get some sleep, and we'll spoil him some more tomorrow."

"All right." Aniyah kissed both of Nick's cheeks, then his forehead. "You sleep well, you hear me?"

"I'm pretty sure they'll give me medicine to sleep if I have trouble." Nick smiled at her. "Go on."

His grandmother's embrace was both softer and sharper at the same time, and he shut his eyes and drank in her comforting scent before she retreated.

Grandma Emerson shook a finger at Nick's sister. "You'll call us if he needs anything."

Emmanuella held up her hands. "The second it comes up, I promise. But you go on. I got this."

Once the two of them were gone, Nick let his head fall into the pillow and exhaled slowly.

Emmanuella leaned back in her chair, but she kept her hand near his arm on the bed. "You doing okay? Want me to get you anything, or give you some time alone?"

"I don't know what I want. Nothing feels real right now." The beep of his blood pressure monitor and occasional whir of his IV machine were comforting, in a way, like anchors. "I can't get over how we were nearly cooked inside the damn elevator shaft."

"Yeah, I'm glad they didn't tell you."

Nick was too. He reached over with his good hand to rub his shoulder. They'd given him enough painkillers it was only slightly sore now, but he was glad he had some of the pain, another link to reality. "Is Jared all right? Have you heard anything about him?"

"He's fine, as far as I know." She hesitated, looking like she wanted to say something serious, but in the end all she said was, "Do you want to go see him? He's next door."

Nick's heart skipped a beat. Yes, he did want to go, but…. "I don't think I can move. I'm so exhausted."

"I can let you sleep."

"I want to keep talking, if that's okay."

"What do you want to talk about?"

I want to talk about Jared. How I feel about him. How I want to pursue something with him but don't know how.

It wasn't the first time he'd nearly come clean with Emmanuella. Not in high school, and not even in college. Sometime in his midtwenties, after his third attempt to date a woman and not being able to accept her invitation to go upstairs because he understood full well how he was cheating her—that's when he'd started wanting to talk this out with his greatest confidant. He'd been too scared, though. He'd managed to distract himself with work for a long, long time.

What if he'd died without sharing this truth with her? Without living it for himself?

But if he was too exhausted to move, he was absolutely too spent to come out, even to Emmanuella. Soon. He'd tell her soon. "Talk to me about anything."

"Want to talk about something silly, or do you want to talk about the accident?"

God, he wanted to tell her. It didn't feel as terrifying right now. Because of the drugs they'd given him? Maybe he should use that. Or maybe he shouldn't. He couldn't decide.

A knock on the door preceded Simon Lane entering with a smile. "Hey. Am I interrupting?"

"No." There. This Nick could answer. "Did you need to run more tests?"

"Nope, not yet. I actually am coming as a kind of intermediary. Jared wanted to come say hello to you, but he didn't want to bother you if you were too tired. Are you up for visitors?"

Jared. Nick's whole spirit soared, and his breath caught. "Yeah. Sounds fine."

It's more than fine. It's freaking fantastic.

Simon's smile widened. "I'll bring him in, then. It'll be a few minutes, because I have to transfer him to a wheelchair and get him mobile with his IV. However, I think Dr. Wu will probably let him take that out soon."

As the door closed, Emmanuella raised an eyebrow at him. "Thought you were too tired?"

"Well. He's coming to me. That's different."

A flutter of nerves made his chest tight. Was that saying too much? Had he sounded too excited? *Two seconds ago you were ready to come out to her. Where'd that fire go, man?* He couldn't recapture it, though. Whether it was old habit or a sign he truly wasn't ready, the thought of being found out filled him with as much fear as it always did. He shut his eyes.

She leaned over and ruffled his hair with her free hand. "All right. But not for long, you got that?"

"I got it."

The door to the room opened, and Nick sat up, dizzy and out-of-body the way he had been ever since the elevator, but this time it was because Jared was coming into the room. Owen held the door as Simon wheeled him in.

It was almost strange to look at him. For hours they'd been in pitch darkness together, touching and talking, unable to see unless Nick's phone lit things up, except for the end when the fire crew had sent the lantern down. Not that Nick didn't know exactly what Jared looked like. Not that he hadn't spent the evening studying him at the country club. But it was part of the dream state to see him now, draped in a hospital gown, full of IVs the same as Nick was, his skin paler than usual. Sallow, his weariness lifting up through his veins. But he was Jared, and Nick welcomed the sight of him.

Nick wondered how Jared saw him.

Jared's smile was worn, slightly shy. "Hey. How are you doing?"

Freaked out. Exhausted. Confused. Strangely lonely. Agitated because of the elevator rides. Missing you. "Okay. You?"

"Good."

Emmanuella rose, patting the bed. "I'm going to get myself some coffee from the vending machine. You boys take your time."

Owen brightened. "No, let me get you some from the doctors' lounge. We have a Keurig. It's better, and it's free. Come on."

They left together, and after Simon parked Jared beside Nick, he followed them. "I'll be at the nurses' station. I'll check back in a bit, but buzz me if you need me sooner."

Once Simon shut the door, they were alone.

Jared spoke first. "How are you, really? Is your shoulder all right?"

Nick touched it reflexively. "It's sore, but it's fine. No fractures, just a lot of pulled tendons. Jack gave me the good drugs." He pursed his lips, then added, "My bigger problem was the elevator ride to and from the CT scanner. I tripped out both times."

Jared looked a little green. "I didn't think about that. How awful. I don't know that I could have done it. I damn well intend to walk down the stairs when they discharge me, no matter what the policy is about wheeling out patients."

It felt so good to sit with him. Part of Nick wanted to address what they'd started in the elevator, but it felt so heavy. "Feels nice to be talking to you with the lights on, without the floor all tilted and death hovering over our heads."

He regretted bringing up the last part. It was too much, ruining the light mood. Leave it to Jared to smooth over it. "Yes, but is it terrible I miss the way you held me?"

Nick couldn't stop grinning. *So bold.* But Jared always was. He reached over and held his palm up, an invitation.

Jared took it, putting his hand in Nick's. It was his hand with the IV line in, a reminder they were both patients.

The things Nick wanted to say came tumbling out. "I'm already tired, thinking of the work ahead of me because of this."

Jared laced their fingers tighter together. "Can I make a suggestion?"

The mixture of boldness and hesitancy in Jared's voice made things purr inside Nick. "Yeah? Let's hear it."

"As a doctor, I think you need to prioritize stress-relieving activities."

Nick had to stifle a laugh. Jared had said something similar in the elevator, and it had definitely been a come-on. He raised an eyebrow at Jared. "As my doctor, huh?"

"As *a* doctor." Jared blushed, and Nick realized this was less come-on now and more sincerity. "As your friend...." He looked away, then at Nick, his gaze bolder. "I think you need to be selfish and take care of yourself."

Just won't come out and say it, will he? Nick settled in to wait him out. "Hmm. How do you figure I should do that?"

Here it was, the stubborn sassiness that both pissed Nick off and drew him in. "I think you need a place where you can let go and be yourself. Someone you can be completely you with, in every way." His chin went up a little. "I want to be that person. The way I used to be. Except this time I won't screw it up."

The hard double thump in Nick's chest tripped his breath. He stopped playfully baiting Jared and waited for him to finish.

Jared threaded their fingers together, and despite his heavy-lidded gaze, he didn't look away. "I'm sorry for the way I treated you when we were young, for the way we parted. It's a long-overdue apology, but I owe it to you. I was wrong in every way. I wanted to help you be your full self to everyone so you could see they'd still love you, but I know now that wasn't what you needed and certainly not the right way to support you. I behaved clumsily, and then when I realized how I'd messed it up, I let my shame keep me away. I wrapped it in bitterness and longing shellacked so hard I wasn't sure anything could cut it—until you held me in the dark in the elevator shaft, protecting me, prioritizing me above yourself. I didn't deserve that."

"Love isn't about deserve."

Jared drew a sharp breath, and he stared, lips parted in surprise, at Nick.

It felt good to say it, Nick decided. He lifted his eyebrows and quirked his mouth in a half smile. "What, you're surprised?"

But then it was Nick who was shocked when Jared ducked his head and wiped at his eyes. When he spoke, his voice was shaky. "Of course I am. Why would I expect that, after all this time? After the way I behaved?" He wiped his eyes again, then sighed raggedly and reached for a tissue from Nick's tray. "I can't believe you said that." He blew his nose. "Actually yes I can. You haven't changed."

"Neither have you."

Tossing his tissue into the trash can, Jared picked up Nick's hand and drew it to his lips, meeting his gaze. "Nick, I want to be with you. I don't care how it happens. I don't care what your conditions are. I think it's going to be almost impossible to hide a relationship with the lives we live now, but I'll figure it out. And I won't ever ask you to do something you're not ready to do ever again."

This was what he'd wanted, wasn't it? To be with Jared. And not only had Jared apologized, he was promising to give Nick the space he needed to bring this part of his life into the open on his own terms.

Why, then, did this make him feel slightly nervous?

Pushing this strange feeling aside, Nick drew Jared to him and leaned forward as far as his shoulder would allow, meeting him for a brief, tender kiss.

"We'll figure it out together," he promised, and laced their hands.

CHAPTER FIVE

JARED FELL asleep in the wee hours of the morning, dizzy and quietly giddy.

I'm dating Nick.

Sort of.

They hadn't called it that, but they'd agreed they would try to see each other, and they'd started texting before they'd gone to sleep that night, resuming as they woke up. It had been funny to do it from the hospital room next door and had made Jared feel like they truly were kids again.

That said, the carnal goodbye kiss Nick gave him before he was released was absolutely R-rated.

With Nick's family waiting for him and Owen and Simon there to take Jared away, Nick said he had to talk to Jared alone, and instead of talking, he pushed him against the back of Jared's hospital room door and kissed him until neither one of them could breathe.

It wasn't a long kiss, but it was intense and full of promise.

But all of this happened behind the door, and once they were in the hallway, they behaved as if they were close friends only.

The thing was, Owen and Simon knew about Jared and Nick, and of course the conundrum was whether Erin and Jack got to know too. It became a hot issue when Owen took Jared to his house to recover upon being released and Jared brought it up, because Owen didn't want to keep a secret from his fiancé, but Jared didn't want to betray Nick any more than he had.

"How is this betraying him? You were confessing your feelings to your friends," Owen pointed out.

"Yes, but I just said I wouldn't tell anyone, and you want me to break that on the first day? It's bad enough I told you before I made my promise."

In the end, Owen agreed to keep quiet until Jared had a chance to talk to Nick about it, and they'd regroup later.

"You're okay with this being a secret, though?" Owen set the mug of coffee he'd made for Jared on the end table beside the recliner he lounged in beneath a woven blanket. "That seems like the hardest thing in the world for you."

Jared sipped his drink. "I'm more concerned about the logistics. My place is out because I live alone, and so is his, because he lives with his family."

"I've always wondered about that, to be honest. Why does the flipping CEO of the hospital live with his mother, grandmother, and sister? It's not like he isn't paid enough to get his own place."

"Well." Jared rubbed his neck. "This is conjecture, mind you. But from what I've heard, and weighing that against how bad things were when his father died, I think Nick has been shouldering a lot of his family's debt. Remember, Collin Beckert's business went on the skids after those asshats from the board thought they needed retribution. And of course once he passed away, Aniyah took it over. I imagine Erin has more intel here because he and Nick were tight in college, but I think Nick was always sending money home, from side jobs at school to the positions he took after graduation. He had a full ride at his university, but he worked his ass off making money any way he could."

"How do you *know* all this? I thought you two were estranged?"

Jared waved a hand airily. "People talk. I listen."

Owen laughed.

"Anyway. I think things have been more stable for a long time, with the Beckert family, but they're so close. Maybe he moved in with them when he came back to Copper Point to save up for his own place, or maybe he just wanted the comfort of people who loved him while he had to deal with those dogs on the board. Maybe he's just a homebody. All I know is his place is out of the question, and so is mine. People see his car parked in my drive overnight, and it'll be all over Copper Point People before we're under the sheets."

"This takes me back to when we'd sneak Jack into the house when he was dating Simon."

"It's worse. There's no buffer over there anymore. When Jack came to see Simon, people could write it off as him visiting all of us. Now it's only me, which is too intimate. They'll think we're having sex."

"Hopefully they'll be right." Shaking his head, Owen nestled into the couch. "I'll never get over how small towns always turn into the background of a Georgette Heyer novel."

Jared raised an eyebrow at him. "You read Heyer?"

"Oh, sure. I read a lot of romance novels in med school. Nothing else took me out of my head after a horrible day quite the way they did. I listen to some on audio while I work out on occasion." He waggled his eyebrows. "They have ones for us now. Gay ones. I especially like the lesbian mystery romances. Kathryn recommends the good ones to me."

Jared had no idea his friend had this side to him. "You're a man of many facets, Owen Gagnon."

The good news was the issue with Erin didn't come up because Jared didn't see him. With Nick gone, Erin was the de facto CEO, and the accident plus patient rerouting had given him plenty to do, even on a Sunday. Owen had to go in to help with a delivery in the evening, so Simon and Jack came over to sit with him.

Simon, it turned out, had spilled the beans to his fiancé, who had mostly pieced things together on his own from something Nick had said in the elevator. Jared probably should have been upset about it, but he couldn't bring himself to reprimand Si, since it suited his purposes so well. While Jack made dinner, Jared grilled the two of them about how their relationship had been when they'd had to hide it because of the hospital's former no-dating policy between staff members.

"It was rough," Simon admitted. "All we wanted to do was let people know, but we couldn't, and we had to second-guess our every move, every gesture, every look. It made me feel seedy."

"It wasn't my favorite thing either, but I think it was harder on Simon than it was on me." Jack flipped the pasta in the pan. "At the time, I was getting to know people, and I'm a more private person by nature than he is. But from his perspective, I think it felt like lying to people he'd known and loved his whole life, doing something he'd never do."

Simon nudged Jared with his foot. "Are you and Nick dating, then, and keeping it secret?"

Was it okay for him to talk about this? Jared decided there was no way he could keep their relationship so secret they didn't share it with their closest friends. He'd have to convince Nick and apologize for jumping the gun. "Yes. And… yes."

Simon's mouth fell open, but Jack only smiled over his shoulder. "Congratulations. From the sounds of things, this is a long time coming."

"Thanks." Jared ran a hand through his hair. "I'm nervous about the secret aspect, but I'm determined to make it work. I don't know *how* it will, but… well."

"Have you been in contact with him today?" Jack asked.

"Some. He's slept a lot, and his family understandably wants to spend time with him. I don't want to interrupt that."

They focused on their dinner instead, which was delicious, and when they were finished, they watched an episode of one of Simon's new favorite Korean dramas on Netflix. There was first, of course, the standard ten-minute lament over the closure of his favorite Asian drama source, DramaFever, which had shut down without warning not long ago. Simon had shed literal tears for a week, often randomly remembering shows he'd never be able to see again or hadn't been able to finish. He was still upset about it, but he was better now.

One episode in, Jared started to get tired, though the two of them didn't leave, only encouraged him to go to bed. "We'll wait until Owen or Erin comes back," Simon said.

"Guys, I'm fine, honestly," Jared insisted.

"Yes, but we're not." Jack waved him toward the stairs. "Go to sleep."

Once he was in bed, Jared texted Nick.

Going to sleep. Hope you had a good day.

He was biting his lip, worrying that was a silly text, when he got a reply.

Can't complain. Got spoiled rotten by three lovely women. You?

Spoiled by my friends. They won't let me be alone.

Same. A pause. *Are you going to work tomorrow?*

No, but I'll have to go Tuesday. You're staying home too, aren't you?

Mmm.

Jared gasped and typed furiously. *You can't seriously be thinking of going back to work already.*

I've been working all day, except when they steal my phone and computer. I'll do more from home again tomorrow, but I think I have put in an appearance by Tuesday.

Jared hesitated, typing several things before settling on, *If you do go in, let me know. I'd like to at least say hello, if I'm free.*

You better do more than say hello.

Grinning, Jared snuggled deeper into the covers.

Nick typed again. *But who knows. I might come find you first.*

It had been a long time since Jared had one of those goofy grins that stretched his face, the ones you couldn't wipe away. *I think you'd better.*

GRANDMA EMERSON had passed the promised pineapple upside-down cake around the nursing station and to the doctors in the emergency room before Nick left the hospital, and everybody took a slice. The cake was warm when she brought it, which in the Beckert household was the only way to serve it. The warm yellow cake, brown sugar, and cooked pineapple scent drew everyone, meaning Nick only got the two pieces she'd cut out for him. He'd tried not to be sullen about having so much of his favorite treat taken away.

However, that evening as he put away his phone from texting Jared, his grandmother pulled a second one out of the oven, one she explained was entirely his. She said she'd warm it up whenever he wanted.

They'd been spoiling him like this all day, acting as if it were some kind of strange holiday undeclared and centered on him. His mother played the stereo, alternating between Aretha Franklin and Etta James (Grandma Emerson's favorite and hers, respectively), and everyone had hummed and danced as they did laundry, cooked, and fussed around the living room where Nick sat going over the files Erin had emailed. When Erin came by at nine to brief him on what had happened during the day and let him know what to expect on his return, they cleared out, but Nick's mother gave him a look that said, *Don't you go staying up too late.*

Erin smiled as they sat together at the table. "You seem well taken care of."

Nick rubbed the back of his head. "Yeah, well." He nodded at the papers Erin had brought. "What do you have for me here?"

Erin sorted through the stack. "I sent you the summary of all the regular business items. What I need your help with are the stickier situations, things we need to take to the board and some things we simply need to act on now because there's no time." He handed Nick a stapled memo. "I met with the insurance adjusters, but they want to interview you and Jared both. Rebecca wants the hospital lawyer to be present at those meetings, and she wants to sit in as a board member and as Jared's personal attorney. She says she's willing to be yours as well, unless you have someone you want to use."

"My usual attorney is at her firm, so it's fine. She can represent me."

"There's also the issue of the consulting firm you wanted to call for. We'll need board approval for that, of course, but I have some names I want you to look at. I want to call a board meeting as soon as possible, but I want everything lined up before then." He tapped his pencil on his notebook. "I think you're right, though. There's no way they'll tell us anything but that we should build a new facility. Apparently it's been suggested for years, but the old board wouldn't have it because of budgetary concerns." Erin pursed his lips. "Quite an irony, given the amount of money they siphoned away. While I'm sure my father will help with this endeavor, the bulk of his fortune went to the cardiac unit and the scholarship fund in your father's name. He might have some contacts in the industry, but I'd rather not use them. And while he and I are finally managing a civil relationship, I'm not ready to work with him on a sustained level, nor do I think is anyone in Copper Point."

"Agreed." Nick wiped his face, thinking. "If we're going to have issues like falling elevators, we're going to need to take action whether we're ready or not. I don't want this to get away from us."

"That's just the thing. The elevator repair itself is going to be incredibly expensive and take a long time. Even if a new building is only more expensive by twenty thousand dollars, we'll be besieged by people who don't understand construction and think we should be economical and recycle the building we have. This is going to hurt us no matter how we slice it." His gaze darted to the plate beside Nick. "Speaking of slice. Is that the remnants of your grandmother's pineapple upside-down cake I see there? I heard there was one floating around the hospital. I can't believe I missed out."

Nick perked up. "Oh, yeah, it is. She made another one, and it's still warm, or she'll make it that way if it isn't. Let's go get you some."

"I won't say no."

Erin looked like a little kid as he sat at the table and waited for a slice of cake, fidgeting and tapping his feet as Nick's grandmother brought two plates over. "Grandma Emerson, your kitchen always smells amazing."

She waved a dish towel at him, but she smiled. "You want coffee with your cake?"

"Oh, no. Water is fine. I need to be able to sleep tonight."

"I'm more worried about you staying awake long enough to drive home." She set a piece of cake in front of Erin and another in front of Nick.

Nick held up his hands. "Grandma, I'm so full I'll burst."

"If you don't eat the cake, I'll put it away after Erin leaves."

Sighing, Nick pulled the plate toward him as his grandmother walked away. "I'm going to need a week in the gym to make up for today alone."

Erin ignored him, his eyes falling closed as his lips sealed around his fork. He groaned as he chewed. "Oh my *God*," he said, mouth half-full. "This is amazing. This is absolutely the best cake I've ever had. It's so *moist*. And I love that it's warm."

Giving in, Nick speared a section of the top of the cake, loaded with pineapple and brown sugar and part of a cherry. He didn't make the sounds Erin did, but he had to agree, it was a perfect cake. All Grandma Emerson's baking was amazing, but this one was the crown jewel as far as he was concerned.

He carved out another bite, this time from the plain cake section, which was moist and soft, springing back as he cut into it. "When I was little and Grandma would take this cake to church potlucks, I'd stand beside it like a carnival barker, selling it to everyone who walked by."

"I'd have walked off with the whole tray." Erin, having finished his piece, mashed some crumbs with his fork and licked them. "I suppose I should get going. Owen had to go in for an OB patient, and Jack and Simon are sitting at the house with Jared. None of us feel right leaving him alone tonight, but at the same time, I don't want to keep them up too late. And since I'll be up early, I should get some sleep too."

Nick thought of his earlier text with Jared. "I'm glad he's staying with you."

"Yes, well, he'll insist on going home soon enough, and if we try to coddle him, he won't have it."

Grandma Emerson stuck her head back into the dining room and looked at Nick's empty plate with a knowing smile. "I'm heading to bed. You boys put your dirty dishes in the dishwasher, and, Nick, go ahead and start it after."

"Yes, ma'am," Nick called.

"Thank you," Erin replied.

Nick walked Erin to the door, but as they stood in the vestibule, Erin glanced into the empty house, then leaned in close to Nick.

"I know you like to keep things private, and I'm not going to pry. But if things are going the way I think between you and Jared, I'm all for it and will support you however I can."

Nick stared openmouthed at Erin. "How—"

Erin gave him a *come on* look. "Nick. I've known you forever, and I got drunk with you in college."

Nick went still. "What happened when we got drunk together in college?"

"You talked about Jared Kumpel every single time."

Nick took a step backward so the wall would support him.

Erin held up a hand. "You only said how frustrated he made you and how you wanted to tell him off, though after vodka you were known to say how much you missed his friendship. Except I always wondered if there wasn't something more to it. Then I watched the two of you play racquetball together, and I was convinced there was."

He needed to deny this, to tell Erin no way, he was imagining things, but Nick was so sideswiped he didn't know where to start.

Worse, Erin kept going. "Then I saw the way you looked at him when the two of you came out of the elevator." When Nick tensed, Erin hurried to continue. "No one else noticed what I did, I'm sure. Except maybe Owen. We've talked about it together, since Jared is his friend. If I'm reading into all of this, I apologize."

There was his escape, except Nick couldn't take it. He pulled Erin deeper into the shadows and pitched his voice low. "I'm not…." A cold sweat broke out across his skin. He'd never said the words out loud. They clogged his throat. "I'm not out. To anyone."

I'm barely out to myself.

"I know." Erin kept his voice low as well. "Which is why I'm telling you like this. I support the two of you. Tell me how I can help."

What was he supposed to say to this? He wanted to tell Erin he could help by butting out and leaving him alone, but he knew he couldn't do that. Shouldn't do that. But saying anything else felt like he might puke up the cake he'd eaten, and dinner too.

Inclining his head, Erin put his hand on the door. "I'm sorry, I've made you uncomfortable. Forget I said anything. But the offer stands. For the record, I know it'll be true of Owen, Jack, and Simon too."

Erin started to leave, and words fell out of Nick's mouth. "Thank you."

He wasn't sure if he meant *for stopping by* or *for bringing my notes* or *for covering for me* or if he actually meant *for telling me you know I'm gay and that you're fine with it*. Maybe it was all of it.

Erin smiled. "Anytime. See you tomorrow."

Head spinning, shoulder aching a little, Nick shuffled into the dining room to collect the plates. Except they were already gone, and he could hear the sound of someone loading the dishwasher in the kitchen.

His stomach turned to lead as he followed the sound. Oh God, who was it? Who had heard them? His mother? Grandma Emerson?

No, it was Emmanuella. When she saw him standing in the doorway, panic-stricken, she put a hand on her hip and cocked an eyebrow.

"What are you looking at me like that for?" She motioned to one of the tall stools at the breakfast bar. "Sit. You're going to fall over, and I'm not having Mom shout at me for it."

Nick moved toward the chair and took a seat in a floating haze. Had she heard them? Had she been in the kitchen? Had they been quiet enough? Should he say something? Should he pretend nothing had happened?

Well, he'd thought she might know in the hospital, but….

God, he didn't know how to behave.

Emmanuella continued to load and start the dishwasher as if nothing was wrong. When she finished, she dusted her hands and turned to him. "Come on. Let's get you to your room. Everyone else is in bed, and I heard you're going to work tomorrow."

Normally Nick would have insisted he could walk to his room alone just fine, but right now he wasn't so sure. He let her herd him up the stairs and down the hall and didn't question it when she followed him inside and shut the door, ushered him to the bed, then sat beside him.

"All right. Now that we're where you know it's private, tell me what has you so spooked. Erin say something? He guess something you didn't want him to? Was it about Jared?"

Nick couldn't breathe for a second. "H-how—?"

Emmanuella tilted her head and looked down the slope of her nose at him. She didn't say anything else.

He was tugged in two directions at once, part of him eager to tell her what he'd wanted to share for years, part of him paralyzed with fear of discovery. As usual, the fear overrode everything. He decided this wasn't the right time to discuss Jared with her. Best to deflect and come up with a better moment later.

Trouble was, he didn't know how to do that with her looking so damned determined.

I'm a CEO of a hospital. I took out a nest of crooked board members. I can handle an interrogation from my baby sister. Except when Nick opened his mouth, all that came out was, “What do you mean, is it about Jared? Why would you guess that?”

“What it’s about is I’d bet my next paycheck you’ve had a crush on him since you were in high school, and now you were trapped in an elevator with him and you both came out looking at each other like you were Jack and Rose in that car in the *Titanic* cargo hold.” When Nick felt the blood drain from his face and possibly the entire upper half of his body, his sister threw up her hands. “See? This is what I’m talking about. I’ve been waiting twenty years for you to confess your orientation to me. You think it’s some big mystery, with the way you won’t date anyone? Figured it was just a matter of time until you introduced me to your boyfriend.”

Nick could only stare at her, drowning in his worst nightmare. It didn’t matter that she was reacting positively. The part of him that was always afraid was too keyed up, too busy connecting every potential dot that might bring his world crashing down around him.

Emmanuella, unaware of this, pressed on. “I’m telling you to your face, bro, that I’m for this. Why don’t you come out and tell me about it so you can quit bottling it up inside?”

Nick honestly thought he might be sick. “Does Mama know? Grandma?”

“That you have feelings for Jared? Or that you’re gay?”

Every bone in his body failed him at once, his stomach twisting into a tighter knot. He slumped farther forward.

She put a hand on his back and stroked him in slow, easy circles. “Nick, honey. I’m not trying to make this about me, but for real, I'm hurt you're reacting like this. You're not happy that I'm happy for you?"

A rough, hollow laugh escaped him. "Wasn't ever gonna tell you."

She smacked him sharply on the shoulder. "*Seriously?* I just *told* you—"

"I wasn't ever going to tell anyone in the family. You're the last people in the world I could tell."

"But *why*?"

His chest was so tight he could barely breathe, his vision blurred by unshed tears as he clenched his hands into fists over his thighs. "Because I could handle anyone in the world rejecting me, but not a single one of you."

She pulled him tight into her arms, drew his head onto her shoulder. "I would never reject you. Not for anything. Certainly not for you telling me the whole of who you are."

A small ball of tightness inside of Nick's chest relaxed, and for a moment they sat quietly as her vow echoed around them and his tears fell softly onto her shirt.

Eventually she started stroking his back again. "As for Mama and Grandma, I don't know. I think they have to suspect something. I mean, *everybody* wonders why you don't date. But then, I assumed we just didn't meet your dates. I never figured out how you got together with anybody, though. You're so busy, and it's not like you sleep overnight anywhere much or stay out late. If you've got extra work, you bring it home."

"Don't date, never have."

She drew back and regarded him with a stunned expression. "Go on, you did so."

He shook his head. "Tried seeing a few women in my early twenties, but I couldn't take them to bed. I was trying to make myself straight, but I knew what I was doing to them and couldn't go through with it. Tried to marry my job after that, which kinda worked."

"What, so you didn't date *anyone?*"

He shrugged. "Hooked up occasionally, but I tried not to. Not much since I came back to Copper Point—only twice, when I was out of town."

"*Baby*. That's not right." She paused. "Unless, are you not interested in sex? Because that's a whole other situation altogether."

"Oh, I'm interested. But denying myself was where I was. I don't want to be there anymore." He ran his good hand over the top of his head. "I want to be with Jared, but I worry a relationship with a closeted man won't be enough for him, and I worry about people finding out."

Rising from the bed, she motioned for him to follow her. "Come on. Let me help you with your hair. You won't be able to do it the way you want with your shoulder. Let's get you some nice waves for tomorrow. You can seduce your doctor or take on insurance adjusters, whatever pleases you most."

He wasn't going to fight her. His hair felt frizzy and dry, his beard a mess. She was right, his shoulder was going to hinder him. If she was offering to play barber, he was willing to let her.

He sat in front of her while she greased his waves and brushed them into place. Having someone else fuss with his head felt good, almost hypnotic. When was the last time someone had done this for him? How old had he been? Over and over she ran the hard bristles, following the pattern of his hair, working in the conditioning oil and taming the curls.

She must have brushed the words out of him too, because all of a sudden he was talking.

"I never knew how you would accept it." He let his head follow the tug of her arm movements. "Coming out wasn't as important to me as family unity or the honor of Dad's memory, so I kept quiet. I figured I just wouldn't get married."

Her brush clipped his ear. "You think any of us want you to deny yourself to preserve some fantasy you have of our family's happiness? You think we can't be unified without you making sacrifices?"

"I think Mom and Grandma would have a hard time with it. A very hard time."

She brushed for a few seconds before replying. "You might be right. But I think they'd come around."

"And what if they don't?"

"You *honestly* think they still wouldn't love you?"

"I think they might love me and be more distant at the same time."

"They might need a minute to adjust, but I'm telling you, they *would* get over it."

"I don't want to risk it. They've given up so much for us."

"They didn't do it so you could be half of yourself."

"If me being my true self means turning the women who kept us above water all these years into angry, bitter strangers, then I don't want my true self."

"Even if it means losing Jared?"

Nick shut his eyes and breathed against the heavy pang in his chest. "Even if it means that. Yes."

She knocked the wooden back of the brush into the side of his head. "That's crap, Nick."

"It's how I feel." He eased a little as she resumed brushing. "Besides. The town isn't ready for a gay hospital CEO. Especially not one dating their favorite pediatrician."

"Oh, that's bull. They already have a gay surgeon, gay nurse, gay vice president, and the pediatrician you want to date is out. Not to mention the gynecologist, the lawyer—there are more damn gay people here than straight, it feels like some days."

"It might be different if it's *me*."

"*Come on.*"

"Fine. I'm not ready. That's the bottom line. While in theory I'd like to be accepted for who I am, I don't know how it's going to play out, and I'm not ready to find out how things will be different. More than anything, I'm not ready for my relationship with Mama and Grandma to change. Because there's no way they'd react like you. Even if somehow I could know for sure they'd come around… no. I can't."

She brushed in silence, then tied his durag around his head with a resigned sigh. "I don't like it. It's not healthy for you. You deserve better."

He patted the blue silk as she tucked the ties, then smoothed her hands over his shoulders. He glanced over his shoulder, smiling softly. "Thanks. You defending me means a lot."

"Course I'm gonna defend you. Even against your damn self." She whacked his good shoulder lightly. "So come to me when you want to talk, all right? I hate how you walk around with the world on your shoulders. You need somewhere to let that stuff out."

Nick thought about Jared, angry and defiant in front of him. Jared soft and sensual in his arms. "You're not wrong there."

CHAPTER SIX

JARED RETURNED to the clinic on Tuesday at ten, three hours later than his normal schedule, which was supposed to be him easing into work. In reality, this meant a greater mess than if he'd come at seven in the morning. The waiting room was full of screaming children and parents at their wits' ends, and the nurses hadn't only double-booked him, they'd triple-booked him with kids in desperate need to be seen. Some of the parents were likely using the excuse to see how Jared was doing. He wasn't the only gossip in town.

Having anticipated this, Jared waved as he entered, pausing to say hello to some of the more upset children, then met with his nurse to strategize how to do the impossible and get all the patients seen without rushing any of their appointments. Once they began the drill, he hit his stride quickly, moving from exam room to exam room as if this were a ballroom dance, pausing to tease the nurses as he washed his hands between patients. The other clinic doctors were cheerful toward him as well, telling him they were glad to have him back, letting him know how much he'd been missed.

Jared was good at his job. He calmed his patients, got them to smile, made them laugh even when they were facing something that frightened them. His exam rooms were full of things to explore for all ages. There were educational toys for the kids, puzzle books for the adults. He also had information and subtle assistance available, health magazines and flyers for networking groups and ways for his patients' parents to reach out to each other.

The problem was he could only go so fast and see so many people. He drew patients from an hour away, bringing in serious money to the clinic and the hospital, but the wait times for his appointments were abysmal. He didn't want to rush his patients either, and if someone needed more time, he gave it to them.

Most parents didn't mind, even if they had to wait or were juggled around, as many of them were today. In fact, the noon patient he saw at one thirty smiled and thanked him when he finally appeared.

"We're just glad you're all right." She shifted her cranky toddler to her opposite hip and put a placating hand on the six-year-old with a fever who was determined to keep his face buried in her hip.

Jared reached for the bucket of stickers and plastic toys, luring the boy from his mother long enough for her to grab a diaper bag and her purse. "Doing fine. Soon Alberto will be too. Oh, and that unicorn duck will definitely help. Everyone who picks that gets better faster."

The mother's grin widened. "You're so good with children. Have you ever thought about having your own?"

He used putting the bucket away to fix a breezy expression onto his face. Usually the parents of his patients stayed well out of his personal life, but then there were always those who wanted to make *sure* he knew they were liberal and accepting, and they often went too far the other direction. He deflected her gently. "Oh, not without a partner to raise them with. But most of the tri-county area's children are patients of mine, and in a way they feel like my own. Even some young adults are former patients, I've seen them so long, so perhaps that's enough."

She raised her eyebrows. "If a partner's all you're missing…."

Yikes. Head the matchmaker off at the pass. "Ah, unfortunately a doctor's schedule makes for terrible courtship." He rose for the door. "Set up a follow-up in ten days, but of course call if he doesn't improve or you have any concerns."

He was at the sink washing his hands when one of the receptionists from the front desk approached him. She looked slightly nervous but also mildly conspiratorial.

He smiled at her. "Helen, what can I do for you?"

She leaned close. "You have a visitor in your office."

He leaned in as well and deadpanned. "Should I be worried?"

Now she blushed, but she had a funny expression on her face. "It's Mr. Beckert."

Jared focused on drying his hands to hide his excitement. Well, he *had* told the man he'd better come see him. "Oh? I'm sure he has something to go over regarding the incident the other day."

"He brought lunch with him from Café Cuore. One of the volunteers went to get it for him."

Jared stilled with the wadded-up paper towel in his hand.

Okay, there was coming to see him, and then there was *coming to see him*. Did Nick not understand subtlety? Did he not get where he was and who was surrounding them? Who was the one in the closet here? Helen was one of the top town gossips, right up there with Jared himself. He had to play this carefully.

"Well." He tossed the paper towel into the basket. "Either he's about to break some bad news to me about what happened with the elevator, or I'm about to get more work as an advisory board member." He tapped his cheek thoughtfully, then regarded her askance. "Do you know if he ordered breadsticks?"

Helen nodded, then frowned. "Well—garlic knots."

God, the woman was *good*. And dangerous. Jared winced dramatically. "Oh, damn, I bet it's bad news about the incident *and* more work for me."

"Except he hasn't done this for any other board members."

No kidding. "Well, Helen, I'll tell you a secret, just between you and me. In the past, the two of us haven't gotten along."

She gasped. "No. Really?"

Oh, but that information would be all over Copper Point before Jared returned to his office. *Good.* Maybe then they'd be less likely to assume they were lovers simply for talking to each other more. "I'm afraid so. But that's the thing about being stuck in an elevator with someone for five hours. It completely changes your perspective on people." He patted her arm. "Going to go get my garlic knots before they get cold. Don't worry, I'll act surprised."

Except after he got over the thrill of seeing Nick standing at the window, delicious in his suit as always—God, and his hair was absolutely excellent today as well—Jared closed the door and folded his arms over his chest. "What's this?"

Nick raised an eyebrow at him, sauntering closer, looking like he intended to make a meal of Jared up against the door. "I was informed you didn't stop for lunch. So as your employer, I'm making you eat."

Jared managed to keep his hands at his sides and not slide them up Nick's crisp shirt and draw him to his lips by his tie. His eyes were rich and full of expression—light and playful, but they hinted at his intelligence too. The whole package turned Jared the hell on. "Well, so you know, your visit is already a point of gossip. I did my best to stop it, but I can only do so much. Unless you changed your mind about this relationship being public?"

Though he'd known the jolt and pullback were coming, it bummed Jared out. Nick wasn't exactly panicked, but he wasn't seducing Jared any longer either. "What do you mean, there's gossip? Because I brought you lunch?"

The man had been back in Copper Point for four years, but he didn't have the rhythm down. "You ordered from somewhere fancy, which you don't normally do. You also don't normally send out people to fetch your food. Then you came to see me. Yes, they're going to talk about it."

"We can't have a lunch together as friends?"

"Sure, but we never have before. And like I said, you didn't simply bring something from the cafeteria."

He sighed. "I should've hidden it in something."

"You could have put it in one of the EMT's organ transplant coolers and they would have been *convinced* you were smuggling me Italian."

Nick made a face. "Gross. Why would I smuggle you food in an organ transplant cooler?"

"Well, for one, they're incredibly sterile. You putting food in them would in fact make them contaminated, but we wash them like crazy anyway. My point is you could disguise it as anything. People in this town notice every little thing that happens, then tell each other about it. You ordered a fancy lunch for two, which wasn't usual. Everyone wanted to see what you did with it."

Nick sank into Jared's desk chair, looking sheepish. "I knew lunch was the way I could see you today, and I wanted it to be nice. I'm sorry."

"You don't have to apologize to me. I'm not the one we're hiding for." Jared slid onto Nick's lap, heart skipping a beat as he worried it was too bold of a move. He smoothed his hand over Nick's cheek to cover his nervousness. "I'm sorry I opened with a lecture. I did try to cover for you, and it's probably good. Can I have a kiss?"

Nick glanced at the door.

Jared nuzzled his nose. "I locked it."

Nick's hand rested on Jared's hip. He nuzzled back but watched the door. "Doesn't that make it more suspicious?"

Now Nick had his head in the game. *Now.* "Possibly, but I can say we were discussing something confidential." Enough. He'd beg for it. "Please kiss me, Nick."

Nick gave him a soft peck on the lips, but he drew away too quickly.

Sighing softly, Jared climbed off Nick, pulled up another chair, and opened the bag. "God, smells great. Can we eat?"

This calmed Nick somewhat. "Yes, let's, before it gets cold. I got the chicken parm pasta special and some garlic knots. You used to love garlic knots when we were younger."

"Still do." Jared withdrew the package of bread and sniffed it. Then groaned. "So good. And Café Cuore makes the best." He offered one to Nick. "Want a bite?" When Nick glanced at the door again instead of accepting it, Jared bopped him on the nose with the bread. "Stop. If anybody comes into my office, especially with you in it, they're going to knock and wait for me."

Frowning, Nick took a bite of the garlic knot. "Why won't they come in if I'm here?" he asked once he was done chewing.

"Because you're *the boss*. And here, I'm also *the boss*. They'll talk about us, though, wondering what we're doing. Don't freak out. Yes, some of them will make innuendos because I'm gay, but plenty of other people will scold them for it."

Nick grimaced. "I wasn't thinking."

"Yes, you were. You were thinking about coming to see me, which I very much appreciate." Jared withdrew the trays of chicken parmesan out of the bag and passed one to Nick along with a set of utensils. "A question for you. When Jack and Simon were dating in defiance of the policy, when did you suspect them?"

Nick paused with his fork over his food. "Hmm. I'd say I started to wonder if there wasn't something the night of Mr. Zhang's emergency. I wasn't sure of Jack's orientation, but that was the first night I began to watch the two of them."

Jared laughed. "My God, they weren't even dating officially yet then. Now I'm thinking back to all the acrobatics we did to hide Jack when he came over and feeling foolish. You knew the whole time. Why didn't you say anything?"

"It wasn't my policy. That was all the board's bullshit. I didn't care who they dated, so long as it didn't affect their performance at work. If anything, they seemed to do better." He looked weary. "But what you're saying, what you've *been* saying, is it's going to be impossible to do this?"

"Not impossible, though we'll have to be a lot more clever. You need to let me drive this bus."

Nick grunted. "I don't care for giving up control."

Jared smiled wickedly around a mouthful of garlic knot. "Mmm." He swallowed and winked. "That's not what I remember." When Nick sputtered and blushed, Jared put down his food and moved to stand between Nick's legs. "Oh, don't be that way. You aren't going to convince me your tastes have changed *that* much." He ran a hand down the side of Nick's face. "You seduced me all sweet, made me melt. Then you wanted me to turn the tables on you and tell you how to take me. You want to keep all the control to yourself right up until you want me to make you beg instead."

Nick swatted Jared's butt. "We're not playing that game *here*."

"I appreciate how you acknowledge we are going to play it." Mostly, though Jared wasn't going to admit it out loud, he liked that they were somehow, this easily, back into the rhythm where they were playing games, period. Jared let his hand fall away. "Tell you what. You figure out where and when you feel okay about it, and I'll meet you."

Oh, but he liked the hungry look in Nick's eyes. *How I've missed this.* However, he didn't enjoy the frustration and defeat he saw in his lover's face. "I don't know how I can possibly find a place or a time that doesn't give us away."

Jared didn't have many ideas either. "Well, what worked for us in the past, as I said, was smuggling. We'd bring Jack over with him lying down in the back seat. Boy did he hate that. Muttered about this town being ridiculous a lot."

"It is." Nick ran a hand over his beard as if he were seriously thinking it over. "I don't know how that would work. My family…."

"Yes, you come with special challenges. If only you lived alone." Jared sighed. "Except I wouldn't wish that on you. I can't stand living by myself. I was about to advertise for a roommate."

Nick sat up straighter. "You can't do that."

"Unless you're going to apply for the position, you don't get a vote. I like people around me, the more the better, and now I go home every night to an empty house. No one to cook for, no one to talk to."

Nick glowered. "I don't like the idea of you cooking for other people either."

Jared kissed his nose. "Figure out a way to get yourself over to my house, and I'll cook for you every single night."

Was it bad to enjoy Nick looking so grumpy? Maybe. But that they were here like this was surreal. Was he asleep in the elevator, dreaming? Had they died after all, and this was heaven?

No. This was, somehow, his life. Apparently the recipe was, put two stubborn men in an elevator, shake slightly, and they reset. Well, Jared wasn't wasting this chance.

Pulling off a piece of bread, Jared offered it again to Nick. "You could come over as a friend, and I could feed you."

"Mmpf." Nick chewed the bite, swallowed, and touched Jared's face. "I'll come over. Next weekend, before we help Dr. Amin. Just don't move in with anyone."

"I won't. For now." When Nick pursed his lips, Jared kissed them. Then he felt Nick's injured shoulder carefully. "Do you still hurt?"

"Only a little."

Jared ran a hand up Nick's neck. "Should I kiss it better?"

"Oh, yes."

Jared kissed him. But his mouth didn't go anywhere near Nick's shoulder.

NICK DIDN'T exactly have a shortage of work in a normal week, but the volume of activity in the one following the accident was definitely off the charts. In addition to his usual work, he also had phone calls to insurance agents and lawyers. To make things even more complicated, both Jeremiah Ryan and Jordan Peterson were calling him more as well. Ryan at least was making sure Nick was all right and ensuring he and Cynthia couldn't do anything more for him, but Peterson sent along yet another request to meet with the full board, assuring Nick this "tragedy with the elevator," as he put it, wouldn't deter their offer. When Nick once again declined, Peterson got angry, called him an upstart, and hung up on him.

Nick felt as if he were constantly warding off a headache.

"What makes me crazy is last week the developers showing interest in St. Ann's was flattering and a reminder to keep ourselves in line," he complained to Erin as they worked on some files together over sandwiches in the conference room on Friday. "Now I feel like we have to view them differently. What if this elevator disaster means we *have* to accept outside help? I don't care for that at all."

"It's too soon." Erin took a bite of his sandwich. "The construction firm the insurance company suggested is assessing the damage and will give us a report later this week, hopefully with a reason for the failure. But I also want to hear from the firm we retain to do the audit."

Nick wanted it all over with so he could plan instead of worry. "Did you get everyone to confirm a date for the emergency meeting?"

"Yes. Next Friday morning at seven thirty. We'll need to be prompt so as not to disrupt the surgical schedule." He stopped typing and picked up a stack of folders, then handed them to Nick. "Here are the auditing firms I suggest we choose from. I had them send over quotes, and I drafted summaries of their strengths and weaknesses. My suggestion is we select three or four and let the board vote from there."

Nick perused the files, taking in Erin's organized spread. "Three is better, I think. These are great. As usual, I couldn't do this without you."

"I feel much the same." Erin resumed typing. "Will you be all right choosing the three candidates for the board? I can give you my input, if you want, but I also am fine confirming your choices or helping you winnow down your last few."

"The latter seems easier, doesn't it? You have so much going on."

"I do. Oh. That reminds me." He passed over yet another folder. "These are transcripts from statements the security guards and custodian gave the insurance company. It's good we're both aware of what they said. I'll be providing copies of all of this to the firm we choose as well."

Nick took this folder from Erin, but he frowned. "Why would you give that to the auditing firm? What would they have to do with it?"

"Transparency is our ally here, in all things."

"But the elevator failure has nothing to do with reconstruction costs."

Erin pursed his lips. “Hopefully.”

Nick leaned back in his chair, eyes wide. “Okay, you have my attention now.”

“Honestly, I don’t know if it’s worth the attention. I might have conspiracy on the brain after all we went through last year. But I can’t stop thinking about the fire chief’s comment that the elevator shouldn’t have fallen the way it did. He talked about how his cousin works in Madison as an engineer and that’s the whole point with elevators, they have brakes and fail-safes like you wouldn’t believe. Despite ours being older, it had to be kept up to code in order to operate. Also, I can hand you the last five years’ worth of inspections showing that everything was up to code and operating effectively. I did extra investigating because I was curious. Everything *should* have been fine. It’s strange how it wasn’t.”

The uncomfortable feeling in Nick’s gut became more pronounced. “You think this was some sort of sabotage?”

Erin waved his hand. “I can’t get too specific based on anything, and as I said, I might be making more out of this than is there. But this is precisely my point. We have local construction estimates coming in, and there will be a separate insurance agent from the elevator company. Now we’ll have a third team in this auditing company, whoever we hire. So let’s let them have all the information possible. Most likely all that will happen is everyone tells us the same thing. But what if someone gives us greater detail, or a slightly different story? We only get that if we’re thorough. And it costs us nothing.”

"I have no objections. But I seriously hope it's you being overcautious. I do *not* need any more excitement in my life."

Erin shut his laptop and focused exclusively on eating his lunch, at least for a few minutes. "In any event, that's settled and rolling. You don't need to worry about it, though I know you will anyway. I'd encourage you to focus on other things as much as possible. Such as visiting your secret boyfriend and taking him Italian takeout, for example."

Nick winced. "God, I should have been more careful."

"Good luck. Hospitals are little petri dishes in more ways than one."

"I hope it's only a metaphorical one. We don't need an E. coli outbreak on top of everything else."

"I can help you invent reasons to meet with Jared in your office. That's probably safer than the clinic."

"He never has time, though. I know I never have a spare moment, but I think he eats standing up more than he sits down."

"He does, from what I gathered while we all lived together. Usually it's a bite at a time between patients from eleven until two, except often he just gives up and waits until he's off work. Owen is much the same, with a bit more leeway. If we could draw a second pediatrician to the clinic, it would be a huge boon to Jared's load."

"Right now let's focus on getting a functional elevator, or a plan for a new building." Nick finished his sandwich and dusted his hands of crumbs to the side of the table before reaching for a napkin. "So. We're helping the Amins unload their van tomorrow, right?"

"Yes, but I doubt anyone will let you lift anything heavy, no matter how great you tell them your shoulder feels." Erin sipped his drink. "I don't know that we have the boat ready yet, but we can have everyone over to our house for a barbecue afterward."

"Mmm, let me talk to Grandma Emerson. She wanted to do something for them anyway, and if we let her and Mom host, they can get things set up while we do the dirty work. Plus we have a swing set up at our house. I keep trying to take it down, but if I bring it up, Mom and Grandma go on about the grandbabies they're going to have playing on it, so I leave it be. I'll make sure nothing's rotten, though, and get new sand for the sandbox."

"Take Jared along with you for the sand, and let him do any hammering." Erin paused. "Actually, maybe you better take Owen. Hammers aren't Jared's strong suit. He tried to repair the mailbox post once and only broke it more completely."

Nick sighed. "My shoulder is fine. Just slightly sore."

"I'll let you tell that to the doctors," Erin said, sifting through his files as he ate.

The nagging over his shoulder aside, Nick liked this. Sitting with Erin, solving problems, planning outings beyond work. They'd done things together before the board turnover, but everything had been tense because they were constantly escaping shadows. Not anymore. Now they were on their own. Things had been good for some time, and they were on track to get better.

Nick gripped the aluminum sides of his water bottle. "I don't want this accident to derail our progress with the hospital. I'll do whatever I have to in order to keep things moving in the direction we want things to go."

Erin glanced up with a quiet smile. "I agree. And I'll be beside you every step of the way."

CHAPTER SEVEN

JARED LOVED the Amin family as soon as he met them.

Uzma ran the show on every level, making the most money as a cardiologist, but she also was clearly the heartbeat of the family, pardon the pun, herding the children, her husband, and her in-laws with firm affection toward the next task. Irfan, Uzma's husband, was quiet and affable, the type of man who seemed excited by the world at large and always eager to see what was around the next corner, but not very interested in organizing it the way his wife did. He was looking forward to taking an adjunct composition position at the college through the rest of the year. Farhan and Zaika, Irfan's parents, were quieter, more focused on supporting their family than interacting with the newcomers, but as the day wore on, they opened up too, Farhan sharing stories of his days as a medical doctor practicing in New Delhi. The children, Samira and Omar, were seven and five respectively, full of curiosity and eagerness regarding their new environment, which was nothing like the Houston they'd just left.

The unloading of the moving van, as well as the distribution of things to the individual rooms, was handled by the company, but Jared, Nick, Simon, Jack, Owen, and Erin helped unpack, assemble, and set up as directed by Uzma. Zaika served refreshments when everyone was tired. As people rested before heading to Nick's house for the picnic, the Amins got to know their helpers.

"Now, let me get this straight. You two"—Uzma gestured to Erin and Owen—"and you two"—she included Jack and Simon in her next wave—"are together. Yes? And engaged to get married?"

"That's correct." Jack placed his hand over Simon's, smiling at his fiancé. "We went back and forth over when would be the best time, but we finally settled on October, and the ceremony will be here in Copper Point. My family will come up from Houston, and I think a few aunts and uncles and cousins from Taiwan are coming over as well."

"We're ready to host everyone, if they want our space," Erin said. "As for our own plans, we're not as formal or as organized."

"That's because someone's always working," Owen chided, but he didn't seem too upset.

Nick sighed. "I'm sorry to say the workload didn't get any lighter with last week."

Everyone talked about how terrifying the elevator accident was, and Jared felt a puff of pride at the way Nick reassured them it was being handled as professionally as possible. Their emergency board meeting had shown him this personally, but he enjoyed seeing his man be all in control like this.

He had his regrets their plans last night had been cancelled because he'd had to fill in for the ER doctor who called in sick, because had Nick been able to comc over as they'd planned, he'd intended to see the CEO surrender all that control. Sunday, they'd said, would be their replacement date.

"What about Jared and Nick?" Uzma asked. "Are either of you seeing anyone?"

"No," Nick said without hesitation. "Both of us are single."

Jared drank his lemonade to hide his frustration.

If he thought he was tormented by hiding things at the Amin residence, though, it was nothing to when the party moved to the Beckert household. At Uzma's, Nick had been friendly and easy with Jared, albeit a little reserved. At his own home, Nick scarcely spoke to Jared.

Jared sucked up his disappointment, put on a smile, and focused on making the Amins feel at home. He played with the kids out back, pushing them on Nick's old swings, thinking of when he'd been the kid visiting and taking advantage of Collin Beckert's quality carpentry skills. He played hide-and-seek too, and when Samira wanted to play doctor, he fetched the spare stethoscope and blood pressure cuff he kept in the trunk of his car and taught her how to use them, then played dutiful patient as first she and then Omar gave him and Zaika excellent medical care at the picnic table.

"You're wonderful with children," Uzma remarked as Zaika led the children inside to wash up before the meal.

Jared folded his stethoscope and blood pressure cuff and put them back in his travel bag. "Well, it is my job."

"That's not what I meant. You're good with them as in you know how to make them feel seen and heard, but you also push them just right. You'd be an excellent father."

Why was everyone bringing this up now? Had there been a meeting? He tried to breeze it off. "Well, first I have to meet the right guy."

The lie burned his throat. Except the truth was, he feared it wasn't a lie. What if Nick *couldn't* be the right guy? What if all they were doing was wasting each other's time?

Uzma smiled warmly and put her hand on his arm. "I hope you meet him very soon."

Her words rang in his head as he waved goodbye to everyone, watching them leave with their loved ones. Or, in Nick's case, remain while Jared went on alone.

Was Nick the right guy? Was this the right thing to do, this secret relationship? It had seemed such an easy decision when it was the two of them, and when he thought about it objectively, he wanted to give Nick this time that he'd asked for, especially since it had been Jared who messed things up when they were young.

Except when it was Jared who stood off to the side with no one but Uzma's children to connect with unless he butted into someone else's union… well, it was more difficult to cling to his nobility. He suddenly wasn't looking forward to the outing on the boat.

Unwilling to go home and face the quiet, he stopped by the grocery store, where he idled through the aisles, filling his cart with things he didn't need, making himself sad as he thought about how fun it had been to cook for other people.

God, when did you become such a mope?

Still, he passed the brand of yogurt Owen used to buy for Erin and couldn't stop a pang. He wanted to buy things like that for someone, to take care of someone. He wanted to take care of Nick the way the others took care of each other.

"Jared?"

Glancing up, startled, Jared saw Matt Engleton at the other end of the dairy cooler, his hand on a half gallon of milk. Jared packed away his morose mood as best he could. "Hey, Matt. How are you?"

"I'm good. Yourself?" Matt leaned on the handle of his cart. "You just get done helping the Amins move in? I heard you had quite a crew there. You should have asked, I'd have helped."

Jared imagined having the cheerful Matt-buffer present, particularly at the Beckerts, and knew regret. "I should have, you're right."

Matt brightened at this, nudging his cart closer. "Well, you can make it up to me by going out with me tomorrow afternoon."

Well, you stepped in that land mine, Kumpel. "Ah, I'm sorry. I already have plans."

"Then tell me what night would work, and I'll come pick you up."

"You're persistent."

"I am. But at least you didn't say pushy."

"You're on the edge." Jared said this, but he couldn't help a smile. "You're too charming for your own good."

"I know, right?" Matt grinned. "So how about it? Can I charm you somewhere other than a grocery store?"

How was he supposed to get out of this? Normally Jared would say he was seeing someone, but if he admitted that and didn't appear with anyone, Matt would think he was lying, or worse, start guessing why he'd done that and possibly put two and two together.

Trying not to sigh, he pinched the bridge of his nose.

"Ah." Matt's voice lost its bright quality. "I'm being pushy after all."

"No, it's—" Jared gave up and exhaled, letting his shoulders fall forward. "It's complicated. *I'm* complicated. It has nothing to do with you whatsoever. You're not pushy. You really are charming."

Matt moved his cart closer, letting the back of his hand brush against Jared's. "I don't think you're complicated at all. And if you think I'm charming, sweetheart, you better not go looking in any mirrors, or you'll captivate yourself." Winking, he went past Jared at a lazy pace. "If you decide you're ready for a date, give me a call. Otherwise I'll keep trying unless you tell me I'm being a bother. Slow and steady wins the race, they say."

Jared couldn't help it, he blushed. For the rest of the grocery store trip Matt's words reverberated in him, giving him a small flutter.

The glow lasted until he let himself into his dark house through the garage, hauling the bags into the empty, unlit kitchen.

"I'm home," he said to the silence, then put his purchases away, the brief tinge of warmth fading in the cold quiet.

"SO DID you hear the news?" Emmanuella asked Nick as he drove everyone home from church on Sunday morning. "Rumor has it Dr. Kumpel was flirting with Matt Engleton at Cub Foods."

It was a good thing she'd made this announcement at a stoplight, or Nick would have swerved or hit the brake too hard. As it was, he only sucked in his breath and tightened his grip on the wheel.

"Well, I suppose he's got the bug to go dating now that all his friends are fixed up." Aniyah spoke mildly, as if remarking on the weather. "Good for him. He was never one who liked being on his own."

"I'm a little surprised he stayed single this long, to be honest. Surprised nobody's *snatched him up before this*." Emmanuella's tone had an extra layer to it, making it clear she was saying all this to goad her brother, though of course only he was aware. "I figured by this time he'd have a houseful of kids."

Grandma Emerson huffed. "That Matt's a kid himself, so he's already got one, if he's sniffing around that boy."

"I'm just saying, anybody interested in Jared had better act fast. But Mama, Grandma, you two like Jared, right? He used to come around all the time when we were kids."

Nick wanted to throttle her. Jesus, this was the *other* reason he'd never told her anything.

Aniyah clucked her tongue and raised her eyebrow at her daughter. "What's gotten into you? Don't tell me you have a thing for that boy. You *know* he don't play for your team."

"Of course I know that, and no, I don't have a thing for him. I'm just asking what you think of him."

"We think he's a fine doctor and a good citizen of Copper Point." Grandma Emerson waved a hand at Emmanuella. "Now lower your voice. I've got a headache."

Happily, the subject of Jared was abruptly dropped, and after a brief moment of quiet in deference to Grandma's head, the conversation turned to what they were having for lunch. As soon as Nick was at home, he paced his bedroom, running his hand over his head and picking up his phone over and over, starting a text three times before giving up.

No. This was a conversation best had in person. Thank God he was about to go see the man.

For a date, dammit. Where there had better be some flirting coming *his* direction.

He was a ball of agitation when he showed up at Jared's house. Even as he tried to talk himself down, confident there had to be an explanation of why he was hearing a rumor about Jared and Matt, the mere thought of the two of them together made Nick's blood boil. As he lifted his hand to press the bell, he realized he'd gone to his first real date in his life—the first that wasn't him trying to lie to himself, anyway—without anything in his hands. He'd been so preoccupied with the rumor that he had no bottle of wine, no chocolates, no flowers. Not so much as a loaf of bread.

What would Matt bring to a date, I wonder?

Before he could decide whether he should nip out and buy something or surrender and knock, the door opened, revealing a flushed and bewildered but smiling Jared. "What are you doing standing there? I heard you pull up, but you didn't knock. Come on in."

He looks excited to see me. Does that mean he didn't flirt with Matt? "I forgot to bring a gift."

Jared's smile widened, making Nick's heart flutter. "I don't care about that. I'm just thrilled you're here." After shutting the door, Jared put his arms around Nick's neck and slid against him. "You can give me a kiss, and that's enough."

Nick couldn't, not yet. When Jared leaned in, Nick pressed their foreheads together and drew a slow breath. "I heard a rumor."

"Well, it's Copper Point, so it fits. What did you hear?"

Why was his heart pounding so much? "I heard you flirted with Matt Engleton at the grocery store."

He hadn't known what to expect, but it certainly wasn't to see Jared tip his head back and roll his eyes. "God, I can't believe *that's* how the little mongers spun the story. But of course they did. *He's* the one who flirted with me, by the way."

Jealousy burned hot and fast in Nick. "But did you flirt back?"

"Well, I had to be diplomatic." Jared arched an eyebrow. "It was actually an awkward moment. I wasn't sure how to handle it. He'd asked me out at the welcome party for Uzma—"

"Wait—he did *what*?"

"He asked me out. I didn't get to answer him, though, before somebody swept me away and got grouchy, so this was his second attempt. Ideally I would have told him no, sorry, I'm seeing someone, but I decided that would cause more problems. So I was trying to work out how to diplomatically sidestep it."

"You could have told him no."

"Well, it would have been awkward, since until you swept back into my life, I was about to tell him yes."

Nick stared at Jared, the ominous lead boot floating over him now crashing down into the bottom of his stomach.

Just as quickly as it fell, Jared whisked it away with a soft smile and a kiss, a sweet brush across Nick's lips that lingered and made Nick yearn all the way to his toes.

Jared nipped lightly at Nick's bottom lip. "I wasn't going to tell him yes because I was in love with him. I just thought, ironically, it was time I moved on. It was almost like you heard my thoughts and came storming over."

"No. I saw the way he looked at you, and I didn't like it." Remembering made Nick glower. "You'd never dated anyone before, since I came back."

Jared raised an eyebrow. "Are you saying you'd expected me to live like a monk? When you hadn't even told me how you felt?"

"No, I…." Nick didn't know what he was saying. All he knew was the gossip had been wrong, Jared was here in his arms, and this wasn't what he wanted to do with their night together. "I'm sorry. I overreacted, and I don't have a right."

"Well, it's fine. I want you to have a right." Jared's smile came back, and he nuzzled Nick's nose, sliding his body to fit against Nick's. "I'm just glad you're here. I was worried something would get in the way and I'd have to eat all this food alone."

Kissing his way up Jared's jaw, Nick whispered against his lover's skin. "I wish I could keep you company every night."

"You're here right now." Jared ran his hands down the front of Nick's shirt. "That's enough."

Yes, Nick was here. Alone in a house with Jared in his arms, the curtains drawn, and no one to interrupt them. The want that had bloomed as he entered turned into a need, and he tilted Jared's head to kiss the place he knew his lover liked. "Let's wait on dinner."

Jared let himself be kissed, then shied away, taking Nick's hand and tugging him into the kitchen. "No way. I went all out for you. Food first. Sex later."

"Bossy," Nick said, but he was smiling.

Winking, Jared smacked him on the butt. "Promise."

The food was excellent. It was a simple stew, seasoned lightly, but it was so good Nick wanted to lick his bowl, and he basically did with the homemade sweet rolls Jared had heaped in the center of the table next to a pot of herbed butter. Even the salad was amazing, a mixture of tossed greens with fresh croutons and a mustard dressing.

"I love all of this." Nick chased the last bit of lettuce from his bowl and patted his belly. "It's perfect."

"Thank you." Jared beamed under the praise as he rose. "There's dessert too, of course. Custard with a dab of whipped cream. I thought about going fancy, but I kept the meal simple in the end. I hope that's okay."

"Simple is good. Fancy is good. Food is good." He kissed Jared's hand as he set down the custard. "*You* are fantastic."

"*You* are a flatterer. More wine?"

Nick did have more wine. And then more after he finished his custard, drinking it seated on the sofa with Jared as they talked about how nice the Amin family was, how cute the kids were.

Emmanuella's comment got under Nick's skin a little, sending him into dangerous waters. "You ever think about having kids?"

Jared shrugged and sipped. "Sure."

Nothing more, just that. Which meant he really did want them and didn't want to talk about it.

Not with his closeted boyfriend, anyway.

Setting down his wineglass, Jared smiled, then climbed onto Nick's lap. "All right." He ran his hands over Nick's hair, along the sides of his neck, and the want from the front door came back in full heat. "We've had our meal."

Goddamn, this sexy man. Nick tugged at the tail of Jared's shirt, slipping his thumb inside the gap below the lowest button. "Mmm, but I'm still hungry."

"Then you'd better do something about that."

Nick wanted to. So much so that he ached. Something about this, though, made him… breathless was too simple a word. He was suspended between the present and the past, remembering and looking forward. It was heady. It was terrifying.

It was wonderful.

Jared pressed their foreheads together, nuzzling their noses. He drifted toward Nick's ear, kissing around the edge, nipping the lobe. "I look forward to making love to Nick the adult."

Nick looked forward to making love to Jared too. Spreading his thighs wider, he cupped Jared's ass and pulled him closer. "We going to get started right here, or you want to go upstairs?"

Jared tapped him on the nose. "Hush. You're not driving the bus right now."

Oh? It was difficult to keep his smile back. Nick raised an eyebrow. "You think so, do you?"

Jared pressed a kiss on Nick's upper lip, on the divot in his chin, on the underside, teasing his tongue against the beard.

Nick couldn't help it. He shivered.

Raising his head, Jared smiled, a mixture of self-satisfaction and softness. "I do think so."

A shaft of ache and melancholy hit Nick out of nowhere, stealing his breath for the span of a heart-beat. *It truly is as if nothing has changed.*

Except it all had. They weren't young men. Time had marched on, as had their lives. Nick was different too. He wasn't consumed with guilt and fear, not like he was then. He was still afraid, yes, but he didn't feel like he was drowning.

Now here they were, with a second chance. The hell Nick was wasting it.

Jared captured Nick's hands, drew them to the front of his own shirt. "Undress me, please."

Excitement kicked in Nick's belly as he complied wordlessly. God, but this was an old game. They didn't need it now, which Jared well knew with the way Nick had tried to jump him at the door. But they hadn't needed it half the time they'd played it toward the end of their time together in high school. They'd simply liked it.

When they'd begun making out, if it hadn't been for Jared's bossiness in bed, they wouldn't have gotten anywhere. Nick knew what he wanted, but when he thought about it too much, he freaked himself out, got too far inside his own head, and shut his system down. The first time Jared had told him what to do had been an attempt to draw him out of his panic. *Keep kissing me.* That had worked so well, Jared kept going. *Touch me. Take off my clothes.*

It didn't take long for them to realize they were onto a kink they wanted to keep. Subtle as it was, it worked for them. Everything got mixed up. Who was the dominant partner here? Where was the give-and-take? It was a concert only the two of them knew how to direct. It kept Nick from feeling guilty, and at the end of the day, it was damn fun.

How much better was *this* going to be with twenty years of growth?

Nick slid Jared's unbuttoned shirt away from his shoulders, revealing an expanse of lightly muscled, pale peach-pink skin dotted with a few more tufts of blond hair than he remembered. When Nick ran his hands over that skin, over the hard rounds of his lover's pectorals, Jared hummed and braced himself against Nick's shoulders.

God, yes, he'd missed this. Every part of this.

Nick leaned forward to press a reverent kiss on Jared's sternum. "This what you wanted?"

"You're on the right track."

Nick smiled into Jared's stomach, sliding his hands down Jared's sides and resting them on his hips. "What were you after, then?"

"Mmm. It just seems like we're both wearing too much, I'd say."

Nick laughed and placed a loud kiss on Jared's navel. "Quit being coy."

The playful edge left Jared's voice. "Take off the rest of my clothes, Nick, then remove your own."

If anyone else spoke to Nick like that, all his hackles would go up. But no one else would know the exact balance between command and invitation, would have known, in fact, to play around first and wait for Nick to say, "Baby, I'm ready for it" before launching ahead.

Only Jared would be this way. Only with him could Nick let go.

Surrender he did. After unfastening the zip, Nick hooked his fingers into Jared's waistband and tugged the fabric away, letting Jared's steadiness and balance even out the last of his nerves. He pulled his own shirt over his head, helped by Jared's long, cool fingers. When Nick got to his jeans, Jared took Nick's face in his hands and kissed him the entire time he worked them down, so that by the time he had them and his socks off, he was panting and desperate.

God, but I've been in love with him all this time. He hadn't dared let himself acknowledge it when they were young, never thought about it until now, but it was the truth.

Would it be enough?

Jared ran his hands along Nick's beard, breaking the kiss to nuzzle his nose. "Stop thinking so much. We can worry about anything you want after."

He was right, Nick knew. It was just…. "I don't want to screw it up."

Arms enveloped him, holding him close, pressing Jared's naked body against his. "You won't. *We* won't. We'll figure this out together. I only want to be with you. Okay?"

"Okay."

"There's lube in the drawer of the end table beside you. Bear that in mind for later. Right now… right now, I want to take you in my mouth."

A hot rush hit Nick like a wind. Oh God, was he going to…?

The look on Jared's face, carnal and dark, told Nick everything he needed to know, sending fire into his gut. "Push me down and make me take it, Nick."

Grunting, Nick kissed Jared hot and hard before anchoring his grip carefully in his soft blond hair and easing that wicked mouth toward his cock. "You do remember everything, don't you?"

Jared's only answer was to cup Nick's balls and suck Nick's length eagerly into his throat.

Nick remembered the first time they'd done this. One day Jared had told Nick to tug his hair until it hurt and push his face onto Nick's cock. He'd worried about it, even as he'd wanted it desperately, and then Jared was looking up at him with a dirty smile and a mouth full of dick and Nick had surrendered to the lust. They'd been so terrified and turned on at the same time, they'd been a mess. That first time he'd stretched Jared's mouth so much he couldn't talk right for a few minutes, which had horrified Nick and made him apologize over and over, but Jared only laughed.

"Don't you worry about stuff like that," he'd told him. "If I don't want it, I'll always tell you. You can let go with me. I like it."

Mouth full of cock once again, Jared gazed up the length of Nick's chest with half-lidded eyes and a sleepy smile, saying the same thing without a single word. *Let go with me. I like it.*

Tightening his grip on Jared's hair, Nick took him at his word.

Jared opened up his throat, wrapped his teeth behind his lips, and sucked Nick in, working the underside of him with his tongue. He made sexy, high-pitched moans that turned Nick on as well as buzzed against the tip of his cock as he thrust forward. For all that Jared was the one with his hair in Nick's fist, his lips split wide and spittle dripping down his chin, he was the one driving the show. The more noise he made, the more he let go and made it clear he was absolutely into this, the more Nick was able to surrender to the feeling, to shut his eyes and thrust, trusting that so long as the hands on his thighs were clawing and clutching at him, not pushing, he had permission to pump into Jared's wet heat until neither of them could stand it.

Nick came faster than he wanted and with little warning, making him feel like he was a teenager again. As Nick caught his breath, Jared popped off his cock and rested his cheek on his thigh.

Jared's lips were swollen, cheeks flushed red. He seemed content, though not sated.

Nick smoothed his lover's hair. "What do you want now, baby?"

Eyes closed, Jared ran his hand over Nick's other thigh. "Push me on my back and hold my hands over my head. Bring the lube."

Nick had been a little winded, but he wasn't now. *All right.* "Couch or floor?"

"Mmm. Couch? Let's be nice to your knees. We're not sixteen anymore."

Nick's heart beat fast as he lifted Jared, arranging him on his back, laying his arms above his head over the armrest. Jared held them there dutifully, waiting as Nick got the lube as well as a condom, which he set on the floor. When Nick knelt in front of Jared on the couch, Jared gave Nick another order.

"Put my legs over your shoulders."

Nick's eyebrows went up. This was new.

Jared's smile was coy. "I've learned a *few* things since you last saw me."

Jealousy pierced Nick, which was ridiculous. He hadn't been celibate either. Yet all he could think of was the fireman Jared dated in college fucking him over a couch with his legs over his shoulders. *Dammit.*

Jared winked at him. "Shh. Stay here with me. Don't drift off anywhere. I'm not bringing anybody else to bed with us. Don't you go doing it either."

Nodding, Nick brought one of Jared's legs, then the other, over his shoulders.

This had the effect, of course, of spreading his naked body, providing Nick with exposure to Jared's balls, his hole, visible through his parted cheeks.

God, he was gorgeous.

Smiling, Jared stretched like a cat as he settled in. "Do what you want with me, Nick. I'm all yours. I can't go anywhere, can't do anything. Can't get off without you."

What I want. Damn, but Nick wanted a lot. He ran his hands down Jared's legs. "So you're just going to lie there, are you, while I have my way with you?"

"Oh, I'm hoping I'm not able to stay still very well, no."

Nick laughed. It erupted out of him, making his chest warm, melting the last of his nerves. Smiling, he kissed Jared's knee. "I missed you."

Jared caressed him back with his leg. "Same."

Nick kissed that leg again, swirling his tongue just above the kneecap as his fingers traveled on a path toward Jared's abdomen. His thumb massaged circles on its way to the center of Jared's chest, heading toward his left nipple before catching it gently between his fingers. As Jared gasped and arched toward the touch, Nick flipped open the bottle of lube, squeezed a bit into his palm, and brought his other hand between Jared's legs.

A rush hit Nick as Jared cried out at the cool touch against his opening, parting his legs more to let Nick in. Nick kneaded gently at the nipple as he teased one finger around Jared's hole, over his cock, greasing him well, taunting him with the thought of touch without actually giving it to him. All the while, Jared writhed and gasped beneath him, shutting his eyes and shaking.

"Please." He kept his hands together above his head as if they'd been tied there, but his arms trembled, making it clear he wanted to tug them down. "Please, Nick, touch me."

Here it was, the switch—just like that, Nick was in control. God, he loved this. "Tell me what you want me to do to you."

"Put it in me. Please."

Nick ran his finger over Jared's puckered, quivering apex. "What do you want put in here?"

"Your finger. Your cock. Anything. *Please.*"

Nick pushed the barest tip of his finger to Jared's hole. "Like this?"

Jared whimpered, trying to bear down. "More. Give me more."

Shifting his body to get a better angle, Nick gave himself a view of his hand splayed against Jared's ass, Jared's body turned up and ready, quivering for him. Nick pressed inside, breaching him with deliberate, aching slowness until Jared's heels dug into his back in desperation.

This was the same. A slightly different choreography, but this invitation to play, to push, to be like this with Jared was so comfortable it was like putting on a pair of shoes he'd been walking past in his closet but had told himself didn't fit. Oh, Jared fit. He fit the curve of Nick's hands, the thickness of his lust, the ease of his soul. He fit the way he wanted to be just a tiny bit dirty, whispering for Nick to spread him, begging him to, but not getting so kinky either of them was uncomfortable.

Jared with him now, in his arms. Laying himself open for Nick, letting him into his body. When he closed his mouth over Jared's cock and inserted a second finger, when Jared arched against him, Nick floated away and dreamed of being able to do this every day.

Once Jared came into his mouth, Nick didn't know how to lead anymore, but that was fine because his lover took over. After a pause to recover, Jared took Nick's hand and led him up the stairs to his bedroom. The curtains were open here, as well as the windows, letting in the early-evening breeze.

Nick's gaze darted to the screen, but Jared soothed him with a kiss on his arm. "My neighbors are gone on vacation. But if you want, we can shut the window."

I need to trust him. Nick shook his head and focused on taking in Jared's room. It was cozy and neat, and the bed was big, full of lush blankets and pillows. "We left the lube downstairs, though."

"Oh, I have more up here."

He couldn't help it. "How many guys you entertaining up here?"

Jared winked at him. "Just the one."

They went onto the bed together—Jared's bed, with Jared's sheets, smelling like him, and the scent was so powerful it transported Nick to the lazy summer days when they would spend the entire day making love, exploring one another inside and out. Back when they'd feared the future, but not each other.

Now Nick was an adult, and he feared everything.

"What now?" Nick's voice cracked at the end. The question was in regards to the next phase of their lovemaking, their day, their relationship. *What do we do now, Jared? How can I walk the path I want without losing you along the way a second time?*

Jared kissed his cheek, drawing him under the covers. "Lie here with me and enjoy the moment."

Nick obeyed, resting his head on Jared's shoulder, fitting their bodies together, letting the contact of flesh on flesh build them slowly toward a second crescendo.

CHAPTER EIGHT

JARED KNEW it would hurt to send Nick away on Sunday night. All evening long, he'd schooled himself to appreciate the time he had with him and not fixate on futures he wanted or thought he deserved. It had worked, at first. He enjoyed their conversations, their teasing, and their lovemaking. Everything about being with Nick felt right on so many levels.

Until he said goodbye and Jared was alone again.

Have I made a mistake?

Am I going to wonder if I made a mistake after every time we're together?

This was the problem with living by himself. He didn't have anyone to interrupt his trains of thought, anyone else's issues to distract him from his own. When he'd lived with Owen and Simon, before either of them had fallen in love with the men they'd decided they would marry, Jared had never been in this scenario. He'd grown accustomed to talking Simon through whatever relationship crisis he was in or talking to Owen about whomever he was angry with at work that week. One of the nurses who had since retired from his clinic used to remark that Jared was the parent of their group, and it wasn't an inaccurate description. He hadn't minded that life, and without realizing it, he supposed he'd set up their little family as his own, with no plan to ever change it. In the back of his head, Jared had intended them to grow old together, married in their own way to one another.

Not for one second had he begrudged either of them their happy ever afters, but he did have to sort out what he was going to do with himself, the man unable to reach for his own because he'd given away his heart to someone unable to share his dreams for a future. At first he'd thought Nick wouldn't return his affections. Now….

Honestly, what now?

He knew he should let go and ride the wave, that in fact this was his only path, but it was so difficult for him. He didn't like surrendering control. In bed was one thing, but in his life was something else entirely. He was the one who gave the orders. In the clinic, in the ER when he took his shift there, and in the house when it had been full of people. He'd ordered Nick around outside of the bedroom before, to disastrous results. Granted, he'd been a teenager, but he knew full well it wasn't his age that had caused the problem. If anything, those old patterns with Nick made him feel like he *was* a teenager again. Nick made him want and crave in a way he hadn't since they'd been together, drawing out parts of him he hadn't realized had been sitting in mothballs since Nick had walked away.

Now he had a second chance, and he wasn't going to screw it up by letting that impetuous, bossy teen self mess things up. It was his turn to learn patience and sit with his insecurities. It was either that, or he couldn't be with Nick.

So he puttered around his house alone, and as had become his habit, he turned on the television to keep him company. He'd never watched television before unless Simon forced him, but he'd started several shows out of desperation, beginning with one Nick had mentioned to him the year before. Owen had teased Nick about being the Fred of their Scooby gang during the embezzlement investigation, and Nick had insisted, a bit tersely, that he wasn't having anything to do with *Scooby-Doo* references, because he was all about *Brooklyn Nine-Nine*. So one night when Jared had been going out of his mind, he'd pulled up the show on a streaming service and was immediately hooked. He'd had no idea the show featured a Black, gay precinct captain who was so stoic and reserved he made Nick look happy-go-lucky. And Nick was right, Rebecca was absolutely Rosa Diaz.

He'd burned through the available episodes quickly, and he'd gone hunting for more. Mistakenly he'd used *Brooklyn Nine-Nine* as a sign that network television had improved since he'd last watched it, but alas, this turned out not to be true. Either that or he wasn't good at sorting through the weeds. Asking the nurses at work wouldn't help either, because they'd suggest atrocious things, he was sure of it. Simon would only tell him to watch Asian dramas, and that was the one positive thing about Simon moving out, that Jared didn't have to suffer through those anymore unless Simon came over.

So he'd done a lot of online searching through *best of* lists and engaged in more trial and error. He leaned on comedies, preferring short shows he could watch or half watch while he made dinner or folded laundry. *Bob's Burgers* was one of his favorites, as was *Jane the Virgin*. He'd recently started *It's Always Sunny in Philadelphia*, which was clever and enjoyable but had to be taken in small doses as too much time with horrible people left a bad taste in his mouth. He was eyeing *Fresh Off the Boat* and *Black-ish* because he'd heard good critical reviews of both and liked the idea of consuming more shows that weren't full of white leads. He'd consulted a list looking for shows with LGBT characters and put a score of others on his to-watch list, including *One Day at a Time*.

The one long-episode drama he watched was *Luther*, because… well. Idris Elba.

He pulled up the show after Nick left, settling into one of his favorite installments, the episode where Luther plays a deadly game of chicken with brothers killing for sport. Jared had already consumed everything on offer several times, but *Luther* was a comfort watch now. He'd started *Luther* because he'd long had a thing for the show's lead (who didn't), but he'd gotten caught up in the character immediately. Nick had regarded him incredulously when Jared said they looked similar, but they did; that, however, was where the similarities ended. Oh, there were times the two of them were alike in how they commanded a situation,

Jared supposed, but Luther was far too hotheaded for his taste. Nick was reserved and earnest; Luther was fiery and explosive, and problematic, though also inherently good-hearted. Though sometimes Nick offered moments where one could glimpse the passion that drove him, he kept his horses tightly leashed and harnessed.

Jared tried to think of what other celebrity actor he might compare Nick to, not necessarily in a particular role but in general. Chris Evans? Too sunny. Mark Ruffalo? No. Too… Mark Ruffalo. Antonio Banderas? No, too effusive. Benedict Cumberbatch? Jesus, no, what was he thinking.

Ricky Whittle. That wasn't bad. Earnest. Quiet. Patient. With a sparkle behind him that made you lean closer.

God, now Jared missed Nick again.

He let Elba's sexy voice wash over him as he burrowed into the couch, where only hours before he'd made love to Nick. What Jared really wanted was to repeat that activity, as well as dinner, then watch *Luther* with Nick, then go to bed with Nick. Everything with Nick.

As he watched television alone, he let himself acknowledge the truth. He'd thought everything was fine when it was just him and Owen and Simon, but the thing was, he knew now he'd been lonely then too, simply better distracted. This yearning in him wasn't new, and the reason he hadn't wanted to move in with Owen and Erin when they'd offered was because he couldn't look away from the truth any longer. He didn't only want company. He wanted a partner of his own.

He wanted Nick.

The problem was, he wasn't sure he could have him. He wasn't sure he *should* have him. But he couldn't do anything else now but play out this hand, to see if there was any way they could find a future together.

He only hoped he wasn't sitting here alone a year from now, hugging a pillow to his chest, convincing himself a pixelated Idris Elba was sufficient company.

ON FRIDAY Nick attended the board meeting, where, after brief deliberation, the members chose to go with the Gilbert Consulting Firm from Madison to review their options for remodeling or renovation.

"I appreciate their long history and work with hospitals," Jack said as the board chatted together after the vote.

"I'm most excited about their reasonable rates." Gus Taylor sipped at his coffee, wincing at his cup before continuing. "They're a decent compromise between the cheapest and most outrageous, but it sounds like they'll give us exactly what we need."

"And they're recommended by that friend of yours, which puts me at ease, Mr. Beckert." Jacob Moore, who was the most hesitant of their board members, nodded to himself as he spoke. "Yes, I think this was a good decision and will be fine in the end."

"The biggest problem will be public opinion," Amanda Rodriguez pointed out. "People hate it when we spend money, and some will think this is a waste."

"It's important we get out in front of it, then," Matt Engleton said, "and make it clear we need to do this to ensure the safety of the hospital and its future."

"I'm excited to hear what they have to say," Owen said.

"Me too," Jared agreed.

As usual, Simon didn't have much to say, though Nick knew he dutifully reported everything that went on back to the rest of the nursing staff and that they appreciated his presence on the board. It was why Nick had pushed for a restructuring of the board makeup when exposing the embezzlement had meant resignations of all but one of the members. Having one less general member and four medical representatives, three physician and one nursing, had been a serious boon for hospital morale, but it also meant efficient policy creation.

Erin let Gilbert Consulting know right away about the board's decision, and the rest of Nick's weekend was full of preparatory meetings via email and Skype with the agents who would be coming on Monday to do an initial investigation. They also coached Erin and Nick through potential press releases, which was the other thing Nick spent the weekend doing, writing up drafts to submit to the paper for their Sunday-night deadline.

Ryan called to check on him Monday morning, making sure there wasn't anything else he could do. "We're not talking about any deals right now. If there's anything else I can do, I hope you don't hesitate to reach out. I consider us business associates, and it's always good business to help a neighbor."

Nick smiled. "My father said the same thing to me every day of his life."

"Well, then I assume that means you'll listen to me." Ryan chuckled. "All right, I won't keep you.

Cynthia will be by sometime in the next few weeks, though, and I hope you spare some time for her."

Nick tensed. "Yes. Of course."

Ryan's voice pitched low, the humor leaching out. "Mind yourself with that Peterson fellow. He's going to make a move on you, now that you're vulnerable."

"Oh, I'm ready for it." Nick leaned back in his chair, staring sightlessly out his office window at Lake Superior in the distance. "I can't decide if he'll make a direct play first, or if he'll undermine me. My gut says the latter."

"Your gut's a smart one. Bide your time."

"I will, sir. Thank you."

It didn't take long for Peterson's wiles to appear, either. Tuesday night when Nick opened the paper after work, instead of seeing an article based on the press release he and Erin had drafted, right on page one, above the fold, was an article that made it sound as if the hospital was wasting funds, and in the middle of it was an interview with Peterson of all people, spinning himself as an expert.

"Piece of work, isn't it?" Grandma Emerson glanced at the paper over the top of her glasses as she snapped the ends off beans at the table beside him. "That paper's always been trash. A real shame, with how much we need journalism in these dark times."

It annoyed Nick that he hadn't seen this coming, that he hadn't prepared. People would be angrier now than they already would have been. He'd been a fool to think a simple press release would be enough. "Should've worked harder to butter up the newspaper. I let Peterson have them all to himself."

"They're gonna do what they're gonna do. But I suppose it wouldn't hurt to reach out. Maybe it's best to let them spin manure now, and then when you know what you want to say, you can take them on with real weapons in your hands. No sense getting in the muck with the fools."

She was right, of course. She always was. It was just that once again, the situation required Nick to humble himself, eating crow in front of people who didn't deserve it, waiting for a safer time to act. For years, this had been his default, and now that he had started to shake out of it, he resented looking weak, as if he had gone back.

But he did it anyway. He drove over to the editor of the paper's house himself and stood on his front steps, metaphorical hat in hand, letting the man bluster and gloat. Let him think he was winning, while all the while Nick took mental notes, hoping there would be enough they could mine later.

Erin called him before he had his dinner, and in addition to reporting what he'd learned from the editor, Nick ended up repeating what his grandmother had said because it was honestly the only thing to do. He wasn't surprised when the texts from Jared started coming through, that giving Jared the same line didn't calm him down.

They're such a rag. They're going to get everyone riled up. God, I hate that this happened. Isn't there something we can do in the meantime? What about posting on Copper Point People?

Nick stifled a sigh. *Throwing gasoline on a fire won't help anything, no.*

I suppose we'd need someone to go in and do it, and everyone connected to us will look connected to us. Dammit. I just hate sitting here doing nothing.

Nick could hear the frustration in his text, could imagine the way Jared paced as he held his phone, the way he shoved his fingers into his hair.

For the first time that evening, he smiled.

He thought about their Sunday together at odd times at work, whenever Jared texted, in the shower, and at night as he lay in bed, staring at his ceiling. It had been a good evening. He wanted another one. Or another lunch, or a walk along the bay.

He wanted to get together with him again, but he didn't know when that would happen. Lunch was often a theoretical possibility, but it didn't matter how he set it up, Jared said it would arouse suspicion among his clinic staff nurses. There were times Jared came over to do rounds, and they had a moment or two if Nick happened to be free, but it wasn't as if Jared had loads of time then either. In the evenings, it was Nick who couldn't get away without raising eyebrows. His mother and grandmother liked him to stay around, and if he went out, of course that was fine, but if he was always at Jared's place, they'd start to wonder.

When their Thursday night racquetball date got cancelled and Jared couldn't reschedule anything for the weekend because it was his turn in the ER, Nick started to get frustrated. The following weekend was out too, as it was the Fourth of July holiday and had been already booked for the long-postponed boat outing with the Amin family. On Monday when Nick sat in the conference room working on the questionnaires for Gilbert, Erin picked up on his mood.

Erin closed his laptop and folded his hands over the top of it. "You're distracted this afternoon. What's on your mind?"

Nick thought about telling Erin it was nothing, but that was a lie, and he didn't have any other person he could talk to. He rubbed his temple and stared at the expanse of table between them. "I don't know how to meet up with Jared without exposing myself."

"So do you plan on dating him but never coming out?"

There was no censure in Erin's tone, only patient curiosity, but Nick still felt pressure from the query. "I've thought about it some. Tried the idea out in my head. I'm not saying no. And I get I should do it for Jared. It's just… I should have done it before everyone was looking at me so hard."

"Well, I don't think you should come out for anyone but yourself." Erin sighed. "I want to think people would come around for you."

Nick shook his head. "It's not that simple. You don't get it."

Erin nodded. "You're right. I don't. But I want to. I'll listen anytime you want to talk."

Nick hadn't planned on it, but talk he did. It started out slow, a rehashing of the talking points about expectations and inertia he'd had with Emmanuella, but then he expanded. "It's not just difficult because I've waited so long. It's always been tough for me to even let myself think about being gay. Looking back, I know I was in love with Jared when we were in high school, but I couldn't see it because I was so caught up in my own denial, my own fear. Fear has always ruled everything for me."

"Why is that?" Erin frowned. "I mean, I understand completely, but your fear seems sharper and more complicated than mine ever was. I never particularly had fears about being gay, though, I suppose. I mostly feared being alone."

"It's one and the same for me. My church isn't the most welcoming place for homosexuality. It's not as bad as some, but it's not open and affirming, either. Especially when I was young, I worried what acknowledging my orientation would cost me in terms of community. While Jared was focused on getting me to accept myself and come out, all I wanted to do was magically become straight so I wouldn't have to face what I was sure was my worst nightmare of a choice."

"You honestly think you wouldn't be allowed in church if you were out?"

"I could go to church. But it might be really different. It probably would be. I don't think I'd be able to be a deacon. There would absolutely be people who stopped associating with me, who kept their kids from me." When Erin made a face, Nick held up a hand. "It's how some people think. It isn't right, no, but I'm not interested in walking away from a whole community that's been so crucial to every aspect of my life and my family's life. That church saved us when we nearly lost our house, when my father died and the business was going under. They kept me going when that old board was jerking me around and pretty much mocking me openly. I get that it might seem an easy choice to some people, to walk away if they don't support me, but that's not how it is for me."

"But surely your family would stand by you."

A thick, heavy bag of emotions exploded within Nick with the impact of that statement. He took several deep breaths and shifted in his chair as he worked out how he wanted to respond.

Once again, something hijacked his consciousness and spoke for him. It led with a story about his father.

"My dad, I swear, never slept. He was up at dawn, fussing with something broken in the house or going over work he brought home—and sometimes he made breakfast for my mother. When I woke up, he was always already dressed, smiling and admonishing us to eat our oatmeal and get ready for school. He sat up with me and helped me with my math homework the night he died. I remember he kept rubbing his chest and didn't look good, but he told me he was fine and I should focus on getting my algebra done. It wasn't until after he was gone, until I was older, that I found out how much he'd been fighting, how things were hard because he'd dared to take on the corrupt hospital board."

Erin appeared stricken. "I'm so sorry for my family's part in your father's struggle."

Nick didn't want to dredge that battle up again. "The point is, he *worked*, and he sacrificed. So who am I to complain because I want…."

"Happiness?" Erin leaned forward, his expression soft. "I don't think your father would begrudge you that."

"He would definitely have begrudged me this particular path to it. His views on homosexuality were stark and clearly stated, repeatedly, directly to my face. He didn't like hearing about it on the news. He didn't like it anywhere. He viewed it as an abomination to God and manhood. He'd have been the first one in line to tell me it was sinful and wrong."

Erin nodded, wincing a little. "I'm not saying it doesn't matter that your father, who you so admire, had unfortunate views about your orientation. Or that it doesn't matter that your church does, because I know it means a lot to you. Surely, though, you see it's not a reason to deny yourself a full life? Your grandmother is the one who always asked me if I was happy, and I've never heard her say anything untoward about Owen and me."

"Yeah, well, there's other people, and then there's her grandson." Nick ran a hand over his hair. "Mom and Grandma didn't talk about it as much as Dad did, no. But I know they wouldn't like me coming out. It's a complicated thing. They can think it's wrong and still be civil to people who are gay. Besides, what you do in your own time is your business. But I'm *their* business. This is about our religion, our family name, and their sense of what a man is supposed to be like. I'm meant to carry on the family name, have all the babies."

"But you can still do both of those things as a gay man. Also, right now, you don't date. Have they pressured you to see women?"

"They used to introduce me, but they stopped when I moved back because I was so stressed with everything going on. It's started to pick up again, though, with things calmed down."

Erin spoke carefully. "Do you think… maybe they know? Or suspect?"

The thought left Nick cold. He'd tried so hard not to dwell on that, even though part of him had never *not* been worrying about it. "It's possible," he said when he was able to find his voice again. "If they do, they're operating on the idea that I'm doing the right thing, not acting on it."

"You're doing an incredible amount of assuming. I know you're going to say I don't know your family like you do, and you're right. But as someone who knows them *a little*, and as someone you've said yourself is good at reading people, please consider you might be letting your fear of their rejection color your thoughts. I'm not saying you're wrong. I'm saying you can't know you're right."

"Well, how do I know how they'll react, then?"

Erin sighed. "I don't know. It wasn't like I formally came out to my father, so I'm not one to talk. Owen simply kissed me in the middle of the bachelor auction. Even if I had made an announcement, though, it wouldn't be the same as your situation. We don't have the relationship you do with your mother, grandmother, and sister. My father's also not a fifth of the person your mother and grandmother are on their worst day."

"The only thing I'm sure of is I have to find a way to at least try to make this work with Jared. I'm willing to walk a bit outside of my comfort zone, but I can't leap off the diving board into the deep end." He glowered. "Though I can't drag my feet so much that he gets a roommate. Especially since I know Matt Engleton will be the first person to apply."

Erin sat up straighter. "Wait, what's this? Jared wants a roommate? Is he having trouble with the mortgage? He told us we bought him out with enough. Why didn't he say something?"

"It's not about money." Too late, Nick realized this was likely information Jared didn't want the others to know, but he couldn't stop the train now. "He's lonely, apparently."

As expected, Erin seemed crestfallen. "Oh, no. I had no idea. Why didn't he—? We *told* him he could move in with us, we said he could have whatever...." His shoulders sagged farther. "Of course he felt like he couldn't say anything to us. I feel awful."

"Please don't tell the others. I shouldn't have said anything."

"How can I not?" When Nick gave him a long look, Erin grimaced. "Fine. But I will find excuses to bother him more."

"I don't think it's that. He misses people around in the morning when he wakes up and when he goes to bed, making dinner with people. It's different, living with someone versus visiting them."

He froze, and as he stared at Erin, it was clear they were thinking the same thing. Except while Erin was excited by the idea, Nick was terrified.

I could be the one to answer his call for a roommate.

"It's perfect," Erin said.

"It's bananas. They'll want to know why I want to move out all of a sudden."

"So come up with a reason."

"Well, the only one I can think of is I want to fuck my secret boyfriend."

"A reason other than *that*. We can think of something if we do it together." Erin tapped his fingers against his laptop, then smiled. "What if we used the truth? You're concerned about Jared. You reconnected with him while you spent all that time in the elevator together, and he confessed things to you he hasn't told other people. One of the things was he's incredibly lonely now that everyone else has moved out. You want to move in with him."

Nick held up a finger. "They'll ask why doesn't somebody else move in with him. They'll want to know, why does it have to be me?"

"Ah, but see, he doesn't want to room with someone he doesn't know well. This is why he hasn't put up a notice about rooms for rent. He can't bear to room with a stranger after rooming with people he was so close to for so long. That's why it can only be you. You were friends for years, and you were quite close. They know this. It's not a lie at all, not a word."

It honestly could work. Goddamn, but Erin was good. "Okay… but what if they suspect me already? What if they suspect the *two* of us already? What if it's worse than you said and they knew about us in high school?"

"You honestly think if they knew in high school they wouldn't have said anything?"

Nick felt dizzy. "I can't even guess at this point."

"Okay. So tell me this. What happens if they do suspect you? What if they call you out? Does the world end?"

The world might end. Except of course that was only a feeling. A huge, heavy one, but it was real. A fear, as Erin had said. Nick shut his eyes. "I don't know."

"Let me rephrase. Is this the kind of risk you feel like you could take, to try to be with Jared?"

Nick swore under his breath and slouched in his chair. "You sure don't pull any punches."

Erin said nothing, only folded his arms and waited patiently for a reply.

Nick rubbed his hair and sighed. "I think… maybe. Yes. I'd have to consider how I'd word it and what I'd do if they called me out, but I feel there's a path here."

His heart beat so hard against his ribs his chest hurt. But for the first time when he thought about this, he knew almost as much excitement as he did fear.

Erin's smile seemed to say he understood this emotion without being told. "Then I'd say you have a legitimate reason for asking Jared to lunch again."

Nick smiled too. "Yeah. I think I do."

CHAPTER NINE

ON THE last Tuesday in June, Jared was weighing a three-month-old baby when Helen stuck her head around the corner of the well-baby room, eyes wide as saucers. “Dr. Kumpel. I have a message for you.”

He didn’t look up from the scale. “Can it wait until I’m finished with my patient?”

“Well—yes, but I didn’t think you’d want it to.” She frowned at the infant. “Why are you weighing babies?”

“My nurse is sick, and I feel bad bothering the float nurses all the time. Besides.” He smiled at the little girl gazing up at him with a toothless grin and caught one of her sets of brown toes. “I love an excuse to spend more time with my angels.” The infant let out a coo that melted Jared’s heart, and he wrinkled his nose and made a goofy face to see if he could coax out another adorable sound as he continued to talk to

Helen, his voice taking on an edge of baby talk. "So what was it you had to tell me, hmm?"

"Mr. Beckert's office called and said he'd like you to stop by. They want to know if you're available for lunch, or if he should catch you after clinic hours."

Jared finally glanced up. "Oh?"

Helen's gaze took on a far-too-interested sheen. "*Also*. He wanted to know if it would be more convenient if he came to you for lunch instead, but he didn't want to intrude if you were busy."

Nick, you need lessons in gossip management. "Well, I should think he's the busier one of the two of us." He returned his focus to the baby, though his heartbeat was quickening now as he tried to guess what Nick wanted and why he hadn't just texted.

Of course, maybe he had. Jared hadn't had two seconds to glance at his phone.

The baby gurgled to get Jared's attention, and Jared blew a raspberry. "What's my schedule?" he asked, then waggled his tongue until his patient giggled.

"You have an hour and a half open starting at twelve thirty, unless we fall behind."

Jared looked up, aghast. "How is my schedule that open?"

"Two cancellations back to back, and we didn't fill them with walk-ins because of the nurse issue. Copper Point People is buzzing about it, parents all up in arms because they think it's unfair."

Everything was normal, then. "Well, I'd say I should decline lunch to help out at the clinic, but how do you refuse the CEO?"

"Should I tell him you'll be up?"

Jared smiled at the baby as he clapped her fat feet together. "*Yes*. Ask him what he wants to eat, then order it for me, would you?" He paused to make one last face at his patient, who was loving this personal doctor theater zone she had going. "I owe him for the last time he dropped by."

"Will do." She hovered, looking as if she wanted to say more, then gave up and disappeared.

Lifting the baby from the scale, Jared drew her into his arms, then leaned in close to whisper, "Your doctor has a date, Danielle."

She cooed excitedly in reply.

At twelve forty-five, Jared finished climbing the last of the stairs to the third floor of the hospital. He wasn't exactly winded, but he was keenly aware he didn't take three flights of stairs on a regular basis. Ironically, despite Nick having been the one with the initial elevator phobia post-accident, he had quickly conquered it and was now riding the elevator with ease when the situation called for it. Jared, on the other hand, had never officially had a panic attack and yet went out of his way to avoid the things. He was about ready to force the issue with himself, though, because he was a little tired of all the accidental StairMaster sessions.

He was catching his breath as he nodded at Wendy and knocked on the open door of Nick's office, brandishing the food bag from India Palace instead of saying hello.

Smiling, Nick rose and came to greet him. "Good to see you."

Nick took the bag from Jared and set it on the coffee table near his sitting area. Then he shut the door, drew Jared against the wall behind it, and gave him the greeting he'd been waiting for.

Jared laced his wrists behind Nick's neck and let his body go slack as Nick ran his hands up his sides and closed his mouth over Jared's in a lazy, sensual kiss that had heat behind it but no rush. It was unexpected and delicious, making Jared's skin shiver and his bones melt.

"Hello to you too," Jared murmured when Nick finally pulled back. Unconsciously, he chased after his lips.

Nick nipped his nose and caught Jared's hand to lead him to the food. "Sit down with me. I have something to tell you. Or rather, suggest to you."

"I love it when you get suggestive."

Nick shoved him lightly, but he was all smiles as they sat. "Let's eat first, though. I'm hungry."

"You're teasing."

Except even as Jared said that, he realized it wasn't true. For all Nick's relaxation, he was a little nervous. He wasn't teasing. He was stalling.

Nick put a hand over Jared's leg. "Don't look at me like that. I'm not here to break up with you. It's a good thing. Let me do this in my own time, all right?"

Jared sighed, and Nick held up a piece of naan laden with butter chicken for him to eat instead of mope.

He did his best not to worry, but his brain went in ten thousand directions, wondering what Nick wanted to tell him, and though he'd said it was a good thing, Jared could only guess negatives. If it wasn't breaking up, it was probably slowing down, which was a laugh because they were already a glacier. If it was that they had to be more discreet, they might as well not speak at all, because they could barely see each other as it was.

Nick flicked the center of his forehead. "Stop it. I can practically hear you worrying. Can you really not think of anything good I might be about to tell you?"

Jared rubbed at the spot where Nick had hit. "It's not that. I just… I don't know. I guess I'm afraid to guess the wrong thing and get my hopes up."

Setting down his tray, Nick turned to face Jared on the sofa, lacing his fingers together. He looked serious, apprehensive… and a little excited. "Well, you'll have to have your hopes up a bit. I can't promise this will work for sure. I have to approach my family, which I think I've worked out how I'll do. But I've been trying to figure out ways for us to be together, and this is the best thing I could think of." He let out a slow, nervous breath, lifting his gaze in an almost shy smile. "If the roommate position is still available, I want to apply."

Jared stared at him as the world became soft and slightly out of focus, his breath abruptly heavy and loud inside his ears. "Is this a joke?" he whispered at last, voice trembling.

Nick's smile faded. "You think I'd make a joke about this?"

"No, but—" Jared's breath caught in his throat, and a tear he hadn't known was there ran out of his eye and down his cheek.

Nick stopped it with his thumb, his expression transforming into something possessive and sheltering.

More tears appeared out of nowhere, surprising Jared as much as they did Nick. Jared reached up to wipe them away, then gave up and searched for a box of tissues. When he couldn't find one and Nick produced a handkerchief for him, a sob escaped as well.

"Sweetheart." Nick stroked his hair, his cheeks. "Why are you crying? I didn't mean to make you sad."

"I'm not s-sad." Shutting his eyes, Jared slouched forward and rested his forehead against Nick's shoulder.

For once, Nick didn't worry about the damn door, too busy comforting him. "You're crying."

"I know. I'm sorry."

"You don't have to be sorry. But what did I say?"

Jared buried his face in Nick's neck. He searched for a less vulnerable reply, then gave up. "That I might not have to be alone."

The arms that wrapped around him felt so good he wanted time to stop. "Have you felt that lonely?"

Jared shrugged, sinking deeper into Nick's embrace. "I tried not to focus on it."

"You should have told the others."

How pathetic should he be? *Might as well dive all the way in.* "You assume I've only felt this way since they moved out."

"*Baby.*"

Jared's heart, fluttering like a nervous butterfly inside his chest, settled down as Nick lifted his face and kissed him again, this time full of promise as well as passion.

"You're not alone," Nick whispered hotly into Jared's forehead as he pulled back. "Neither one of us is anymore."

Sighing, Jared relaxed into him.

Nick stroked Jared's hair, his low, rumbling voice quiet in Jared's ear. "So am I to take it this is a yes, you'll have me?"

"Of course it's a yes," Jared said, and held tight to his man.

NICK WANTED to figure out how to talk to his mother and grandmother about moving in with Jared right away, but the universe, as it was wont to do, heard he had an agenda and rushed to fill his plate with other things.

The Fourth of July holiday wasn't as big a to-do in Copper Point as Founder's Day, but New Birth always hosted a community picnic at the church before the fireworks show over the bay, which meant Nick and his family had plenty of work to do, organizing and planning, setting up, and in the case of his grandmother, mother, and sister, cooking up a storm. His grandmother baked three different cakes, including the beloved pineapple upside-down, and his mother and sister contributed homemade potato salad and macaroni and cheese. They were all Emerson family recipes passed from Great-Grandmother Dinah-Jo, whose family had owned a restaurant before leaving South Carolina in the Great Migration. All the Beckert family dishes would be given pride of place at the picnic, and Nick would be obliged to show up early and help set up tables, solve crises, and corral the boys who liked to get into trouble when they thought nobody was looking.

The picnic went off without a hitch, and he settled in his family's row of lawn chairs along the greenbelt park with an exhausted but satisfied sigh to watch the fireworks show. The next day, however, he got up bright and early once again, because it was time for the long-put-off boating adventure with the Amin family.

He didn't begrudge this event at all, one because it meant he got to be with Jared, and two because the Amins were quickly becoming some of his favorite people. Uzma's practice was thriving, as everyone had known it would be, with such a desperate need, but she was so warm and bright that simply having her on staff seemed to make the hospital function better. The day spent on the water was wonderful too, the children's excited cries a joy only second to Jared's eager smiles as he played with them.

He would make a good father, Nick acknowledged.

I wonder what it would be like to see him playing with our children.

The thought left Nick dizzy.

Unfortunately the holiday wasn't the only thing distracting Nick. Peterson's newspaper sabotage had brought forth the bitter fruit he'd hoped for, and both at the picnic and as Nick set up his family's area at the fireworks, several people had come up to let him know what they thought of him wasting taxpayer money on a frivolous exercise. Since the article in the paper, Nick had received countless letters, emails, and phone calls from concerned citizens, but by Monday after the holiday, the situation became so intense he had to suspect it was coordinated, likely once again by Peterson. It wasn't yet enough that they worried for the two members up for reelection this fall, but it was getting close.

And while Nick was trying to figure out what to do about that, he got a text from Cynthia Ryan letting him know she'd be stopping by that afternoon and hoped he could spare some time for her.

Both Peterson and the Ryans had become thorns in Nick's side in different ways. At first Jeremiah Ryan's attention seemed supportive, and Nick had welcomed it, but he was calling an awful lot, being excessively helpful, a bit pushy, and very "you should do it this way, son." Nick started to wonder if he could trust the man's offers of help. Peterson was a horsefly dogging him, and Nick had no illusions this stint with the newspaper would be the only roadblock he threw up.

All this and he *still* hadn't worked out how to talk to his family about moving out.

As he was about to pack up for the day, Wendy buzzed him with a call he couldn't ignore. Allison Christy from the Gilbert Consulting Firm had an update for him on line one.

"Nick, good to talk to you." Christy's voice was warm and soothing over the line, but professional. "Do you have a few minutes for me to go over our initial findings? I'll give a full report at the meeting next week, but I wanted to let you know what we plan to say so you have some advance preparation."

"Absolutely." He settled into his chair as he fished out a legal pad and a pen. "Let's hear it."

"Well, I don't think most of it will be a surprise. It's as you suspected. The hospital needs a lot of work in some subtle but critical areas. There are a few things I'd advise you to address immediately, regardless of any decisions you make, but as a whole it wasn't difficult to see a picture of what should be done from a third party's perspective. The hospital isn't modernized in a number of aspects, and the physical structures aren't possible to be modified without considerable expense. Plus the location could be better. There are mild mold issues in the basement, which isn't a good look for a hospital, but more important is that the reason for this is the building was built too close to a small subterranean stream. We recommend building a new facility without a basement and with targeted, modern systems designed to grow with new technology on a site cleared of location issues and more accessible to ambulances and the public. We found three potential sites, two of which are already on the market. Another option would be to stay in your location but build in the parking lot, which is not on the river, though you will be limited to further expansion in the future should the city ever grow."

Nick flipped the page of his pad and continued writing furiously. "But Copper Point has only seen decline in growth in the past twenty years. Is that honestly something we should be concerned about?"

"Looking at a longer-term pattern, the area has fluctuated significantly and could grow again. Also, St. Ann's remains the only hospital in a large radius. Should there be any nearby growth, the hospital will grow as well."

"I see." Nick finished writing and set down his pen. "This is excellent information. I have no idea what we'll do with it, but it's good fodder for us as we decide how we'll move forward."

"Additionally, I'd like to talk about the elevator shaft. It's a major complication. I would not recommend repairing it if you're at all considering new construction or a buyout. It will be more expensive and complicated, we believe, than you've been quoted.

The damage is oddly extensive, and repairs should only be undertaken if you decide to remain entirely as is. I also want it clear we in no way advise you take that path."

Nick ran a hand over his face. It was what he'd expected, but it was heavy to hear. "I'll bear that in mind as well. Thank you."

"I regret to inform you there's more. We're investigating, but we have concerns about the other quotes you were given regarding the repairs. As I said, the difference is significant, and we don't understand the logic behind them. If it had been only one construction firm, we'd have written it off, but that both insurance company and the manufacturer's estimates came so far under is concerning. We're currently reaching out to them to see if they have explanations they'd like to share, or if there might be some other cause for the discrepancy."

Nick would bet money the newspaper would run a story about the expensive estimates from the Gilbert firm as soon as they appeared. "Can you send over your itemized figures and rationales? I'm going to have an uphill battle selling this to the public, I'm afraid."

"Absolutely. In the meantime, if you need anything at all, let us know. As we discussed, meeting with the community is part of our services offered, but if you need us to come sooner, just let me know."

"I'll think about it. I suspect it'll be better if we handle it ourselves, though. Copper Point can be funny about outsiders."

"Understood. Well, you have my number. Please feel free to call anytime. Give my regards to Erin and the rest of the board."

After hanging up the phone, Nick pressed his hands together and rested the tips of his fingers under his chin as he stared at the paper for several seconds. Then he hit the intercom and buzzed Erin.

"Mr. Andreas. Can I have you for a few minutes?"

"Certainly. I'll be right over."

Erin came in looking about as haggard as Nick felt, but he gave his boss all his attention. "What is it?"

Nick gestured to a chair. "I'd like to share with you the initial findings from Gilbert."

Erin was immediately focused. "What did they say?"

Nick handed him the notes he'd taken during the phone call. "No surprises. It's as you said. We need to build a new hospital. I assume they'll give us a quote at the meeting next week."

Erin scanned the papers. "What's this about the elevator?"

"That's the interesting bit. She said not to renovate at all until we know which direction we're going. She also suspects we were misquoted by the contractors because their teams' initial workups indicated it would be more expensive than we were told, by a significant margin."

"Why would they give us bad numbers?" Erin set the pad down. "What construction companies gave us the estimates? Someone local?"

"No. Our insurance company sent someone from Eau Claire, and the elevator company sent someone from Madison."

"We should have someone here look at it, then."

"Let's wait. We have the report from Gilbert with a quote from a construction company on their end. I don't know that we need three to go to the board."

"Speaking of, how do you think this is going to go over with the board?"

Nick shrugged. "I have no idea. The elected officials are already feeling the heat, and we haven't begun to discuss anything controversial yet."

"The advisory reps are getting letters too, and it's the talk of the hospital cafeteria." Erin pursed his lips. "This is all Peterson's doing, isn't it?"

"Obviously. And don't think it'll be the end of his chess moves either. But don't despair yet. I think the board will hold together. Rebecca is a good leader."

"You're right. We have an exceptional team. I think Matt Engleton is an excellent vice president to Rebecca."

At the mention of Engleton's name, Nick grimaced.

Erin, focused on the notes in front of him, missed it. "There's so much potential in our board now. The diversity of experience, background, and culture better represents Copper Point and a more prosperous future for both St. Ann's and the community at large."

"We have to make sure this elevator crisis doesn't sandbag them. It's no good if the board is ready but they can't get reelected." Nick rubbed his beard. "It's a little sobering, how Gilbert said our one option we don't have is to remain as we are. Because it means if we don't build, we have to privatize or be absorbed by a corporation. I don't think either option is good for St. Ann's or Copper Point."

"One step at a time." Erin pushed to his feet. "Is there anything else, or do you mind if I go finish my work? Owen is off soon, and we were going to make dinner together."

Soon, if I play this right, that can be me with Jared. "Go on. I'm about to head out as well. We'll talk more about this tomorrow. Hopefully they'll have sent the report by then." He winced as he glanced at his phone and saw another text. "Oh, damn. I can't leave yet. Cynthia Ryan is stopping by."

Erin raised his eyebrows. "Oh?"

"She's on her way through to Duluth for a meeting or something and wanted to say hello."

"Going to dinner with her, then?"

Nick hadn't thought about it, but he supposed that was the expectation. He *should* have thought about it, but he'd been so consumed with everything else. Also, it was possible he tried to avoid thinking about what the Ryans might be expecting of him, particularly Cynthia. He sighed. "If my mother finds out she's in town, my life is over."

"Well, best of luck to you. Let me know if you need anything."

"Will do."

As soon as Erin left, Nick put in a call to Café Cuore, securing a reservation for an early dinner. When Cynthia texted him to let him know she'd arrived at the hospital, he closed up his laptop and hurried down the stairs to meet her in the lobby.

"Cynthia. Good to see you again." He hugged her lightly. "You look well. How's your father?"

"He's busy as a bee, just the way he likes it." She raked him with her gaze and lifted a brow. "*You* look stressed."

"You know how it goes." He gestured to the parking garage. "I made us a reservation at an excellent Italian restaurant in town. Can I treat you?"

"Of course you can. But you're going to tell me everything that's going on with the Gilbert report on the way."

Exactly what Nick had been afraid of. He tried to brush this off with an easy smile. "Oh, if you really want to help me relax, you'll tell me stories and let me *not* think about that business for a while."

She indulged him a bit, regaling him with the events of her last business trip to California as they drove to the restaurant and got settled in at their table. She was a lovely woman, highly intelligent and absolutely beautiful. She reminded Nick in many ways of his own mother, down to her sense of humor and her shrewd way of handling obstacles. Were he straight, he'd have allowed himself to be maneuvered into her orbit long ago.

"What are you thinking about with such an expression on your face?" she teased him as she sipped at her wine. "You're always so serious."

I'm wondering why I keep hanging out in this limbo, not embracing the false identity that would come with marrying you or some other woman, not admitting to the people I love who I truly am. He sighed into his water glass. "Boring stuff."

"Hmm." She didn't buy his lie at all, which didn't surprise him.

She didn't push him, though, which he appreciated. She'd make someone such a good partner. He hoped she wasn't part of their parents' conspiracy to get them together, that she wasn't waiting for him. He doubted it, given how put together she was. But if he'd somehow accidentally led her on by his stasis, he had no idea how to apologize.

Putting down her glass, she leaned over the table. "All right. No more staring broodingly at me. Tell me what you're thinking about so hard."

Dangerous, treacherous waters. But he owed her this, he suspected. "Expectations. Duties. How to meet them without harming other people."

Her laughter was soft and wry. "That's the most Nick Beckert answer I've ever heard, I think."

"Well, duty is important to me."

"That much is abundantly clear." She poured more wine into his glass. "The thing is, while duty is important, it's worthless if it drags you down. You're a wonderful man and a credit to your family, but you can't maintain your presence if all you think about is others. You can give endlessly, but only if you keep your well filled."

He drank deeply of the wine, drowning his instinct to tell her this was the one thing he couldn't do, because filling his well meant exposing a part of him he knew no one wanted to accept. Except he knew at the same time she was right. Emmanuella was right. Erin was right. He should be able to be his full, true self *and* embrace the legacy his father established. They shouldn't have to cancel each other out.

It dawned on him, as he sat here with her, that though he thought he'd been hiding, he'd actually been holding his breath all this time. He'd *wanted* to embrace himself before anybody goaded him about it. So what was standing in his way? What obstacle was left?

Realizing he'd been brooding again, Nick held up his hands in surrender. "My apologies. I'm a terrible escort today."

Cynthia gave him a sly smile. "Am I keeping you from someone you'd rather be brooding with, by chance?"

Something about her tone made him pause, and the look in her eye drew the words out of him before he could think to call them back. "It would be incredibly rude of me, if that were true."

"Not in the slightest. We're friends, Nick. It's no secret our firm would love to work with St. Ann's, but our relationship is more than business. Our families know each other. What I've always admired most about you, even beyond your sense of duty to your family and community, is the way you see and support people, including me. Not once have you regarded me as anything less than a competent woman with a voice worth hearing. Who would I be if I didn't extend that same courtesy back to you? If there's someone else you'd like to be with tonight, I'm not going to stop you from going to them."

Nick stared at her, barely able to breathe.

She knows. In that moment, he was convinced of it. That pronoun had been chosen with such care. The expression on her face, her warm, gentle smile, telling him without a word she was his sister and would stand by him—*she knew*, somehow. Cold terror swept him as he feared that perhaps Erin had called it and despite Nick's efforts, everyone knew.

Was Nick's greatest secret not a secret at all?

Still relaxed, Cynthia waved down the server. "I think it might be best if we made this just a drink and not dinner. I'm thinking room service and a long soak in a hotel tub is what I want this evening."

She collected the bill and deftly provided her card before he could object, but when she started to rise, he caught her hand.

"Thank you," he said quietly. He hoped she understood what he was grateful for.

Her easy reply told him she did. "If you ever need anything, Nick, you call me. I've been waiting a long time to support you the way you've supported me." She winked at him. "Just don't take too long until you have the right person sitting beside you at this table, you hear me?"

He smiled back at her. "I'll do my best."

JARED WASN'T going to bring up Nick potentially moving in with him to any of his friends, but the subject came up on its own when he went over to Simon and Jack's the week after the Fourth of July holiday for what everyone had started calling their monthly family dinner. Originally family dinners had been weekly and on Sunday, but with everyone's busy schedule, monthly was so much easier. Sometimes they had more than one a month, for special occasions. Sometimes because of scheduling they ended up practically back to back or nearly two months apart. They moved the meal anywhere from Friday night to Sunday night, depending on who was on call and who had what community obligation. Sometimes they met at a restaurant, sometimes they brought takeout to someone's house. Their gathering meal could be anything from a light brunch to a full-on five-course dinner. The one requirement was they all had to attend. Everyone stayed as long as possible, and everyone spilled the tea on whatever was going on with their life.

Sometimes, though, the others spilled the tea for them.

The family dinner was at Simon and Jack's condo this time, Jack making miso-marinated salmon steaks and a wild rice pilaf to go along with his arugula salad and hot-and-sour soup. Jared had brought some bread and wine, Owen and Erin had brought more wine and a homemade pie for dessert, and the evening was shaping up to be delicious and perfect in every way.

But Jared didn't have even half a glass of wine down before he was seated on the couch with all eyes on him.

"Jared." Simon regarded Jared with concern. "Is everything all right with you?"

Something about the way Simon asked made Jared pause. "I'm fine. Great, actually. Why do you ask?"

Simon and Erin exchanged knowing looks. Jared turned to Owen beside him, confused, but Owen was equally serious. Jack, finishing up the last details of the meal in the kitchen, glanced up from his work as if he too were eager to hear about Jared's state.

Jared pursed his lips. "Okay, guys. What's this all about?"

The others glanced at each other, clearly silently deciding who was going to do the explaining, but unsurprisingly it was Owen in the end who spoke up. "Well, we heard a rumor you're holding out on us, not letting us know you feel lonely."

Nick, you blabbermouth. How much did you tell them? Jared cleared his throat and sipped his wine. "I see."

Simon leaned forward. "Why didn't you say something to us? We would have helped."

Owen appeared equally affronted. "Did we make you think you couldn't talk to us for some reason? Is that why you refused Erin and me when we tried to get you to move in with us?"

"Would you have rather moved in with Hong-Wei and me?" Simon added.

"*Stop.*" Jared held up his hands, sloshing the wine in his glass dangerously. "I don't want to move in with any of you, and no one has made me feel unwanted." He sighed. "My loneliness isn't even new, I'm afraid, only more impossible to ignore with the rest of you settled into your own partnerships. There are goals for my life I've put off too long, and it's time I start pursuing them."

Erin's eyes widened. "Does this mean you and Nick…?"

Jared shrugged. "I don't know. It's complicated."

Simon looked worried. "I heard the rumor that he's thinking of dating Cynthia Ryan."

Jared pinched the bridge of his nose. "Nick isn't going to date Cynthia Ryan. We're dating each other, albeit quietly. We're both trying to make this work. In fact, he told me last week he wants to move in with me."

Everyone spoke at once, congratulating Jared and telling him how wonderful this was. Only Jack seemed taken aback. "You mean he's thinking about coming out?"

"I don't know if it'll come to that. But we'd live together as housemates, at least to everyone else. It would give us time to get to know each other properly."

Erin nodded. "And it would give Nick time to warm up to the idea of being exposed. This is a huge step for him."

Simon wasn't impressed. "This isn't a good deal for you, though. You've always been out. And you want a relationship, right? One in the open?"

"I'd like one, yes. But for now, I want whatever I can get with Nick."

They left the discussion there and turned the conversation to other people, but Jared was aware Owen and Simon in particular hadn't completely liked this notion of him settling for what to them was half a relationship. As predicted, while the others did dishes and cleaned up, Owen pulled Jared aside to the deck and spoke quietly with him.

"Are you really okay with this?" he asked Jared. "Having your whole relationship be hidden?"

"That's all it's ever been with Nick. Why is everyone so concerned about it now?"

"Because there's something about the two of you moving in together that feels huge, and yet it's going to be under the radar. I guess I wanted more progress for you. Can he even come to family dinners? How much can we acknowledge him before other people see through the ruse? Do you understand how much you'll have to modulate your reactions to him in public and how hard that will be once you get close to him in private?"

Yes, Jared had thought of all this. "I don't see what else there is to do, unless I insist he come out. Which as I told you is a great way to drive him off."

Owen grimaced. "Maybe you should. Maybe if he can't be there for you, you shouldn't give this a chance."

The thought made Jared's chest ache. "That's not fair."

"It absolutely is fair—to you."

"I thought you liked Nick. And you were the one who told me I was horrible for forcing a choice on him when we were teenagers."

"I do. I like him a lot. But I like you more. And I never said you were horrible." Owen sighed. "Look. Do what you need to do. Just be careful, okay? And be smart. At the end of the day, I don't want you to feel lonely. The thing is, you're not sixteen. You're thirty-six. You've already given so much of your life to waiting for him. There are other guys out there interested in you, guys who won't make you feel this way."

Immediately Jared thought of Matt. "Yes, but they're not Nick."

Owen put an arm around Jared's shoulders. "Then I hope, for your sake, he comes around."

CHAPTER TEN

NICK KEPT putting off talking to his family about moving out, which he knew was a problem, and yet every time he tried to work up the courage, he failed. Thus it ended up that suddenly it was the last week of July, and he hadn't brought anything up to his mother and grandmother. His furtive dates, such as they were, with Jared were fewer and farther between, and it was clear Jared didn't like the delay. Nick knew he was taking too long.

It came to a head late one Sunday night while he did the dishes with Emmanuella.

"You going to tell me why you've been looking like a cat in a room full of rocking chairs?" She bumped him with her hip when he glanced over his shoulder at the darkened stairs. "Mom's out at that meeting, and Grandma already took her pills. She's dead to the world. Spill it."

Nick wiped the towel carefully over the glass pan he was holding as he searched for the right opening. There wasn't one. He might as well dive in. He kept his voice low, though, because he didn't trust his grandmother not to walk in at the wrong moment. "I want to move in with Jared."

Emmanuella dropped a colander in the sink. "You're going to come out?"

He swatted her with his towel. "*Chill*. No. I want to move in with him as a friend."

She snorted. "Everybody's going to see through that one."

His chest tightened. "You think?"

"Well… they're all going to wonder, anyway. Including Mama and Grandma. They already despair that you don't date. You shack up with a gay man? They're gonna talk."

Exactly what he was afraid of. "So you're saying don't do it?"

"I'm saying nothing of the sort. But you're fooling yourself if you think you can play the roommate card and call it good."

"Look, I got a plan."

She passed him the colander after shaking the water from it. "Well, let's hear your pitch."

"I'm gonna tell them I'm moving in with him because he's lonely. Used to have a house full, but they all got married and now it's just him. They know how we were tight back in the day, and we reconnected during the accident. He's looking for a roommate, but I'm the only one who can fit the bill, because with Jared, it's got to be someone he knows well." He held out his hands, grinning in self-satisfaction. "Solid, right?"

She only shook her head. "You're gonna fall on your ass so fast."

His shoulders sank as he lowered his hands. "Why? This is a good argument. I worked hard on it."

"It's all focused on saving Jared. It has nothing to do with you. Also, you're taking the wrong approach. You're asking their permission. You should *tell* them what you're doing."

His whole body tensed. "I can't do that."

"Why the hell not? You're a grown-assed man. You're the CEO of the hospital, the head of this family. You have every right to move out if you damn well please. Honestly, it's weird you're still here, much as I love having you around."

Okay, that one hurt. "You know I moved in here because of the stress of this job when I took it—"

"Yes, yes. But that's over now. Been over for a long time. Even considering the mortgage on this house, Mama could take it over and you could go get your own if that's what you were after. The point is, it's not weird for you to say it's time for you to move on. And if you want to move on with Jared, that's your business. But keep it all about *your* business." She pursed her lips and scrubbed at a pan. "You can talk about Jared's pain if you insist, but most of it needs to be about you and what you need, what you want."

"And what if they're angry? What if I let them down?" *What if they know the truth?*

"Of course they'll be angry. They're entirely too used to having their own way. But this is something important to you. Incredibly so. You're not ready to tell them the real reason, but you have to find a way to come close. Because if living with him works out, at some point you're going to have to confess."

He held up a hand. "I'm not ready to think about that."

"I know. I'm doing it for you. Don't tell them the truth, but consider it while you approach them. Be honest inside."

"What if they figure it out, though?"

"I don't understand why you think it's so awful that they see who you are. You're letting this fear rule you."

"Because they might reject me."

"Hon, you have *got* to stop obsessing over this. If they only accept the false version of who you are, it's practically the same thing." She put a soapy hand on his. "You're wading in slowly for them as well as you. Think of it that way. They'll take some time to come around, but they'll get there."

They did the rest of the dishes in comfortable silence. As they finished up and Emmanuella loaded the soap into the dishwasher, Nick let out a breath.

"Friday. I'll tell them after dinner on Friday."

Emmanuella lifted her head and raised an eyebrow at him. "No excuses?"

"No excuses."

"You freaking out?"

"Yes."

"Well, go ahead and have your panic, just so long as you stick to your deadline and remember you're not getting permission, you're letting them know."

"I'll try."

She patted his shoulder and kissed his cheek. "You'll be fine."

JARED WAS edgy, waiting while Nick took his time talking to his family, trying not to let it bother him that a single conversation seemed to take an inordinate amount of time.

When twelve days had passed since he'd reassured his friends that everything would be fine and yet somehow nothing had changed, Jared decided he couldn't handle staying at home alone, and went on a long walk, meandering through his neighborhood, waving to people he knew, sometimes stopping to chat. It was a nice evening, the lake breeze cool and invigorating, and he wandered all the way to campus town and the coffee shop.

Café Sól had been around for about five years now, resurrected from a previous incarnation by August Taylor. Gus had been a business student at Bayview University and a frequent customer at the formerly failing shop. Gus made renovations of the shop a project for his master's thesis, and when he presented it to the town council, they gave him a small grant. Now it was a thriving business.

Gus often worked the espresso bar, and he was there as Nick walked in. "Hey there, Dr. Kumpel." It was a teasing greeting. The two of them were close enough friends that they called each other by their first name, but Gus called him by his title or "Doc" half the time.

"Hey yourself." Jared glanced around the shop, which as usual was bustling with college students studying and a few locals chatting quietly over cups of tea and coffee. Sliding onto one of the stools at the bar, he put his hand on his chin and frowned at the strange glass apparatus Gus was playing with. "What in the world is that?"

"My new vacuum coffee maker." Gus's gaze sparkled as he tweaked the flame on a burner beneath the bottom glass globe and settled the top canister so the water magically drew into it from the bottom. Looking more than a little like a mad scientist, he measured freshly ground beans into a cup and weighed them on a scale before dumping them into the upper chamber and stirring gently. "Would you care to try the first pot with me?"

Jared wasn't going to sleep tonight anyway. "Why not?"

Gus was a kid with a new toy as he fussed with the machine. Jared backtracked on that thought as soon as he had it, though. Was it technically a machine? It didn't appear to plug in. Relative to the computer-driven coffee makers he was used to, it was such a simple thing, and yet with all these tubes and complicated steps it was something else entirely.

"Is this coffee supposed to taste different?" he asked.

One glance from Gus and he could tell he'd asked just the right—or possibly wrong—question.

"*Yes*. The vacuum brewing process preserves the flavor of the coffee and doesn't kill it by boiling it. It's a bit more complex than what most people are used to, but it's worth the extra effort. The aroma is more intense as well, which makes the experience more pleasurable."

Gus kept going, talking about the history of coffee makers, and Jared drifted off, thinking once again of Nick. He hoped he was doing the right thing by letting him talk to his family at his own pace. It was *so* difficult not to be bossy and tell him how to behave.

What if Nick had decided he didn't want to move in after all? What if he couldn't do it because he didn't dare disturb his family? Jared could hardly complain about it, but he didn't like how he felt, sitting here empty, alone, restless.

If only he hadn't fallen for such a difficult man.

"Now for the test." Gus rubbed his hands together as he fussed with the burner again and stirred the coffee once more. The coffee returned to the bottom beaker as Gus watched, eyes full of stars. Jared watched too, interested now that things were actually happening.

"Here you go." Gus handed a cup of steaming coffee to Jared. "Go ahead. Tell me what you think."

After a sniff, which did indeed prove far more aromatic than run-of-the-mill coffee, Jared took a hesitant sip. Then his eyebrows rose. It was rich, subtle, and delicious. "This is not bad at all."

"I know, right?" Gus leaned on his elbows. "I first read about this type of coffee maker in a magazine, and I tried it when I was in San Francisco at a coffee bar there. I wanted one for the shop."

"You wanted to try it for yourself," Jared corrected, taking another drink.

"Both, really." Gus smiled at someone over Jared's shoulder. "Hey, Matt."

Sitting up straighter, Jared turned on his stool. Sure enough, it was Matt Engleton standing in the doorway, and when he saw Jared, his smile widened. "Hey, Gus. Jared. What are you two up to?"

"Trying out vacuum coffee. Want to get in on it?" Gus asked.

Matt grinned. "Obviously."

Gus motioned to the chair beside Jared. "Have a seat."

Jared hid his wince in his coffee cup. Matt Engleton wasn't what he needed right now, but what was he supposed to do? Get up and leave? He should, but he'd drink this coffee first, then conveniently get an important text calling him away. Hmm, should it be business or personal?

The coffee was seriously good, though. It was a shame to rush it.

Matt elbowed him gently. "So, stranger. How have you been?"

Shrugging, Jared set his mug back down. "Can't complain. Not trapped in any elevators lately, so that's something."

Matt shuddered. "That's one of my worst nightmares, ever since I was a kid. I would have been a ball of panic. How did you get through it?" Wincing, he held up a hand. "Sorry if this is something you don't want to talk about. Feel free to tell me to mind my own business."

Jared smiled. "No worries. As for how I got through it… Nick, I guess. I couldn't have endured it alone. Certainly I wouldn't have gotten out of it with as little trauma as I did. We took turns boosting each other, but mostly we were each someone to face the terror of it with. You'd think so few floors would have been not such a big deal, but it's all darkness and unknown when you're trapped in a sealed box."

Matt shook his head. "I'm not glad it happened to anyone, but had it been a patient or a visitor? I keep worrying about the liability lawsuit. Someone slipped and fell in our store two years ago on a piece of flooring that had come loose. The customer didn't fault us, but because they broke their hip, the insurance company forced the issue and sued us for the entire medical procedure."

"Yikes." Jared frowned. "I hadn't even considered that. I wonder what the case will be with our medical bills. I suppose the hospital will absorb them. I wonder who handled that, though? I'd say Erin."

"I'd agree." Matt leaned on his elbow, resting his chin in his hand. "God, but I get the feeling the next few hospital board meetings are going to be intense."

Gus snorted. "The next *few*? Someone's in dreamland. What's more interesting is that all the decisions we make will affect those of us up for reelection this fall."

That was right—when Nick appointed people after the embezzlement, they were filling the vacated seats until they could be properly voted on. Everyone had undergone a special election after the appointment, but to preserve the rotation, some of those terms were up again now. The advisory seats were never voted on, because they had no power. But being on the board as an observer meant Jared had a more acute understanding of what was going on and what tensions arose for the board members.

Term lengths were three years, which hadn't changed, but the first thing the new board did was implement a three-consecutive-term limit for any standing member and a two-consecutive-term limit for any advisory member. They further cemented this rule into law by making it so that if this were to be changed, the county would have to approve it by a supermajority and reconfirm it by a second supermajority. There would never be a decades-long fiefdom of embezzlement again, if they had their say.

However, embezzlement was old news. Now the issue was facilities and the future, and the young, inexperienced board had been thrown in headfirst. The last few meetings, full of reports from Gilbert, had been rough.

"Are you still getting emails and phone calls about the consulting firm?" Jared asked.

Since the question pertained to both Gus and Matt, they regarded each other before they took turns answering. "Some," Gus said, "but mostly people tell me what they think when they come into the shop. I appreciate that, actually. Gives me a chance to discuss it properly."

Matt nodded. "I'm the same as well, and I agree. Jacob's having a rough time of it, though. He's too introverted to argue with people like that."

"Hopefully the public meeting in a few weeks settles things, but knowing Copper Point, plenty of people would complain if we handed them checks."

Matt held up his hands. "I don't want to talk politics. I came in here to let my hair down a minute. I've been smiling at customers all day, and I'm done."

"So glad you think of my shop as somewhere you don't have to smile," Gus quipped wryly, but there was a friendliness in his teasing.

"Do you two hang out together a lot?" Jared asked.

Gus rolled his eyes as he set a cup of coffee in front of Matt, a mild queen-out gesture. "Lord, I haven't been able to shake this one since the third grade when I started bringing salt and vinegar potato chips in my lunch."

"You brought the chips so I'd keep coming over," Matt retorted without looking up. He sipped the coffee, then did a double take. "Damn, Gus. What is this?"

"Vacuum coffee. Be nicer to me, or I won't give you more." To Jared, Gus said, "We were best friends the way you and Simon and Owen were. Except we dated in middle school until we figured out we were better friends than lovers."

"Are you truly lovers in middle school?" Matt objected.

"You're such a contrarian."

Jared smiled into his cup. Ah, but they made him miss Simon and Owen.

And Nick.

As if sensing his rival, Matt turned to Jared, charm on. "So. What brings you out this evening, my good doctor?"

"Oh, you know." Shrugging, Jared ran his finger around the rim of his mug. "My house is too quiet. Drives me nuts sometimes."

"You should come here more often, then." Matt grinned. "That's right, you've never lived alone, have you?"

Grimacing, Jared shook his head. "I had a roommate ever since college. The *same* roommates. I keep thinking I'll grow accustomed to living on my own, but I don't think I'm suited for it."

Gus, having returned from giving a customer a refill, crossed his legs. "You should rent out a room."

"Maybe." Jared needed to tread carefully in this discussion. "I can't live with just anyone, though, either. I don't like the idea of bringing in a stranger. I was spoiled, living with my made family."

"What about moving in with one of them?" Gus suggested. "Owen and Erin have to have enough room they wouldn't even notice you."

Jared winced. "No way. I couldn't do that. They're making their families now. I wouldn't want to get in the way."

Matt raised an eyebrow. "Can't say I'd expect them to see it that way, though."

No, they didn't. Jared cleared his throat. "Anyway. I actually may have a lead on something, but it's not for sure. If it doesn't work out, I'll probably get over myself and consider a roommate."

Gus shook his head. "You need to get yourself your own husband and adopt a pile of babies. I've never seen someone more suited to be a father."

You'd think there was bourbon in thc coffee, the way Jared was spilling his secrets. "I wouldn't want to adopt. I'd want to hire a surrogate."

Gus smiled. "Now you're going to tell me each of you would father one of the kids, aren't you?"

Jared rubbed the side of his beard self-consciously, then held up two fingers.

Gus laughed. "You'd each have two? Jared. We've got to get you a man. And he'll need to be young to keep up with *your* dreams."

A customer called Gus away, or perhaps Gus called himself away, giving his friend the opening of a lifetime.

Matt didn't miss a beat. "Jared, go out with me."

If I weren't completely hooked on someone else, kid, this would be a perfect setup. Jared tried to shrug it off with a wry smile. "What, you're telling me you want to have my four kids?"

"I'm telling you I want to date you. But yeah. Four kids sounds great. Mostly, though, I think you are. You're smart, sexy, handsome, and kind. I'm funny, charming, and cute. We'd make a great couple."

Jared didn't know what to say. He wanted to tell him no. To say he was in love with Nick and they were about to move in together, taking the first step toward the happy ever after he'd always dreamed of. But he couldn't be sure the moving in was happening, and even if it was, he wouldn't be able to acknowledge what it meant to anyone. He couldn't tell Matt he was rejecting him because he was hung up on someone else, not unless he was careful Matt didn't guess who the someone else was.

And all the while Jared had to keep himself braced for the possibility Nick would decide he couldn't do this. Or that by the time he figured it out, it would be too late for the dream of four kids. If Nick even shared it at all.

Matt rubbed his neck. "I didn't think it was *that* difficult a decision, or one which would cause you to make such a face. Is it such an awful idea?"

Jared smiled, but his weariness and jagged edges shone through. "No. But I'm… in the middle of something complicated—and private. So it isn't the best time. Sorry."

"Ah. So you're saying I'm too late?"

"About twenty years too late, yes."

"Well, that's hardly fair. I was only seven then and barely knew what gay was. I did know I liked Gus *a lot*, though." His expression became easy and, yes, Jared had to admit, charming. "Fair enough. I won't ask you again. But I won't accept a no from you either, if that's okay, or a yes. Can you give me your answer when things get uncomplicated for you?"

Jared sighed. "Lord, sometimes I despair of it ever happening."

Matt stopped smiling, looking concerned. "You're a great guy, and you said it yourself, you shouldn't be rattling around in that house alone."

"What, first you want a date, and now you're proposing? You work fast."

"You know what I mean. I'm serious." Matt frowned. "All right, it's settled. It's not my favorite thing, but we're going to be friends. Forget dating for now. I know you think I'm young and silly, but maybe you need some young and silly. You're not going to sit at home alone. You're going to come hang out here, and go to movies with us, and dinner—"

"How much free time do you think I have?"

Matt ignored him. "Since you're the one with the fancy house, we'll make dinner there and hang out. The three of us."

"I *do* have other friends, you know."

"Well, they can come too. Sometimes." Matt held out his hand. "Will you give me your phone so I can share my number?"

Jared unlocked his screen, opened an empty contact, and passed it over. "Not going to demand I give you mine?"

"This way the ball's in your court, and if you don't want to call me, you won't, no chance of me being bossy. But I think you will. If not, it's a small town. If you look like you're lonely later, as a friend I'll ask you what's wrong and if I can help the next time we bump into one another."

Jared shook his head, but he couldn't help smiling. "You're not bossy. *I'm* bossy. *You're* stealth."

"But in a *good* way."

Gus returned, taking pains to look breezy as if he'd just finished up, but there was no question he'd waited until deeming things were settled before reentering. "So. What'd I miss?"

Matt passed Jared back his phone. "The three of us are going to hang out. Jared will set things up. We're going to be friends now."

Gus blinked, clearly not anticipating this reaction.

Laughing, Jared eased into his chair and gave in to the unfamiliar but not unwelcome banter of his newfound companions.

NICK HAD never been more nervous for a meal in his entire life.

On the surface everything was the same as it always was. It was Friday night. He was home a little bit late, but that in itself wasn't unusual. His mother and grandmother had made the dinner together and held it in the oven as he hurried home, but as he washed up, his sister leaned around the door of the bathroom and gave him a quiet pep talk.

Because tonight was the night he told them he was moving out.

"You can do it," Emmanuella said as he splashed water on his face and breathed into a hand towel. "Don't look so guilty and nervous. Just tell them matter-of-factly this is happening. Thank them for everything and assure them you'll be ready to help whenever they need so much as a light bulb changed. But tell them. Don't you let him get away."

The way she said it made Nick pause. He lowered the towel and met her gaze in the mirror. "What do you mean, let him get away?"

Emmanuella came into the bathroom and shut the door. "Kayla Jenkins saw him at Gus's shop last night, getting flirted with by Matt Engleton. Rumor is Matt asked him out in front of everyone, and Jared gave him his phone number."

Nick's heart lurched sideways. "He wouldn't do that." *Would he?*

"I know he wouldn't. Got to be the rumor mill taking things out of hand. The point is, other people are sniffing around your man. One man in particular is focused on him on a regular basis. Are you going to let that happen because you're afraid to have a damn dinner table conversation?"

Jaw set, Nick folded the towel and put it back on the hanger. "No."

Emmanuella nodded approvingly. "Come on, then."

Nick felt as if he were going into battle, not heading down the hall to have a meal. He supposed he was. The trick was, he wasn't supposed to let it show on his face, and he didn't know how to do that.

This idea that Matt was making moves on Jared was focusing, though. He wanted to throw all this over and send a text right now asking for details. Except he'd look like a fool, especially given how that had turned out the last time he'd gone on a jealous tear.

No, what he had to do was inform his mother and grandmother he was moving out, and put a stop to this hedging in by Matt. He'd find a way to make it clear Jared wasn't available without coming all the way out of the closet.

Except wouldn't it be a lot easier if you were?

His mother was taking her seat, and his grandmother was putting the last dish on the table as he entered the dining room. As usual there wasn't only a roast, there were also boiled potatoes, rolls, two heated vegetables, and two salads, one pasta and bean, one lettuce. When Jared used to stay over and witnessed one of these meals, he'd whispered to Nick and asked who else was coming to dinner and why everything was so fancy. Nick had explained this was how every meal was at his house. Jared had accepted this at face value, but Nick's other childhood friends had told him it was weird, and eventually Nick asked his family for an explanation. His mother said it was Grandma Emerson's pride to serve bountiful meals, that she'd fed all the workers in her husband's factory as it came into its bloom in Milwaukee, had entertained the election officials as they worked the precincts and the community leaders who made sure everyone was taken care of, and that she just couldn't seem to quit the habit.

When he'd been a growing boy with the metabolism of a fighter jet, the overladen tables had been heaven. As a man in his midthirties aware heart disease ran in the family and who didn't want a rounded belly before his age and desk job gave him one whether he wanted one or not, Nick fought the huge portions ladled onto his plate and the starch and carbohydrates at every meal. For this alone, in all honesty, he'd do well to move in with Jared. Knowing his grandmother, she'd bring over a pot of food every night, adding him to her rounds of personal deliveries.

If she wasn't angry with him for leaving.

Tonight the meal was beef pot roast and roasted vegetables, but also a broccoli rice casserole made with cheese and not one but two cream soups. The sweet rolls were fresh baked and piping hot. The salad was the only healthy thing on the table, though it had been tossed with a heavy dressing.

God, but it all looked delicious.

His grandmother smiled at him as he headed for his chair. "Nick, honey, let me get you some water."

"I'll get it." Grabbing the stone pitcher from the buffet, Nick waved her into her chair. "You sit."

She didn't sit, fussing with a relish tray on the counter. "You know I eat like a bird." She wrested the pitcher from him. "Go on, you've been at work all day. Sit down, let me do my own job."

"How was the hospital?" his mother asked as she passed the napkin basket. "Everything okay?"

"Everything is fine. We're getting ready for the public meeting in August."

His grandmother leaned over him to pour the water. "Everything going all right?"

"'Bout as good as it can."

"Well, we'll all keep you in our prayers." Grandma Emerson took her seat and folded her hands. "Speaking of. Nick, go ahead and say grace."

Nick led them through the mealtime prayer, his mind half wandering, trying to decide where and when he should start the conversation. Right away? In the middle of eating? When they were done? He should have talked to Emmanuella about this.

What was Jared doing tonight? Was he talking to Matt? How often was Matt contacting him, anyway?

"You look like you've got something on your mind," Grandma Emerson remarked when Nick remained quiet as they passed the food.

Emmanuella all but kicked him under the table. He didn't need the prompt, though. He understood he wasn't going to get a better opening.

Clearing his throat, Nick passed the pot roast to Emmanuella and scooped broccoli casserole onto his plate. "Well, there is something I need to tell everyone, something I've been thinking about for some time now." He wiped his mouth with his napkin and tried to quiet his heartbeat. "I'm going to move out and live on my own. Well, with a roommate."

Both women put down the dishes of food they'd been ready to pass and began to protest at once. "Boy, what are you talking about?" his mother demanded, as his grandmother muttered, "I just knew he was cooking up something foolish, but I never dreamed he'd lost his damn head completely," as she glared at the ceiling as if it might rescue her from her ridiculous grandson.

Emmanuella, bless her, jumped right into the fray and took hold of the conversation. "What are you two making noise like that for? He's a grown man. He can move out of the house if he wants to."

Their mother humphed. "It's so sudden. What brought this on? And what roommate?"

Nick held up a hand. "It's something I've thought about before, but the timing or opportunity never felt right. That's changed. I'm going to move in with Jared Kumpel."

The table went completely silent.

Nick continued as he'd rehearsed, trying not to sweat. "As I told you, Jared and I rekindled our friendship during the accident. In the elevator we talked through a lot of things from our past, and then some. He told me was how much he hates living alone, and I was ready for some independence, but not complete solitude. Like him, the idea of rooming with a stranger is uncomfortable. I did that while I was in school and the first few years I was working, and I didn't care for it. But living alone wasn't for me, either. With the two of us, we solve all our problems. But I wanted to make sure you understood I'll come over anytime you so much as needed something from a high shelf. And of course I'll go to church with you every Sunday."

He paused, waiting to hear what they would say in reply.

His mother pursed her lips and folded her napkin over and over in what Nick thought of as her *I don't care for this at all* gesture. Emmanuella watched everyone like a hawk as she loaded potatoes and pot roast and carrot into her roll. Grandma Emerson kept her gaze squarely on Nick, and he understood she was scanning him, peeling layers from him as if he were an onion she suspected was rotten at its core. Whether this was simply her habit—because he could be full of gray hair himself and so long as she was alive, she'd still view him as a little boy—or whether she smelled the rat he truly did have buried in his tale, he couldn't say.

It took everything in Nick to project a neutral countenance instead of sweating. *Yes, Grandma. I'm moving in with my boyfriend. This is all a pleasant lie. A fiction I'm making to keep the peace. To ease everyone into the transition.*

Eventually his grandmother let out a long, ragged sigh. "Not much I can say about it, I suppose. I expect you to remember where you come from and who you are, no matter where you are. And I won't have you bringing shame to this family."

"*Grandma*," Emmanuella scolded under her breath.

Nick didn't sweat, but he flinched on the inside.

Oh, there was no question about it. She suspected. She might know the whole truth, as he feared.

Funny, in so many ways this was the worst-case scenario, the only one worse being where they came out and asked him if he was gay, forcing him to admit it or lie. He wondered what his answer would have been. All he knew was as his grandmother stared at him, as her words hung in the air and he knew exactly what she meant, he didn't feel the shame he thought he would have.

Only sadness.

"I would never do anything I find shameful," he replied.

He saw the surprise in her eyes as she noted his careful wording. His mother lifted her head too, and the sorrow cut him as he felt the curtain fall across the table, sheer but weighty, a net of steel. A divide separating them, invisible but present. One that wouldn't easily go away.

So this was how it would go after all. They understood what this was, didn't like it, but would let him pretend.

It was there, under the heaviness of his mother's and grandmother's gazes, that Nick was finally able to understand this compromise would never be enough for him. He had only just begun to walk through the door he'd been pressing his hand against for twenty years.

A door they've known about but had hoped I would keep closed.

He lowered his gaze to his plate, full of food he was no longer hungry enough to eat.

CHAPTER ELEVEN

NICK WAS moving in at last.

Jared was so excited he barely knew how to contain himself. He'd hardly slept at all after Nick had called and asked, out of nowhere, if this weekend was too soon to move in. Jared had wept like a fool as he told him he could come over that moment if he wanted, though he was a little glad Nick waited for the morning. He was too busy arranging and cleaning and, if he were honest, daydreaming. They were going to buy furniture together, and set up rooms together, and pick out new drapes—*couple things* the likes of which he'd give himself nosebleeds over if he let himself dwell on them.

They would eat dinner together Saturday night, making it together in their own kitchen. Their kitchen. *Theirs.*

It was almost too much.

The only downside was Nick was adamant Jared not help him pack up or load anything from his house, saying he preferred to do it all on his own. Jared didn't understand why he couldn't help, especially if he brought the rest of the guys to split the load. Nick had insisted he didn't have many things so it wasn't an issue, but Jared was sure there was something more to it.

Whatever. It was about to happen. It wasn't quite the way he'd imagined, but it was closer than he'd dreamed.

He paced back and forth all morning, counting the hours until Nick would arrive, like a child waiting for Santa. He wondered what they'd do together first. Have sex? Seemed obvious. But sometimes Nick liked to torture him. He might be feeling moody because of his family, as evidenced by not letting Jared help him move out. So maybe they should stick to something low-key.

God, but it was going to take everything in Jared not to blast himself at the man and do him in the doorway.

By eleven he'd already cleaned every room in the house and emptied out a dresser for Nick as well as a drawer in the bathroom. He was debating baking some bread to keep himself from going crazy when his phone buzzed in his pocket. It was a text from Nick.

On my way over.

Jared allowed himself a foolish grin, a girlish twirl, and a flop on the sofa.

When Nick pulled into the driveway, Jared was on the porch ready to meet him with a wide smile on his face. He tried not to bounce on his heels, but he didn't manage it. "Hey," he said when Nick got out of the car.

"Hey yourself." Nick slung a bag higher on his shoulder.

They stared at one another, a little eager, a little awkward. Finally Jared gestured to the door. "Well, *entrez-vous*."

Nick's mouth quirked in a half smile as he came up the stairs. "Technically you should say just *entrez*. If you say *entrez-vous*, it sounds as if you're asking me if I want to come in."

Jared blinked. "Are you pulling my leg?"

Nick slapped Jared's ass on the way by. "Nope. I paid more attention in high school French than you did, plus I continued on in college."

Rubbing the slightly stinging spot on his rump, Jared followed Nick inside. For someone who didn't want to be found out, he sure was casual about PDA. He closed the door behind him and turned toward Nick. "So how much stuff do you have—?"

The rest of his question was cut off as Nick cupped Jared's face and closed his mouth over Jared's.

Jared softened immediately, dissolving into Nick's embrace, allowing himself to be pressed to the door, his hair, neck, and torso mapped by Nick's seeking hands as Nick coaxed Jared's mouth open to let him inside. Jared didn't require much convincing. Essentially, Nick asked, and Jared gave him what he wanted, tangling with him, shifting his head, yielding his mouth and his tongue. When Nick finally broke the kiss, Jared was breathless and fully aroused, gazing hazily at his lover.

Nick brushed his lips across Jared's nose, smiling.

Jared threaded his fingers over the fuzzy back of Nick's head. *I can kiss him anytime I want to, now. For as long as I want to.* He kissed Nick's chin. "Welcome home."

They lingered together a second longer, but then they put themselves to rights and brought the last of Nick's things in. He didn't have much, mostly clothes and a few boxes. It worried Jared a little, making him think this was an experiment for Nick, not a real move. But he didn't want to bring them down, so he didn't push. *He's here. He'll go get more things later, in his own time. Enjoy him right now.*

There was plenty to enjoy. Nick had been in the house before, but now he was establishing himself in the place. Putting clothes in drawers, books on shelves, toiletries in cupboards. Jared's favorite thing Nick brought was a bright-red mug, narrower on the bottom than the top, that had his name and title stamped on one side and the St. Ann's Medical Center logo on the other.

"It was a gift from Wendy my first year on the job, for Boss's Day," Nick explained when Jared remarked on it. "I like the shape and size of it. Perfect for my morning cup of coffee."

"That brings up a good question. What's your morning routine? Do you like coffee at a particular time? Do you work out? When do you shower?"

"I use the PT gym equipment to work out when I arrive at the hospital early enough, but otherwise I go to the community center a few times a week. I prefer to get to the hospital by seven so I have some time to myself before the day gets going. At home—at my grandmother's house, I mean—she'd have oatmeal waiting for me, and some bacon and eggs and toast, but I only ate the oatmeal."

"Oatmeal's my breakfast of choice as well. I prefer steel-cut in the slow cooker because I can set the timer so they're done at exactly the right hour. If you want, I can make enough for two. I usually go in around seven also, either to do rounds or catch up on charts, so our timing is about right. I'll set the timer on the coffeepot for then too. Unless you're fussy about having pour-over coffee instead of automatic drip?"

Nick blinked at him. "Why would I be fussy about something like that?"

"Everyone has something they're fussy about. A coffee-brewing method is an easy one to pick. Have you not seen how many different ways Gus makes coffee in his shop?"

"Gus's shop where you gave Matt Engleton your phone number, you mean?"

Jared blushed and averted his gaze. "And here I thought I was the gossipy one." He cleared his throat. "You don't need to worry about Matt."

"I think I'll decide that on my own, thank you." Nick didn't seem too upset, though, too busy looking around, taking everything in. "It's weird to think I actually went and did it. Moved out, I mean. Good weird, but still weird."

Jared couldn't stand it anymore. He had to bring it up. "You hardly brought anything."

"Yeah, well, every time I packed something up, Mom and Grandma hovered over me, acting like I was carrying out a family heirloom. I decided to start with the essentials and bring more over casually. Honestly, I don't have a lot of stuff to begin with. Most of what I have at their house are things from when I was younger. Old comics, board games, movies, yearbooks, things that meant something to me in high school and I can't throw away but don't exactly need to cart around."

"Mmm." Jared leaned against the counter. "Not me. If the situation were reversed, I'd show up in a U-Haul."

"Well, it's convenient, then, that I came to you." Nick stepped into the living and dining room areas, craning his head back to take in the ceiling. "I like this place. It's older, but it's been remodeled?"

"Yes. The inside was completely redone before we bought it. All new wiring, floors resurfaced, walls and ceilings restructured. They even moved the stairs. The garage wasn't attached either, but the breezeway was added, a huge plus. Basement partially finished as well, except that's largely empty as Owen had used that as his weight room."

Nick perked up at this. "Weight room? I could get into that."

"We'll have to refurnish it, as Owen took his equipment with him when he moved out. He had a TV rigged up and everything, though half the time he listened to music or books."

"Do you know what I could really use? A home office. I sort of made do with the dining room table and an old writing desk in the foyer, and it's not the same as a space you can make your own mess in."

"Then a home office you shall have. Would you like it to be upstairs, or down?"

They wandered through the house together considering options, starting with the small space on the first floor Jared currently used as his own office, storing tax receipts and various thises and thats. It wasn't very large, however, and as Jared pointed out, better suited to someone storing things rather than hanging out in it. "I'd give it to you if you wanted it, because all this junk could be anywhere. But since there are two open bedrooms upstairs, I'm thinking you'd rather have one of them."

"I'll need to use a room for my clothes and make it look as if I'm living there. I could double it as my office."

Oh, yes. There was that part of this arrangement, wasn't there? "Well, you can have both rooms, then. It depends on what you want to use each one for. Simon's old room is smaller but cozy. Owen's is larger and better suited for an office if you want to put in bookcases and things like that."

Nick rubbed his chin as he followed Jared up the stairs. "Bookcases, huh? I could make my own little library. Sweet."

"We'll get you a reading chair and a nice lamp. I'm assuming you read as much as you ever did?"

"Not as much as I'd like. Never enough time in the day. I try to make time before bed, but sometimes I can't focus on anything." He stuck his head into Owen's old bedroom, which now only had a bed and a dresser in it. "This would make a good office, you're right. Those windows look over the backyard?"

"They do. And we could move the bed to the attic. We might want to move Simon's old bed and shift this one to the spare bedroom—your fake bedroom." Jared paused. "I mean, I assume you'll be sleeping with me?"

Nick turned around and favored Jared with a smoldering smile. "Oh, I'll be sleeping with you, yes. I'll need to be good, though, about keeping everything of mine in that other room. I'm fairly sure my grandmother and mother suspect me, which means they'll come over here and make an excuse to verify." He frowned. "I hope they come over, anyway."

This was a lot of work to avoid a conversation, but it wasn't Jared's conversation to have. *Focus on the fact that he's here with you.* "Well, do you want to shop for furniture in town, or online?"

Nick rubbed his chin. "I'd rather do it in town, but I don't know I want the fuss it'll cause."

Okay, Jared had put up with about as much of this as he could take. "Look. You can't hide the fact that you're living here. You can offer an alternative version of why that is, but people are going to notice you're driving here instead of your grandmother's house. Where you buy furniture isn't going to change that." He decided not to mention the subliminal PDAs or he might not get more in the future.

"I know, I just…." Nick sighed. "You're right. Fine. Let's do it in town."

Jared checked his watch. It was Saturday, and not even noon. "Want to go now?"

Nick laughed. "Right now?"

"Petersen's Home Furnishings is open until three. We can pick out some things, eat some lunch, then come back and hang out until it's time to go shopping for dinner. Which I can make for you or we can make together."

Nick put his hands in his pockets, considering. Then he cast a wry smile Jared's direction. "Add in a little window-shopping at the clothing store and you're on."

"Clothing store? You need clothes?"

"Yes. I'm going to buy my new roommate a tie." Nick's expression was wicked. "Matt works the weekend, right?"

Jared laughed. "Yeah. I think he does."

"That settles it, then." Nick caught Jared's elbow and led him toward the stairs. "Let's go shopping."

SHOPPING WITH Jared was, in essence, Nick's second covert date with his lover. Third, he supposed, if he counted lunch with him at the clinic. Of all their times together, however, the outing to find office furniture and settle him into their now-shared home was both the most dangerous and wonderful experience he'd had with Jared.

It was fun to shop together. Jared emphasized how this was largely about creating a space for Nick, insisting he needed it as a man with so much on his plate. Jared's protective instincts, his determination to make him feel at home, moved Nick. "I want you to think of what colors you like for your office," he kept saying. "We'll repaint it however you want."

When Nick suggested he'd like to paint the walls a rich hunter green, they found rugs and furniture to match. Jared found a lush paisley overstuffed chair and ottoman and a lamp he said would go great in the corner, as well as a long row of bookshelves that went with the woodwork of the large desk Nick selected. They found a desk chair and love seat as well.

"So what do you say?" Jared asked as they left. "Curtains next, paint, or lunch?"

"Oh, I want to buy you that tie." Nick aimed them toward Engleton's.

Like most professional adults in Copper Point, Nick shopped regularly at Engleton's Fine Clothing. The department store in what was left of the mall didn't quite have the style he wanted, and he liked supporting local retailers, even if it meant paying a little more. They had an exceptional selection of suits and business casual wear, but they also had a nice range of upscale shirts, sweaters, and higher-end jeans and khakis.

He didn't need anything in the store today, but as he entered with Jared, he scanned the racks, taking everything in as if he were here to make a major purchase. What he was truly looking for, of course, was the store manager. Not a difficult thing, as Matt Engleton had spotted them and was already headed their way, salesman smile firmly in place. Except Nick felt there was something extra in his expression, put there for Jared.

Jared leaned in close to Nick, whispering before Matt came close enough to hear. "Not that I'm not flattered by your urge to piss a circle around me, but how are you going to do this without letting him know you're gay?"

"I don't know," Nick murmured through his own smile. "I haven't thought that far ahead."

"Might be something to consider. Just saying. Unless today's the day you plan to come out to everyone." He ran a hand across Nick's elbow before pulling away and greeting Matt with a wave. "Hello again."

"Hello yourself." Oh, but he put far, far too much suggestion in that greeting, especially compared to the more formal one Nick received. "Mr. Beckert. Good to see you as well. What can I do for you two fine gentlemen today? Looking for anything in particular?"

A leash for you. Nick didn't say that, but he was a little pricklier than he should have been as he put a hand on Jared's shoulder. "I'd like to buy Jared a tie. Something fancy and unique, but in line with his taste."

If Matt found anything about Nick's declaration strange, he didn't let his reaction register at all. "Certainly. Let's see what we have on the rack, but if none of those are to your liking, I have more in the storeroom."

Matt led them to a tall vertical spinning display of multicolored neckties. "So we have a couple of styles here. There's the traditional tie, coming in more muted colors with the occasional red or blue or yellow for vibrancy, and then we have the more artistic top-shelf tie sets. Not exactly novelty, but a bit more daring than the traditional. Some of them are subdued in color but not design, and the fabric texture might be slightly elevated. But these tie sets come with matching silk squares and cuff links."

Jared tucked his hands behind his back and leaned over as he inspected the rows of ties. "I like these. I was trying to wear bow ties for a while, because the kids like them so much, but these are fun too."

"We have bow ties as well." Matt pulled open a drawer in a display, revealing a set of bow ties as jaunty as the traditional counterparts. "They don't sell as well, but we keep them on hand, in patterns as well as in solids. We also have significantly more we can order, if you decide bow ties are your thing."

Jared turned to Nick. "I don't know, what do you think? Should I be the bow tie doctor?"

Nick's mouth quirked in a smile. "I thought you were the K-pop-performing doctor."

"Yeah, well. That's only in the hospital. This is for every day. We haven't done any of our musical numbers lately anyway, and we do more than just K-pop now, you might have noticed."

"I did notice. I liked the Ariana Grande one you did a few months ago." Nick fingered a bright lavender silk bow tie. "You're right, you haven't been doing as many lately, though."

"Well, it's tough to rehearse now that we don't all live in the same house. We tried for a while, but… you know." Jared shrugged. "People get busy."

He could try to brush it off as much as he wanted, but Nick could tell losing this tradition with Owen and Simon bothered him. Ever since before Nick had come on as CEO, the trio had performed crazy lip sync dance numbers to Korean pop songs when a peds patient was released from the hospital. Shortly after Jack showed them up by legitimately performing Asian pop with members of his string quartet at a Founder's Day event—they could all sing as well as they played—Jared, Owen, and Simon had branched into domestic pop too, which frankly went over better with the kids. The thing was, Nick knew at the end of the day it was Jared who loved performing most of all, and he hated seeing it end.

"You guys have so much in your repertoire. You could recycle things," Nick pointed out. "But make those guys get together and practice with you. How long can it take?"

"Well, part of it is the increased surgery schedule. Before we weren't very busy, but now we always are. I can't make patients wait for surgery or discharge because of a song. Maybe I should switch to magic acts. That would be something I could do on my own. And I could justify a fun bow tie fetish."

Matt perked up. "That sounds great! I used to dabble in magic in high school and college."

Jared let go of the ties, all his focus on Matt. "Oh? Let's see a trick."

"Well, I don't know about a trick, but I do have an imaginary coin." Matt withdrew his hands from his pockets and held out his left palm, which was empty, and made a circle with his right index finger, as if tracing an invisible quarter. "You can't see it, but it's there. Now, if you believe a little harder and use your imagination—" He closed his left fist, then tapped the back of it with his right hand a few times in various places. When he opened it, there was indeed a quarter in his left palm.

Jared stared at the coin, mouth hanging open. "How did you do that?"

Nick glared at Matt's palms. Yes, how had he done it? And damn it, how had he stolen Jared's attention like this? This hadn't been in the plan.

Matt held up the coin by two fingers and winked at Jared. "Ah, but this is an imaginary coin, remember? If you don't keep believing in it, it'll go away." He nodded at Nick. "I don't think Mr. Beckert believes in my magic. He's trying to catch me up. If we're not careful…." He closed his fist over the coin, tapped around it once more, and sure enough, as he lifted his other hand with a flourish, the coin was gone, no sign of it even as he turned both his palms around.

Jared's whole face lit up. "That's *amazing*. Perfect for kids too. Can you teach me?"

Nick grimaced. *Oh, hell.*

"But of course." Matt made a small bow. "You have my number. Let me know when you'd like a lesson."

"I absolutely will." Jared turned to Nick, beaming. "Magic tricks. Do you think I could pull them off?"

It was the way he'd been so eager to get *his* approval, not his rival's, that undid Nick. He returned Jared's smile. "Yes. I think you can do it. I'll help you practice every night."

He'd spoken sincerely, intending only to show Jared his support, but no sooner were the words out of his mouth than he realized how it sounded, what he'd accidentally done.

Matt frowned. "Every night?"

Jared appeared torn as he glanced at Nick, silently pleading for a way to respond. Of course, this only increased Matt's alarm.

Nick, however, was finally feeling pretty good. He rubbed his chin and cast an apologetic glance at Matt. "Ah. Well, we're housemates now."

It was absolutely delicious the way Matt's eyes widened. "*Housemates?* You're living together?"

Jared fidgeted, clearly unsure how to play this. "I… well, yes, as of today, in fact." He cast a pointed glance at Nick that said, very plainly, *Rescue me.*

Nick was happy to, especially since Matt had watched each one of Jared's glances and read more into them than Jared intended. With anyone else, Nick would have panicked, but with this guy…. "We were both looking for different living arrangements, it turns out, and so we teamed up. We've been friends for a long time, after all."

Matt nodded dumbly. He seemed a bit in shock.

Jared apparently didn't know what to do with himself and kept touching the hair at his ear and casting awkward glances at Nick. "So. I suppose I should pick one of these ties."

Nick shook his head. "Oh no, I'm buying you at least five."

"*Five?* That's too many."

"Five is the minimum, so you'd better start picking."

Matt plastered on his salesman's smile and gestured to the display as he backed away. "I'll leave you gentlemen to it, then. Let me know if you need anything."

As soon as they were alone, Jared leaned into Nick's side and jabbed him lightly with his elbow. "I think you broke him."

Nick thought he had too, and he wasn't sorry. "All I did was tell the truth."

"Yes, but you enjoyed it a little too much."

"Are you telling me you want him to keep flirting with you?"

"No," Jared said, but Nick took note of the heaviness of the word.

Matt Engleton was a rival to be feared.

Neither one of them brought up Matt again as they focused on the ties. There were so many options to choose from that they began making piles. Jared was drawn to the bright colors, though not all of them would look good on him. Jared's favorite was one called Stratos, full of bold red, blue, gold, and black and accented with geometrics, but it didn't suit his coloring at all.

"It would look amazing on *you*, though," Jared pointed out, holding it up to Nick's neck. He smiled. "Yes, it's perfect."

"I'm not really a bow tie kind of guy."

"Maybe you should be. We could set a new Copper Point trend. And then—*oh*." Jared's face lit up. "I know. You could get some bow ties, learn magic with me, and be my assistant when it worked with your schedule! That has to be good hospital PR, right?"

It was fortunate no one else was in this section of the store, that the only person paying attention to the two of them was Matt. Because Nick couldn't help how he smiled at Jared, couldn't contain the thrill he had at the image his lover had just conjured. Nick would be in the middle of paperwork or a boring meeting, but then Wendy would call, or better yet Jared himself would appear and lead Nick down to the patient wing, where they would perform together for children. But first they'd have a little time together in Nick's office, or a quiet space somewhere else, for Jared to fuss over Nick's tie, straightening edges and smoothing it out.

And wouldn't it be even better if everyone knew the two of you weren't simply living together, that you were together, full stop?

The thought came out of nowhere, arresting Nick with dual tracks of longing and fear. He wanted that imagined future so much his teeth ached. At the same time, he feared it because he couldn't imagine it actually coming to pass, not for him, not as perfectly as he saw it in his mind. For that fractured second, though, he felt the possibility of it, and he yearned for it.

Let me have this. Let me have this with him. Somehow.

He shook himself out of his distraction and fingered the tie Jared had picked out for him. "I'd love to be your assistant. It sounds wonderful."

His expression soft, Jared leaned into Nick. "Then we'll have to pick you out some ties too." He straightened as he realized how close he stood to Nick, how much he touched him, and some of his light went out as he stepped away. "Sorry. I'll do better."

The words pierced Nick, twisting darkness over his private fantasy of being exposed. "Let's find some ties," he said quietly.

Find ties they did. They made two piles, ties for Nick and ties for Jared, the Jared pile of course being much larger.

"I feel like I have too many," Jared said, worrying his bottom lip.

"Just get what you like. This is all on me."

Mmm, but Nick liked the way that made Jared blush. He also liked that Jared didn't argue any further, just kept making selections.

Funny how the ties spoke to their individual tastes and styles but also joined them at the same time. Nick had selected most of Jared's ties, and Jared most of Nick's. In addition to the dark-colored Stratos, Nick ended up with a bright-red tie with subtle paisley and stripes and faint white spots, and another red one called Cinnamon Stripe that had bold red stripes next to patterned red and black with white spots. Jared's favorite he selected for Nick was called Tangelo, a plain orange tie with fabric so softly patterned it drew the eye, and against Nick's dark skin it made his whole face seem to glow. Nick's favorite, though, was one called Teal Pond, a dark, almost denim-blue background with teal, brown, and gold paisley.

Jared meanwhile stayed in lighter colors, pinks, blues, purples, and greens. One tie was vibrant purple with white flecks. Another Nick selected because he suspected the kids would love it. With bright colors in an abstract paisley, Park Avenue worked with Jared's fair complexion because the base was light blue. Many of his ties had a blue base. The most charming tie, though, was Brisk Energy, a lavender and pink gradient tie with subtle geometrics.

But they also got a few ties that matched in pattern while varying in hue. The idea was Jared could wear the one tie and Nick would wear the counterpart on the days they did magic tricks. The problem was, by the time they had all the ties tallied, they had over twenty between the two of them.

"I want to get something for you too." Jared shifted to the spinning rack of tie tacks and tie bars without waiting for permission. Nick didn't argue, nor did he interfere with Jared's selection. He was too lost in a new fantasy, one where every day of the week he went to work either wearing a tie matching Jared's or the pin Jared had gifted, a quiet but constant reminder that Nick was taken. Tied and pinned down.

They took their stack of purchases to the counter, and Matt met them at the register, still wearing his official smile. Jared, giddy from the experience, explained their plan to him as he rang up the pile of Nick's ties and tie bar, holding a few of them up to Nick's neck to show them off.

Matt nodded and smiled, but as Jared turned away with his bag to tuck his wallet into his jeans and Nick slid into his place at the register, Matt lifted an eyebrow at him as if to say, without a word, *You're just friends, are you?*

Nick lifted both his eyebrows in reply and stared right back. *Absolutely not.*

He wasn't sure if it was a good idea, but in that moment he didn't care. Something told him Matt understood the whole of their game.

Matt busied himself with ringing up Nick's purchases. He was yielding… for now. A second glance at him included a warning, though. *I won't stand in your way. But you'd better not hurt him.*

Nick nodded curtly and cast his gaze at the nest of ties, at the bright and pastel colors tangled together.

JARED HAD thought about looking up some magic tricks as soon as he got home, but the door was barely shut before Nick took him into his arms, divested him of his shopping bag, and pulled him forward for a kiss.

It was a soft, slow claiming, but everything about it promised the kind of contact Jared had dreamed of since the Sunday Nick had stayed over, except this time Nick wasn't going to go home afterward and leave Jared feeling bereft. Nick was already home.

Jared surrendered immediately, giving up on every other idea he'd had for how the evening would go, content to let Nick back him toward the couch, to lie down on it and extend his hands over his head as Nick settled himself atop him, never moving too far away from his lips. He shut his eyes and melted into the feel and taste of Nick, the joy of having him here, now.

Nick had no hesitation tonight, not a moment's doubt as he peeled away first Jared's clothing and then his own. With one hand he braced himself against Jared's shoulder, the other hand holding on to Jared's hip, his mouth sliding a patient, erotic path, lingering in the divot of Jared's clavicle, the rise of his sternum. When insistent fingers tugged at one nipple, Nick's mouth closing over the other, Jared let out a sigh and arched his back, his cock filling with his desire.

"I want to savor every inch of you," Nick whispered into Jared's chest, punctuating the thought with a flick of his tongue. "I want to take you to our bed and make you cry out all night long."

Jared cried out now, heart catching on that word. *Our.* He rested his hands on Nick's hair, kneading into it. "Do it. All of it."

"I want to mark you, leave evidence of my claim across your skin. Hidden where only we know where it is, but waiting all the same, for you to undress and be reminded. For you to disrobe for me and show me that you're mine, and I'm yours."

Jared whimpered and slid his body suggestively against Nick's.

Nick buried his face in Jared's abdomen, kissing his way along the slope to the erect cock that bobbed for him. "I want to suck you until you don't know how to speak, to work you open until you're so pliant and ready you spread open for me, then gasp as I enter you."

Hands tight on Nick's head, Jared pushed him farther down. *Go ahead and get started on that.*

Nick went, but after he spread Jared's legs open, he only kissed his thighs, as if he knew this would drive Jared out of his mind and wouldn't have it any other way. "I want to do this or a variation on it every single night, in every room of this house. Then I want to take you to bed, to our bed, where wc sleep together, twined limbs, bodies tangled in our shared sheets, losing ourselves in each other, our dreams, then waking up together. Every single day."

Jared almost sobbed. "*Yes*."

It was the sound of his surrender, of yielding, except Jared had already given in long ago. He was Nick's for whatever he wanted tonight, and what Nick seemed to want was for Jared to stop thinking, stop being anything but pleasure. This was something Jared could easily give him. As Nick closed his mouth at last over Jared's heat, as he gently cupped his balls, Jared melted further, giving up all his control to Nick.

Only give this to me, Nick telegraphed as he sucked Jared's orgasm down.

Only to you, Jared replied with his body, his mind, his soul, his everything.

When Jared was wrung and spent, Nick smoothed his hand over Jared's quivering thigh. Jared's leg was bent double where Nick had pressed them together. "Still keeping lube in the end table drawers?"

"N-n-no, I…." Jared rested the back of his hand over his eyes as he fought for breath. He'd been too busy fantasizing about couch canoodling. "I hadn't thought that far ahead this time. Sorry."

Rising, Nick took Jared's hands and helped him onto unsteady legs. "I'm ready to take this show upstairs anyway."

Clinging to his arm, Jared took in their clothing explosion. "What about all this?"

"We'll let the maid get it," Nick quipped, urging him forward.

"I actually have a housekeeper. Two of them, in fact. When the three of us lived together, we used to take turns cleaning, but it's too much on my own. Don't worry, it's no one who will spread gossip. Jack hooked me up with Mr. Zhang's friends who relocated here. They have the massage place out in the old mall, but they do cleaning too. They do excellent work. I had Jack teach me enough Mandarin I could leave thank-you notes."

Nick nodded. "I know the place you're talking about. My grandmother loves them, and I've gone with her a few times myself. I didn't know they also did cleaning."

"I've gone for massages too. I hate how they have to go to such lengths to make it clear they're not *that* kind of Asian massage place, but I think at this point their reputation speaks for itself. They're good, but the flexibility of being able to walk in whenever you need your shoulders straightened out is highly attractive all on its own. Anyway. They know some English, but even if they figure out exactly what we're doing here, they aren't going to spread rumors the way other cleaning companies would. Maybe they'll talk to each other, but that doesn't bother me."

"Me either. It sounds perfect. I'll contribute to their fee, of course." Nick swatted lightly at Jared's ass. "Right now, though, you're getting in the shower."

Jared's eyebrows rose. "Am I?"

"You are. And I'm coming with you."

They made out leisurely under the spray, their kisses heating as Jared pulled the handheld arm down and aimed it at his own backside. He yelped when Nick took over, but didn't fight him, only spread his legs wider and let the water sluice between his cheeks and against his balls. Jared wondered if they'd end up having sex in the shower, but no, Nick dried them off and led them to the bedroom, where he put Jared on his hands and knees, stood beside him at the edge of the mattress, and—

"*Ohgod.*" Jared's elbows gave out as Nick kissed his way down Jared's crack, parting his cheeks with his palms as he ambled toward his target.

Nick remained unhurried, rimming him as if he had nothing else to do that day, week, or possibly the rest of the year. Only when Jared was whimpering and desperate did Nick pull away, find the lube from the bedside drawer, and slip a finger inside.

When Nick sat on the mattress, still fingering him, Jared happily followed the nudge to take his lover into his mouth, working his cock with the same slowness his ass received. He didn't attempt to hurry the pace or take them in different directions, only did as Nick bid him.

It felt good to let go. To enjoy sex with his lover, in his house, in *their* house. It felt good to brace himself against the mattress, face turned to the side as Nick pumped into him, to tangle with him on the comforter, kissing softly.

What was truly wonderful, though, was slipping into sweats afterward and padding to the kitchen with him, making grilled cheese sandwiches and tomato soup for a simple supper, watching a random home and garden show on the television while they ate, then holding hands as they went upstairs, standing beside each other at the sink as they brushed their teeth. Then they shed their clothes and climbed into bed in the darkness, where they kissed some more and giggled like little boys, then held each other and went to sleep.

In the morning, Nick was there when Jared woke up, the first light of dawn cast across his face, dancing on his long lashes. Heart caught in his chest, Jared burrowed under the covers and curled up beside him, reaching out to stroke the silky, springy curls.

Oh, but he could get used to this.

CHAPTER TWELVE

NICK WOULD have loved to spend a lazy Sunday with Jared in bed, but he knew today more than any day it was vital he return to the house to take his family to church.

He left his lover buried in the comforter, indulging in a moment to run his fingers through Jared's hair, memorizing the shivering feel against his skin before straightening his tie and heading out.

His family was ready and waiting for him as he arrived, except only Emmanuella was happy to see him. His mother had her arms folded and seemed like she wanted to lecture but was holding her tongue, and his grandmother simply didn't look at him. It was an awkward ride across town, and not even finding his grandmother's favorite gospel hits station on satellite radio eased the tension.

Of course, he found no relief in church itself.

Nick had been coming to New Birth since he was very young, except for the decade or so he'd been away to college and then working out of town, and even then he'd come back regularly. While he hadn't been born in Copper Point, it was the only place he could remember, and church growing up had been as much of a home as his own house. His family had always been involved in everything regarding church. They were all in the choir, and Nick had been an usher since age fifteen, but his father had also been a deacon, and his mother was in charge of Sunday school until six years ago, when she said it was time for her to retire. In fact, his mother kept her hand in there somewhat, overseeing lessons and filling in whenever a teacher called in sick. Ever since coming back to town, Nick had been a deacon too.

He'd no sooner parked the car than he was surrounded by what felt like half the congregation: men wanting to chat, women wanting his attention, children looking up at him with bright eyes. Today, though, the glances were a little troubled. It was Copper Point; everyone already knew Nick had moved out and where he'd gone.

The notable exception was James. He grinned as he congratulated Nick on his change of address and promised to stop by with a loaf of banana bread as a housewarming gift.

Pastor Robert didn't preach against homosexuality every single Sunday. It was more like once a month, and it seemed to be part of a standard package. The week after Owen and Erin got engaged, Pastor had emphasized that while homosexuality was an abomination to God, good Christians didn't reject people who were sinners.

Being gay wasn't condoned and absolutely wasn't encouraged. It didn't mean automatic expulsion, but there were unstated rules on how someone gay would behave. James was Exhibit A. He'd never formally come out, and he *never* held hands in public, but everybody knew he was gay, and most had seen him with a boyfriend at city festivals and out to eat. Every now and again someone questioned whether or not it was right for him to lead the choir while being gay, but since Pastor wasn't making a fuss, no one else did more than talk. However, nobody who belonged to the church had ever been a married homosexual.

All of this was subtext. The sermons were pulpit policy. They'd made Nick's stomach turn when he was a teenager, sending him home with a stomachache so acute he couldn't eat dinner too many times to count. Nick didn't digest them any better as an adult. Because all he heard was, *We will still love you if you're a sinner, but you're not a full person, not once you come out.* Gay people weren't to be hurt, but they certainly weren't accepted in quite the same way.

He knew some version of this sermon was going to come again today, but this time that not-exactly-subtle message would be aimed at him.

As he walked with his mother on his left and his grandmother on his right, Emmanuella drifting alongside them, waving to people as they approached the front door, the walls of the world seemed to be pressing in on Nick's body. He felt as if when he went inside the structure of the church, it would crush him like a weight, stealing his breath. People spoke to him, smiled at him as they waited for the service to begin, told him what a wonderful job he was doing at the hospital.

However, that wasn't all they brought up.

"Heard you moved out of your grandma's house." One of the other deacons raised his eyebrows meaningfully at Nick, and others around him hurried to chime in.

"Oh, but he didn't just move out. He moved *in*."

"Yes, with that gay pediatrician. Where in the world is your head, son?"

"You got something you want to tell us?"

Some of them laughed at this joke, but one older woman didn't so much as crack a smile. "This ain't no joke, folks. How's this look, Nick, to have you potentially influenced in such a manner?"

And just like that, the mood shifted.

"It's not right."

"No, sir, it ain't."

"Nick, you gotta reconsider."

Nick did his best to smooth things over, mostly avoiding the topic as best he could, nodding and smiling at them, teasing them about butting into his business, thanking them for their concern. He understood completely this was all it was. Their objections were well-meant, voiced in order to protect a member of the community.

It hurt that he hadn't come out and the censure had already started.

He was relieved when his grandmother said she didn't want to linger after the service and asked to be taken home. The ride back wasn't any less awkward than the one there, but Nick preferred the quiet of his family's awkwardness to that of the church at this moment. He looked forward to his grandmother's cooking, even if he had to endure her glaring at him while he enjoyed it.

But to his shock, when he started to come inside the house, his grandmother shook her head.

"You should get on home to that boy. He's probably waiting for you."

Nick's blood ran cold, his entire body abruptly leaden. "But—Grandma, I always eat Sunday lunch with—"

Unsmiling, she withdrew a bag from the vestibule and passed it to him. "Go on. You've made your choice." She pushed the bag into his arms and turned away, speaking over her shoulder as she disappeared inside. "We'll see you next week."

His mother followed with another cool glare tossed his direction. Emmanuella was the only one who lingered, casting worried, frustrated glances between the women and Nick. She took his hand and squeezed it. "Are you okay?"

No. He wasn't. But he gripped her palm to reassure her. "I'll be fine. Go on with them. You know they're not as level about this as they seem."

She hesitated, then nodded before heading inside. "I'll call you later, okay?"

Reeling, Nick drifted back to his car, where he sat for several seconds, digesting what had just happened.

He peeked into the bag she'd handed him. It contained a dozen fresh-made sweet rolls, carefully wrapped.

He drove home in a daze, taking the long way around the bay to where Lake Superior officially began. He stopped his car at the lookout point, stared out at the gray-blue expanse of water, and lost himself in the waves, in the peacefulness of the quiet, letting it eat his loneliness. He thought about the day they'd all spent on the boat, of the hope and happiness he'd felt then. He remembered the brightness of Jared's face and how he'd thought about having children with him.

Moving more quickly now, he got in the car and hurried back to Jared's house. Nick worried Jared wouldn't be there, that since Nick had said he'd be gone through lunch, Jared would have left to eat somewhere.

Maybe he's gone to eat lunch with Matt. Nick's heart twisted, and he drove a little faster.

But Jared's car was in the garage, and when Nick rushed into the kitchen through the side door, Jared was there, leafing through a cookbook. He glanced up in surprise.

"Oh—I thought you weren't—" He got a better look at Nick's face and shut the cookbook, crossing to touch his shoulders. "What happened?"

Nick didn't know what to say. For several seconds he stared at Jared, vulnerable and helpless.

Jared lifted a hand to Nick's face, stroked his cheek, smoothed over his hair. "Have you eaten?"

Throat thick, eyes dangerously blurry, Nick shook his head.

"Then let's make lunch together. And perhaps we'll treat ourselves to something sweet after. What would you like?"

A pineapple upside-down cake, so I can eat it warm and fresh from the oven, with the sun streaming through the window. Nick swallowed the lump in this throat. "Maybe some oatmeal cookies?"

Jared kissed his cheek and took his hand, leading him to the counter.

IN JARED'S opinion, no matter how you sliced it, board meetings were exceptionally dull.

Administration was not his forte. He enjoyed interacting with patients. He wanted to be with people, particularly children. He liked cracking jokes, being in charge of the room, and making people feel better. Meetings, in contrast, were about getting things done, except he never seemed to be a person in charge of doing anything. He was always the guy who listened, maybe made a suggestion, but it would never go anywhere until more debate and fussing happened, if it went anywhere at all. He had yet to be involved in any organized body that met to make decisions that didn't ultimately chase its own tail.

He had to say, since the incident with the elevator, things had gotten a lot more interesting in the board room, but unfortunately, it wasn't interesting in a good way. Everyone was cognizant of the precarious financial situation St. Anne's was in, one made worse because now they had to figure out a way to fund a new hospital without upsetting the community. A daunting task, especially for a brand-new board.

"I'm passing around the figures from Gilbert's most recent report," Erin said as he walked around the room handing out papers. "We've discussed this already in general, but now you have before you the specific breakdowns for their assessments. If you continue reading, you'll see an additional paragraph outlining the full details of why the Gilbert firm believes these costs are accurate. We have asked for this level of accounting from all the other places that have given us estimates, but they aren't able to provide much detail."

Gus grimaced at the papers in front of him. "Well, okay. Nothing about this is very good, is it? I mean, why won't the other companies give us detail, especially when faced with the discrepancy?"

Beside him Matt had a similar expression. "Honestly, this is looking like a conspiracy."

Amanda waved her papers at Matt and Gus. "It's that Peterson guy, no question. He's got to be behind this."

"But what good would having them lowball the figures do?" Simon asked.

"Who knows? Maybe they wanted us to commit to repairing only to find ourselves in over our heads when the adjusted estimates came in. Maybe they planned to win the bid so they could drag it out and take more time and allow more of Peterson's plans to unfold." Erin grimaced. "All I can tell you is that Peterson wants this hospital, and since we've said we won't agree with his plans willingly, he intends to bend us to his will by whatever means necessary. Consider this part of that scheme."

Jacob, always a little nervous, began to pale. "What are we supposed to do?"

"First of all, we calm down." Rebecca stared at her papers and tapped her pencil against the table beside them. "We can't assume this is Peterson and his plan, even though it probably is. We have to have proof, and a clear trail. And intent."

At the head of the table, Nick glanced at Erin, who nodded before Nick began to speak. "Well, funny you should mention that. I don't have documents yet to support this, and I'm going to have to ask this information stay inside this room for now. But we received word this morning from Gilbert there is possible evidence—possible, mind you—that the elevator had been tampered with, and this was the reason for its failure."

For several seconds, the entire table was silent.

Jared didn't know what to say. He couldn't think. Tampered with? As in sabotage? That meant someone wanted the elevator to fail.

That meant someone wanted him… and Nick….

He glanced at Nick, who regarded him with a grave expression. Jared reached for the glass of water in front of him. Good God.

Owen was the first to come out of his stupor, fueled by rage. "So you're telling me someone wanted to hurt people? In our hospital? Are you kidding me? Why don't you have the police involved in this?"

Nick gave him a long, weary look. "We had this argument the last time there was a problem with the hospital. The police in this town are not exactly the sort you run to when you have a problem unless you have them in your pocket. Until we have proof and can rule out this wasn't done by someone who has the police on their side, we have to keep this between us and Gilbert. Gilbert is fully aware of what they've discovered. They also understand the situation with Copper Point law enforcement. They were the ones who advised Erin and me to keep this quiet until they had at least some discernible proof, which they're searching for. Once they have that, it doesn't matter whose side the police are on. They're going to have to take this seriously, especially once we share this with the newspaper."

Simon, who had been sitting quietly through all this, finally came to life. "Oh my God. Do we have to play amateur detectives again?"

Erin shook his head. "No. We have Gilbert doing our work for us this time. They've asked us specifically to stay out of it and let them do their job. We trust them, and we're hoping you all will too. They're looking for the security guards who were working that night, though so far they haven't had any luck. Those two are suspicious because they quit a month after the accident and now can't be found. But that's the big problem—they can't be found. Gilbert is going to keep looking, though. They're going to make some time to meet with the board extensively before the public meeting next week."

Amanda winced. "I forgot about the meeting. How are they going to explain all this to the community? Do they think they'll have answers by then?"

Nick looked grim. "No. They won't have anything at that time, unless some weird miracle falls in their laps. Which means you all need to brace yourselves. The public meeting is going to end up being more vague than we'd planned, and people won't be happy. You're going to get more phone calls. I'm sorry."

Everyone glanced at Jacob, but surprisingly he seemed calm. Nervous, but resigned. "Obviously I'm not eager for that, but this isn't just about my discomfort any longer. This is about the safety of the community. My mother visited the hospital the day of the accident. She could have been in that elevator. I'll think about it every time someone shouts at me on the phone."

"It's vital we don't tell anyone about our suspicions until we have all of the information," Erin said. "Not about the elevator being tampered with, not about the discrepancy in the quotes. This is absolutely a game of PR at this point. If someone tampered with the elevator, they had a goal in mind. It probably wasn't to kill someone, though it does seem like they weren't particularly concerned about people's safety. Likely they wanted to damage the reputation of the hospital, and thereby the reputation of Nick and me and all of us here in the room."

"So what we do now?" Simon asked.

Jack had been quiet the entire time but now signaled Nick that he wanted to speak. He was consistently the only one who attempted to follow rules of order to keep the meetings from becoming a shouting match. "It seems to me we're in a waiting period. We can't do much until Gilbert comes back with the information. We need confirmation that something was indeed wrong, or acknowledgment they can't prove anything either way. We could attempt to figure out who might want us to fail or what else they might be after, but everything at this point is conjecture. I agree, if we attempt to solve this on our own, we might harm the investigation. Personally I think we should continue as we have been and focus on drafting up potential marketing plans for bond issues or however else we would like to raise the money should we need to for a new hospital."

"I agree," Rebecca said. "It's difficult to sit here powerless, but it's essentially what we are. The only ace we have is making sure we know who our allies are and gather them close. We can list our enemies, but a stronger position might be to identify friends. Who are the possible donors? Who are the people who will come forward for us? Who is going to stand with us? Who is going to get in the way? These are all things we can determine now at least to some degree. That's work we can do. Everything else is spinning conspiracy theories. I don't think that gets us anywhere we need to be."

The group descended into a bit of a chaotic discussion for the next fifteen minutes, everyone largely agreeing with what Jack and Rebecca said but wanting time to work out some of their own feelings regarding what they thought might be happening. For his part, Jared was glad when the meeting adjourned and he could follow Nick to his office and discuss some of these things with his boyfriend face-to-face.

"I can't believe someone might have actually tried to hurt us on purpose." Jared paced in front of Nick's desk. "I understand the odds they were targeting you and me specifically are low, but the end result is that someone nearly killed us." He stopped in the middle of the carpet, clenched his fists, and set his jaw. "How in the hell is wrecking an elevator going to get anyone anything? Why would someone do that, and in a hospital of all places? I've already sat up nights thinking of terrible scenarios. What if it had been an elderly couple in the elevator, or a patient? What if it had been someone trying to go to surgery, or a child? A woman in labor?"

Nick wasn't pacing, but he looked as grim as Jared felt. "I understand completely. Gilbert explained this to us on a conference video call, and both Erin and I were so taken aback we couldn't speak for several minutes. Yes, if this is true, it adds a terrible layer to what is already an awful situation. However, to be a bit mercenary—I didn't want to bring this up in the meeting and engender false hopc, but if we can catch who did this and they have any kind of capital, we can consider our new hospital paid for without a single dime from the county."

Jared frowned at him. "I don't understand what you mean."

"I mean we'll sue whoever did this. And if they have money enough, we will take them for every penny they have."

Jared felt a little dizzy. "I suppose this is why you're the administrator and I'm the doctor."

"It was actually Rebecca who thought of it. I brought her in early because I wanted to advise her both as the president of the board and as a lawyer. It was the first thing out of her mouth."

Jared laughed. "Okay, that sounds like Rebecca."

The door was shut, so Nick didn't hesitate to take Jared into his arms, kissing him on the mouth before drawing his head onto his shoulder. "I'm one hundred percent with you on how upsetting it is. I want to catch whoever did it, but we need a lot more detail. Happily, we have Gilbert on the case."

"No *Brooklyn Nine-Nine* references?" Jared traced Nick's ear. "Let's watch more of that tonight, by the way." It was a rerun for both of them, but their first time watching together.

"Can't. We're going over to Owen and Erin's, remember?"

Jared had forgotten. He sighed. "We've barely had a week together. I want more alone time with you."

"I don't plan on going anywhere anytime soon."

"I know. I just want to be greedy."

The truth was Jared looked forward to bringing Nick to one of the family dinners as his official significant other. Once inside their protected space, he wouldn't have to watch how much he touched his lover or mind how lovingly he gazed at him. They could be themselves, could enjoy each other and their company.

He thought about how great it would be all afternoon, to the point he got distracted as he saw patients. "Sorry, busy day," he apologized to one of the mothers with a toddler on her lap.

She smiled. "It's all right. I understand." She nodded at his purple-and-pink bow tie. "I love your new look, by the way."

"Thanks. I'm practicing some magic acts to go with it, for when I release inpatients. Not quite ready for prime time yet, but I'm getting there. I'm better on the ones Mr. Beckert helps me with. He's kindly agreed to act as my assistant."

"It's good to see you two so close," the mother remarked. Then she paused, clearly searching for how to phrase what she was about to say. "I heard… that you were living together now?"

Jared paused as he opened the baby's chart. This wasn't the first time a parent had wanted to discuss his new living arrangements, and there was definitely a pattern. Some were excited for him, convinced he and Nick were going out, no matter what Jared said. Some, however, behaved like this mother, oddly cautious. Jared didn't know what this reaction meant.

"Yes. We're housemates. I wanted someone to share the mortgage with, and it turned out he was looking for something new as well. It all worked out."

"I see." Her smile had an odd tinge to it.

He was in a funky mood when he left the clinic, deciding to hang out in the lobby instead of trekking all the way up the stairs when Nick was due at any second. While he waited, playing a puzzle game on his phone, Uzma came up to him. "Good afternoon, Dr. Kumpel. Done for the day?"

"Yes. Waiting for Nick. What about you? On your way home?"

"I am, thank God. I'm ready to go home and put my feet up and watch a silly movie." She shifted her purse higher onto her shoulder, leaning forward, eyes twinkling. "How are things with you and your new *housemate*?"

Jared hesitated, unsure of how to respond. "Just fine…."

"Good." She winked at him as she turned away. "I'm rooting for you."

She put him in a better mood, and by the time Nick came down, Jared was smiling again. They went home long enough to change and make out a little on the couch, then headed straight over to Erin and Owen's place, where the others were already busy in the middle of meal prep. They welcomed Nick and Jared with open arms and hugs, teasing them for being late and assigning them tasks.

They talked about the board news, everyone wanting to process it more, but since it was a depressing topic with nowhere to go, they didn't linger on it. Instead they focused on Simon and Jack's upcoming wedding.

"I can't believe it's finally almost time! Only two months away." Erin nudged Simon with his elbow as they sat on the couch with their desserts. "Are you ready?"

Simon shuddered. "Absolutely not. It's gotten so out of hand. Between my family and Hong-Wei's, there are so many people coming who want things to be just so—the only thing the two of us want is to get married."

Jack gave his fiancé a reproachful look. "They're coming all this way, and they're being incredibly supportive. The least we can do is accommodate a few special requests."

"Well, you know you can count on us," Owen said, and everyone agreed.

On the surface they were simply having another lazy night with the group, another family dinner. Nothing extraordinary happened. For Jared, the moment was huge. He wasn't the odd man out. He wasn't lonely and trying to hide it. True, he was there with his closeted boyfriend. But for now, it was enough.

When they went back to the house afterward, he and Nick held hands, and they barely made it into the kitchen before they started kissing. They laughed into each other's mouths, explored each other's bodies, unable to stop touching as they wound through furniture and bumped into walls on their way to the stairs and the bedroom.

The house was filling, slowly, with Nick. The kitchen had pears in it, because he liked them. He left his keys on the island or on the stand in the hall by the front door. His shoes seemed to be everywhere at once, never tucked away, simply discarded wherever they fell off his feet. His toiletries were in the cupboard. His books and magazines were littered here and there, as were suit coats and ties. Owen's former bedroom had been cleaned out and painted, and the furniture was due to be delivered the day before the public meeting next week.

The tie bar from Jared was always placed with care on the dresser in the room where Nick kept his clothes. He wore it every day.

They had room for improvement, Jared knew. He wanted Nick's dresser in their bedroom. He wanted to walk along the park with Nick and hold his hand, or at least not worry about whether or not they looked too much like a couple. He wanted to tease him in the grocery store without being cognizant of the eyes on them.

He wanted to not catch his boyfriend trolling Copper Point People, trying to discover evidence of their affair, face furrowing in worry whenever he found something.

Jared wanted these things, but he had so much, he reminded himself. He wouldn't push.

It was enough. He'd make it be enough.

CHAPTER THIRTEEN

IT TURNED out Jared was not a natural-born magician.

He'd long ago lost track of how many YouTube videos he'd watched and how many books he'd read revealing the secrets of magic tricks. The key for him was practicing the sleights of hand, making them so automatic he could misdirect. Jared wanted to use a magic trick to distract, reward, and even possibly aid in therapy for his patients. All of this was so ahead of the horse, though, when he couldn't reliably stick a quarter behind his fingers as he waved them in the air, let alone sneakily slip it into his pocket. He practiced for hours in front of the mirror as well as in front of Nick. Unfortunately, it was clear he wasn't even adequate, let alone proficient.

"Maybe you're going about this the wrong way," Nick suggested one night when Jared was particularly frustrated. "Maybe you shouldn't focus on being an expert magician."

"What do you mean?"

"I think you should allow your patients to see you making mistakes. Maybe you could *teach* them magic tricks. Maybe you could let them see you doing magic badly. There's a lot of ways you could spin it."

It was a brilliant idea. Some of the older patients might find it preferable. He scratched his beard. "Okay, so let's say I went with one of these angles. How do I use my assistant? Because I still want to do that."

Nick considered this. "Well, if I were better at the tricks, we could do an act where you did the trick badly and I did it well."

Jared smiled wickedly. "Now we have to have a contest. Get on over here and show me what you've got, Mr. Beckert."

It shouldn't have surprised Jared to discover Nick was a far better student of magic. He struggled with some of the more complicated tricks, but he picked up many of the basic ones in only a few nights' worth of practice. The devil wasn't apologetic about besting Jared either.

"So we're going with you're the bad magician and I'm the good one?" Nick's eyes danced with mirth.

In answer, Jared threw a pillow at him.

Secretly, of course, he was thrilled they were finally able to put their long-awaited plan into action. On the day before the public meeting, the time had come for them to put their lessons to the test.

Jared was discharging a little boy who had been suffering from acute bronchitis. When Jared said he needed to call in his assistant to help with his trick and Nick came through the door, the child and both adults lit up.

"Mr. Beckert. It's so good to see you," the mother said, her whole demeanor changing.

Jared raised an eyebrow. "Do you two know each other?"

Nick nodded. "Yes. Bobby and his family go to New Birth Baptist. How are you folks doing today?"

"Fine, fine." The father put a hand on his son's shoulder. He was standing a lot straighter now that Nick was here. The mother was still beaming, and Bobby stared up at Nick as if he were a rock star.

Bobby's gaze shifted to the bow ties. He pointed first at Nick's, then at Jared's. "You're wearing the same tie."

Nick crouched to be at Bobby's level, smiling a patient smile that made Jared's heart expand. "*Almost* the same. Can you tell me how they're slightly different?"

Bobby studied the two bow ties carefully for several moments. "They have some different colors."

Nick nodded approvingly. "That's right. Can you tell me what the two different colors are?"

"Yours is red, and Doctor's is blue."

"Excellent job. I think you deserve to see some magic." He glanced up at Bobby's parents, then back at Bobby. "What do you think? Would you like to see a couple magic tricks?"

Both Bobby and his parents agreed, and so Jared made a great show of setting up his trick on the bedside tray, and without trying to, he managed to completely screw it up.

"Oh dear," Jared murmured.

Nick rubbed his chin thoughtfully before picking up the quarter from the red cloth Jared had spread across the table. "Dr. Kumpel, would you let me give this a try?"

With a slight incline of his head, Jared gestured to the space in front of Bobby. "By all means."

With thc deftness Jared envied, Nick handily performed the trick, first making the quarter "vanish," then magically making it appear from behind Bobby's ear. Bobby and his parents clapped, and Nick took a small bow.

Jared clapped as well. "Well, I'm not good at magic, I guess. I suppose I should just stick to medicine."

This part they had also rehearsed. "No, I don't think so," Nick said. "You can't quit practicing when something doesn't go the way you want it to. You have to keep trying. You can't give up when something's difficult."

Jared turned to Bobby, leaning down close as Nick had done. "Do you know, Bobby, I think Mr. Beckert is wise."

Bobby nodded, clutching the quarter Nick had given him as if it were the most sacred talisman in the world.

"That went well, didn't it?" Nick said as they walked away from Bobby's room.

"Yes, I think it did." Jared waved at a passing nurse, who waved back. The two of them were getting a lot of attention as they headed down the hall, everyone commenting on the fact that they wore matching bow ties.

Nick ignored their groupies and kept his focus on Jared. "Bobby is a good kid. I know his family from church, but I remember his mom from school. She was only a few years behind us. I think she works for the quarry as a receptionist, and his dad works in the mines themselves."

"I could tell they have a lot of respect for you. That was cool to see. It made me feel like I was dat—" He cut himself off in time. "—living with a celebrity."

Nick's face clouded a little. "It was always the same way with my dad. Wherever we went, everybody looked up to him. He knew it too. He understood who he was to the community and took his position seriously."

"I think your dad could only be proud of how you filled his shoes," Jared said quietly.

To this, Nick made no reply.

It wasn't the first time Nick sobered when they discussed his family, especially his father. As usual, when Nick took his leave to go to his office and Jared went to the clinic, Jared thought about the reassurances he wanted to give his boyfriend, the things he'd like to point out about what Nick had done, how much he'd achieved, and how unfair it was for anyone to judge his life by something that was an integral part of himself. But he never said any of these things, aware Nick wanted to sort this out on his own.

In any event, Nick was more preoccupied about the public meeting than people's opinion of him. That night Erin and Rebecca came over to the house, rehearsing their parts in the forum and imagining multiple reactions, laying out possible countermeasures that would give Gilbert more time to finish their investigation. Jared kept them supplied with coffee and snacks, but since he felt like he was mostly in the way of the discussion, he ended up reading a book in bed until they were finished. When Nick finally came upstairs, he looked wrung out.

Jared pulled him onto the mattress and wrapped his body around him. "Is everything all right? Can I help?"

Nick reached to pat Jared's arm, lingering to squeeze it gently. "This is a huge help. As for whether or not everything's okay, I doubt it, but we'll shake that out tomorrow."

Nick had left for work already when Jared woke up the next day, and Jared's own clinic time was tight, as he was required to leave at three on the dot to make it over to the board meeting before the public meeting. He managed to be only ten minutes late and slid into place beside Owen.

Allison Christy led the meeting, letting the board know everything Gilbert had discovered so far, which wasn't anything beyond what Nick had told them. People asked a lot of questions, but as far as Jared could tell, nothing new was on the table. What he did take away from the meeting was that hell was about to rain down on them.

"Our anticipation is whoever did this to the elevator will ensure there's significant resistance at the public meeting today. We've monitored some online chatrooms and listservs, and there's a major antiboard effort. Unfortunately, we don't think at this time it's in our interest to push too hard against them. It's almost better to allow them to feel they've won, for now. If they think they have you over a barrel, they might not take additional measures to pressure you until we can identify them. And we do believe we can identify them."

Jacob looked grim but determined. "So the phone calls will keep coming?"

"Yes. Please save any correspondence you receive and send it to our office, and sum up any live or phone conversations. We doubt there will be any real leads there, but we don't want to miss anything."

Jared rode over to the community center with Nick, holding his hand from the passenger side of the car. He studied his boyfriend's face quietly. There was no fear there, only determination.

"You really are amazing, you know?" Jared squeezed Nick's hand. "You care so much about the hospital, this town, and all the people in it. I'm so incredibly proud of you. I hope at least some of the people tonight can see how wonderful you are."

Nick parked the car and killed the engine. He didn't look at Jared, but he didn't let go of his hand, and after several seconds, he lifted it to his lips and kissed it.

"Thank you. For saying that, for being here with me."

I'll always be with you.

The words were on the tip of Jared's tongue, but for some reason they wouldn't go past his lips. Concerned, he swallowed them down and found a smile instead. "Shall we go inside?"

Nick smiled back, and after they exited the car, they walked together to the community center, where a large crowd had started to gather.

Jared allowed himself one more moment's concern over why he'd hesitated to speak out loud, then pushed this aside and focused on being there for the board, for St. Ann's, and for Nick.

THE PUBLIC meeting went as poorly as Nick had anticipated it would.

Some people came with legitimate questions and concerns, but as Allison had warned them, a significant force was present only to stir up trouble. He wondered, as he stood under the shower spray after the meeting was finished, trying to drown out his headache, if perhaps he should have made more of an attempt to round up their allies, or if it was best to let the opposition win for now. It didn't sit well with him to have the board demeaned, to see public opinion dipping so low after all their work.

There'd been a marked absence of New Birth members there, which had surprised him and left him a little depressed. He'd looked for his family but hadn't seen them either.

He couldn't wait to go to bed and put this behind him.

When he came out of the bathroom, though, Jared waited for him in the hallway, appearing slightly agitated. "Your sister is here to see you. She's waiting downstairs." He bit his lip and lowered his voice. "Is that okay? Sorry, I didn't know what to do."

"It's fine." Nick kissed Jared's cheek and briefly curled a hand around his hip. "Baby, go ahead and get some sleep. You look worn out."

"Not as worn out as you. I could make tea or coffee…."

"I got this. Promise." He smiled and ran a hand along Jared's cheek. "Get some sleep. I'll be along in a bit."

He waited until Jared disappeared into their bedroom, and then, after donning a T-shirt from the room where he kept his clothes, Nick padded down the stairs in bare feet, his thin sweatpants whispering against his legs.

Emmanuella was in the kitchen, water for tea already going on the stove. She smiled over her shoulder as Nick came closer. "Hey there. Good job tonight. That was a tough crowd."

"You were there?" He started for a stool at the bar, then stopped as he saw the plastic-covered plate on the island. It was his grandmother's coffee cake, no mistaking it.

Emmanuella pulled plates from the cupboard and set them beside the cake before peeling it open and carving off two slices. "We all were, way in the back. Except Grandma left early because she said, and I quote, 'Those fools aren't worth the time of day.'"

"I'm hoping she meant the audience, and not the board?"

"Of course she meant the audience. She rushed home to bake this and insisted I bring it to you. I wasn't told, but I know full well I'm supposed to find out how you are. So, how are you?"

He sighed. "I'm all right, I guess. Tired. There's a lot more to this than I'm at liberty to say."

"We figured." She pushed a plate and a cup of tea toward him. "Here. She'll want to know if you liked it. She worried it was too dry because she was in a rush."

The cake wasn't dry. It was perfect, doing more to heal Nick than anything else could, save the shelter of Jared's arms. "It's delicious."

"Good. Well, when you finish your slice, give me a tour. This is a nice place you two have got."

Nick did give her a tour, starting with the basement, where he explained his dream setup for weight equipment, ending in his newly finished office that smelled faintly of paint. Emmanuella smiled as she ran her hand over the furniture and the shelves, which so far didn't have much on them.

"This is fantastic. You should bring more of your things over here. Make it more homey. But it's already great. I love this space for you, like a lush Nick oasis."

It was indeed that. Nick liked how she approved of it. "I'm eager to sit in here on a long snowy winter's day, reading and listening to music. Jack's setting me up with a killer stereo system. Should be here next month. Jared told me to get a TV so I can watch the game, if I want."

"Listen to your man and get yourself a TV. You deserve all of it."

Nick tucked his hands into his pockets and rocked on his heels, gaze fixed on the floor. "Are they… still mad?"

Emmanuella shrugged. "I don't know if they've ever been *mad*, exactly."

He snorted. "I haven't been allowed at Sunday dinner since I moved out. They're mad."

"They're working it through. I don't think they're keeping you away because they want to be petty. I think that's still a bridge too far for Grandma. They think about you, though. You notice they tend to visit you Sunday afternoons."

"Do they talk about me? Do they… know?"

"Oh, they know. But they don't talk about that. About you in general, yes. More every day, especially with all the stuff you have going on. I feel like they're trying to find their way through this. I'm doing my best to nudge them forward. I hope you don't think I'm dragging my feet or siding with them."

He looked up immediately. "Absolutely not. Why would I think that?"

Her smile was a little sad. "You're not the only one who worries what people think, okay? You're my brother. My one and only. I want you to be happy, and I want us on good terms. But I want our whole family to be at peace too."

"That's what I want as well. It's all I've ever wanted."

"Funny, I think the four of us are in complete agreement there. How I see it is, everyone's taking their time to get their feelings in order. They're trying to work out how to process this. Personally, I think it's not half as much about you being gay as it is about them having to face how much of their own dreams they put on you, how much you were willing to bear."

"I think religion has a place in this too."

"Well, yes, but I don't think it's the greatest obstacle. Honestly, if you'd gotten a woman pregnant and abandoned her, that would have been a far, far greater sin to them, and you know it. Your orientation is something in their minds that means a harder life for you. They don't want that."

He frowned and met her gaze. "Is that what *you* think?"

"I don't. I mean—yes, I know it means a few more challenges for you, but I also see how happy Jared makes you, and I can glimpse the edges of how much lighter and happier you'd be as your full self. That's worth overcoming any obstacle in my book, and I want to be part of it."

He let out a ragged breath, pressing a hand to his chest as her words pierced him. "I want that too. More every day."

"But you're not ready yet."

He shook his head. "Not now. But… soon. When all this with the hospital is over, maybe."

She shook her head. "You do it when it's right for you, whenever that is. Take your time, get yourself in order, and then, when you're sure, don't let anything else stand in your way. Give yourself that gift, all right?" She took his hand and squeezed.

He pulled her tight into his arms. "Thanks, sis."

She hugged him back. "Anytime."

AS FOUNDER'S Day passed and September approached, Nick and Jared began to find a routine. The gossip around them had died down, most people either believing their story or acknowledging they simply weren't going to admit what was going on and, at least to their faces, allowing them their fiction. Most people were more worked up over what was going on with the hospital than who the CEO might be dating, filling the newspaper with op-eds and letters to the editor, spouting off on Copper Point People or personal Facebook posts. Jared sometimes listened to concerns in his office, though most of those he had to wrap up and ask that they write him an email as he had too many patients to work into a single day to allow for political diversions. Because the Gilbert Group wanted more time for their investigation, the board said that while they were leaning toward new construction, they were exploring options and would go into further details at their November meeting.

More interesting than the developments (or lack thereof) in the situation with the hospital was the slow, incremental thaw between Nick and his family.

Jared figured out early on that when Nick's grandmother, mother, or someone from the church came to visit him, it was Jared's job to make himself scarce. He handled this disappearing act in a number of ways. But like his magic, he was never very good at it. What he wanted to do was stick around, to know if they were making Nick feel better or worse.

It would be a lot easier if Nick's family issues were as cut-and-dried as his own. Jared had never looked back at his own parents, feeling he was better off without them, and he didn't see a reason to change his opinion now. For half a second he considered this might've been the wrong approach, as he'd watched Nick struggle so valiantly to reconcile his orientation with his community, but then Jared decided this was the key point. Community.

Nick belonged to both his family and his church in a way Jared had never known and doubted he ever would. Despite Nick's fears, Jared was certain both would accept him if he came out. Of course there would be friction, and they'd have to acknowledge he wasn't the man they thought he was, but that was the point. The Nick Beckert they thought they knew didn't completely exist. He had an extra bit of a rainbow shine to him they didn't particularly want, but without it he wouldn't be Nick at all.

They'd come around to it, though. Jared would bet his house on that fact.

Jared had nothing remotely like this in his background. His parents would be happy to have him in their life, but the acceptance was a false front, and they had nothing powerful behind their affection. They would never stand up for Jared the way Nick's family did for him, sending Emmanuella over with coffee cake on the night of the public hearing despite their being somewhat at odds. They would never make careful, cautious inroads toward familial peace the way the Beckerts were. No, the Kumpels were all about their way or the highway.

Jared had been fine with the highway.

Jared wanted to say this to Nick, but it felt like it wasn't his place, so he simply removed himself. When someone from the church or Nick's family came over, unless it was Emmanuella alone, Jared pasted on a bright smile and made an excuse to leave.

Not one time did Nick attempt to stop him or tell him once he returned that he should've stayed.

It became his habit rather quickly during these outings to end up at Café Sól. At first he tried to run errands, but they didn't always need anything, and he tended to buy the weirdest kinds of garbage when he was on one of these exiles. He learned it was best to put himself somewhere that he couldn't cause trouble or inspire him to buy another case of toilet paper. This meant going to a friend's house and saying things he shouldn't, or going to Gus's and drowning his sorrows in a cup of coffee.

On a crisp Sunday near the end of September, when Jared walked into the coffee shop, Gus was wiping off a table and stopped to wave at him. "Back again, I see."

"Can't stay away." Jared didn't waste a lot of energy forcing a smile, only glanced around for an empty table away from the afternoon crowd. "Busy in here."

"Yep. It's freshman orientation day, so we're full of parents and soon-to-be students learning all about Bayview University and thc joys of Copper Point. They put us in the booklet, and I offered up a buy-one-get-one coupon, so we're a popular spot." Gus gestured to the coffee bar at the back of the store. "I think there's a free stool next to Matt, though."

Sure enough, there was, and it was the only empty space left in the entire shop. "Thanks," Jared said, trying to sound grateful instead of miserable.

It wasn't the first time he'd run into Matt when he'd left the house so Nick could have it to himself. Matt smiled at Jared as he slid onto the stool. "Hey there, handsome. What's up with you this fine afternoon?"

"Nothing much. Just needed fresh air." Jared grimaced as he glanced around the busy shop. "I think I maybe should have gone to the park instead."

"Nothing says we can't go there now together." Matt motioned to the college-aged barista. "Place your order to go and we'll head on out."

Objectively Jared understood he shouldn't be going on outings with Matt, particularly when he was feeling sullen because he had to leave the house he shared with his boyfriend. But what frustrated him even more was that he wasn't sure how to politely back out of this. Likely Matt understood what he and Nick were doing. So from that standpoint, he could definitely have said to Matt he needed to decline because his boyfriend wouldn't like it. However, his boyfriend also wouldn't like him calling him *boyfriend* to anyone outside of their tight circle.

Maybe Jared should start sitting alone in his car somewhere quiet when he left the house.

"Hey." Matt's voice was full of concern. "Is everything okay? You seem upset. If you'd rather not go anywhere with me, I completely understand. I only want to help."

Something about the gentleness in Matt's tone undid Jared. "Thank you. I do think I want to leave. But if you can put up with me being a little moody, I don't think I'd mind the company."

They were quiet until they stood next to their cars, which happened to be only a few spots away from each other in the parking lot. Matt, with his hands in his pockets, raised an eyebrow. "Shall I drive, would you like the honors, or would you prefer to walk?"

"If you would drive, I'd appreciate it."

Matt took them around the same meandering paths Jared often drove when he needed to think, weaving through some of the prettier residential districts before ending up at the road leading along the bay. This meant they passed Erin and Owen's house.

"I heard they finally set a date," Matt said. "March, right?"

"Yes, though they're still waffling a bit."

"Dad was all over me to offer them some kind of discount if they used our formalwear, but I didn't want to be pushy. I figured it would look awkward since we didn't offer the same deal to Dr. Wu and Simon."

"You can tell your dad he can bank on their business." Jared smiled sadly as his friends' house vanished from view. "They're both big on local support. And despite what people think, it's not going to be a high society wedding. They've toyed more than once with the idea of running down to city hall."

Matt was quiet for a second. "Is it difficult watching them be able to have a public relationship when yours has to remain quiet?"

Jared couldn't decide if he was surprised Matt was so bold, or if somehow he'd seen this coming all along. Eventually he chuckled. "So you *do* know what's going on."

"I figured it out when Nick gave me the stink eye as he bought every bow tie I had, telling me to back the hell off. I was fairly sure it wasn't because he was a possessive roommate. It makes sense. I knew you were hung up on someone, and you said I was twenty years too late, so that meant someone from high school. I thought maybe it was someone who didn't reciprocate your feelings. I was a little bit shocked to discover it was someone who wasn't out. This probably marks me as naïve, but I really thought those days were behind us."

Oh, but it was so tempting for Jared to spill his guts. He made himself take several long, slow breaths before speaking, choosing his words carefully. "I don't feel like I can discuss much about his situation without his permission, but the one thing I can say is living with Nick has taught me it's far, far more complicated than I ever dreamed."

"While I appreciate this in the abstract, I resent what it means for you in the specific."

First Owen and Simon, and now Matt. Jared stared out the window sadly. "You know, I've never resented Nick or my situation. I've disliked it intensely, but I don't resent it."

"But how? You have to at least a little. It isn't fair to you to have to wait for him."

"Whoever told you love was about fair?"

This only made Matt angrier. "It's not right for you, is what I'm saying. You've waited for him this entire time. You're putting your dreams, your life, everything on hold because he can't… what? Come out? Embrace his whole self?" When Jared tensed and started to interject, Matt held up a hand. "I know. You're going to tell me I don't understand. You're right, I don't. In fact, I don't want to understand. Because I don't care about Nick, not nearly as much as I care about you. Somebody should be thinking about your happiness in all of this."

"What a coincidence. That's the same way I feel about him."

"But he doesn't feel the same way about you. If he did, he wouldn't—"

"I don't want to talk about this anymore."

"Fine," Matt said gruffly.

Except it wasn't ten seconds before Jared's emotions bubbled over. "It's pretty rich for you to assume you know how much Nick cares for me. You think you can look at our relationship from the outside, one where we can't be ourselves in public, by the way, and think you understand his feelings. What seems like nothing to you is actually a monumental step for him. I understand that. Do I sometimes wish he could step further faster? Of course I do. But I don't love him for who I want him to be. I love him for who he is. I love him for who we are together. I love him for who he is even when he's not with me. I've loved him when I thought he hated me. So why would I give a second thought for how hard it is for him to take these last few steps?"

"It's just every time I see you, you're a little bit sadder. I know how I would take care of you, how I would treasure you, and I don't feel like he's doing half of that—"

"It's not up to you to treasure me or to make me happy, nor is it Nick's job. I'm not with him because I expect him to make me happy. I'm with him because I love him."

"Even though loving him might mean you never get to have those beautiful dreams you told me about? The dreams I would be so ready to start with you right now?"

Yes.

The full truth of that word hit Jared like a cold Lake Superior wave.

He *did* love Nick more than he loved his own dreams. He was willing to wait, even if it meant the chances for other things he'd wanted passed him by. Even if at the end of the day he and Nick didn't work out. Because the chance they might work was worth it.

More than anything else, Nick was his dream. Not only being with him, but Nick, full stop.

Jared lifted one hand, then the other, to his face in an attempt to hold back the tears.

How could he know peace and emptiness all at once? How could comprehending his feelings on this level bring him a sense of understanding and the need to run away as far as he could go?

God, but he needed to be alone.

Right now. He needed to be alone right now.

"Stop the car."

All the anger leached out of Matt like a deflated balloon. Wincing, he held up a hand. "I promise I won't say another word about it. I'm sorry, I totally stepped over the line. You don't have to get out of the car. Just tell me where you want me to go, and I'll take you there."

"You don't need to apologize. I want to be alone is all. This exact second."

"We're in the middle of nowhere. There isn't a house or side road for another five miles." Matt was starting to panic. "Please tell me where you want to go. I truly am sorry."

The whole world began to spin, and Jared honestly thought he might be sick. "*Please stop the car.*"

Matt stopped. He didn't exactly slam on the brakes, but Jared's head jerked a little as Matt pulled to the side of the road. Jared didn't waste time. He threw the door open before the car had come to a complete stop and started walking as soon as the door closed behind him. He didn't bother giving Matt any further directions. He didn't tell him to wait, didn't tell him to leave.

I'll apologize later, he told himself, and then, with a watery sigh, he let the overwhelming emotions overtake him.

He could feel the sob inside him desperate to get out. He tried waiting for it, tried walking faster as if he could catch up to it. Nothing worked. In the end he crossed the road, found a sunny spot overlooking the water, and stared straight ahead, waiting.

Waiting. That was one thing he was good at.

He wasn't sure how long he sat there, because he wasn't marking time, only breathing, letting his sad, lonely truth resonate inside him. When he heard the footsteps behind him, his initial response was to shut his eyes. He was just working out how he was going to tell Matt to go away, searching for the level of gentleness and firmness to mix inside his voice, when first one hand and then another fell on his shoulders, one on either side. He glanced to the right and saw Owen standing there, looking almost as weary as Jared felt. When he glanced to the left, he found Simon, whose tears were flowing freely.

It was then, finally, the dam inside Jared broke.

Crouching forward so he was almost in a ball, he let the sobs roll out of him, silent at first, and then loud and ugly, the kind of cries he couldn't allow himself alone. This was sorrow he could only handle in the company of his best friends.

They sat beside him, wrapping him into their embrace, resting their foreheads onto his back until he could sit up enough for them to lean into his hair.

"You never had to do this by yourself," Owen said, his voice rough with emotion.

Jared laughed then, the sound a little manic and full of bitterness. “I didn’t want to do it at all.”

Simon punched him lightly in the arm. “We hurt when you hurt, you know? We always will.”

There was absolutely nothing to say in reply to that. The only thing Jared could do was close his eyes and let himself cry.

CHAPTER FOURTEEN

THE DAY of Simon and Jack's wedding donned bright, breezy, and warm.

While they'd initially wanted to have it at Owen and Erin's house, the ceremony had finally been established at a local park near the bay to accommodate the ever-burgeoning guest list. Jared and Owen, as members of the wedding party, were completely absorbed with work and preparation, and Erin had fallen naturally into a managerial role. For a while Nick helped Erin, but he soon discovered he was better suited to a remixed version of what he did every day: greeting and glad-handing. While Erin put out fires, Nick shook hands and smiled, smoothing over any rough edges Erin didn't have time to manage. When guests began to arrive, Nick made sure everyone knew where to go and felt comfortable as they waited for the ceremony to start. If a family member from either groom needed something, Nick got an available person to run and fetch.

It felt good, like he'd found his place with the others.

Unfortunately, such a concentration of Copper Point residents with nothing else to do gossiped, and Nick and Jared's relationship was still prime dish. Something about the atmosphere of a gay wedding gave everyone ideas. It didn't matter that whenever he and Jared spoke to one another, in view of others, they were careful. People saw what they wanted to see.

The nail in the coffin of his fantasies that he could go on pretending people bought his lie came when Jack's mother greeted him after he'd been fussing with Jared's tie.

"And so is he *your* partner?" she asked in a polite, interested voice.

Nick had almost choked as he'd rushed to assure her no, Jared was just his roommate. He hated how he had to lie to her, but today of all days he couldn't afford a slip.

He was pivoting fast toward a moment of decision. People suspected, but more than that, it bothered him increasingly with each passing day to keep up the fiction. Being Jared's lover openly only when he was with Jared's close friends wasn't enough. He wanted what the rest of them had: public recognition.

As he watched Jack and Simon say their vows, as he saw their friends and family so supportive and happy for them, for the first time in his life, Nick's jealousy and desire to have this kind of experience for himself was louder than his fears of what might happen if he dared to claim it. Why *couldn't* he have this?

How much would his world change if he came out? How much of the potential disaster was real, and how much of it had he built up in his head?

The only way to find out was to give in and let go.

At first he tried not to watch Jared during the ceremony, but after about five minutes he allowed himself to gaze upon his lover, who looked so handsome in his tuxedo and paisley cummerbund, with matching bow tie of course. Jared was beautiful, glowing, radiant, thrilled for his friends, eager to be part of their shared future. Soon they'd be repeating this celebration for Owen and Erin.

Would Nick be hiding half his life then the way he was now?

Would Jared have the patience to put up with him, if by the time that second wedding came around he still wasn't ready to step forward?

Nick never stopped asking himself these questions during the rest of the ceremony and the first part of the reception. He watched Jack and Simon and Erin and Owen flirt with one another, feed each other food, lead each other onto the dance floor. Jared remained alone, sitting at the front of the room with the rest of the wedding party, though Nick noticed Matt kept dropping by to say hello. Simon and Jack had offered Nick a place with them up front, but he declined, thinking it would be better to sit with his family and the general audience, for appearance's sake. Now his decision was nothing but torture, reminding him his determination to maintain appearances separated him from the place he wanted to be, literally and figuratively.

He couldn't laugh with the people he wanted to laugh with. He couldn't dance with the man he wanted to dance with. He couldn't be with the man he loved.

As if they understood the precipice he stood on, his family kept silent beside him. Emmanuella had sent him a text asking if he wanted to slip away and talk, but he sent a decline. He didn't have words for this.

Eventually he did have to get away. After excusing himself from his family's table, he stepped out of the reception tent and headed toward the ridge lining the bay. He offered polite smiles and waves to other guests as he passed them, but he quickly aimed himself at a darker area where no one stood. He needed time alone.

The waters were calm tonight. Many barges passed on the lake beyond the bay, and everything was dark, lit only by the sliver of moon. A handful of stars danced overhead, and the breeze was cool and pleasant.

When he heard footsteps, he saw Owen approaching him. His friend's tie had come undone, and his hair was messy, caked with sweat, as if he'd been dancing his heart out. Now his expression was serious.

Nick knew what was coming. In fact, he was surprised it had taken this long.

Owen planted himself in the grass beside Nick and spent a few minutes rocking on his heels, sharing the view. "I've put off having this conversation with you for as long as I possibly could. I hope you take this in the same spirit as when you took me up to the rooftop and gave me a talking-to about my intentions for Erin." Grimacing, Owen rubbed at his jaw. "He's hurting, Nick. I'm not sure how much you can see, how well he's hiding it from you. But two weeks ago, Simon and I got a frantic call from Matt Engleton to come pick Jared up from the middle of nowhere because he'd insisted on getting out of the car and was sitting on the side of the road. When we got there, Jared broke into sobs. I've never heard sounds like that from him before, and I never want to again."

The image Owen's words painted rocked Nick to the core. "What happened? Why didn't anyone say something to me sooner?"

"No one said anything because what he was upset about was you. Not anything you did, not anything that you'd said. Just that Matt had dared to question whether or not the situation of hiding your relationship was fair to Jared, and after angrily defending his right to stand by and wait for you, Jared broke down. He never offered any explanation to us, and we didn't ask. We didn't need it. We've understood what's been going on for a long time." Owen shook his head. "I'm not going to tell you when it's right for you to come out. It's rough, because I truly understand how much you care for him. I've seen the two of you together. It's the weirdest thing, because it's not as if we're watching a new relationship, either. You're the oldest married couple I've ever seen. You really are good together. But I can't stand to see Jared hurting so much. And to be honest, I think if you'd seen him that day, you wouldn't be able to stand it either."

Nick was having difficulty tolerating it, and he hadn't borne witness. He couldn't even muster up jealousy over Matt's involvement. For once he was glad the man had been there. Pinching the bridge of his nose, he let out a long sigh. "I don't know what to do."

Owen's laugh was bitter. "No offense, but I think you know exactly what to do. In case we're not on the same wavelength, though, I'll spell it out: you need to make up your mind. You're either preparing to have a proper relationship with Jared, or you need to start making an exit strategy."

Exit strategy. Hearing the words out of Owen's mouth made Nick feel sick. "I don't want to leave him, ever."

He let out a breath and teetered slightly where he stood. He hadn't censored himself, hadn't weighed his decision. He'd simply said, out loud, what was on his mind. And there it was, the truth he hadn't let himself fully embrace but had been dancing around all evening long.

He wanted this life with Jared more than he didn't, and he wanted it right now.

He was ready, at long last, to come out.

When he staggered a second time, Owen steadied him with a hand on the shoulder. "Easy there."

"I don't how to do this." Nick steepled his fingers over his face, but nothing was going to stop this crazy spinning sensation. "I don't know what I'm supposed to do now."

"Well, I don't think you have to do anything tonight. Acknowledging this is a plenty big step." Owen wouldn't let go of Nick's shoulder. "However, it's time you talked to Jared. Something tells me you said more to me about this than you have to him."

Nick laughed. "I hadn't even discussed this with myself. I've acknowledged it somewhat to

Emmanuella, but the closest I'd come was allowing myself to feel jealous. You just launched me into the master class."

"I hope you know I respect how difficult this is for you. And while I'm standing here making confessions, I'm sorry I never noticed you were one of us in high school. I understand you didn't want to be noticed, but I was sure I had a good idea of who the closeted kids were. In hindsight, that was an arrogant thing to assume. I don't know if you would've wanted to be in our group, but if my youthful idiocy kept you from feeling you could reach out, I apologize."

"I never wanted to reach out to anyone. It was my plan to find a way to make myself straight so I could be the man everyone wanted me to be. It was Jared who woke me up to the fact that this was a fantasy that would never come to pass. He tried to tell me then I should be myself, that I wasn't fully me unless I let my whole truth out to everyone in my life. Back then it was a truth I didn't want to hear. I wasted a whole lot of our lives trying to find compromises so that I could live the life other people wanted for me." He smiled sadly at the dark water. "Funny how that was so much simpler when I was busy being dogged by those jerks on the old board."

"It's easy to hide when you're persecuted. Peacetime brings out the want in all of us." Owen let go of Nick's shoulder with a small pat. "I'll let you stay here alone a bit and digest what you've just coughed up. Don't stay away too long, though, because when I left, Jared was already wondering where you were."

Jared. Nick wanted to talk to him. He wished they could leave now and go to the house, but that was without question too rude to be considered. Still, having come to this revelation, Nick didn't want to sit on it alone.

They'd both been alone long enough.

"Would you send him out here to talk to me?"

Owen grinned. "Absolutely."

JARED WAS standing at the edge of the dance floor, flirting with the idea of having a third glass of wine, when he saw Owen motioning to him from the other side of the tent. "Just a moment," he said to the woman telling him a story he'd only been half listening to. "I'll be right back."

Owen's expression had him nervous. Had something happened? His instincts told him this had to do with Nick. He'd tried not to watch his boyfriend too closely, lest he give them away, but he'd known something wasn't right. At first he'd caught himself wishing the night would go by quicker so that he could ask what was wrong, but then he remembered he was at Simon and Jack's wedding and gave himself a stern talking-to. Nick was a big boy. Another few hours wouldn't kill him. What was important right now was being present physically and mentally for his friends.

That said, as soon as he and Owen were out of earshot of the other guests, Jared didn't hold anything back. "What happened? What's the matter with Nick?"

"Nick is fine, but he does have something he wants to talk to you about." Owen gestured across the greenbelt toward the bay, where a solitary figure was silhouetted against the water.

Something about the slouch of Nick's shoulders made Jared's heart ache. He wanted to rush to him, but instead he glanced around nervously. "I don't know if I should. Too many people can see. I've felt like people might be figuring it out."

Owen smiled enigmatically before squeezing Jared's arm. "Go to him. It'll be fine. I promise." With that, he returned to the hubbub of the reception.

Confused and unsure of what was going on, Jared crossed to his lover, trusting Owen wouldn't send him over if it wasn't okay. He glanced over his shoulder a few times, but after about twenty feet, the gentle swish of the water against the shore ahead of him was louder than the din of the party behind him. He knew Nick could hear him coming, but he didn't turn around, only continued to stare out the bay.

"Nick?" Jared spoke softly, as if someone might appear and give him a reason to be cautious. "Owen told me to come find you."

For a second, Nick said nothing. But just when Jared was about to repeat himself, Nick let out a long, slow breath. "I'm going to come out."

At first, Jared wasn't sure he'd heard properly. He'd waited so long for those words, he couldn't believe this was happening. But there wasn't a question.

Nick was ready.

Jared opened his mouth, intending to say something reassuring and supportive. Instead he only managed a soft cry as his knees gave out, and suddenly he was sitting on the dewy grass.

Nick crouched beside him immediately, face full of concern. "Are you all right?"

Jared felt ridiculous. "I'm fine. I don't know why—" He cut himself off as another wave of dizziness hit him.

Nick took hold of his shoulders. "You're not fine. Should I call Owen?"

"No." Jared wanted to lean into him, held himself away out of habit, realized what Nick had just said meant the days of holding himself back were possibly over, and his head spun all over again. Giving up, he braced himself with a hand on Nick's wrist. "I think I underestimated how much I've been waiting to hear that, is all. I'm sorry. This isn't about me right now. I'm not trying to steal your moment—"

His voice broke, and he clamped a hand over his mouth.

Nick pulled him into his lap and folded him into his arms.

Jared resisted, his gaze pulling away toward the party. "Someone might see us."

"I don't care."

"Yes, you do. You care quite a bit. And I don't want you to think I don't respect that."

"I know you do, and I appreciate it. But I meant what I told you. I'm ready. I'm nervous, but I'm ready."

Jared had a thousand questions. What had brought this on? Was it the wedding? Was it something someone had said? Had this been brewing for days and he simply hadn't said anything? Most likely it was all of the above. And honestly none of it mattered, not at this second.

Drawing back, Jared looked into Nick's eyes. "You're not doing this alone. I want you to know that first of all. It's okay if you decide it'll take you months for the next step. It's okay if it takes you years. But I want you to know that I'm right here with you, whatever happens."

Nick shook his head. "It's not okay for it to take years. It's hurting you now, while I try to work this out. That's not okay for me."

Jared grimaced. *Now* he knew what had motivated Nick, and he didn't care for it. "Owen shouldn't have said anything."

"Yes he should have. I would've preferred it to come from you, but I understand why you didn't speak up. I both appreciate it and am saddened by it at the same time. But the truth of the matter is I'm doing this for me as much as I am for you. In fact, I've been thinking about this for a while. The wedding drove it home. Ever since you walked back into my life, I've been in limbo between two worlds. I always knew I couldn't have it both ways, but I was too afraid to choose. It feels selfish to reach for this, but I'm going to have to work through those feelings. Because I'm not willing to let that fear stand in the way of the happiness I know you and I can have together. It's the happiness I owe to myself." His eyes became shiny, his voice a little shaky. "In my head, I keep framing this as a choice between my family and my lover, but at the end of the day, that isn't it at all. It's just a question of whether or not I allow myself to be who I am or accept a life that's only a fraction of who I know myself to be."

Holding Nick's face in his hands, Jared pressed a tender kiss to his lips. "I'm so proud of you. I can't say it enough. I've always been incredibly proud of you. But right now, hearing you talk like that about yourself, I'm absolutely bursting with it."

Tears streamed down Nick's face. "I love you. I've loved you since we were in high school. I've never stopped, not for one day."

Jared choked on a laugh that was half a sob. "It's exactly the same for me. And I'm going to love you until the end of time."

For a blissful few minutes they sat together, listening to the water, feeling the grass tickle their legs. He let Nick decide when it was time to return to the party, giggling as they brushed grass and dew off their clothes. When Nick reached for his hand, he gave it gladly, enjoying the feeling of walking with his lover in the dark.

He was ready to let go as soon as they came too close to the reception, but he wouldn't be the first to make a move. In every way, he'd follow Nick's lead. However, Nick made no effort to separate them. If anything, his grip became tighter.

"Are you sure about this?" Jared asked. He spoke as quietly as he could, but they were so close some people probably could hear them. "You don't want to talk to your family first?"

"I'm going to lead you to your table. That's all."

Nick spoke with firm resolution, but sweat beaded on his brow as they wove through the tables and the murmurs from people who saw them together began to rise around them. Jared did his best to keep his composure. All eyes were on them, all talk was about them. It was as if he were in high school again, walking through the lunchroom for the first time after he'd admitted to someone in the locker room he was gay. The difference was there was no hostility here, only curiosity.

Well. There was a *little* hostility.

He'd done his best to stay out of Grandma Emerson's way ever since Nick moved in. He always liked the Beckert family and had fancied them on more than one occasion as something of a surrogate for his own fractured unit. He'd known as soon as he and Nick took this relationship seriously he'd be cast as the villain of the piece by Nick's family, and he'd tried to make peace with that. But it was difficult to see the sharp gazes following him now from the Beckert matriarchs.

As promised, Nick did nothing more but walk him to the front table, to the place where Owen and the others lingered, but he did so holding Jared's hand the entire time. He looked as if he wanted to give him a kiss on the cheek before he left. Apparently he decided this was a bridge too far right now, and settled for stroking his thumb on the back of Jared's hand before smiling softly and weaving his way through the crowd.

Feeling dizzy again, Jared sat. The others huddled around him, their faces full of questions, concern, and hesitant joy. Rebecca and Kathryn beamed at him from across the room, giving him enthusiastic thumbs-up.

Jared smiled back, nervous, but letting himself dare to believe for the first time in a long time that everything might, just might, be all right after all.

CHAPTER FIFTEEN

NICK WAS surprised at the comfort that came from claiming Jared's hand.

The attention he got as he walked back to his family's table was essentially everything he'd ever feared. People looked at him differently. The simple act of taking his boyfriend's hand had altered the image of who he was.

What, him too? He could read the unspoken question on their faces.

Yet the reality of coming out, even in this casual way, wasn't half as bad as his imagination had made it out to be. He'd never accounted for the power that came with accepting his full self. People had talked to him about it, assured him it was important, and it wasn't that he disbelieved them. He hadn't understood the resonance, however. He was the same man, but now he was *more*. *All* of him was here and accounted for, swelling inside him to the point he felt like he pulsed with it.

Fullness. He overflowed with himself, a sense of identity he hadn't known to dream of seeping into every pore of his body. He felt it all the way to his core. Strength untold. Happiness beyond measure.

Relief. So much relief.

He'd acknowledged his relationship with Jared, and by extension, he'd acknowledged himself—in public. It was the smallest of first steps. But now he felt emboldened, ready for more.

Unfortunately, his biggest challenge beyond this initial leap was already before him.

He'd intended to tell his family before making his relationship with Jared public, right up until the moment when he changed his mind. Standing before the stony faces of his grandmother and mother, taking in the nervous countenance of Emmanuella, he didn't have any regret. Asking permission, doing anything that made it sound as if this were a debate, wasn't a good way to go. This would be a difficult conversation no matter when they had it. However, he wasn't going to change his mind.

He inclined his head in greeting as he resumed his seat beside them. When he spoke, he kept his glance on the dance floor, but he watched his family out of the corner of his eye. "Do you want to go somewhere and talk?"

His mother clucked her tongue and shifted in her seat, muttering under her breath. His grandmother remained perfectly poised, though her expression had managed to harden even further. She too focused on the dancers. "We're at a wedding right now. It's Simon and Jack's time."

Translation: *we're not going to make a scene in front of other people*. Fair enough. "When would you like to meet?"

He tried not to hold his breath.

"We'll talk at dinner after church tomorrow." Grandma Emerson didn't leave room for argument in this declaration.

"I'll come by to pick you up at the usual time."

Except his chest constricted, fearing her next words would be to tell him not to bother coming at all, that she didn't want him going with her to church.

"We'll be waiting."

His grandmother stood in the slow and careful way she had, gripping her handbag in front of her like a tiny shield. "Aniyah, come with me to get some punch."

Nick rose quickly, pulling back both of their chairs and offering his hand as his grandmother wove her way through the tight space. She accepted it once for a bit of balance, but otherwise she held herself regally and walked away, Nick's mother following close behind. As soon as they were gone, Nick collapsed into his chair.

Emmanuella scooted over and grabbed his hand. "Holy shit. You want to give a girl warning? I thought I was going to pass out. What were you thinking?"

He glanced around, saw how many people were watching them, and leaned in closer to her. "Let's take a walk and have this conversation without as many ears."

He didn't take her to the same place he'd had his heart-to-heart with Jared, walking her instead toward the brightly lit gazebo at the main part of the park.

"How angry are they?" he asked.

"Plenty. But then, they've known this was coming. You're going to get the most grief for not coming to them before you pulled a stunt like that."

"It wasn't a stunt. I wanted to hold his hand, so I did."

She waited until they passed a small group of people chatting amongst themselves before she spoke again. The people smiled at them politely, and from the way they regarded Nick, he could tell they hadn't yet heard the news about him.

Once they were alone, she turned to face him. "So after all this time, after being so cautious, you're going to come out by acting as if you've been out all along?"

"There isn't exactly a manual for this. But yes, I always knew when I got to this point, I would simply be. What, did you think I was supposed to hold a press conference?"

"Obviously not. It's just… I don't know. I mean, how is this gonna work? Will you let people walk up and ask you if you're gay? If they do ask you, what'll you say?"

"If they come up and ask that boldly, I'll tell them it's none of their damn business."

She shook her head. "I can't believe how blasé you are about this. I thought you'd be more worked up."

He snorted. "I'm glad to hear you have so much confidence in me."

"You know what I mean."

"Honestly? It feels good. Terrifying, yes. But I feel like I let out a huge breath. And I haven't done anything yet. Time will tell how it shakes out, but at least in this second it feels like the worst is behind me."

"You're one hell of an optimist. You haven't even been to church yet."

"True. But see, I always knew that would be rough. I always knew all of it would be rough. But so far the anticipation was a lot worse than the jump."

"Let me know if you need me to push a trampoline underneath the cliff."

That made him smile. "Will do."

He didn't sit with his family for the rest of the evening once he returned with Emmanuella. He wandered the edges, amazed at how little the stares bothered him, hoping this could last.

He was about to head back to Jared when he felt a hand on his arm, then one on his other arm as well. Rebecca and Kathryn had claimed him.

They didn't waste any words, only dragged him to an open table and plunked him down. "So you're doing it?" Kathryn squeezed him. "I wasn't seeing things, right? You were holding Jared's hand? The two of you, you're together? You're coming out?"

Nick glanced between the two of them. "Wait, are you telling me you knew all along?"

Rebecca waved a hand. "Suspected, suspected. But we were convinced when you moved in with Jared. Don't look like that. I think the straights were largely confused. They wanted the two of you to be an item because it made good gossip, but they weren't ready for the reality. You only have to look around this room to have that confirmed."

Kathryn punched him lightly. "How come you're not sitting with him?"

"Well, I was trying to have a chat with my family. But my grandma got up and left the table."

Kathryn nodded as if this were completely to be expected. "Did you soften her up at all before this? Or did you sideswipe her?"

"I didn't mention anything specifically. But I'm pretty sure they've seen this coming." He let out a slow breath. Then another.

Rebecca grinned. "Feels good, doesn't it?"

He smiled. "Yeah. It really does. I'm waiting for the next shoe to fall, but I feel as if I'm riding the dragon instead of hovering beneath it."

"Oh, there's gonna to be shoes falling." Kathryn sighed. "Are you going to church tomorrow?"

He nodded. "I figure that will be the worst."

"Probably so." She shook her head. "I can't bring myself to go back most of the time. They turned away at a time I needed them. I've been able to forgive everyone individually, but I have a hard time with the place itself. I know you know this, but you have to get ready to face the truth that some of the people there are always going to look at you differently once they hear. I don't know if you can mentally prepare yourself for that, but do your best. And remember, at the end of the day, there are other places you can make a community." She smiled wryly. "Hey, we got enough people now we could even make a club. Queer Folks of Color of Copper Point. The potlucks will be out of this world."

He couldn't tell if she was joking or not, but he wanted to join that club.

When Rebecca and Kathryn finally let him go, he joined Jared and the others where they were seated near the front of the room. His initial giddiness was wearing off. Though earlier he'd thought he might attempt to dance with Jared, now mostly he wanted to go to bed. He was fully prepared to suck it up and stay for the long haul, but he hadn't stood with the others for five minutes before Jack and Simon came up to them with a knowing smile.

"We wanted to let you know," Simon said, "that we don't have a problem with you leaving early. In fact, we think you should go right now."

Jack held up a hand before they could protest. "You have a lot to discuss. And not to be rude, but we have enough people to see here that we don't need to worry about whether or not the two of you are okay. You've seen us get married, and you were here for our party. Now go have the conversations you need to have."

After a round of hugs and a few tears, especially on Simon's part, Jared and Nick did just that.

They didn't say much on the way to the car, but it wasn't a time for talking. No one had come up to either of them except for their closest friends, and Matt in particular had become abruptly absent. They didn't hold hands as they walked, but they stood closer together, no longer policing their body language. In the car, however, they embraced one another, lingering for several seconds before pulling away.

"You okay?" Jared touched Nick's face as he studied him carefully.

Nick nodded, turning to kiss Jared's hand. "Yes."

Once they were at home, they moved upstairs to the bedroom, peeling out of their formalwear. As Nick folded his suit over a chair, he smiled wryly. "Well, I suppose I can move my things in here now."

Jared, in his undershirt and briefs, wrapped his arms around Nick's naked torso. "I saw there wasn't much conversation with your family, except for Emmanuella."

Nick nodded. "I don't think it was all bad, though. Granted, they were never going to do much in front of people. But it went about as I expected. Still taking them to church tomorrow, and we're going to talk afterward."

"Church. Are you ready for that? This is possibly a silly question, but do you want me to come along?"

Nick laughed. "Not a good idea."

"I figured, but I had to offer."

Nick kissed Jared's fingers. "Let's go to bed."

Their lovemaking that night was slow and easy. Though tomorrow would bring new challenges, this moment was about shelter and quiet rejoicing. Being with Jared always felt like coming home, but tonight it was as if everything had been made brighter, sharper, more vibrant.

Nick woke early the next morning, without an alarm. He went to the basement to run on the treadmill with his headphones on, and when he emerged to the main floor, Jared was making oatmeal and sausage, coffee percolating as Prince played in the background. Nick meandered to the stereo as he mopped his brow with his hand towel, noting the album was *The Hits/ The B-Sides*.

"I figured I couldn't go with you, but I could send you off with a nice breakfast," Jared said.

"Thanks, baby." Nick kissed his boyfriend's cheek, lingering a little. "I'm gonna shower quick. Keep it warm for me?"

Jared did. When Nick returned, dressed in his Sunday best, "When Doves Cry" was playing. He shook his head. The shuffle gods had interesting senses of humor.

Nick dished himself some food and sat next to Jared at the breakfast table, tapping his toe to the beat.

Jared smiled at him. "You're in a better mood than I thought you'd be."

"Nervous as hell. Feel like you could launch me to the moon. I don't need this coffee, I'll tell you that." He took a big sip of it. He set his mug down and rolled his shoulders. "I don't know. I feel weirdly amped. It's going to be terrible, I know that. I can't explain why I'm so buzzed now when before I felt so subdued."

"It feels good to acknowledge yourself. Like you're letting in clean air."

"I do worry it's going to mess up all the stuff with the hospital. Maybe I should have waited."

"It's not going to mess up the hospital. We're stuck there until Gilbert gives us something, so you might as well be happy and whole while you take your licks. And you don't have to make those kinds of decisions, putting the hospital's needs above your own."

"I hope you're right." Glancing at his watch, Nick wiped his mouth and rose, bending to kiss Jared's cheek. "I gotta go."

Jared caught his hand and squeezed it. "Good luck."

He'd timed it so he arrived at his grandmother's house just as they were ready to leave. She'd said they were going to talk after the service, which meant they weren't going to talk until after the service. Getting there early would only mean feeling awkward and making everyone more upset than they already were.

The three women were waiting for him on the front porch as usual, and there was no mistaking his mother and grandmother in particular had taken great pains to look extra nice this morning. His grandmother and mother were subdued on the ride over, not saying much. His sister tried to make conversation that included everyone, but no one else wanted to talk, too aware of the spaces between them.

But that gave Nick a little hope. If things didn't get any worse than they had been, he could handle it. If they didn't outright disown him, he felt confident with time he could work them back around, or at least help them to a new normal.

He didn't even have the car parked at church, however, before he knew *this* aspect of his life was going to be as bad as he had feared, possibly worse. Kathryn had warned him, but he hadn't been prepared. It cut to feel the same gazes that had always regarded him with support and admiration suddenly regarding him with suspicion. Granted, some of them were more judgmental than others. Some seemed shocked, much like the ones at the wedding reception. But some of them hurt. His second-and-third-grade Sunday school teacher was curling her lip at him as if he were the dirtiest scum who'd ever crossed her path, not the man who only last week she'd thanked as an example to the community.

The worst were the parents who touched their children's shoulders and pulled them back, as if wandering too close to Nick might lead to something untoward. What did they think would happen? That he'd haul them away and turn them queer like him?

He understood now why Kathryn said she couldn't come back. He hoped he didn't end up in the same situation.

Some people, though, made a point to smile at him, to come up and say hello and let him know everything was normal. One of them was James, whose always-bright smile had something extra in it. A silent welcome, a whisper of encouragement. His handshake lingered too. Nick had the feeling more banana bread would appear in his mailbox in the future.

He decided it was time to take another step forward. Before James could let go of his hand and slip away, Nick stopped him with a gentle grip on his arm. "We never get a chance to talk. Maybe you can come by for dinner sometime. Jared and I would love to have you."

His pulse filled his ears and his throat felt as if it were closing once the words left his lips. He eased, though, as James smiled, a wide, dazzling grin. "I'd love to come."

As expected, Pastor Robert approached Nick soberly and requested they get together soon to talk. That said, Pastor felt like a chaotic neutral. He certainly wasn't acting as if nothing had happened, but he didn't seem ready to condemn Nick to hell for unforgiveable sins, either. Nick told him he'd give him a call.

Instead of paying attention to the sermon, he tried to sort out his emotions. He marveled a bit at how calm he'd managed to stay, unsure how that had happened. As he probed deeper, he felt a few tender, terrible feelings, and he wondered if he was experiencing some kind of shock. It was as if his brain could only process so much and had decided for now it wasn't going to think about what coming out would mean to his church life, not yet. He needed to be careful, to make sure his fragile new beginnings had a chance to bloom.

His family left immediately after the service, not lingering to chat as they normally did. This he'd expected. However, he *was* surprised when, as soon as they were in the car and driving out of the lot, his grandmother started to speak.

"You sure have made a mess."

Nick glanced at her in the rearview mirror. Her face was hard and wooden. He returned his focus to the road. "Sorry, Grandma."

She clucked her tongue. Another glance in the mirror showed she was looking out the window with her lips pursed tight. "I sure thought you'd grown out of it. That damned elevator is what started it all up."

"It started when I was born," Nick said gently. "If you're gonna try to say Jared made me this way, it'll never fly."

His mother, who had been silently fuming, stopped holding her tongue. "You haven't acted on it this whole time. Why *now*?"

"Oh, Lord," Emmanuella murmured under her breath.

Nick did his best to maintain his patience. "Mama, I say this with respect, but you have no idea how much I have *acted on it*. And I honestly don't think you want to know."

His mother's face was red, her voice rising. "Couldn't you have let things stay the way they were?"

Grandma Emerson held up a hand. "We will not be so uncivil we yell in this car. We can wait to finish this until we get to the house."

No one said anything else until they were inside the house, but as soon as they were there, it all started up again.

Nick's mother aimed a finger at him, her eyes full of fury. "I want to know why you had to do this. I want to know why you couldn't have kept things going the way they were. They were good. Everything was just fine."

Finally, Nick lost his patience. "Just fine? I'm so glad you understand my state of mind, Mama."

"Don't you talk back to me."

"Don't you tell me how I feel or how I should live. This is my life. This is my happiness, my journey to find the person I want to spend the rest of my life with. It was only ever going to be a man. And before anybody tells me it's a sin—if you can stand here and tell me loving one of the most respected doctors in this community and wanting to make a life with him makes me a sinner, you go ahead."

"It's *God's Word*," his grandmother shot back.

"Well I'm God's creation, and I'm here to tell you I came as is, so call me a Biblical conundrum, I guess. But even if I allow you that, Grandma, even if you insist who I am is a sin, are you honestly going to say this is the most important thing about me? Does that negate everything else I am, everything else I've done? Not to the church, but *to you*?"

He waited, but she said nothing, only pursed her lips tight and stared back.

The fire was lit in him now, and he kept going. "All these years when everyone else was coming out, I stayed in because I didn't want you to look at me the way you are now."

His mother couldn't contain herself any longer, either. "This isn't what we want for you. Your life has been challenging enough as it is. Do you really need to make it more complicated? Do you need homophobia thrown at you on top of everything else?"

"What in the world do you think *this* is, Mama? You say you want to make things easier for me? Then accept me. You want me to be happy? Acknowledge me. Because pretending to be someone I'm not isn't happiness. It isn't a full life. This whole time you think I've been safe in my closet, I've had to look at *myself* in the mirror, and there have been plenty of days I was so grim I felt dead inside. So lonely and hollow I absolutely had moments I wanted to die because I didn't see a way out. Is that the kind of less complicated you're talking about? If so, I'm not interested. All I want is who I am on the inside and the outside to match. I want you to love the whole of me. I want to be able to love the whole of me."

Holding up his hands, he backed toward the door. "You know what, I'm gonna let this sit for a bit. I do want to talk to you. I do want to be part of this family. It's incredibly important to me. But I think this is all I can take for today."

He turned around and left before any of them could say a word, climbing into his car and driving away in a daze. He went home. It wasn't until he parked the car and was stumbling toward the garage door leading into the kitchen that he realized he thought of this house as his home. *This* was his safe place now.

As Jared opened the door, his arms open wide to gather Nick in, Nick allowed the protective walls he'd erected in church to fall away, let his sorrows pour out. As he settled into Jared's embrace, he shut his eyes and swam away on his lover's quiet promises that everything was going to be all right.

ON SUNDAY afternoon, Jared and Nick went over to Owen and Erin's house. Jared did his best to field the conversations Nick didn't want to have, working with this script they'd agreed on.

"Yes, Nick and I are going out," he told Simon's mother as they sat together near the fireplace in the main room. "We've been seeing each other for a while, but because Nick wasn't out, we chose to keep it private."

"But you're already living together!" Madeline's eyes twinkled with mischief. "So this must be serious?"

It was impossible for Jared to stop his gaze from traveling across the room to land on Nick. "Yes. It is."

The questions and curiosities they received here were all friendly, as expected at the private reception of the wedding of two gay men. The real test would be on Monday when they went back to work. But this was a nice wading in, especially for Nick, who wasn't used to having this part of him public.

Still, it was good to go home and have it be just the two of them again. Nick looked exhausted, and Jared wanted to treat him a little. "Why don't you take a long soak in the tub, and I'll make us dinner. Take the portable stereo in with you and a glass of wine. Shut the world off for a while."

Groaning, Nick slouched and leaned his head on Jared's shoulder. "Not going to argue with you."

As soon as Nick was up the stairs, Jared searched through his cookbooks, trying to find the perfect soothing recipe. He debated between fancy and simple, and in the end decided to split the difference with chicken tortellini soup and homemade rolls. He put the bread together and set the dough to rising, then wrote a short grocery list. Before he left, he penned a quick note on the counter to let Nick know where he was going.

There were stares at the grocery store—he was definitely the hot gossip topic of the day. Unlike at the wedding or Owen and Erin's house, here no one came up to ask for confirmation or offer their congratulations, but Jared wasn't surprised. Even if some of these people were on Jared's side, none of them knew him well enough for that kind of intrusion. He was a little surprised, however, that overall they seemed more standoffish than he'd expected. *He* wasn't the one who'd come out.

Though Owen and Simon had warned him about this. They'd pulled him aside the night before and explained what had happened to them once they were in serious relationships. People, even the ones who said they were all for marriage equality, began treating them slightly differently once they were in committed, public relationships. For Simon, it was a phenomenon he'd been well aware of for years, as someone who'd regularly dated. Owen, who had never dated in town before Erin, had been quite surprised. The idea people preferred gay men not to be sexual wasn't novel, but it was strange to experience it live and in person. Simon said people's awkwardness had increased once he was engaged.

"Just be ready for it," Owen had said. "People understand they shouldn't be bigoted, and some really want to be tolerant, but when it's right in front of them, they're uncomfortable. And because it's a heterosexual-centered world, their discomfort is your job to fix, in their mind."

"Oh, and don't forget racism." Simon's mouth flattened into a line. "Every day I discover another 'nice white person' who feels entitled to come up to me and call my husband a slur. Sometimes me too. Sometimes it's as if they can't figure out what they want to be more upset about, my homosexuality or the fact that I wanted to marry an Asian man. Hong-Wei doesn't talk much about what it's like for him, but I know it's worse."

As Jared walked through the grocery store and felt the eyes on him, he wondered if he should have taken their admonitions more to heart. He also worried, for the first time, if he might receive even more censure from the public because he was a pediatrician. There were already parents who wouldn't send their children to an out gay doctor. Would there be more parents who felt they needed to go elsewhere once they knew Jared was actually in a relationship? Would he now have to deal with the racial bigots as well as the homosexual ones? Seemed so.

Kathryn had mentioned this issue with her practice, about mothers who would drive two hours for delivery just to make sure they weren't in the hands of a lesbian Black woman. Jared felt foolish for thinking he would somehow be immune. He hoped he'd be exempt, but for the rest of the night, he mentally prepared himself for the worst.

When he went to work the next morning, he discovered he hadn't been overreacting at all.

"I have *how many* cancellations?" Jared stared at the receptionist in disbelief.

The woman blanched, looking uncomfortable. "Five. And six tomorrow. I'm sorry."

Grimacing, Jared went back to his office.

There were four other doctors in the St. Ann's Family Clinic, everyone practicing family medicine except for Jared. One was an elderly gentleman who hadn't retired because they couldn't find anyone to take his place, and the other three were around Jared's age. Two of the physicians were women, the other a man, but to Jared's knowledge every last one of them was straight—if they were bi or pan, they were playing things close to the vest, which he could hardly blame them for. They were married, and they all had children. Dr. Franzen's kids were grown with children of their own, but the other doctors were constantly juggling school performances and field trips against their on-call duties. None of them were Jared's best friends, but they got along decently well. Even the ones who came from evangelical Christian backgrounds.

Each of them made a point to stop by his office that day. The two he'd thought would perhaps shut him out now that he was dating someone went out of their way to give him a cheery hello and mention Jack and Simon's wedding. No one said a word about his dating Nick, but in their own way they tacitly let him know it wasn't going to interfere with their relationship. Because the doctors set this standard, the nurses followed suit, all but a few, and so did the receptionists.

In the afternoon, Helen stopped by with the most stunning news yet. "I wanted to let you know, because I didn't think anyone else would tell you. The other doctors made it clear to us at the front desk they weren't taking any new patients this week who were children. They said they'd reconsider their position in a month, but right now they were all too busy to take on what they already had a competent doctor for."

For a moment, Jared couldn't speak. When he did, his throat was thick with the emotion. "Thank you, Helen."

He'd texted Nick several times during the day, asking him how things were going for him. From the sounds of it, his experience was a remix of Jared's own. No one could cancel an appointment with the CEO of the hospital, but they could certainly let him know in subtle and overt ways what they thought of him. For Nick it focused on people regarding him differently, as if he had been lying to them all this time. Jared had tried to get him to go to lunch, but Nick had said for now he didn't want to fan the flames. "Maybe later in the week."

They were going home together, so when Jared finished, he waited in the lobby, reading the news on his phone and sipping a cup of coffee from the gift shop. He was used to the stares by now, to the point he thought they might be easing up a little. *Perhaps this will be easier than I thought.*

And that's when his parents walked into the hospital.

He didn't react right away. He assumed they were here to visit someone. This wasn't the first time their paths had crossed in town. In general, when overlap like this happened, they politely ignored each other. If his parents felt like greeting him, Jared would be civil, but that was as far as he would go. He didn't want to greet them today, so he kept his focus on his the website he was surfing.

"Is it true?" Jared's mother's body was tight with fury as she walked up to him. "Is it true you're dating *that man*?"

Oh, they were going to do *this* dance? And with an audience no less. Jared put his phone down, his smile brittle. "If you're going to cause a scene in the hospital, I'm going to have to ask you to leave."

Jared's father was beet red. "So you're not denying it?"

Picking up his phone again, Jared tapped a quick text to Erin. Then he laced his fingers over his abdomen. "I'm dating Nicolas Beckert, yes. I have no reason to deny it. But this is no business of yours."

His mother looked as if she honestly might have a heart attack right here in the lobby. Jared wondered what her position was on being operated on by a Muslim woman.

His mother's voice shook with her rage. "If you continue in this relationship, you won't be part of this family anymore."

Jared leaned forward, his eyes narrowed. "I haven't been a part of this family for a long time. And if you're going to be racist, I'm not interested in having anything to do with you."

His mother stopped forward, clearly determined to hit him, and Jared made no move to block her. He wanted the slap. In his mind, it would feel both like a cleansing and a cap to this strange day: the long-overdue final break in his relationship with his parents, a throwback to his youth when she'd struck him for indiscretions serious and dubious. This wasn't an indiscretion on his part, but having some sort of physical reminder, a ringing blow to his cheek, would keep him from reaching back if later he thought perhaps he should give them another chance.

The sound of footsteps on the stairs told him the security he'd asked Erin to send were on their way, and for a second he worried she wouldn't get to hit him. Why he was so disappointed in that he wasn't sure, but before he could analyze it, she finished closing the distance between them, and even as the security guards tried to pull her back, her palm connected with the side of his face.

The blow was hard enough to send his head to the side, wrenching his neck a little. His father tried to land a blow of his own, but the security guards caught him first, restraining him the same way they had his mother. There was quite a crowd of onlookers around them now. Essentially everyone who was on the first floor was watching, as well as some people who had drifted down from the second.

At the bottom of the stairs were Erin and Nick.

Deliberately not touching his throbbing cheek, Jared calmly regarded his red-faced parents. "And now we're done. This is the last time we'll speak. You won't approach me again. If we see each other on the street, we'll be strangers to one another. When I have children, they won't know you as grandparents. If I'm trapped in another elevator, don't feel compelled to visit me afterward if I've nearly died. Because from now on, you don't have a son, and I don't have parents. It's clear this will be the best arrangement for everyone involved."

Turning away from them, he walked toward Nick, who stood beside the stair door with his usual inscrutable expression. Except Jared knew how to interpret this one. His lover was furious.

Jared smiled as he took Nick's arm. "Sorry to disturb you. Do you need some more time, or are you ready to go?"

Not looking away from Jared's parents, Nick shook his head. "I'm ready to leave. Let's go home." Then he shifted his gaze to Jared's swollen cheek. "Should I call Jack to check you out?"

"No need. I can take care of myself at home. Let's go." Taking great care to let everyone see who wanted to, Jared leaned forward and placed a gentle kiss on his lover's cheek.

Then, with every bit of pride he had left in him, he took Nick's arm and led him to the parking garage.

EMMANUELLA CALLED Nick every single night after Jack and Simon's wedding.

She texted him often during the day as well, but every night once he was home from work and had finished dinner, she called him up and asked him about his day. He could tell by the background noise that she was doing this in the middle of the living room, in full earshot of their mother and grandmother. When they spoke on the phone, they didn't discuss anything about the family, but in her texts, she kept him updated and essentially let him know the door wasn't closed.

They're going to come around. They don't let me know it, but they pay attention to every bit of gossip that has to do with you. I heard the two of them talking the other day after Jared's parents showed up at the hospital, and they were so worried something might have happened, that one of them could have come with a gun. It played into their deepest fears. To be honest with you, I think the hardest thing for them is exactly what Mama said, that they didn't want anything this difficult for you.

Nick didn't doubt she was right, but it frustrated him. While he appreciated they didn't want him to face difficulty, he wished they'd work harder to understand he'd rather face prejudice than live a lie. Now that he'd stepped out of the closet and could see how much he needed that truth, how much denying himself for so long had hurt him, he knew he could only go forward, not backward.

The trouble was, there were plenty of struggles before him that being out made more complicated. The whispers around town were one thing, the subtle change in perception from the hospital staff another. But he was fighting this battle of what to do about the new building. Gilbert hadn't gotten anywhere in their investigation, and he acknowledged he might have to face a scenario where they never uncovered anything.

At the end of the day, they had to repair the elevator or build a new building, and they'd need money from somewhere. A bond issue was the most logical choice, but it had already been an uphill battle with Peterson's bad press souring the water, and Nick had to do public glad-handing with people looking at him like he was an alien.

If his coming out affected the hospital's ability to reorganize itself, he didn't know how he was going to handle that.

To make things even worse, two weeks after Jack and Simon's wedding, Jeremiah Ryan removed one of Nick's last emergency props.

"I'm going to be straight with you," Ryan said as he sat across from Nick in his office, his tone a mixture of disappointment and frustration. "I'm not pleased. I didn't think Collin's son would be the kind of man to betray me this way."

Nick blinked a few times, racing to figure out what was going on. "I'm sorry you feel I betrayed you, sir. How—?"

"*My daughter*, man. You've been stringing her along all this time, and now you're seeing someone else. One of your *doctors*—a *male* doctor."

It hurt Nick more than he'd anticipated to have Ryan upset with him. "I didn't mean to mislead your daughter. From my perspective, I was being polite to a colleague, one I enjoyed working with. I appreciate the counsel and advice both of you give. I'm sorry to hear learning the truth of my orientation lowers your opinion of me."

Ryan sighed. "I thought we had an understanding here. I thought I'd made it clear I wanted you as a son-in-law. You're not a fool. There's no way you missed that."

"I did suspect, yes. In my defense, it wasn't something I could easily explain, especially since I wasn't out. I apologize if either of you were hurt, however inadvertently."

"Well." Ryan threw up his hands. "I appreciate your apology, but I need to back off from this for now. I'm rescinding my offer to invest in St. Ann's. Most of my interest came because of you anyway, and my hopes for a relationship with my daughter. This said, I do feel you are a bright individual and will do well. So once things have cooled a bit, I might just be in touch again."

Nick's throat was a little thick. "I appreciate that, sir."

He wasn't sure exactly why he was so bothered. The board didn't want an outside takeover, so he was never going to do anything with Ryan's suggestion. However, he did think highly of Jeremiah, and Cynthia too. He probably should have given some more overt clue so Ryan hadn't thought there was a chance.

He didn't even have one day to cool off from the Ryan visit before he received a phone call from Peterson. This one had nothing to do with his coming out, which was a relief, but the subject matter wasn't any more pleasant.

"A little birdie told me you're considering a bond issue." Peterson laughed. "I think you'll have trouble with that. It's not going to matter if you had your fancy firm give you more information. You're never going to get your tiny town to cough up enough money to give you what you want."

God, but Nick hoped Gilbert discovered evidence pointing directly to this asshole. "We'll see what happens."

"That we will. Oh, and don't count on any lingering trails of sabotage, either."

Nick stilled. "Excuse me?"

Peterson was a cat with cream. "You heard me. I know what you're trying to do, and it won't work. You won't find a thing. Which is such a shame. If you could prove sabotage, you could get whoever had done it to pay for everything. But you have to have proof." He clucked his tongue.

Now the man was taunting him. Nick didn't need this. "Thank you for your concern about our hospital. But as I've said several times, we have no intention of doing business with you or your firm."

"That's all right. I have patience. When you get forced out of your job, I'll make sure the next CEO I deal with has more sense than you. It's a shame the brand-new board has such work cut out for it. Really hope they can all get reelected."

"Goodbye," Nick said, and hung up on him.

He left work early, sending a text to Jared saying he was going to walk home. He took a circular route to get back to the house, willing the fall air to clear his head. He passed the Amin place, where Zaika was in the yard, and she waved hello to him. The children played in the yard as well, while their grandfather fiddled with the lawn mower in the driveway.

Seeing them made Nick sad. He was tired and lonely, and he wanted his family back. He needed to sit at the kitchen table with his grandmother, vent his frustrations about the bond issue, and hear her wisdom on the matter. He longed to watch his mother be indignant on his behalf and listen to her insist he could do anything he put his mind to. He wanted to dream about getting married to Jared and having kids with him, and he wanted to have his family be excited for them when he shared those goals. He didn't like how such an idyllic moment at the Amin house made him wonder whether he would ever have this for himself.

Nick was exhausted by the time he got to the house, his thoughts crushing down on him like weights. He craved a day off from this, one where he didn't have to worry if he was making a huge mistake and how many people his actions harmed. He didn't want to worry that everything he'd worked for with Erin might be about to go down the tubes, whether he may have inadvertently been the cause of it. He needed to be able to be himself in every way, without worrying about what it might mean for his job, for his family, and for his friends.

He hadn't so much as taken off his suit coat when someone knocked on the front door. Nick's heart grew heavy as he looked through the peephole and saw Pastor Robert standing on the stoop.

"Nick." Though he smiled, Pastor looked as weary as Nick. "Mind if I come in?"

"Of course." Nick held the door open wide. "Can I get you something to drink?"

"Glass of water would be great, thanks."

Nick's hands felt leaden as he carried two glasses to the living room. He was nervous, yes, but he felt relieved too. This wasn't going to be a pleasant conversation, but putting it off wasn't going to make it any better.

Pastor accepted the water, took a drink, then cradled the glass in his hands and stared at it for several seconds. Then he sighed. "I suspect you know why I'm here."

"I assume it's because you heard rumors I'm not only living with Jared, I'm dating him."

Pastor lifted his gaze. "And are those rumors true?"

"They are."

Another sigh. Pastor stared at the water again, then shook his head. "Aw, son."

The disappointment in the voice of such an important man in Nick's life hurt. No denying that. What else was coming? Condemnation? Rebuke? Outright rejection?

Lord, he was tired.

Nick cleared his throat. "My orientation isn't something about me that I can change. I've always known that, but for a long time I thought I could compromise by denying myself. It took falling in love with Jared—to tell the truth, rediscovering a very old love—to realize there is no compromise when it comes to accepting yourself. You are who you are, and if you cut off that part of yourself, you're not a whole person."

Pastor stayed quiet for almost a full minute. When he finally spoke, it was as if he were selecting each word carefully from a shelf and squaring it up before letting it come out of his mouth. "I respect the difficulty of your path and your need to express this full self, as you put it. As your friend, your elder who helped raise you, and simply someone who cares a great deal about you, I have faith this relationship with

Dr. Kumpel won't change who you are at your core, that this will make you happy in the way you need to be. However. As your pastor, I can't condone this. I can't in good conscience tell you anything except that I fear for your immortal soul."

Nick's hand tightened on his knee, and he drew a breath to slow his temper. "How God sees me or doesn't see me because of the way I am, the way He made me—I can't let someone else get in the middle of that. If He honestly wants me to be half of myself in order to be in His Kingdom, that's something the two of us will have to wrestle with when I go to meet Him. But I'll tell you, I don't believe that's how He works. I can't accept He'd make me this way and then tell me I could only be saved if I carved out a part of myself straight people don't have to. And to be honest, denying who I am isn't something you told me was part of a healthy relationship with my Maker. You can't tell me to come as I am and not hide my light under a bushel but then say you don't like the color of my light."

"And if your light involved murder or adultery? What would I say to that?"

"Murder and adultery harm other people. Me holding Jared's hand and building a family with him hurts no one. That's a rude, insulting comparison, and you know it."

Pastor's lips thinned. "You're bordering on out of line yourself right now."

"Why? Because I don't want to be equated with people who kill or emotionally wound their partners? Gosh, I can't imagine why that would upset me."

Pastor held up his hands. "Look. I understand, I do. Personally, it's not the hill I want to die on. But while theoretically I could change the rules of our church, you and I both know if I did, even for you, it would divide the community in an incredibly harmful way. As I'm sure you know, there are other men and women in the church who are homosexual, but they live their lives quietly, out of sight. If you were to do that, it wouldn't be such a big deal. That's pretty much the arrangement."

"It's not an arrangement I'm interested in."

"Given that, I'm sorry to say that you'll have to resign as deacon. That's the very least that'll happen. As for whether or not you can remain… I don't know. It's going to cause a huge fuss."

Nick thought about Kathryn, about her decision to walk away. He thought about his mother and grandmother and their frosty silences. He thought about how easy it would be if he simply gave this up, chalked it up as a casualty.

Then he considered how hard he'd worked to get this far in his life, how much he'd already sacrificed or had outright taken from him, and his will hardened like a piece of iron.

"I suppose you'll have to deal with a huge fuss, then."

Pastor ran a hand over his hair and rose. "All right. I'll see what I can do. I'm not promising anything, and no matter what, you're going to have to *work* to get people to see things your way. But I'm not going to fight you."

The corner of Nick's mouth lifted in a smile. "I'm used to fighting."

They embraced, and after Nick saw Pastor to the door, he flopped onto the couch and closed his eyes, willing the tension of the meeting to melt away.

He hadn't meant to fall asleep, but the next thing he knew, Jared was leaning over him, looking concerned.

"Are you okay, honey?" Jared asked, lightly touching his face.

Nick caught Jared's hand and kissed it. "I'm just fine," he said, and the truth was that as long as Jared was there, it wasn't a lie.

CHAPTER SIXTEEN

IT PAINED Jared to see how much Nick hurt.

"I wish there was something I could do." He said this to Owen one day as they sat alone in the doctors' lounge at the beginning of November. The two board members up for reelection, Ram and Amanda, had just cleared their hurdle, but only by the skin of their teeth. It was generally considered that the college vote had carried them through, as they were both professors. "He has so much pressure on him. He feels like he needs to do everything perfectly, better than perfectly, and worst of all, I know he's not wrong. He has to work harder to prove himself. I want to support him, and I don't feel I'm doing enough."

"Frankly I'm surprised at how little you're bossing him around." Owen sipped at his coffee. "I know you're trying to be good, but it's not like you, honestly."

"Well, I'd love to tell him what to do, but this is hardly the time for it."

"True. But that subtle *here's what you should do* attitude is kind of who you are. It has to be part of what he loves about you. I think you should lean on your strengths. I'm not saying nag him, but there's got to be a way for you to stop holding your breath. You want to help? Figure out how to be that part of yourself with him."

At first, Jared wasn't sure what to do with this advice. Every night Nick came home from work looking weary, and when Jared asked what was troubling him, he said it was the hospital funding. He and Erin were getting ready to announce the bond issue and special election for next May, but he was nervous about it passing. He worried often that his coming out had put things at risk.

This made no sense to Jared. Yes, there were some bigots, but overall when they went out together as an official couple, people smiled and waved to them more than they didn't. If anything, he thought their relationship might be a selling point. The people who found them distasteful had always found them distasteful.

The problem, he realized one night when they were out to dinner together, was one of perception.

They'd gone to Café Cuore, and the hostess greeted them with what Jared had thought was extra warmth. The server was equally pleasant. They got a few curious looks, yes, but on the whole their relationship was old news now, and most people simply went on with their lives. When Jared mentioned this to

Nick, however, Nick seemed unimpressed, or at least too distracted by worries of what voters would think.

Jared put down his fork and frowned. "But *these* are voters. They're not throwing you a parade, but they're treating you like everyone else."

"I can't know for sure my coming out won't affect the hospital until the vote actually happens. And this isn't to say Peterson doesn't have something up his sleeve, some plan to make sure it doesn't work. I'm half afraid to start anything lest I give him more ammunition."

"What do you mean, start anything? What would you start?"

Nick shushed him. "Keep your voice down."

"You honestly think he's here?"

"I think he managed to infiltrate the hospital, nearly kill us, gloated about it to me, and gleefully reminded me we can't get anywhere without proof. I think he's capable of about anything."

Does he have to do anything, though, when you're doing so much to yourself? Jared wished he knew how to say that out loud.

The next day he went to Rebecca, because he wanted an expert's opinion. "How much of this is legitimate, what he's fearing?"

Rebecca sipped her tea. "More than you'd like to admit."

This wasn't what Jared wanted to hear. "We need to help him. We need to canvass or something. We need to find the evidence to pin Peterson down, if Gilbert won't."

"I think Erin mentioned something about an ad campaign at the last meeting. But you're saying actively go door-to-door?" She considered the idea a moment, then shrugged. "It's not bad. What's the message? Outside of the obvious pitching of the hospital."

"What do you mean?"

"I mean, you're fighting subtext, right? So what are you striking back with? Are you showing them the board is united behind Nick? Do you want to underscore our diversity? Do you want to play to the voters' egos? Do you want to let them know someone sabotaged the hospital? Do you want to sell this as Copper Point strength? What's the angle?"

Jared's head swam. "All of it. I want to do all of that. We'd need to discuss the sabotage part with the full board since we'd agreed not to disclose that, but everything else… yes. Can't we do everything at once? I mean, the people who want to be against us will be against us no matter what we say. But the people who want to move forward will be drawn in by everything, and we sell it that way. We say, 'You voting like this takes Copper Point forward.' Ego appeal and all."

"You've got quite a slogan right there. St. Ann's Medical Center: Moving Copper Point Forward."

Jared clapped his hands. "That's *it*. Goddamn. Thanks, Rebecca. I'm taking this to Erin right now."

Erin was as excited as he was by the slogan, by all of it. "I say we get not only the board but the staff of the whole hospital out campaigning. We can go door-to-door, but we can have events too. We could host a fair at the community center, a kind of wellness clinic and family fun night in one. We could have the blueprints for the proposed hospital there and take community input for what they'd like to see in a new building."

Owen was into it too. "Maybe Jack could invite some outside specialists to come show what a more advanced hospital could offer. And that Ryan guy, the one with all the facts and figures, maybe he could show people what improvements would do for the community."

"I think Ryan is out. His daughter might be in, though. It doesn't matter, because we have all the information from Gilbert. We could go to the city council and see what they thought of it, maybe get them to offer insights. Hell, maybe they'll campaign with us."

Erin nodded. "There's a lot of possibility here. It's sooner than we'd planned to act, but there's nothing wrong with that. The question now is at what point are you bringing Nick into this? You'll need board approval, but you should run everything by him first as a matter of courtesy. I'm surprised you didn't start with him."

"It's to try to take some of the pressure off of him that I fell into this rabbit hole in the first place. I feel like all he can see is the negative lately, and I wanted to show him we can turn this around and make it work in our favor. That his coming out wasn't a liability. That he didn't trade his power for his identity. I feel like he knows this, but he needs help seeing it. But you're right, I need to tell him, and in a way he won't immediately dismiss because he's being a Negative Nancy."

"Wine and woo him," Owen suggested. "Honestly, I don't know why you're overcomplicating this. He's not the only one who's had his perspective blown out of the water. The two of you have always communicated with power struggle. Even when I didn't know you were secretly going out back in high school, that's how you operated. Maybe that's what he needs. Lock horns with him in a way that lets him cool off, then show him the same blueprint you showed us. And if he resists, just woo him a second time. You seriously can't lose here."

Wine and woo him while locking horns. It was so simple and so obvious. Why hadn't Jared seen it? He'd been so busy not telling Nick how to come out, staying out of his way, he'd quit doing one of the things that was, as Owen said, the hallmark of their relationship.

Well. That cease-fire ended now.

"I gotta go," Jared said, rising.

Owen smiled over the rim of his coffee mug. "Have fun."

NICK WAS exhausted in a to-the-bone kind of way, as if he'd been hauling around different-sized boulders but had to be careful so no one noticed what he held. He was worn out from the constant arguments with himself, trying to decide how much of his caution was overdone and how much of it was protective. He was weary from judging every interaction, weighing the other person as friend or foe, from sitting up late in the dark long after Jared was asleep and worrying over whether he handled this or that conversation properly. He understood objectively that he was making all of this worse, that his overthinking everything wasn't helping, but it wasn't something he could stop.

He was tired, but he was also restless. If Jared wasn't with him to select a television show or a song, he flitted from one thing to another until eventually this too made him exhausted and he gave up. Several times he'd woken up in the middle of the night to his brain already churning, and he'd gone downstairs to pace like a caged animal. Twice he'd come close to asking Jack for something to settle his nerves, but he held off because he didn't know when he *wouldn't* be anxious, and the CEO using anti-anxiety medication seemed like another thing to worry about people discovering.

His thoughts were a train he wanted to get off of, but he couldn't find the station.

What made him the most frustrated was he knew this was upsetting Jared. He tried not to worry him, but of all the people in his life, Jared was the most difficult to deceive. Plus he was the only place Nick could let himself go. There were times he couldn't stand it, he *needed* to lean against his boyfriend while they watched television, to shut his eyes and breathe in the scent of him for half an hour. If he didn't have this outlet, this touchstone, he wasn't sure he could keep going.

He was having one of those days on a Sunday in the middle of November. He'd taken his family to church as usual, but everything was still awkward on both fronts. Church itself remained an exercise of walking on coals, and as far as his family went, though he'd graduated to resuming dinner with them after, it was chilly and awkward, and he always left feeling heavy. That day he'd hoped to come home and bury himself in Jared, but his boyfriend wasn't there. He scolded himself for being disappointed. What, was it Jared's job to sit around and wait for him?

He fussed with the television and the stereo, then flipped through a magazine, never landing long on an activity, lest his thoughts catch up with him. When he heard Jared's car pulling into the garage, he sighed in relief and went to wait for him in the kitchen, a compromise to rushing out to greet him as he truly wanted to do. His heart beat faster as the door opened, even as he hurried to hide his neediness.

Then he got one look at Jared's face and forgot everything he'd been thinking about.

Jared seemed… different.

He was slightly out of breath, as if he'd run beside the car instead of driven it. His eyes had a wildness to them, a sparkle that made Nick pause. He looked dangerous.

It reminded Nick of the way Jared had been that fateful day when they were young and Jared had stalked across Nick's bedroom, pushed the handheld game out of his hands, and straddled his lap. The day that had ended up with both their pants around their ankles and Nick holding their cocks together in his grip as they thrust their tongues into each other's mouths.

Backing up, Nick took hold of the edge of the counter behind him.

The expression on Jared's face didn't change as he set his keys aside and placed himself in front of Nick. "You and I need to have a chat."

Normally that would be an ominous phrase, but the way Jared purred the syllables made *a chat* sound like *sex*, and Nick's dick responded accordingly. "What did you want to… chat about?"

"A lot of things." Jared nudged Nick's legs apart and stood between them, running one hand up the center of Nick's chest. "I have some ideas on how we can best sell the bond issue. I already ran them by Erin, and I think you'll appreciate them. But before we get to that." He trailed long fingers along Nick's jaw toward his ear. "First, I owe you an apology."

And now *apology* sounded like *blow job*. Nick felt hypnotized. It had been a while since Jared had come at him like a panther. He'd forgotten how much it turned him on. "Wh-why do I need an apology?"

"Because I took things a little too far. I was trying not to be bossy, but I forgot that at least most of the time, you *like* me this way. In private. You need to be the boss at the hospital, and you're damn good at it. Most of the time in our relationship, we share the lead. Sometimes, though, you need me to take it away from you. You've needed me to do that for some time, but I was trying so hard not to get in your way over coming out, I missed the cues. So, I'm sorry, honey." He ran his thumb over Nick's bottom lip, tugging it away from his teeth. "I'm going to make it *all* up to you today."

Yep. Nick's dick was *all* the way at attention. "What is it you want me to do?"

Jared placed a soft kiss on Nick's lips. Then he took his hands and tugged him toward the stairs. "Follow me."

Nick went willingly. Goddamn, but yes, he liked this side of Jared. Bossy, sexy, confident. He only liked it in Jared, though, because he was the only one Nick had ever gone to bed with who knew how to balance it. He wasn't arrogant about it. He wasn't shaming.

He took Nick's control only on a sixth sense of when he knew his partner wanted it taken, or in this case, needed it. And he always gave it back in a manner that made Nick feel superhuman. It was the sweetest space. He could be a little bit submissive without giving up an inch of pride.

He needed that so much right now.

In their bedroom, the curtains were drawn, and Jared kept them that way, lighting a few of the accent lamps. When Nick started to undress, Jared waved a finger at him. "No. You're not in charge at the moment. You need a day off from everything. You're not allowed to so much as think without my permission, not for the next several hours." He winked and slid a hand underneath Nick's shirt. "Doctor's orders."

Nick grinned even as the boulders he held started to lose some of their weight. "Playing doctor, are we? That's a new one." A terrible thought stole the light from his heart. "Did you do this with the fireman?"

Jared tweaked his nose. "Stop thinking. But for your information, no, I didn't play doctor with the fireman. I didn't play with anyone like I do with you. I couldn't."

More of the boulders fell away. "Me either."

"Hold up your arms so I can undress you."

"Yes, Dr. Kumpel."

Jared's smile sent a delightful shiver down Nick's spine. "See? I've only given you one order, and you're already more relaxed. Just think how you're going to feel after several hours."

This. This is what I've been missing, who I've needed to give it to me. Nick arched an eyebrow as

Jared worked the T-shirt over his head. "Hours, huh? You've got that kind of stamina?"

Jared cupped Nick's face and nipped at his lips. "Be a good boy, and I'll let you find out."

Nick shut his eyes and leaned into his lover. "I love you so much."

This time the kiss on his lips was slow and sweet. "I love you too."

He let everything go as Jared undressed him, surrendering not only his control but every one of those heavy thoughts as Jared first peeled his clothing away, then led him to their bed. He lay back on the comforter, able to do nothing but moan in pleasure as Jared kissed his way down Nick's body, covering every inch of his torso in carnal trails, kneading his hips in a gentle massage. He writhed as Jared pushed his feet to the mattress and mapped his groin with the same tender lovemaking, kissing around his cock but not on it, laving his balls and teasing his taint, tickling his thighs with his tongue. When Jared finally sucked him down, Nick gasped, thrusting forward to meet him.

He was surprised when Jared got him off without further teasing, but then, as instructed, he hadn't been thinking, only following the pleasure as Jared laid it out for him. He came into Jared's mouth, then lay gasping on the bed, his body so heavy he couldn't move.

Jared wasn't done with him, though. While Nick's head spun, Jared kissed Nick's abdomen as he got to his feet.

"Lie here and rest. I'm going to draw some water for a bath."

Nick nodded, letting his eyes fall shut as Jared walked away. He focused on the sounds of the room, the faint whisper of traffic from the street, a man calling his dog at a neighboring house. He heard the water running in the bathroom, a lulling rush. His mind started up a bit, but only to hope Jared stayed with him as he bathed.

He must have dozed, because abruptly Jared was touching him, calling for him to rise and follow, and the water had stopped. When they got to the bathroom, to Nick's delight, it was full of candles, and an open bottle of wine and two glasses sat on the counter.

Jared shed the robe he was wearing, revealing his nakedness, then climbed into the water, gently tugging Nick after. "Come sit in front of me. I'll wash your back. Then we'll sip wine and loll here until the water gets cold."

Nick approached the tub dubiously. "Are we going to fit in here together?"

"Oh, it'll be a near thing, but I don't think we'll have to call emergency services to get out or anything." After scooting the wine closer and fussing with his phone, Jared patted the edge of the tub. "Come on."

Prince, of course, started to play. "Call My Name," one of Nick's favorites, of which Jared was well aware. The languid sound wrapped around him, making him feel easy and good. He laughed as they struggled to fit in the water, displacing it so much it sloshed a little over the edges. But eventually they got settled and Nick nestled against Jared's shoulder, his glass of wine resting on the ledge.

"This is good." Nick ran his hand over Jared's wet thigh. "Sitting with you, a glass of wine, listening to Prince while soaking in hot water. Only way it gets better is if we have a bigger tub."

"Do you remember the day I figured out what 'Alphabet St.' was about?" Jared stroked his fingers in Nick's hair.

Nick laughed. "Oh my God, I still laugh sometimes when I hear it."

"How was I supposed to know anything about oral sex with women? I was so panicked, though, when you were such an expert on it. I'd finally convinced myself you were into me, and then I thought I was wrong."

"Hey. I could have been bisexual."

"Yes, well, my thinking was exceptionally binary at that point. I was obsessed with trying to read every tea leaf that would tell me if you were into me or not."

"I was into you."

"I caught up eventually." Jared kissed his hair. "Those were some magical years. I didn't always like hiding, but I loved being with you. You were my whole world when we were together, and when we were apart, all I did was think of you. I'm sorry I messed it up."

"We both messed it up. And anyway, that's the past."

"I know. But I regret we didn't have more time together." He trailed fingers across Nick's chest, leaving a river of water. "We have the time now. And I'm not wasting a second of it. Not ever again. I'm going to treasure you, Nick. Every single day. I can't take away the things that make life difficult for you and wear you down. But I can be a safe place for you, and I can support you. And I can remind you of things you can't always see so clearly from where you're standing." He kissed the side of Nick's head, leaning against his temple. "You're doing a great job. You've done incredible things, and you're going to keep doing even more. You've gotten so much done in such a short amount of time, and you did it with the care and meticulousness that's your hallmark. I'm so incredibly proud of you. I hope you're proud of yourself."

Nick's eyes had fallen closed in the middle of Jared's speech, but when he got to *you're doing a great job*, Nick surrendered and let his tears fall. They were tears of exhaustion, of relief, of gratitude. Of love.

This is what I needed. To be this version of myself, in this way, with this man.

"Thanks," he whispered at last.

"Everything's going to come around." Jared kept stroking Nick's arm. "The hospital funding and rebuilding. The bond issue. Your family. *Our* family. It'll take time, and there will be bumps in the road, but we'll get there. I know you'll work hard no matter what, but I want you to know I'll always be here beside you." He kissed Nick openmouthed on the back of his neck. "And tonight, I'll be inside you."

Nick laced his fingers with Jared's, tipping his head forward and giving him better access to his neck.

He groaned in pleasure as Jared touched him, kissed him, washed his body. He sipped the wine Jared brought to his lips, allowed it and the heated water to spin him gently away from his cares. When Jared let out the water and had him rise, Nick went, feeling as if he were floating now, listing a bit as Jared toweled him off.

Jared led Nick to the bed once more, this time sending him facedown. Jared switched the music to the bedroom stereo, and Nick smiled into the comforter when "Alphabet St." started playing.

Then he sucked in a breath as he felt hands against his thighs and a hot mouth sliding along his crack.

His legs trembled as he rose to his knees, as Jared parted his cheeks with his thumbs and licked inside in time to Prince's beat. Occasionally his hand would slip down and stroke Nick, ensuring he was at nothing less than full hardness, but mostly Jared stayed at his post, writing the alphabet with his tongue against Nick's ass.

"Can I fuck you, baby?" he asked once the song was finished.

Nick whimpered and let his knees fall apart wider in response.

He kept finding new depths to release into. When Jared's slick fingers entered him, working him open and preparing him, Nick tumbled further away from his worries. When Jared's cock pushed at his entrance, he thought of nothing but this moment, of connecting with this man, of tumbling into blissful, wild places with the two of them alone. When Jared pounded into him, Nick let his body go slack, taking it, eager to have it, riding the wave of pleasure Jared asked him to accept.

They came one shortly after the other, and Nick, completely spent now, drifted into a sort of bliss coma. He lay there as Jared cleaned him up, not so much as shifting until Jared came back to bed, spooning up behind him.

"I'm going to go make us dinner now." He kissed Nick's shoulder. "How about you stay here and sleep until you're rested? I'll keep everything warm in the oven until you're awake. And then we can watch *Luther* together while we eat."

It sounded wonderful. It sounded perfect. All Nick could manage was a small grunt of acknowledgment, though, as he drifted away, every one of his cares behind him, his mind and body insulated by the safety and security of Jared's love.

CHAPTER SEVENTEEN

A WEEK before Thanksgiving, Jared stood on the doorstep to Pearle Dinah Emerson's house, straightening his tie and squaring his shoulders as he waited for someone to answer the bell. He'd already run his plan by Emmanuella, who had approved after a few edits and cautionary pieces of advice. Jared made note of everything she said, thanked her for her help, then asked when the best time to visit was.

Now here he was.

Aniyah answered the door, her expression cool and unreadable. "Come in." She held the door open wide for him.

This had been an appointment, set by Emmanuella, so his arrival wasn't some dramatic surprise—Emmanuella's first edit.

With a murmured thank-you and incline of his head, Jared entered. He glanced at Aniyah's feet and the entryway for clues as to whether or not he should remove his shoes—he couldn't remember if he had when he was younger, but since Simon had adopted the practice in deference to his spouse, Jared was more cognizant of the rule. Aniyah wore house slippers, and there were several pairs of shoes by the door. At their house, Nick did tend to shed his shoes for the most part as soon as he'd entered. Jared decided to err on the side of caution and stepped out of his loafers.

Aniyah raised an eyebrow at him but made no comment. "We're in the parlor." She walked away.

Jared followed her.

Grandma Emerson and Emmanuella sat near one another, Grandma Emerson in the tall wingback chair on the end, Emmanuella adjacent to her on the sofa. Aniyah headed for the seat near her daughter, gesturing at a smaller chair opposite her mother for Jared. "Have a seat."

Jared went to the chair, but first he withdrew the package he'd carried from his jacket. He set it on the table in front of Grandma Emerson. "These are for you, Mrs. Emerson. Some fresh roasted beans from Gus's shop and the strawberry hard candies from the hospital gift shop."

She eyed the package with reluctant approval. "You do your homework." Her gaze narrowed. "But if you've come here because you think my grandson needs some white boy to intervene between him and his family, you can take your present and go."

"I wouldn't dare to think such a thing." He paused, then smiled ruefully as he stared at the coffee table. "All right. I'll be honest with you. I would. I would boss anyone around for Nick's sake, if I thought it could make him happy. But I know most of the time it wouldn't do that, and in this instance, it would upset him a great deal. So let me revise that to say no, I'm not here because I think Nick needs saving."

Grandma Emerson harrumphed. "Why *are* you here?"

"Because I want to tell you about something the rest of us are doing to help Nick, and I wanted to make sure you knew you were invited to participate." He cleared his throat. "Also, I wanted to let you know my intentions toward him. I understand you're coming to terms with his orientation in your own time, and I don't want to get in the way, but I'm not waiting any longer, either. It's not good for Nick, and it's not good for me."

Aniyah pursed her lips and leaned forward. "Who are you to decide what's good for him?"

"His boyfriend. But I don't decide *for* him. I decide *with* him." He held up his hands, losing the patience Emmanuella had cautioned him to keep. "He has so much riding on him with the hospital, but also all the pressures he puts on himself to maintain a certain image. I respect his standards for himself, but I also try to give him a place where he can let go from that, just for a little while. My schedule doesn't allow me to dote on him quite the way a stay-at-home partner would, but I keep track of him at work, and my network lets me know when I should make time to pop by to say hello and cheer him up or appear with lunch."

He stopped himself, taking a slow breath before continuing. "This isn't what I came here to say. My point is that I care about him. I understand caring for him means caring for the three of you—and this is easy, because I've always had the highest regard for you and the deepest respect. I hate seeing you at odds with him…" Emmanuella's eyes widened, and she shook her head imperceptibly. He gave a slight nod to let her know he understood and wasn't taking that any further. "…but I also understand this is complicated and a matter between your family. I don't expect you to welcome me in. But I do—"

The emotion came out of nowhere, choking him up, surprising and disarming him. He froze, blinking, unsure of how to proceed, panicking as a tear ran down his cheek. He wiped at it furiously. "Sorry." He attempted to laugh it off, but it sounded hollow. "I'm not sure—" His voice cracked, and he stopped talking, glancing around desperately for a tissue.

What was wrong with him?

A box appeared in front of him, handed over by Aniyah. He took two with a murmured thank-you and dabbed at his eyes.

In the silence, Grandma Emerson spoke. "I heard about the argument you had with your folks in the hospital lobby."

She'd spoken quietly, but the words were a punch to Jared's gut. He wiped at his eyes again and took a steadying breath. "I—yes. They…." He didn't know how to finish that sentence. *They're terrible racists, and I'm embarrassed by them.* That's what he wanted to say.

But in that moment, he only felt hollow and sad. Why?

Grandma Emerson continued, her voice firm. "I'm curious as to how a man comes before me, wanting me to reconcile with my grandson, when he can't reconcile with his own parents."

Ouch. He glanced up at her, surprised. If she'd heard about the lobby, then she'd heard everything, right? Yes, looking at her face, he could tell her question was more complicated than it felt on its surface. Or maybe it wasn't. She wanted him to answer, to answer honestly, but…

But *ouch*.

He would do it for Nick, though.

Clutching the tissues tight in his hand, he looked her in the eye. "I can't reconcile with them." Another tear ran down his cheek, but he didn't stop it. "They found out about Nick and me in high school, and they showed me their true colors in a manner I can't forgive, because they've made it clear they don't intend to change their ways. I can't be family with people consumed by hate."

"So you won't have family at all?"

God, why couldn't he quit crying? He didn't want them to think he was trying to put on an act. "I'll have the family I've made with others. And hopefully with Nick, a family of my own."

Aniyah perked up at this, surprised, cautious. "You… you mean to have children?"

"Yes. I want to have four, but of course it all depends on what my partner wants. It was always my dream to have two fathered by each of us. And if it was Nick, I wanted to find a Black surrogate so—" He wiped at his eyes again, swallowed. "I'm so sorry. I don't know why I can't stop crying."

"You plan to have this large family with Nick," Grandma Emerson said, her tone heavy, "but you'll stand back if we don't accept you? Let all that family be embraced but you?"

Jared's tissues were ragged strings now, useless. "I… I don't want to get in Nick's way. Not of his family."

Aniyah snorted. "You honestly think he could let you stay in the cold like that?"

Jared's heart constricted. "But if you're holding back because of me—"

He stopped as he saw their faces. They weren't holding back. Not anymore. Somehow in the middle of that, they'd changed.

Also, too late he realized he'd been arrogant again, thinking this was all about him. It was maybe tangentially about him, but at its essence, this remained about Nick through and through. They were still working their way through this. But they were coming around. And when they did, they'd embrace him too.

Family.

"Give the boy more tissues, Aniyah. Emmanuella, pour him some coffee. And, Jared, tell us about whatever this is Nick needs help with."

"Forget about that." Aniyah passed the box of tissues to Jared with a light in her eyes. "I want to hear more about this surrogate mother."

Jared blew his nose, then smiled. "Well, at home I have a binder. But I do have some websites bookmarked I can show you."

As he pulled out his phone, Aniyah moved over and patted the space between her and Emmanuella. He went, showing them the first website as he sat. But as the two of them looked, he glanced up at Grandma Emerson.

"Mrs. Emerson, I'll come show you as well once they're done looking."

She waved an impatient hand at him. "Let them take their time. I'll wait for the actual great-grandbabies. And stop calling me Mrs. Emerson. You're to call me Grandma."

Jared's heart swelled. "Yes, Grandma Emerson."

JARED HAD explained his plan for public awareness regarding the new hospital, but Nick didn't fully appreciate the depth of it until he saw it in action.

He'd personally felt they could wait to call for the bond issue, had wanted to study things more before acting. It was Erin who convinced him to move forward.

"I appreciate your hesitation, and normally I'd be all for it. But the truth is, we have a ton of data already, and we know Peterson's goal is to undermine us before our special election. So why not get ahead of him? He's been working on public opinion. Let's not let him have it to himself any longer."

And so they'd begun. The board met in yet another emergency session, hammered out a plan, and started their attack. They began with a press conference the Friday before Thanksgiving, Erin and Nick unveiling the full results of the Gilbert study, including the reports of sabotage. They'd consulted with Allison Christy before they let this out of the bag, and she'd agreed it might not be a bad play. Maybe, she said, someone would even come forward.

So that's what they did. They told the public absolutely everything that had happened, put all the information online, and made sure people knew they'd work with the authorities to find the culprit, but in the meantime they were going forward with the firm's recommendations to rebuild the hospital. They unveiled Gilbert's blueprints and dossier full of proposed amenities, and they were clear about projected costs.

Then they unleashed the hounds.

Before the press conference, the board members had all identified at least one individual within the community friendly to their cause and willing to write a letter to the editor of the local paper, and they deployed those individuals now. They also took to the streets, canvassing door-to-door with flyers giving information about the project and a number to call if they had any questions. Several doctors and nurses had been roped in as well, and when Dr. Amin went door-to-door, she brought her entire family.

But what surprised Nick were the churches. Several of them came forward on their own, asking how they could help, and Erin gave them canvassing packets and sectors of the town and surrounding county to reach out to, and on Saturday, they all got to work.

One of the churches was Nick's, and the representative leading the charge was his grandmother. When he heard about this, he hurried to meet her. She only smiled at him and patted his arm, saying she knew he was busy and didn't want to take up too much of his time.

She also leaned in close and said, "That boy of yours is a good one."

Nick stared at her, dizzy. "I know. I'm glad you agree."

"Bring him by for lunch tomorrow after church. Oh, and I expect you both for Thanksgiving. I'll be making pineapple upside-down cake."

His breath caught. So they were okay? Just like that, they were okay?

Grandma Emerson's gaze narrowed, but there was a brightness in her eyes he hadn't realized how much he'd missed until now. "We still need to talk, as a family. We need to do a lot of talking. But since it's clear you intend to make that man part of your family too, you best bring him along for the conversations. Is that clear?"

Nick's eyes filled with tears, but he didn't allow them to fall, just pushed them back with the force of his grin. "It's clear, Grandma. We'll be there for Thanksgiving."

She didn't smile, but she did pat him on the shoulder, and her grip lingered for several seconds before she walked away.

Cynthia Ryan showed up as well, bringing a team of volunteers from Milwaukee. She waved at Nick when she saw him, and when he introduced her to Jared, she grinned wide and gave them both a huge hug.

As she pulled away from Nick, she whispered in his ear, "Don't worry. I'll get Dad to come around."

Jack had been put in charge of out-of-town media, and he was often in front of a television camera or calling in to a radio show, explaining what was going on in Copper Point and always pushing their message, St. Ann's Medical Center: Moving Copper Point Forward. He told the story of how he'd come to the small town seeking a quiet life but had been pleased to discover how welcoming and culturally diverse it was, thanks to the college and staff at the hospital. He talked about how excited he was by the improvements at St. Ann's, which he considered to be on par with those of any hospital in the area. "We have an unprecedented level of talent for such a small region. I don't think people realize what a treasure they have right under their noses. I hope they choose to invest in taking care of that and growing it, rather than letting an outside company swoop in and undo everything this town has worked so hard for."

That was usually when he deferred to Nick to explain the takeover threats looming if the bond issue didn't pass, and for him to make his plea to anyone who had information on the sabotage.

"We'll protect any whistleblower who comes forward. Our goal is to safeguard health care in this town above all else, and finding proof of the saboteur would go a long way toward that."

No one had come forward yet, but Nick kept making the plea all the same.

He canvassed as well, sometimes with Jared, sometimes with Erin, sometimes with his church, sometimes on his own. He quickly wished he had done so long ago. He learned more about his town—the good and the bad—than he ever had before. What they wanted, what they needed, what they feared, what motivated them. Some of his interactions confirmed his own fears about how he was judged and what sorts of double standards existed for him and him alone because of who he was—the color of his skin and who he chose to love.

But there were plenty who went out of their way to let him know not only did they support him, they believed in him. They told him how much they appreciated his leadership, told stories of how certain doctors had affected them personally. Some got a mischievous look in their eye and offered their congratulations to him and Jared, saying how much they loved the story of how they'd fallen in love while trapped in an elevator.

Nick never knew what to say to that one, but thankfully it only came up when Jared was around, and he handled it. With a wink, Jared would put a hand on Nick's arm and reply, "Oh, I was in love with him long before that."

By the time mid-December rolled around, public polling was starting to shift in their favor. It wasn't enough, not quite, but it was a decent start. "We'll just keep wearing them down," Jared would say whenever Nick worried they wouldn't be able to swing sentiment in time for the vote. "The story about the sabotage is getting a lot of traction. You should see the theories running on Copper Point People."

Nick shuddered. "I'd rather not."

"The point is, they're on our side, mostly. All it's going to take is a few more nudges, and they're putty in our hands."

The nudge came sooner than they'd thought, and from an unfortunate corner: just before Christmas, the mayor of Copper Point had a heart attack.

He was in the middle of a city council meeting when it happened, and the entire board ended up in the waiting room with his wife while Dr. Amin performed the quadruple bypass surgery. It was so complicated she asked Jack to assist, and because of the high-profile nature of the patient, Erin and Nick both went to sit with Penny Wagner while they waited on news of her husband. They started to leave when Dr. Amin came out post-surgery, but Penny gripped their hands tight, unwilling to face the news alone.

"He's going to be fine." Dr. Amin smiled at Penny. "He'll need a great deal of rest, and I want to talk to you both about dietary changes he needs to make, but the bottom line is the prognosis is good."

"Oh, thank God." Squeezing Erin and Nick's hands, Penny started to cry.

Amin was a wily one, though. Because this wasn't all she said to the Wagners, and before the mayor was discharged, Nick was summoned to the mayor's hospital room.

"Dr. Amin explained everything to me." The mayor looked weary but determined. "How lucky I was to have a hospital with not only a cardiac unit but a specialist such as Dr. Wu on staff. That if it weren't for St. Ann's being what it is, I would have most likely died on my way to a larger hospital. How if St. Ann's isn't supported by the community, it'll turn into a critical access only hospital, with no supports like the ones I just enjoyed. She made it clear all this was your doing, and the new leadership of the board. So I want you to understand you have my full support, and I'll see to it you have the support of the city council as well. We'll be behind this bond issue, and we'll back it publicly."

Nick couldn't believe this. He tried to gather himself as best he could, inclining his head in acknowledgment. "We're grateful for your support."

"No, sir, it's the other way around. And to this point, I'd like to ask you to be the marshal for the next Founder's Day parade. It was when I asked Dr. Amin to be it that she set me straight on everything. She'll be deputy marshal, though."

Nick couldn't help a smile. "I'd be honored."

The mayor was true to his word. The holidays weren't over before he had the city council marching to his new tune, and though he was confined to bed rest, *they* were out in force with the rest of the canvassers, on his order. His wife went for him in his stead, tearfully telling his story and sharing her gratitude to St. Ann's Medical Center that she still had her husband. Sometimes she canvassed with the staff nutritionist, who had been working with her to prepare more heart-healthy meals better suited to the mayor's new diet.

Public opinion was shifting now, and not slowly anymore. Surely Peterson would try something again soon, but this time Nick would be ready for him.

On New Year's Eve, when Nick was trying to leave his office, the janitor came to see him.

Nick knew the man vaguely, had said hello to him in the halls, but that was as far as their association went. Something was clearly troubling the older gentleman, however, and Nick invited him to sit and had Wendy bring them some coffee to drink. He also had her shut the door on her way out.

After a few minutes of polite conversation, Kevin gripped his cup tightly and confessed why he'd come to see Nick. "I should have come forward sooner, but I was too nervous. I think I might know who sabotaged the elevator."

Nick sat up a little, trying to tamp down his eagerness. "I'm listening."

Kevin worried the rim of his cup, not meeting Nick's gaze. "I'm not sure, is the thing. I don't want to get people in trouble if I'm wrong. But I don't want people trying to hurt the hospital to go free. And I feel guilty with everyone else working to help, and I haven't said anything."

Every fiber of Nick's being vibrated. "It's all right. All I need is the information you have, and we'll investigate from there. If it comes to nothing, it comes to nothing."

"Well—see, I don't know if I trust the police. They pulled one over on my cousin years ago, and I don't think they've changed much since then."

"I fully understand." Nick decided to take a risk. "If it's any comfort to you, we'll be giving this information to the private firm helping us as well as the authorities. And I'll have to talk to Rebecca about how to best go about it, but perhaps we can share our discovery with the police… slowly."

Kevin brightened. "I love Rebecca. She's amazing. My—" He stopped, his nose going a bit red, but then he carried on, his voice a little softer. "My husband and I both like her a lot."

It hit Nick then, confirmed by the way Kevin was looking at him, the silent message conveyed by the man in front of him. *The fact that you're gay too is the only reason I came forward. The only reason I trust you.*

Nick smiled. "I didn't know you were married, Kevin. But I'm realizing I have a lot to learn about the deeper workings of my own hospital. Jared is usually the first to point this out to me."

Kevin's ears were red now too, but he seemed significantly more relaxed. "The two of you are good together." He winked. "You should get married too."

"I'm not at all opposed to the idea."

Kevin's smile lingered a little longer, and then he lowered his gaze to his mug. "There were new security guards the night of the accident, you know."

Nick nodded. "We've wondered about them too. We got statements from them, and once we knew about the sabotage, we tried to check the surveillance footage, except it had all been erased. They both quit a month after they started, which was suspicious, but we don't have any evidence. We wanted to follow up with them recently, but we can't locate them. The information they gave us on their employment forms was fake."

"That's the thing." Kevin held up his phone. "See, I thought they seemed odd right off, so I snapped their picture when they weren't looking. I have a clear shot of both of them near the elevator control room, which they have no business being in. Also, my husband thinks he might know one of them. He swears he saw him last week."

Nick's heart beat wildly in his ears. "Kevin, I would be so grateful if you'd email that photo to me and to Erin and have your husband give a statement to the authorities. Or even simply to Rebecca. I promise you, if they didn't do anything, they won't be charged."

Kevin nodded, as if this was exactly what he'd expected to hear. "But they probably did it, didn't they? And would turn on the one who hired them, unless they're sure the crooked police won't touch them.

Because this is the other thing I worried about. Maybe everyone's already been paid off."

"Well, this is why I bet Rebecca will make sure there are reporters with her when she takes them to the district attorney."

"She's the greatest, isn't she?"

"She really is." Nick nodded to Kevin's phone. "And so are you, sir. So are you."

EPILOGUE

THE DAY of the Founder's Day Parade was bright and sunny, and almost too warm.

"I'm going to roast in this suit," Nick complained as Jared fussed with his bow tie.

"We'll tell the kids to spray you with their water pistols." Jared smoothed the tie in place and stood back to admire his work. "You look perfect."

Jared didn't look so bad either. They were wearing matching ties, their way of staying together despite the fact that they'd be stationed a significant way apart during the parade. Nick was the parade marshal, near the middle of the front behind the combined college and high school marching band, and Jared walked along with the extensive St. Ann's float, passing out flyers and doing magic tricks that produced tokens valid for spending at the St. Ann's booths that would be set up near the community center once the parade was over. He'd do all this wearing his white doctor's coat, which looked significantly cooler than Nick's.

"I heard you talking to Rebecca this morning," Jared said as they drove to the parade route. "Any more news?"

Nick waved at someone over the top of his steering wheel as they passed. "We should be getting a check by the end of the year." The security guards had confessed everything as soon as they were confronted, especially with Rebecca making it clear if they didn't, they were looking at even more jail time. Peterson's hands were of course on everything, but his company and the insurance companies whose agents had made illicit deeds without their knowledge were eager to settle out of court, shoving Peterson out the airlock as quickly as possible. "We should be able to cut the amount down from the bond issue that passed to almost nothing. It'll all be in the paper tomorrow, but I think she had a news van with her, so maybe on the news tonight too."

"Excellent. Oh, speaking of news vans—I think there will be some at the parade and celebration after. We're hot items right now, our little hospital."

"Good. We'll take the publicity. It's like free ads every time they do this. If it keeps up, we might have to expand the blueprint for the new building."

Jared smiled. "I hear Jeremiah Ryan is coming."

Nick grinned. "Yeah. He wants to take us to dinner afterward. Cynthia will be there too."

"Can't wait."

Jared kissed him goodbye when they got to the start of the route, leaving him to go to his own post. Dr. Amin and her family waved to Nick from their car, which was one ahead of Nick's. They were in a classic Cadillac convertible, but Nick was in a brand-new Chevrolet Camaro, courtesy of the local dealership. His job as parade marshal, apparently, was to simply sit on the back of the car, wave at people, and if he chose, throw candy to the kids.

He chose to throw the candy.

It was a heady feeling, being parade marshal. To sit in the back of that car and be driven through town as if he were the biggest celebrity they could arrange for, to be cheered and waved at everywhere he went. Oh, there were some actively lowering their hands and turning away, but they were few and far between, and they got dark looks from their neighbors. The mood right now was celebration, and everyone loved the narrative going for St. Ann's and its CEO.

It was also fun to ride behind the bands, to hear them blasting out pop songs arranged for instruments, to watch the college kids weave and dance around the high schoolers who were mostly trying to stay in their regulation square. The Amin kids were in the car ahead of him, eyes as big as saucers as they took in the town waving and cheering for them.

When they got in front of the mayor's stand, though, the band stopped to perform a song. This was standard, Nick supposed, so he settled back to enjoy it.

Except as they began to play, he recognized the opening notes of Prince's "Kiss." He also noted the band wasn't staying in front of the mayor, but instead was weaving its way backward and forming up around him, facing him.

And out of nowhere, there was Jared, wearing his doctor's coat with the collar up, a microphone in his hand as he belted out the words over the top of the band, singing them off-key at Nick. And dancing.

He looked ridiculous, as silly as he did when he did the K-pop lip syncs with Simon and Owen. In fact Owen and Simon were there, as well as Jack and Erin, playing his backup singers and singing just as badly. But Jared was the star of the show, having a great time, and it was clear he was doing it all for Nick.

Smiling, Nick leaned back and grooved along.

When the song was over, the crowd cheered, and Jared climbed over the side of the convertible to sit beside Nick.

"I love you," Nick said, laughing.

"I love you too." Jared raised an eyebrow and looked near the side of Nick's head. "Oh—hold on. There's something…." He reached behind Nick's ear, plucked at the air, and reemerged holding a gleaming golden ring.

The crowd around them went wild. The trumpets in the band blasted their enthusiasm.

Nick's heart swelled, but he played along. "Now how did that get there?"

"Magic." Jared slid the ring on Nick's finger. "And would you look at that, it fits. Well, what do you think?"

In answer, Nick took Jared's face in his and kissed him soundly.

Read More About Copper Point Medical in…

www.dreamspinnerpress.com

Copper Point Medical: Book One

The brilliant but brooding new doctor encounters Copper Point's sunny nurse-next-door… and nothing can stand in the way of this romance.

Dr. Hong-Wei Wu has come to Copper Point, Wisconsin, after the pressures of a high-powered residency burned him out of his career before he started. Ashamed of letting his family down after all they've done for him, he plans to live a quiet life as a simple surgeon in this tiny northern town. His plans, however, don't include his outgoing, kind, and attractive surgical nurse, Simon Lane.

Simon wasn't ready for the new surgeon to be a handsome charmer who keeps asking him for help getting settled and who woos him with amazing Taiwanese dishes. There's no question—Dr. Wu is flirting with him, and Simon is flirting back. The problem is, St. Ann's has a strict no-dating policy between staff, which means their romance is off the table… unless they bend the rules.

But a romance that keeps them—literally—in the closet can't lead to happy ever after. Simon doesn't want to stay a secret, and Hong-Wei doesn't want to keep himself removed from life, not anymore. To secure their happiness, they'll have to change the administration's mind. But what other secrets will they uncover along the way, about Copper Point… and about each other?

CHAPTER ONE

Dr. Hong-Wei Wu cracked as he boarded the plane to Duluth.

He'd distracted himself on the first leg of the flight from Houston with a few drinks and the medical journal he'd brought in his bag. He nibbled at the in-flight meal, raising his eyebrow at their "Asian noodles" beneath a microwaved chicken breast.

He realized how long it would be until he ate his sister's or his grandmother's cooking again, and his chest tightened, but he pushed his feelings aside and focused on the article about the effects of perioperative gabapentin use on postsurgical pain in patients undergoing head and neck surgery.

When he disembarked at Minneapolis to transfer to his final destination, the reality of what Hong-Wei was about to do bloomed before him, but he faced it with a whiskey neat in an airport bar. Unquestionably he'd require some adjustments, but he'd make it work. If he could succeed at Baylor, he could succeed at a tiny hospital in a remote town in northern Wisconsin.

Except you didn't succeed. You panicked, you let your family down, and you ran away.

The last of the whiskey chased that nagging bit of truth out of his thoughts, and when he stood in line for priority boarding for his last flight, he was sure he had himself properly fortified once again.

Then he stepped onto the plane.

It had fewer than twenty rows, and either he was imagining things, or those were propellers on the wings. Was that legal? It had to be a mistake. This couldn't be a commercial plane. Yet no, there was a flight attendant with the airline's logo on his lapel, and the people behind Hong-Wei held tickets, acting as if this was all entirely normal.

He peered around an elderly couple to speak to the flight attendant. "Sir? Excuse me? Where is first class?"

The attendant gave Hong-Wei an apologetic look that meant nothing but bad news. "They downgraded the plane at the last minute due to low passenger load, so there isn't technically a first-class section. You should have received a refund on your ticket. If you didn't, contact customer service right away when we land."

Hong-Wei hadn't received a refund, as he hadn't been the one to buy the ticket. The hospital had. He fought to keep his jaw from tightening. "So these are the seats?" They were the most uncomfortable-looking things he'd ever seen, and he could tell already his knees were going to be squeezed against the back of the person ahead of him. "Can I at least upgrade to an exit row?"

The attendant gave him an even more apologetic look. "I'm so sorry, those seats are sold out. But I can offer you complimentary drinks and an extra bag of peanuts."

An extra bag of peanuts.

As Hong-Wei stared at his narrow seat on the plane that would take him to the waiting arms of his escorts from St. Ann's Medical Center, the walls of doubt and insecurity he'd held back crushed down upon him.

You shouldn't have left Houston. What were you thinking? It's bad enough you ran, throwing away everything your family sacrificed for. Why did you take this job? Why not any of the other prestigious institutions that offered for you? Why didn't you at least remain close to home?

You're a failure. You're a disgrace to your family. How will you ever face them again?

"Excuse me, but do you mind if I slip past?"

Hong-Wei looked down. A tiny elderly white woman smiled up at him, her crinkled blue eyes clouded by cataracts. She wore a bright yellow pantsuit, clutching a handbag of the same color.

Breaking free of his terror-stricken reverie, Hong-Wei stepped aside. "Pardon me. I was startled, was all. I wasn't expecting such a small plane."

The woman waved a hand airily as she shuffled into her seat. "Oh, they always stuff us into one of these puddle jumpers on the way to Duluth. This is big compared to the last one I was on."

They made commercial planes *smaller* than this? Hong-Wei suppressed a shudder.

With an exhale of release, the woman eased into the window seat in her row.

More people were piling into the plane now, and Hong-Wei had become an obstacle by standing in the aisle. Consigning himself to his fate, he stowed his carry-on and settled into the seat, wincing as he arranged his knees. When he finished, his seatmate was smiling expectantly at him, holding out her hand.

"Grace Albertson. Pleasure to meet you."

The last thing he wanted was conversation, but he didn't want to be rude, especially to someone her age. Forcing himself not to grimace, he accepted her hand. "Jack Wu. A pleasure to meet you as well."

Ms. Albertson's handshake was strong despite some obvious arthritis. "So where are you from, Jack?"

Hong-Wei matched Ms. Albertson's smile. "Houston. And yourself?"

"Oh, I grew up outside of St. Peter, but now I live in Eden Prairie. I fly up to Duluth regular, though, to see my great-granddaughter." She threaded her fingers over her midsection. "Houston, you say. So you were born here? In the United States, I mean."

"I was born in Taiwan. My family moved here when I was ten."

"Is that so? That would make you… well, do they call you first- or second-generation? Bah, I don't know about that stuff." She laughed and dusted wrinkled hands in the air. "My grandmother came here when she was eighteen, a new bride. Didn't speak a word of English. She learned, but if she got cross with you, she started speaking Norwegian. We always wondered if she was swearing at us." Ms. Albertson lifted her eyebrows at Hong-Wei. "You speak English quite nicely. But then I suppose you learned it growing up?"

"I studied in elementary school and with private tutors, but I struggled a bit when I first arrived."

What an understatement that was. It was good Hong-Su wasn't here. Even Ms. Albertson's status as an elder wouldn't have protected her from his sister's lecture on why it wasn't okay to ask Asian Americans where they were from. Though simply thinking of Hong-Su reminded him he wouldn't be going home to her tonight to complain about another white person asking him where he was from.

Have I made a terrible mistake?

Ms. Albertson nodded sagely. "Well, it's a credit to you. I never learned any language but English, though my mother told me I should learn Norwegian and talk to my grandmother properly. I took a year of it in high school, but I'm ashamed to tell you I barely passed the course and can't remember but three or four words of the language now. You must have worked hard to speak as well as you do. I wouldn't know but that you were born here, from the way you talk."

Before Hong-Wei could come up with a polite reply, a bag hit him in the side of his head. A steadier stream of passengers had begun to board the plane, and a middle-aged, overweight businessman's shoulder bag thudded against every seat as the man shuffled an awkward sideways dance down the narrow aisles. Either he didn't realize he'd hit Hong-Wei or didn't care, because he continued single-mindedly on… to the exit row.

Well, for that alone, Hong-Wei resented him.

His seatmate clucked her tongue. "Some people have no manners. Is your head all right? Poor dear. Let me have a look at it."

Definitely a grandmother. Hong-Wei bit back a smile and held up his hands. "I'm fine, but thank you. It's close quarters in here. I think a few bumps are bound to happen." Hong-Wei was glad, however, he was in the aisle and not the frail Ms. Albertson.

"Well, scooch in closer, then, so you don't get hit anymore." She patted his leg. "I'll show you pictures of the grandchildren and great-grandchildren I'm flying north to see."

Not knowing what else to do, Hong-Wei leaned closer and made what he hoped were appropriate noises as Grace Albertson fumbled through her phone's photo album.

He was rescued when the flight attendant announced they were closing the flight door, and a series of loudspeaker announcements meant for the next several minutes conversation was impossible, so outside of Hong-Wei's polite decline of Ms. Albertson's offer of a hard candy, he settled into silence.

The engines were loud as they taxied on the runway, so loud he couldn't have listened to music even if he had headphones. He wished he'd bought some in the Minneapolis airport, or better yet had made sure to pack some in his carry-on. He supposed he could ask for a headset from the flight attendant, but they were always such poor quality, he'd rather do without.

Headphones were just one thing he should have prepared for. He'd rushed into this without thinking, full of the fury and headstrong nonsense Hong-Su always chided him for. It had felt so important to break away when he'd been in Houston, pressed down by everything. Here, now, with the roar of takeoff in his ears, with nothing but this last flight between him and his destiny, he didn't feel that sense of rightness at all. He had none of the confidence that had burned so strongly in him, fueling his wild reach into the beyond.

I can be a doctor anywhere, he'd told himself defiantly as he made the decision to take this job. *I can do surgery in Houston, Texas, Cleveland, Ohio, or Copper Point, Wisconsin. The farther away I am from the mess I made, the better.*

Trapped, helpless in this plane, his defiance was gone, as was his confidence.

What have I done?

He was so consumed by dissolving into dread he forgot about his seatmate until they were in the air, the engines settling down, the plane leveling out slightly as Ms. Albertson pressed something that crinkled into his palm. He glanced down at the candy, then over at her.

She winked. "It's peppermint. It'll calm you. Or, it'll at least give you something to suck on besides your tongue."

Feeling sheepish, this time Hong-Wei accepted the candy. "Thank you."

She patted his leg. "I don't know what's waiting for you in Duluth that has you in such knots, but take it from someone whose life has knotted and unknotted itself more than a few times: it won't be as bad as you think it is, most likely. It'll either be perfectly fine, or so much worse, and in any event, there's not much you can do at this point, is there, except your best."

The peppermint oil burst against his tongue, seeping into his sinuses. He took deep breaths, rubbing the plastic of the wrapper between his fingers. Any other time he would say nothing. Here on the plane, though, he couldn't walk away, and he had no other means to escape the pressure of the panic inside him.

Talking about it a little couldn't hurt.

"I worry perhaps I didn't make the right choice in coming here."

He braced for her questions, for her to ask what he meant by that, to ask for more details about his situation or who the people saying such things were, but she said only, "When you made the choice, weren't you sure you were right?"

Hong-Wei sucked on the peppermint as he considered how to reply. "I didn't exactly make a reasoned choice about my place of employment. I all but threw a dart at a map."

Ms. Albertson laughed. "Well, that explains why you're so uneasy now. But you still had a reason for doing what you did. Why did you throw a dart at a map instead of making a reasoned decision?"

His panic crested, then to his surprise rolled away under the force of the question, and Hong-Wei chased the last vestiges to the corners of his mind as he rolled the candy around with his tongue. "Because it didn't matter where I went. Everything was going to be the same. Except I thought… I hoped… if I went somewhere far enough away, somewhere as unlike the place where I'd been as I could possibly get, maybe it would be different."

"Ah." She smiled. "You're one of *those*. An idealist. Just like my late husband. But you're proud too, so you don't want anyone to know."

Hong-Wei rubbed at his cheek. “That’s what my sister says. That I’m *too* proud, and my idealism holds me down.”

“Nothing to be ashamed of. We need idealists in the world. No doubt wherever you’re going needs them too. Good for you for taking a leap. Don’t worry too much about it. Even if it’s a disaster, you’ll figure it out, and you’ll make it work.”

“Except I don’t want it to be a disaster. I want to make it right, somehow.” He thought of his family, who had regarded him with such concern when he’d said he was leaving. *I want to become someone they can be proud of, instead of the failure I am now.*

“Of course you don’t. No one wants trouble. Sometimes a little bit of it isn’t as bad as we think.” Covering her mouth to stifle a yawn, she settled into her seat. “You have to take risks. You’ll never win anything big if you don’t.”

As his seatmate began to doze, Hong-Wei stared at the seat ahead of him, her advice swimming in his head. *Take a risk.* Without meaning to, he’d subliminally internalized this philosophy by accepting this job and moving here. The trouble came with his logical brain trying to catch up.

His whole life, all Hong-Wei had done was study and work. He’d been at the top of his class in high school, as an undergraduate, and through medical school. He’d been praised throughout his residency and fellowship and courted for enviable positions by hospitals from well beyond Baylor’s scope before any of his peers had begun to apply. A clear, practical map for his future had presented itself to him.

He still couldn't articulate, even to himself, why he'd leapt from that gilded path into this wild brush, navigable only by dubious commercial jet.

Coming to Copper Point—the town seeking a surgeon the farthest north on the map, a town nowhere near any other hospitals or cities of any kind—felt like an escape that settled his soul. He knew nothing about Wisconsin. Something about cheese, he thought he'd heard. What it *felt* like to Hong-Wei was a clean slate.

Would it truly be different, though? Certainly it wouldn't be Baylor, but would it be different in the right way?

Grace Albertson had called him an idealist with a smile. Hong-Su had always chided him for it. What he needed from Copper Point was some kind of signal that they valued him, idealism and all. That they appreciated the fact that he could have gone anywhere in the country but he'd chosen them. An indication that here might be the place he could find himself, make something of himself. One small sign to show they understood him. It didn't seem too much to ask.

Ms. Albertson woke as the plane landed, and Hong-Wei helped her gather her things, then escorted her down the long walkway to the terminal and out through security.

"You seem to have found some of your confidence while I napped," she observed.

He wasn't sure about that. "I've decided to accept my fate, let's say."

She nodded in approval. "Remember, mistakes are the spice of life. If you arrive and it's a disaster, embrace it. I promise you, whatever you find when you land, if you're lucky enough to get to my age, when you look back at it from your twilight years, you'll think of it fondly, so long as you approach it with the right spirit."

They had come to the end of the walkway leading into the waiting area. Hong-Wei turned and made a polite bow to his companion. "Thank you, Ms. Albertson, for your advice and for your company. I'll do my best to remember what you've said."

She took his hand and held it tight in her grip, smiling. "Best of luck to you, young man."

Hong-Wei watched her go to her family, watched them fold her into their embraces with no small bit of longing in his heart. Turning to the rest of the crowd, he looked for the welcoming party from Copper Point, ready to see what happened next on his adventure.

No one appeared to be waiting for him.

Hong-Wei paused, confused and concerned. There should be a large group, composed chiefly of the hospital board, poised with smiles and coming forward to greet him. They'd mentioned how eager they were to see him and assured him they'd have a delegation sent to collect him in Duluth. It wouldn't be difficult for them to identify Hong-Wei—they'd seen his photo, and there were at best four Asians in the entire airport. The waiting area was small as well. The entire airport was small. What was going on?

All his apprehension came rushing back, swamping the peace Grace Albertson had given him.

This is going to be a failure before I even begin.

Then he saw it—just as he'd asked for, there was a sign. A literal sign, small and white, and it had his name on it, sort of. It read DOCTOR WU in block letters, but underneath it was the Mandarin word for doctor in hànzi followed by Wu, also written in Chinese character. Except it wasn't quite the right word for doctor, and the character for Wu wasn't the one Hong-Wei's family used. The order was also incorrect, with the character for doctor written before Wu—in Mandarin, the proper address would be *Wu Dr.* instead of *Dr. Wu.*

Still, Hong-Wei *had* asked for a sign, and here it was.

The man who held the sign appeared to be alone. He was young, about Hong-Wei's age, perhaps a bit younger. He looked nervous and haggard. He was also, Hong-Wei couldn't help noticing, attractive. *Cute* was definitely a word that described this individual. Light brown hair, bright hazel eyes, a thin strip of beard on his chin, the suggestion of muscles beneath a tight shirt....

The man's eyes met Hong-Wei's, and something crackled in the air.

Hong-Wei threw up walls as quickly as he could. *No.* Good grief, no. He'd said he would consider opening up, but he wasn't interested in romance, or even simple sex, and absolutely not with someone associated with the hospital.

But those eyes. And he'd made a sign. An incorrect, awkward sign. Hong-Wei could tell by the way the man smiled at Hong-Wei—uncertainly, hopefully—that the Chinese had been his idea.

Gripping the strap of his bag tightly, Hong-Wei stepped forward and did his best to meet his disaster head-on.

NO ONE had told Simon the new doctor was beautiful.

He hadn't wanted to drive the hour and a half from Copper Point to Duluth and back again to pick up the new surgeon, especially when he'd been asked at the last minute during an extended shift. He'd worked odd hours seven days in a row, and then they'd wanted him to fetch the doctor everyone had been raving about as if he were some kind of second coming for St. Ann's? It wasn't as if Simon could refuse, though. Erin Andreas, the new human resources director and son of the hospital board president, had asked him personally.

"It's fitting for the surgical nurse to pick up the new surgeon, don't you think?" Andreas had punctuated this remark with a thin, apologetic smile. "I'd originally planned to go myself with a team of physicians, but everyone was summoned for call, and I have an internal crisis I need to deal with. So, if you would do this for us, please."

He hadn't waited for Simon to agree, only given him directions on when and how to meet Dr. Wu. He'd also sent along another copy of what Owen called That Damned Memo, the one reminding everyone of the strict new penalties for dating between staff members. Simon had no idea if Andreas meant it for him or for the new doctor.

As he clutched his hastily cobbled welcome sign, his pulse quickening with each step the surgeon took closer, Simon decided he'd definitely been the memo's intended target. Dr. Wu could have starred in an Asian drama, he was so beautiful. In fact, he looked a lot like Aaron Yan, one of Simon's top five favorite DramaFever stars. He was also *tall*. Simon wasn't particularly short, but he was compared to Dr. Wu.

Tall. Handsome. Chiseled. Short black hair, not dyed, artfully styled into messy peaks. Dark eyes that scanned the airport terminal with sharp focus, then zeroed in on Simon. A long, defined jaw lightly dotted with travel stubble below the most articulate set of cheekbones Simon had ever seen.

I'm going to work beside this man every single day. Hand him instruments. Follow his every instruction. Except if he smells even a fraction as good as he looks, I'm going to pass out in the OR before the patient arrives.

Mentally slapping sense into himself, Simon straightened and smiled, holding his sign higher as the man approached. "Dr. Wu? Hello, and welcome. I'm Simon Lane, the surgical nurse at St. Ann's Medical Center. It's a pleasure to meet you."

Dr. Wu accepted Simon's hand, but he also looked around, searching for something. When Simon realized what it probably was, he lowered his gaze, his cheeks heating.

"I… apologize that it's only me here to greet you. We're a small hospital, as you know, and the team members who planned to greet you were all called away on emergencies. I hope you're not offended."

Wu cleared his throat, not meeting Simon's gaze. "Of course not."

Simon was sure Wu was at least a *little* offended, which made Simon feel bad, but it wasn't as if the man didn't have a right to be upset. It was also pretty much on par for the administration to shove a nurse into the middle of its mess to take the heat for a mistake he had nothing to do with.

This wasn't the time to feel sorry for himself or sigh over the man. Dr. Wu had traveled a long way and deserved some professionalism. Forcing a smile, Simon gestured to the hallway. "Shall we collect your luggage?"

Wu adjusted his shoulder bag and nodded, setting his jaw. "Please."

They walked in silence to the baggage claim area, where the rest of the flight from Minneapolis was already gathered, for the most part. An elderly woman in yellow, surrounded by children and adults, waved at Dr. Wu as he passed, and he waved back. Simon almost asked if it was someone the surgeon knew, decided that was a stupid question, and kept his focus on the matter at hand. *Professional. Be professional.*

"It says your bags will appear at the second claim."

Dr. Wu glanced from side to side, then raised his eyebrows in a look of quiet disdain. "Well, if not, there are only the two."

Simon followed his glance. "I guess there are. I never thought about it. I haven't been to any other airport baggage areas. I haven't so much as been on a plane, myself." Realizing he should probably not have said that, he rubbed his cheek. "Sorry, I didn't mean to give away that they'd sent the B-team to escort you. I may not know anything about the rest of the world, but I'm an expert on Copper Point."

For crying out loud, Lane, the man is going to think they sent the village idiot to fetch him. Except even as he thought this, Simon noticed Dr. Wu was smiling a real smile.

It was gorgeous. If the man sent too many of those Simon's way, he was going to need a cardiologist, not a surgeon.

The baggage carousel hadn't started to move yet, so Simon filled the gap with conversation he thought might interest Dr. Wu. "The administrators told me to take you out to eat before we headed to Copper Point, but if you're too tired, we can skip that. I think someone stocked your condo with some starter groceries, but we could also stop somewhere on the way to get anything you might need." He paused, biting his lip and glancing sideways at Dr. Wu. "I should warn you. Our grocery options are seriously limited in Copper Point. I mean, we have food, obviously, but because the population is small and homogenous, anyone who wants to cook beyond the church cookbook greatest hits has to drive to Duluth or order online. A good friend of mine is a bit of a gourmand, and he's always complaining about it. So if you want, we can stop at a store too. But it can also wait."

Crap, now he was babbling. The carousel wasn't moving, though, and the surgeon wasn't talking. A stolen glance revealed he was still smiling, however. *Wider* now, in fact.

Simon swallowed a whimper and clenched his hands at his sides. When he spoke next, his voice cracked. "It's nice to have someone new come to town, and we do need a surgeon at the hospital. An official surgeon on staff, I mean." He could tell his cheeks were blotchy, the stain of his blush leaching onto his neck. "Sorry. I talk too much when I'm nervous."

Wu's voice was like warm velvet falling over him. "I'm sorry I make you nervous."

He *did* make Simon nervous, but Simon didn't want his new superior to know that, and he *especially* didn't want him to know why. "I… you… you don't make me nervous. I mean… I feel bad that you had to be met by me, is all. You deserve a better reception. I'm sure the hospital will make up for it once we arrive in town."

"Your reception is more than adequate. Thank you for coming."

Dr. Wu sounded almost gentle, and Simon couldn't breathe. Also, he was pretty sure his entire face and neck were as red as a strawberry.

The baggage carousel began to move, collecting suitcases spit from the chute, and Dr. Wu stepped away from Simon to retrieve his bags. "Where was it you thought of stopping for dinner?"

Simon fumbled for his phone and called up the list of food options Andreas had given him. "There's an Italian restaurant with good reviews. Oh, but it's in the other direction." Most of the places were, though. He resigned himself to returning home after midnight. Trying not to let his frustration show, he rattled off the other choices on the list. "There's a place called Restaurant 301. 'American classics with a local bent.' I'm not sure what that means, but I could look at the menu. There's another Italian restaurant. Wow. There are, like, five." He scrolled some more. "Tavern on the Hill has Greek wood-fired pizza." He frowned. "What makes pizza Greek? Is that really a thing, or do you think this is a gimmick to punk tourists?"

Dr. Wu had ducked his head, and when he lifted it, he looked as if he were trying not to laugh. Before Simon could apologize for whatever foolish thing he'd said, the surgeon spoke. "I'd prefer a burger and a beer somewhere low-key, to be honest."

Simon was sure *low-key* was nowhere on Andreas's carefully curated list. He opened Yelp, typed in *burger*, and scanned the results. The first hit immediately jogged his memory, and he knew where he wanted to take Dr. Wu. “What about Clyde Iron Works? It’s a lot more casual, but the food is good, and they have an extensive list of microbrews. I won’t drink, obviously, since I’m driving.”

“Sounds perfect.”

Once Wu had collected his suitcases from the belt, Simon claimed the handle of the larger one. “Let me take this. You have your carry-on and the other.”

Dr. Wu hesitated, then inclined his head. “Thank you.”

As Simon had feared, the surgeon’s suitcases completely filled his trunk and much of the back seat. “Sorry we’re so cramped.” Simon’s cheeks were hot with shame as he paid the ticket and drove them away from the airport. “I was going to borrow my friend’s car, which is bigger, but it ended up in the shop.”

“It’s not a problem.”

At this point Simon couldn’t tell if Wu was simply being nice, or if he didn’t mind. Uncertainty made him babble again. “You’ll meet Owen soon enough. He’s one of my best friends from middle school and the anesthesiologist at St. Ann’s. He was on the original team that was coming to meet you. Kathryn, another friend of mine and our resident OB-GYN, was going to come too, but too many of her patients had babies.”

Wu gazed through the window, taking in the scenery as they passed. “You mentioned you knew Copper Point well. Have you lived there long?”

Simon laughed. “My whole life, and possibly my previous one. I’m one of those people who can trace a great-great-grandparent to the town. When I was four, the town had its one hundred fiftieth anniversary, and they put me on a float in some kind of settler getup with the other kids who were descendants of the founding families." Come to think of it, that meant he'd stood next to Erin Andreas, who would have been just a few years older.

"Tell me about the town. I saw a little online, but of course it's not the same thing as firsthand experience."

"Well, it's on the bay feeding into Lake Superior, and it's one of the first settlement areas in what was the Northwest Territories. Lots of fur trading here before that. The European settlers came for the mining, I think." Simon bit his lip. "Okay, so I don't know the *history* of Copper Point so well. But I can tell you that we have a sandstone mine—I think it was copper the first time, but it's sandstone now—and a college. It's called Bayview University, but it's a small liberal arts college. We have a campus town, which has more places to eat than our downtown and some fun shops. Because we're so far away from everything, our Main Street does okay, even with the big box stores. It's a midsized town, but it's small enough everyone knows everyone. Sometimes more than you want.

"You're moving here from Houston, right? I looked it up while I was waiting. Wow, it's really big. Did you come there from somewhere else in Texas before you went to school? They didn't tell me much about you. I know you were born in Taiwan and did your residency at Baylor, but that's about it." Simon's hand brushed the sign between them, and he decided this was a good time to get his apology over with. "Sorry if the sign was over-the-top. I misunderstood and thought you were more recently from Taiwan than you are."

Dr. Wu glanced at the sign with an affectionate smile. "No, I liked the sign. Thank you. I moved to Houston from Taipei with my family when I was ten. It worked out that the university I wanted to attend was in the same city, and I was fortunate enough to be matched with Baylor for my residency."

"Wow. I would think you'd have more of an accent, if you moved here that late."

"My sister has one, sometimes, but the two of us worked hard to practice our American accents as well as our English. It was important to us both to blend in." He shook his head, rueful. "We watched *so many* movies. She would find the scripts, and we'd read along with them."

Simon hadn't meant to confess, but the road ahead of him was hypnotic, as was Dr. Wu's low, smooth voice, and it tumbled out of him. "I wish I could do that to learn Korean or Chinese. I watch so many Asian shows on DramaFever, but I've only learned how to say *I'm sorry* and *thank you* and *I love you*, and I'm not entirely sure about the last one."

There was a moment's awkward pause where Simon cringed inwardly and Dr. Wu said nothing.

"You… watch Asian television?" Wu said at last.

Simon nodded, refusing to be uncomfortable about his confession. "The romances. They're my favorite. I stumbled on one on Netflix one day and loved it, and of course Netflix kept recommending more, and I was down the rabbit hole. I found out there was an entire network devoted to them, and it was all over. Now I watch the new ones as they're released, but I've also gone back and watched a lot of older ones as well." He resisted the urge to apologize for himself and forged on. “I think it's better than most of the stuff on American television. It makes me wish I could travel.”

“Is there some reason you can't?”

Simon shrugged. “I haven't had the opportunity, I guess.” Deciding to be honest, he added, “Also, I'm a little scared. I used to want to go everywhere, but the older I get, the more impossible it seems. I still want to do it, but I don't want to go by myself, and….” He forced a smile. “Anyway. You're certainly not scared. I look forward to working with you, Dr. Wu.”

Wu made no reply to this, only stared out the window, an unreadable expression on his face. Simon was working up to apologize for whatever it was he'd said wrong when he noticed the surgeon had closed his hand over the edge of Simon's cardboard sign, holding on to it like an anchor.

Maybe he'd messed some things up, but he'd done the sign right. At least he had that going for him.

THE RESTAURANT Hong-Wei's escort took them to had a funky urban-industrial theme, and the menu was more than promising, full of burgers, pasta, and as Lane had said, a vast selection of local beer. Hong-Wei ordered two different types and a large bacon cheeseburger, as well as a side of onion rings.

Lane, who had a smoked salmon salad, blinked as he watched Hong-Wei dig into the beer-battered rings. “So… you're not a health-conscious doctor, then?”

Hong-Wei shrugged as he wiped his mouth with a napkin and dusted crumbs from his fingers. “My mother and grandmother always nag me to eat properly, so whenever I escape their influence, I tend to go wild." He pushed the basket of rings toward Lane. "Try one. They're excellent."

Lane held up a hand and shook his head, eyeing Hong-Wei curiously. Hong-Wei retreated into his food and drink, reeling a bit from Lane's declaration that Hong-Wei wasn't scared. Now he felt as if the pressure was on, which was difficult since the closer he got to his new reality, the more terrified he became. Junk food and alcohol seemed the best refuge.

He liked hearing Lane talk, so he searched for a prompt. "You told me about the town. What about the hospital? My schedule didn't allow me to come to Wisconsin for a proper visit."

As Hong-Wei had hoped, Lane relaxed and launched eagerly into speaking about the hospital. "St. Ann's is a small critical access hospital, which I suppose you already knew. I guess the thing I can tell you that's most important since it sounds like you've always dealt with large hospitals is small hospitals have a different feel. I worked at a larger hospital after finishing my degree, and the atmosphere at a place like St. Ann's is very different. Unlike large hospitals where there are multiple floors and departments separated from each other, we're all in each other's laps at St. Ann's. There's only one nurses' station. One doctors' lounge. One bank of elevators, though we do have a service elevator in the laundry area. Technically we have one hundred beds, but because of the way the critical access rules read, we only ever use seventy-five. Also, though everyone has their specific role, we fill in everywhere. I'm supposed to be the surgical nurse, but I do whatever shift needs doing. The doctors are in the same predicament."

None of this had come up when the administration had interviewed him, Hong-Wei thought as he sipped his beer, but he wasn't surprised. He wondered how much else he could get Lane to confess. "What's the work environment like? Do people get along? Are they competitive with one another?"

Lane seemed confused. "Competitive? I'm not sure what you mean. As far as getting along… well, it depends on who it is. Owen—he's Dr. Gagnon—is known for being difficult, but I think that's overblown, personally. The nurses gossip a lot, which I don't care for, but it's not like anybody can stop that either." He sighed. "The hospital board is a little… scary. They're all old, which would be fine, but they're a total good-old-boys club. The hospital CEO is a solid guy, I always thought. He was friends with one of my friends in high school. The HR director, though, is the son of the hospital board president, and he makes me nervous. You know Roz, that woman from *9 to 5*?"

9 to 5 was one of the movies he and Hong-Su had used to improve their English. "I'm familiar with her, yes."

"He reminds me of her, sometimes. I feel like everything I say goes directly to the board."

Lane toyed with his straw, first with his fingers, then with his lips as he stared off to the side, ostensibly considering something deeply. Hong-Wei paused with an onion ring halfway off his plate, arrested by the sight of Lane's full lips teasing the straw.

Stop it, he chided himself. *He's a nurse. Your nurse.*

The spell was broken when Lane sat back, a determined look on his face. "I'm going to tell you this because you're going to hear about it eventually anyway.

We've had our share of scandals recently at St. Ann's. The CEO before Nick Beckert was fired due to embezzlement, and before the air was clear, a married clinic doctor was caught sleeping with his nurse. It was like watching a soap opera live at work, except it got ugly and made the papers and the TV news. I don't think the board was paying as close attention then as they are now, though they've been worried about money since forever. Anyway, we got a new CEO, and the new HR person. The latter is really bringing down the hammer." Lane aimed his fork at Hong-Wei. "Don't be fooled by how Erin Andreas appears either. He seems small and sweet, but he smiles while he bites you. He's already fired four people since he arrived last month."

Interesting information. Hong-Wei digested it as he drank more beer. "Has he fired any doctors?"

Lane laughed, the sound startling for its bitterness. "Are you kidding? Not a chance. The doctors are never wrong." Apparently remembering he was in the presence of a doctor, Lane averted his gaze and cleared his throat. "I mean, the hospital gives doctors the benefit of the doubt, always."

"That will be an interesting change, then." Hong-Wei picked up his burger and took a bite, thinking as he chewed. "I've been a surgical resident up until now. Things were my fault even if I was at home sleeping when they happened."

"Nothing will be your fault. I thought things would get better once we switched to the electronic record-keeping system, because finally the doctors couldn't blame us when we couldn't figure out what their insane handwriting meant or when they wrote the order wrong and the pharmacist yelled at us. Now they still ask for the wrong dose of medicine, and when the pharmacist says an order would kill the patient and calls to tell them so, we get yelled at for letting them interrupt the doctor."

The beer was unloosening things in Hong-Wei, making it easier to laugh. It also silenced the voice warning him not to notice how the lighting in the restaurant was making soft halos dance on top of Lane's light brown hair, casting pleasant shadows across his broad shoulders. "This sort of thing happened to me in my residency as well. I hadn't planned on passing on the experience to my nurses, though. I thought I'd prefer to be a competent surgeon instead."

Oh, but Lane had a nice smile. "About that. I don't know the full story, but I heard the other doctors and some administrators talking. I hear you're an exceptionally good surgeon, or that you have some kind of special skill? I didn't understand all of what they were talking about, but what I gathered is we're very fortunate to have you at St. Ann's."

Hong-Wei held his glass to his lips longer than necessary as he tried to decide how to reply. He hadn't given the full truth to St. Ann's in his interview. Had they uncovered it on their own? It didn't matter, he supposed, but it made him uneasy. The whole point in coming here had been to step back and be a simple general surgeon.

He cleared his throat and set down his glass. "I had many places to choose from for my postresidency employment, yes. I decided to come to St. Ann's, however, because I wanted a more intimate, uncomplicated hospital experience."

"Well, I don't know about uncomplicated, but you'll probably get more up close and personal with people than you care to." Lane's smile was crooked, apologetic, and impossibly endearing. "That includes me, I'm afraid. We have a few other backup nurses trained, but in the same way you're the only surgeon at St. Ann's, I'm the only surgical nurse. So we'll be seeing a lot of each other, Dr. Wu."

"Call me Jack."

Lane's eyebrows lifted. "Oh, that's your first name? Huh, not what I expected. Do most people in Taiwan have Western names these days?"

The beer had relaxed Hong-Wei's tongue to the point of no return. Or perhaps it was Lane's smile and gentle eyes. "No. Jack is the name I use with people outside my family, since Americans don't have an easy time with Asian names."

"Would you mind telling me your given name? I'll use Jack if you prefer, but I'm curious about who you really are."

Who you really are. He was both Jack and Hong-Wei equally at this point, but Lane was so clumsily charming, Hong-Wei couldn't resist him. He shifted on his chair. "Wu Hong-Wei." Why did he give it in Taiwanese order instead of Western order, with his surname first? Now he was just being silly.

You're an idealist. Grace Albertson's voice came back to him. Hong-Wei had to agree. Though now he wondered if he didn't have to admit to being a romantic as well.

"Wu Hong-Wei."

Hong-Wei shivered and went still.

Lane's pronunciation came out as clumsy as any American's attempt, maybe worse because he was clearly trying to mimic Hong-Wei.

Ever since the airport, the yearning to connect had been apparent in Simon Lane's gaze, but now Hong-Wei saw the truth behind the nurse's longing for what it was, a truth his escort probably didn't want him to see. He'd come all this way to pick up the new surgeon because he'd been asked, because he was a nice guy… and because he was lonely.

Without a moment to prepare for the attack, Hong-Wei's walls crumbled into dust.

He finished off the first beer and picked up the second, indulging in a long draught. "You may call me Hong-Wei if you like, Simon."

Simon smiled so wide it lifted his ears and made his hazel eyes twinkle.

Losing himself in that smile, Hong-Wei couldn't remember why, exactly, he shouldn't pursue a flirtation with his nurse. Something told him the harder he tried to resist Simon Lane, the more he'd be sucked in.

A relationship wasn't the adventure he'd come to Copper Point to pursue, and yet every instinct Hong-Wei had told him Simon would be the adventure he ended up taking.

Author of over thirty novels, Midwest-native HEIDI CULLINAN writes positive-outcome romances for LGBT characters struggling against insurmountable odds because she believes there's no such thing as too much happy ever after. Heidi is a two-time RITA® finalist, and her books have been recommended by *Library Journal*, *USA Today*, *RT Magazine*, and *Publishers Weekly*. When Heidi isn't writing, she enjoys cooking, reading novels and manga, playing with her cats, and watching too much anime.

Visit Heidi's website at www.heidicullinan.com.

You can contact her at heidi@heidicullinan.com.

COPPER POINT MEDICAL: BOOK TWO

Where happy ever after is just a heartbeat away

THE DOCTOR'S DATE

HEIDI CULLINAN

Copper Point Medical: Book Two

The hospital's least eligible bachelor and its aloof administrator hate each other... so why are they pretending to date?

Dr. Owen Gagnon and HR director Erin Andreas are infamous for their hospital hallway shouting matches. So imagine the town's surprise when Erin bids an obscene amount of money to win Owen in the hospital bachelor auction—and Owen ups the ante by insisting Erin move in with him.

Copper Point may not know what's going on, but neither do Erin and Owen. Erin intends his gesture to let Owen know he's interested. Owen, on the other hand, suspects ulterior motives—that Erin wants a fake relationship as a refuge from his overbearing father.

With Erin suddenly heading a messy internal investigation, Owen wants to step up and be the hero Erin's never had. Too bad Erin would rather spend his energy trying to rescue Owen from the shadows of a past he doesn't talk about.

This relationship may be fake, but the feelings aren't. Still, what Erin and Owen have won't last unless they put their respective demons to rest. To do that, they'll have to do more than work together—they'll have to trust they can heal each other's hearts.

TUCKER PAWN
SECOND HAND
A TUCKER SPRINGS NOVEL
MARIE SEXTON
HEIDI CULLINAN

A Tucker Springs Novel

Paul Hannon flunked out of vet school. His fiancée left him. He can barely afford his rent, and he hates his house. About the only things he has left are a pantry full of his ex's kitchen gadgets and a lot of emotional baggage. He could really use a win—and that's when he meets El.

Pawnbroker El Rozal is a cynic. His own family's dysfunction has taught him that love and relationships lead to misery. Despite that belief, he keeps making up excuses to see Paul again. Paul, who doesn't seem to realize that he's talented and kind and worthy. Paul, who's not over his ex-fiancée and is probably straight anyway. Paul, who's so blind to El's growing attraction, even asking him out on dates doesn't seem to tip him off.

El may not do relationships, but something has to give. If he wants to keep Paul, he'll have to convince him he's worthy of love—and he'll have to admit that attachment might not be so bad after all.

DIRTY
LAUNDRY
A TUCKER SPRINGS NOVEL
HEIDI CULLINAN

A Tucker Springs Novel

Sometimes you have to get dirty to come clean.

When muscle-bound Denver Rogers effortlessly dispatches the frat boys harassing grad student Adam Ellery at the Tucker Springs laundromat, Adam's thank-you turns into impromptu sex over the laundry table. The problem comes when they exchange numbers. What if Adam wants to meet again and discovers Denver is a high-school dropout with a learning disability who works as a bouncer at a local gay bar? Or what if Denver calls Adam only to learn while he might be brilliant in the lab, outside of it he has crippling social anxiety and obsessive-compulsive disorder?

Either way, neither of them can shake the memory of their laundromat encounter. Despite their fears of what the other might think, they can only remember how good the other one feels. The more they get together, the kinkier things become. They're both a little bent, but in just the right ways.

Maybe the secret to staying together isn't to keep things clean and proper. Maybe it's best to keep their laundry just a little bit dirty.

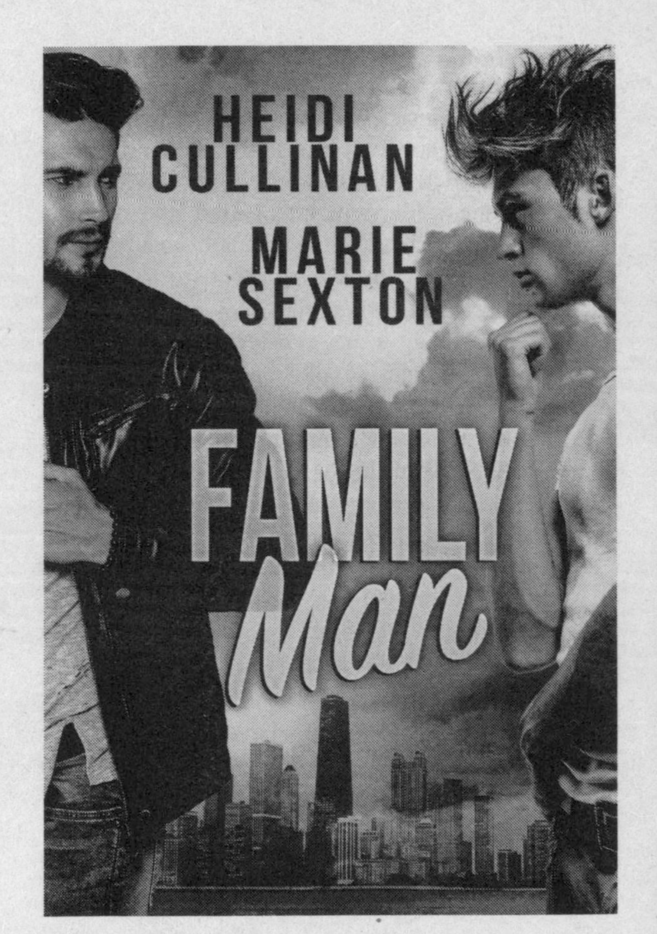
HEIDI
CULLINAN
MARIE
SEXTON
FAMILY
Man

Sometimes family chooses you.

At forty, Vincent “Vinnie” Fierro is still afraid to admit he might be gay—even to himself. It’ll be a problem for his big fat Italian family. Still, after three failed marriages, it’s getting harder to ignore what he really wants.

Vinnie attempts some self-exploration in Chicago’s Boystown bars, far from anyone who knows him. Naturally, he runs smack into someone from the neighborhood.

Between working two jobs, going to school, taking care of his grandmother, and dealing with his mother’s ongoing substance abuse, Trey Giles has little time for fun, let alone dating someone who swears he’s straight. Yet after one night of dancing cheek-to-cheek, Trey agrees to let Vinnie court him and see if he truly belongs on this side of the fence—though Trey intends to keep his virginity intact.

It seems like a solid plan, but nothing is simple when family is involved. When Vinnie’s family finds out about their relationship, the situation is sticky enough, but when Trey’s mother goes critical, Vinnie and Trey must decide whose happiness is most important—their families’ or their own.

NEVER
A HERO
A TUCKER SPRINGS NOVEL
MARIE SEXTON

A Tucker Springs Novel

Owen Meade is in need of a hero. Sheltered, ashamed, and ridiculed by his own mother for his sexuality, his stutter, and his congenital arm amputation, Owen lives like a hermit, rarely leaving his apartment. He hardly dares to hope for more… until veterinarian Nick Reynolds moves in downstairs.

Charming, handsome Nick steals past Owen's defenses and makes him feel almost normal. Meeting his fiery, determined little sister, June, who was born with a similar amputation, helps too. June always seems to get her way—she even convinces Owen to sign up for piano lessons with her. Suddenly the only thing standing between Owen and his perfect life is Nick. No matter how much he flirts, how attracted to Owen he seems to be, or how much time they spend together, Nick always pulls away.

Caught between his mother's contempt and Nick's stubbornness, Owen makes a decision. It's time to be the hero of his own story, and that means going after what he wants: not just Nick, but the full life he deserves.

DREAMSPINNER
PRESS
dreamspinnerpress.com